The Architecture of the Arkansas Ozarks

Donald Harington

The Architecture of the Arkansas Ozarks

The Toby Press

Paperback Edition, 2004

The Toby Press LLC
POB 8531, New Milford, CT. 06676-8531, USA
& POB 2455, London WIA 5WY, England
www.tobypress.com

ISBN 1 59264 073 7 *paperback*

A CIP catalogue record for this title
is available from the British Library

Typeset in Garamond by Jerusalem Typesetting

Printed and bound in the United States by
Thomson-Shore Inc., Michigan

To the memory of my father (1905–1977)
and my mother (1905–1983)

The true basis for any serious study of the art of Architecture still lies in those indigenous, more humble buildings everywhere that are to architecture what folklore is to literature or folk song to music and with which academic architects were seldom concerned.

...These many folk structures are *of the soil*, natural. Though often slight, their virtue is intimately related to the environment and to the heartlife of the people. Functions are usually truthfully conceived and rendered invariably with natural feeling. Results are often beautiful and always instructive.

FRANK LLOYD WRIGHT
from *The Sovereignty of the Individual*

Chapter one

We begin with an ending: the last arciform architecture in the Arkansas Ozarks. Years afterward, waking up one morning in his bedroom at the governor's mansion in Little Rock, Jacob Ingledew was to remember the home—house, hive, hovel, we should not call it merely "hut"—of Fanshaw. There was, clearly, not a straight line in it, not a corner, not an edge, and Jacob Ingledew was to wake up one morning and stare at the four-cornered ceiling of his bedroom in the governor's mansion, and think: *box*! Immediately he would jerk his elbow into his wife Sarah's ribs, waking her, and declare, "That's the trouble, Sarey! We've done went and boxed ourself in!"

"What?" she was to answer, rousing from good sleep. "You thinkin about them delegates from Washin'ton, hon?" No, he would not have been thinking about the delegates to Washington, but at her mention of them, he was to give over to sleep again in an effort not to think about them, and he was to forget Fanshaw's home and forget feeling boxed, and go on forever dwelling in boxes of various shapes and sizes.

The home of Fanshaw—our illustration is purely conjectural, based largely on word-of-mouth description; like structures in some of the other illustrations in this study, it no longer exists; Jacob Ingledew moved it, after Fanshaw left, to his backyard, where he used it as a corncrib for several years until it logically fell victim to rot and termites, and disintegrated—looks deceptively small; actually both pens (it was bigeminal, or, to employ the term that we will have frequent recourse to, was an architectural "duple") were nearly ten feet high and almost thirteen feet in diameter; Fanshaw, who was uncommonly tall for his race, over six feet, was required to stoop only slightly in order to exit his door, while his wife did not have to stoop at all.

Fanshaw was stooping to exit his door when Jacob Ingledew first laid eyes on him. Jacob Ingledew with his brother Noah had come with two saddlebagged mules some six hundred miles from Warren County, Tennessee, their birthplace and rearing-place; on a hazardous journey into an unknown wilderness the two brothers had palliated their nervousness by virtually chain-smoking their pipes, with the result that their supply of tobacco had been exhausted for nearly a week before they stumbled upon the village—or camp—of Fanshaw. It was situated in a clearing on the banks of Swains Creek approximately where Doc Plowright's spread would later be, in a narrow winding valley that snaked along through five mountains, each a thousand feet higher than the valley. At the first sight of it, Noah Ingledew retreated, refusing to go nearer. From the woods on the hillside, Jacob Ingledew watched the camp for three and one-half hours before Fanshaw emerged, stooping, from his house. Jacob decided that the village, which consisted of twelve other dwellings similar to the one in our illustration, must be deserted except for Fanshaw. A field to one side of the village was devoted to the cultivation of corn, squash, beans, and, Jacob had been pleased to see, tobacco. Although Jacob, like all Ingledew men, was uncommonly shy, so great was his desire for tobacco that, after bobbing his prominent Adam's apple a couple of times, he began walking toward Fanshaw. Instantly Fanshaw saw him and kept his eyes fastened upon him the whole length of his approach. Jacob Ingledew walked slowly to signify he was friendly.

Fanshaw descried a man of his own height, tall, dressed in buckskin jacket and trousers, wearing a headpiece made from the skin and tail of a raccoon, thin, blue-eyed, brown-haired, long-nosed, and carrying not a rifle but a half-gallon jug with corncob stopper.

Jacob Ingledew saw a man of his own height, tall, dressed in buckskin moccasins and leggings that covered only the legs, the space between breeched with a breech clout, wearing a headpiece (actually just a bandeau) of beaver skin, eagle fathers in the roach of his hair, muscular, dark-eyed, bronze-skinned, long-nosed and naked from the waist up except for a necklace of several dozen bear claws.

Jacob Ingledew spoke, rather noisily from nervousness: "How! You habbum 'baccy? Me swappum firewater for 'baccy. Sabbe?"

"Quite," said Fanshaw. Jacob Ingledew misinterpreted this as "Quiet," and began looking around, wondering if the others were sleeping, although it was well into the afternoon. Actually, Fanshaw had spoken in the manner of his namesake, George W. Featherstonehaugh, a British geologist who had explored the Ozarks a few years previously and had been welcomed by Wah Ti An Kah, as he was known before his fellow tribesmen jokingly nicknamed him after their guest because he spent so much time in dialogue with the visitor, even to the point of taking pains to master the visitor's language.

Fanshaw's dwelling, like the others, was made of long slender poles cut, appropriately enough, from the *bois d'arc* tree, or Osageorange (I will discuss in due course the significance of the name *bois d'arc*, still today called "bodark," which fits so perfectly with all the other thumping arks of our study). Both ends of these poles were sharpened and then the poles were bent like a bow and the ends stuck into the ground, forming a large arch which was actually a parabola—and most architectural historians agree that the parabolic is the most graceful, not to say strongest, of all arch forms. As may be seen in our illustration, these arched poles were interwoven as they crossed in the smoke-hole at the top; the result was literally a paraboloid, an inverted basketry paraboloid. Marvelous! Over this framework reeds, cattails and other thatch materials were interwoven; as a shelter it was weatherproof; a negligible amount of water poured through the smoke-hole during a heavy rainstorm but was absorbed by woven mats covering the earthen floor which were hung out to dry in the beautiful sunshine that often comes to the Ozarks.

Portable? Yes, "quite portable," Fanshaw explained later that afternoon when both men were warmed by firewater, Tennessee sour mash nearly comparable, or possibly even superior in some respects, to the Jack Daniels of our time... and Fanshaw's cured tobacco wasn't such a bad product itself. Jacob Ingledew was on his third pipeful. (Noah Ingledew still wouldn't come out of the woods. Noah Ingledew never would work up the nerve to come and talk to Fanshaw, even though Jacob later told him, "Why, that injun kin talk ary bit as good as you or me. Better, mebbe.")

"A gentleman and his squaw," Fanshaw explained over the firewater, "can lift and transport their domicile over great distances where the woods are not, or, where the woods are, disassemble and reassemble. If Wahkontah—he whom you address 'God'—wanted gentlemen to stay in one place he would make the world stand still; but he in his infinite wisdom made it always to change, so birds and animals can move and always have green grass and ripe berries, sunlight to work and play, and night to sleep, always changing, everything for good, the earth and bodies of the skies, forever and ever..." At that point a pretty Indian woman appeared briefly in the door of Fanshaw's house and spoke gently to Fanshaw in a language that Jacob Ingledew had never heard, then withdrew, presumably into the second of the two units in the duple. Fanshaw chuckled and said to Jacob Ingledew: "The lady thinks I talk too much." He stood up and gave Jacob his hand, saying, "Do come again, brother."

But it was a long time before Jacob Ingledew visited again and that was after Fanshaw had come to him. "Jist too blamed tard to 'sociate," Jacob explained, pointing at the work that he and his brother were doing, the construction of their cabin (see our illustration to the following chapter). There had been some argument between the brothers over settling here. Noah Ingledew did not want to build in the vicinity of Indians. Jacob Ingledew liked the landscape, and besides, these Indians were friendly, and besides that, there were only two of them, Fanshaw having told him that the other members of the tribe had gone off on a hunting trip over a year previously and had not returned. As a result of having imbibed Featherstonehaugh's firewater too freely, Fanshaw had broken his leg in a fall from his horse at the outset of the hunting trip, and was required to remain behind. He was skeptical that the others would return. He hoped they would, of course, but it had been such a long time since they had gone hunting, and he had had plenty of spare time to imagine the worst: they had met their enemies the Cherokees and been defeated, or met the blue-coat government men who forced them westward into reservations. He did not know. He still walked with a limp.

Jacob and Noah Ingledew worked from sunup to sundown for a fortnight building their cabin. For a discussion of their methods, we must await the next chapter, but suffice it to say here that this work was drudgery, although it lasted only a fortnight. At the end of that time, Fanshaw sought Jacob out (Noah scampered off into the woods as the aborigine approached and wouldn't come back until he had left, a couple of hours later). Jacob Ingledew passed his jug to Fanshaw, realizing that now his cabin was nearly finished he could get his corn planted but even so it was going to be a dry summer, "dry" before he could get a new run of whiskey made. He told Fanshaw that he was just too tired at the end of each day building his cabin to visit him again.

Fanshaw studied the Ingledew cabin, scratching his chin. He just looked at it for a long time, walking all the way around it like a bird studying some other bird's strange nest. Not portable, he observed. But worse, to his point of view, it was all square, foursquare, quadriform, there was not a curved edge to it, not one. After passing the jug back and forth between them for a while, they got into a long argument about architecture. I will repeat here only the end of the argument, the point at which it stopped. Although we may be sure that Fanshaw did not have the word "organic" in his vocabulary, let alone understand what is meant by organic architecture, he had a sense of a dwelling's belonging to the landscape and fitting in with it, and he was trying to boast of how his own dwelling expressed this feeling in a way that the Ingledew cabin did not. He looked out across the rolling hills and pointed toward the gently rounded double-top of what later would be locally called Big Tits Mountain. "My house," he boasted, "is of the same shape."

"Yeah?" said Jacob Ingledew, and pointed toward the peak of what later would be called Ingledew Mountain. "Wal, how about that un?" The top of Ingledew Mountain forms a triangular peak of almost the same geometric angles as the gable roof of the Ingledew cabin. Fanshaw just looked at him and grinned.

Fanshaw changed the subject by inquiring whether or not Jacob's "lady" was "at home." Jacob Ingledew blushed and hemmed and hawed and said he aint never had ary, for the fact was that an Ingledew man brave enough to approach a savage Indian would never, could never have approached a female, at least not one above the age of, say, eleven. Jacob Ingledew changed the subject by saying that there wasn't nobody here but him and his brother, and his brother wasn't here right now because he was scared shitless of Indians, although in most other respects his brother was brave and fearless and had recently killed a panther by ramming his fist down its throat, although he had a few ugly scars on his arm to show for it.

After a couple of hours of drink and talk, Fanshaw got up to go. "Stay more," Jacob invited him. "Hell, you jist got here." But Fanshaw politely explained that his lady would be unhappy if he tarried further, and he must return to her. The pattern of this parting would be duplicated on a number of subsequent occasions, always with Jacob inviting him to "stay more"—this was not necessarily because Jacob Ingledew craved his company, although he did in fact very much enjoy Fanshaw's visits, but a matter of formality, a custom let us say, of his people. One always urges a departing guest to remain. Yet Fanshaw could not help but remark upon this custom to his wife because among his own people the exact reverse is the case: when a guest has stayed as long as he wants to, his host senses it and sends him packing with an Indian expression which, if translated into modern idiom, would most literally be "Haul ass" or perhaps even "Fuck off." Fanshaw's wife was amused by the term "stay more" in the Indian equivalent into which he translated it for her. In time, it got to where whenever Fanshaw was leaving his house to go visit Jacob Ingledew, he would tell his wife that he was going to Stay More. Some folks even today think that it was Jacob and/or Noah Ingledew who gave the town its name, when in fact it was an aborigine, and the significance of the name, in its rustic ambivalence, is going to have, we will find, many ramifications, some of them poignant. We must not allow ourselves to feel that this is entirely a happy story.

But it is of Fanshaw's house that I should speak. Why was it bigeminal, that is, a duple? Not visible in our illustration is the other door, on the other side—the west door to the other unit. There may or may not have been an interior connecting door as well; unfortunately, information on this point has been impossible to obtain. One would logically think that there was an interior connecting door, one would *want* to believe so, at any rate, but Jacob Ingledew, who was, on at least several occasions, inside the dwelling, simply neglected ever to mention whether or not there was an interior connecting door. The first time he asked Fanshaw why his house was bigeminal (which wasn't the word he used; he said "divided" although that is not accurate, for, as one can see, the two units of the building are not divided at all, but very strongly conjoined), Fanshaw simply replied that it was "traditional." Later on, when Jacob Ingledew raised the matter again, Fanshaw could only explain: "That is hers, this is mine." Naturally Jacob Ingledew would have been too embarrassed to ask Fanshaw whether this meant that they slept separately.

It was learned that Fanshaw himself had not built his house. He had helped to build a number of others, but he had not built this one. He explained. Among his people, the most desirable and eligible young gentlemen are actively sought out by the maidens for the purpose of—he could not remember the English word for it, but it is the state of being man and squaw. The maiden expresses her wish for the young gentleman of her choice by giving him a piece of bread made of maize. Of course the young gentleman has the right to reject her proposal by returning the maize-bread to her. But if he wants her, he keeps the bread. Together they plan a public festival at which they will announce their wish to enter the state of man and squaw. The whole village, then, as a token of joy, build the dwellingplace for the couple in one afternoon. That is the entire ceremony.

"It is simple," Fanshaw observed. "No words need be spoken, other than many exclamations of joy by the people as they build the domicile. A lodge-raising is a most noisy festival, but it is not in words. Much meat is eaten. The blessed couple afterward are too full of meat

7

to do the—I did not ever learn what you call it in English—the, when in darkness, one-on-top-together-fastened-between. Do you know it? No? Pity. It is with much joy." There was a legend among his people that this frolic was responsible for the girl's production of an infant after nine moons. But Fanshaw's lady had never produced an infant, although, with little else to do but tend their garden patch and hunt an occasional wild turkey, they spent most of their time in one-on-top-together-fastened-between.

It could be a superstition, of which there were many, and while Fanshaw was of the opinion that the efficacy of superstitions was in direct proportion to one's belief in their efficacy, there was no denying that many superstitions were useful and never failed. In the course of time he imparted several of these to Jacob Ingledew. The root of the buckeye tree, crushed and dropped into a pool of the creek, is a quick way to catch fish, by poisoning them. In time of famine, when other meat is scarce, do not disdain the ordinary mud turtle; his flesh consists of seven tastes of meat: pork, beef, mutton, venison, chicken, duck and fish. Fanshaw taught him many natural herbal remedies for the thousand ills that flesh is heir to, although most of these happened to be identical with ones that Jacob Ingledew already knew, learned from his ancestors. They discovered also that they had in common their beliefs in the importance of doing certain things, such as planting, by the dark of the moon or the light of the moon.

One of their few disagreements, which provided much fuel for their debates, was over the existence of God, or Wahkontah, as Fanshaw called him (it translates as "Mysterious Spirit" rather than the more common "Great Spirit" of other tribes). Jacob Ingledew felt that there was no such thing as God, or, if there were, he was a senile loafer who had created the world during his energetic youth but was now too old to care for it or take care of it. This notion greatly incensed Fanshaw, and in the intensity of their debates they almost came to blows. But they never fought, physically; I have always been curious as to which of them would have won if they had; it would have been a very even match.

But Fanshaw was a man of prayer. The door of his house, that is, the door of his half of the house, faced the east, whence, his people believed, all good things came (a peculiarly harsh irony in view of the fact that the displacing white settlers came from that direction). Each morning, at dawn, he would rise and perform his matinals, facing east. Our illustration attempts to show his house as illuminated by the long light of this early moment; imagination must visualize Fanshaw standing outside his door facing east. The first morning Jacob Ingledew spent in Stay More, sleeping on the ground by his mule tethered half a mile up the creek from Fanshaw's, he woke to the sound of Fanshaw's morning prayer, and, having never in his life heard anything like it, went to investigate, hiding in the woods near Fanshaw's camp and watching him. The closest sound it resembled was that of a screaming panther, which Jacob had heard on many occasions, the most recent being just before Noah had rammed his fist down one's throat. Jacob was astonished to discover that the sound was being produced by the vocal apparatus of his new friend Fanshaw (and possibly, in the back of his mind, after listening to Fanshaw's Dawn Chant to its conclusion, he felt that Fanshaw was crazy, and this may have been the real reason, rather than fatigue, why he did not soon return to Fanshaw's house). Long afterward, Jacob Ingledew could do a reasonable imitation of the Dawn Chant, to awe his descendants, frightening the younger ones, and from one of his descendants in turn I have heard it; it lies beyond my power of words to reproduce; I can only say that it began on the highest pitched note that the voice could reach, and after traveling up and down the scale in a nonmusical but nonverbal manner for several long minutes that evoked abstractly supplications and petitions of all manner, ended abruptly on a note that can only be called a sob of frustration. It was this last that most puzzled Jacob Ingledew, but it was a long time before he could get up his nerve to ask Fanshaw what it meant. Jacob returned to his cabin site to find his brother Noah saddling one of the mules. "Shitfire," Noah said, "I'm a-gorn back to Tennessee, Jake." Jacob explained that it was only the aborigine singing some kind of morningsong, but it was only with much conciliation that Jacob persuaded his brother to stay.

It was at the height of one of their arguments about God, much later, that Jacob said to Fanshaw, "If you believe in him so durn much, how come when you git to the 'amen' part of yore prayers, you make this here noise that sounds like you feel it aint nary bitty use nohow to be prayin?" Fanshaw stared at him for a long moment before saying, "Oh? You listen to my 'prayers'?" Jacob said, "Hell's bells, a body caint help listenin to 'em." "Be glad then," Fanshaw retorted, "that there is only me. If my tribesmen were here, we would deafen you." But he relented, and explained to Jacob that the sob of frustration did not mean that he thought his praying was futile but rather that he was, at that point, given to understand that Wahkontah had chosen, for reasons of His own, to deny Fanshaw's requests. We all want. We must always continue to want, to desire, even if our wants are not gratified. What did Fanshaw want? He could not tell Jacob; to tell another mortal what one wants greatly decreases one's chances of getting it—no, it is a *guarantee* that one will not get it.

But Jacob Ingledew, for all his rough frontiersman demeanor, was a man of good mind, and he could guess the source of Fanshaw's frustration: surely it had to do with the rest of his tribe not return- ing. He felt sorry for Fanshaw, but of course if the rest of the tribe *did* return, which he doubted, he himself would have to move on. He had been told before leaving Tennessee that within a few short years, now that Arkansas had achieved statehood and was no longer a territory, every Indian would have to leave the state.

In the fall, when they were sampling the first run of Jacob's Arkan- sas sour mash whiskey (Fanshaw had helped him harvest the corn, and had shown him how to grind it, Indian-fashion, by placing it in a hollowed-out rock—of which there are many in the Ozark streams—and pounding it with a stone pestle), Fanshaw happened to pop a question:

"Why do we drink this stuff?"

"You don't lak it?" Jacob said. "I 'low as how it aint near as good as that I brung from Tennessee, but..."

"Oh, it is fine. Ripping stuff, old boy. I simply raise the philo- sophical question: why do we drink it?"

Jacob pondered. "Wal, I kinder relish the taste, myself."

"Yo. But do we not more relish that which it does to us?"

"I don't feature drunkenness. I know when to stop."

"Yo. But in between? Between drunkenness and sobriety there is a wide country, and what is the Name of that Country?"

"Joy?"

"No. Not if, by joy, you mean that kind which, although you have never felt it and thus cannot understand it, comes to the gentleman when with the lady in one-on-top-together-fastened-between. Not a bit of it, old fellow."

"Wal, what do you call the Country, then?"

"*Importance*," Fanshaw uttered, and let the word hover in the air between them like a hummingbird before continuing. "We know that we are nothing, you and I. And it is true, we are as nothing in the sight of Wahkontah. We are but flies he swats in sport. But the *pe-tsa-ni*—firewater—permits us for a while to forget this. The fire burns away our personal insignificance, and leaves us for a while a great sense of importance."

"But aint that joy?"

"Not like—" Fanshaw began, but stopped and contemplated Jacob for a moment before declaring, "My friend, some day you must experience the one-on-top-together-fastened-between."

Jacob kicked a small rock around on the ground for a while and then drew some doodles in the dirt with a stick, and at length said, "Aw, shoot," and, changing the subject, proposed their topic for debate that day: Which enjoys life more, a short-tailed dog or a long-tailed dog? (Both Fanshaw and Jacob Ingledew had dogs. Fanshaw's dog was short-tailed, Ingledew's was a long-tailed hound bitch; these animals had fought one another at first but later seemed to be on amicable terms.) Fanshaw agreed to this topic of debate, and for the next hour the two men matched oratory, but, since there was no referee, the victor could not be decided and each man felt that himself had won.

These debates between Fanshaw and Ingledew were both a sport and a diversion: they gave the two men something to talk about, because often there would be nothing to talk about after exhausting the usual run of topics: weather, crops and the existence of God. A few years later, every little settlement in the Ozarks had its debating society, and it is thought that their repertoire of topics for debate originated with Jacob Ingledew and Fanshaw. Which is worse, a cold or a hangover? Which is the superior tree, the oak or the pine? Which is worse, blindness or deafness? Which makes better whiskey, spring-water or rainwater? Is the earth round or flat? And so on. It was the last named topic which, next to their debates about the existence of God, provided the liveliest disputation.

Fanshaw's people had long believed that the earth was round and revolved slowly around the sun. This notion struck Jacob as fantastic and incredible. "If thet were so, everbody would git throwed offen it!" was his first reaction to this preposterous concept. Jacob began to believe that such a crackpot concept was the result of living in a round house, and he said so to Fanshaw. But Fanshaw proceeded by skillful argument to state his case, and Jacob lost ground, inch by inch, until he was left with only one line of defense: "Wal, if the earth is round, then we must be on the top side of it, and all them pore devils on the bottom has fell off."

To this, Fanshaw propounded an original explanation of gravity which I would like to dignify with the title Fanshaw's Law of Grav-ity, for, if it is correct, he goes far beyond Newton in explaining that mysterious force, namely, that all objects, all matter, actually weigh twice their apparent weight; the other half of their actual weight cre-ates a counteracting "pull" which is the gravity for the objects on the opposite side of the round globe. Thus, all matter is exerting an even outward pull from the center of the earth which is matched by the inward pull that we ordinarily think of as gravity. This concept was almost beyond Jacob's power of comprehension, but Fanshaw made it clear and simple by saying, "In other words, everything is holding everything else together."

After Fanshaw had left that day, and Jacob's brother Noah came back from where he was hiding in the woods during the Indian's visit, Jacob told him that the Indian thought the earth was round.

"Shitfire, why don't ye quit wastin yore time with him?" Noah said. Jacob repeated in detail Fanshaw's arguments for the earth being round, including his theory of gravity. Noah, however, remained unconvinced. *Every*body of any sense knew that the earth was flat.

(And indeed, the debating societies of every little settlement in the Ozarks would continue year by year to have this topic in their repertoire, until finally, years later, somebody brought in from St. Louis one of those disturbing volumes known as a "textbook.")

Early winter found the two friends hunting together, Jacob with his flintlock, Fanshaw with his bow. Again, it would be difficult to decide which of the two was the better marksman; they were both deadly accurate. Jacob's weapon seemed more effective in killing a bear rather than merely wounding it, but on at least one occasion Jacob's life was saved when, charged by a wounded bear or panther who still had enough life to bite and scratch, he fell and would have been mangled save for the speedy and accurate arrows of Fanshaw.

Fanshaw's bow was a large one, made of well-seasoned wood from the *bois d'arc*, coincidentally the same tree that his house was made of. A small but illuminating digression on language is necessary at this point, to help us get all our arks together. *Bois d'arc* is of course French and may be translated as Bow Wood, which is one of its names, the others being ironwood, yellowwood, hedge, mock orange, and Osage-orange, the last two referring to the fruit, which is a large yellow ball vaguely resembling an orange but which, as any schoolboy who has ever bitten into one has discovered, is quite bitter. "Osage-orange" is so called because the Osages used it to make their bows with, also their houses.

Arc, and also ark, comes from an Indo-European word root, *arkw*, which means bow or arrow (it is uncertain which; perhaps both together as a unit, since one is no good without the other). The Old Norse *arw* supplies our word for arrow. In almost all Indo-European languages, *arkw* is the root of such words as arc, arcade, arch, architecture, archer (shooter of arrow), arciform, arcuate, etc. Arc is also an obsolete form of ark, which meant originally a chest, box, coffer and hence a *place of refuge*, as in the Biblical Noah's vessel and as in all over this present book. Both Chaucer and Milton were wont to spell an arc as curve or arch as *ark*. The name of our state, Arkansas, is thought to mean in Indian the smoky, *bow*-shaped river, since Kansas means smoky river and ark means bow (although we should all know that Arkansas does not rhyme with Kansas and is accented on the first syllable). The name of our region, the Ozarks, is said by one early authority (Schoolcraft, who should know) to be compounded from "Osage" (our Indian again) and "Arkansas," which makes just as much sense as the usual idea that it comes from the French, *Aux Arc*. Therefore, when we speak of "the bois d'arc in the arciform architecture of the Arkansas Ozarks," every unit in this sentence can be traced to the same root.

What does it feel like to live inside Fanshaw's house? To settle this question once and for all, I propose that an enterprising group of students reconstruct an example of it, out in the hilly woods, and spend a night in it. And record their dreams the next morning. Many other tribes of Indians lived in the Ozarks down through history, and many of them lived in recesses under bluffs, caverns if you will, and these were rounded and curvilinear too. It is probably difficult to adapt rectilinear furniture to a curvilinear dwelling, but Fanshaw didn't have any.

One more round thing, and then we must search for the end of this chapter. In Fanshaw's garden there had grown a plant which Jacob Ingledew had not seen before. Luxuriant green bushes produced a rounded green fruit which, when ripened, turned red, but had a taste that was not sweet like other fruit but tangy, almost acrid, and produced a feeling of voluptuousness. Upon inquiry from Jacob, Fanshaw said this plant was called Tah May Toh, which could be translated as "love apple." Even now in early winter Fanshaw had a supply of green ones which were still turning ripe. But he failed in his attempts to get Jacob to sample one. Jacob, perhaps out of a growing sense that all round things, all concepts of roundness, and the supposedly round earth itself, were somehow alien to him, was suspicious that the Tah May Toh was poisonous, and he never ate them. (Later generations of Ingledews would learn to love them, and in fact the only "industry" that ever came to Stay More, unless you want to call Vernon Ingledew's Ham Processing Plant an industry, was a factory for canning these love apples.)

"It don't matter to me whether the earth is round or flat," Jacob said to Fanshaw one evening in the late winter. "I aint gonna git to the other side nohow."

"Where *are* you going to get to, old chap?"

"Huh? I've done got there."

"The time has come, now, when we must at last cultivate a topic of discussion which, hitherto, we have avoided: why did you come here and build upon this land?"

"Hit was gittin jist too durn crowded back in Tennessee," Jacob said. "I purt nigh couldn't lift my elbow 'thout hittin somebody and the preachers was so thick a feller couldn't say 'heck' without gittin a sermon fer it."

"But you have never even asked for permission to build here. Stay More is the land of my grandfathers."

"'Stay More'?"

Fanshaw chuckled. "Yo. That is what I have come to call it."

Jacob Ingledew repeated the name a couple of times, and himself chuckled. "I reckon that'll do as well as ary other name."

"But you cannot," Fanshaw said.

"Cannot what?"

"Stay more."

"Says who?" Jacob demanded. "You fixin to try to run me off?"

"My grandfathers are buried here."

"My grandchildren will be buried here."

"Ho. Where is their grandmother?"

"I'll find one, by and by."

"Ho."

Then Fanshaw told him the story of the origin of his people. Once upon a time a snail was washed far down the river by floods. He was a good snail but he was alone. Wahkontah, in appreciation of his goodness and in pity for his loneliness, caused the snail to sleep for a long, long time. During the sleep, the snail's entire body was changed. When he awoke he started back into his shell, but it was far too small. Then he looked at himself, and, seeing that he had long legs, he stood up and walked about. As he walked he kept growing. Hair grew on his head, and from his shoulders long, powerful arms grew. This new creature remembered his former home, and walked far back up the river to the home of the snails, but he could not live with them, and he went in search of some place he could call home. When he grew hungry, Wahkontah gave him a bow and arrow and taught him how to get food. Day by day he went out in search of a home. At last the man, for such he had become, came to the hut of a beaver. The old beaver came out, and said, "Who are you and what do you want?" The man told his story and said he was seeking a home. The young man and the beaver were about to fight, when the beaver's daughter came out and said she would teach the man to build a house, so that he would not have to trespass on others. To this arrangement the old beaver finally agreed. So the beaver's daughter and the young man went away together, and she taught him how to build a house of bent bois d'arc poles and to thatch it. Because of her kindness, Wahkontah changed the beaver's daughter into a maiden, and she became the squaw wife of the man. These two were the first of the people, and that is why they wear the beaver skin ornament.

"What is the origin of *your* people?" Fanshaw then asked him. Jacob, although an ungodly man, knew the story of Adam and Eve. He told this to Fanshaw, who listened attentively. When he had finished, Fanshaw said, "I now propose the topic for our next debate: Which is greater, the story of the snail and the beaver or the story of Adam and Eve?"

The two men debated this topic at length. Fanshaw pointed out that while there is a distinct reference to the paraboloid house of the man and woman who were snail and beaver, there is no reference to any sort of house for Adam and Eve, neither before nor after their Fall. What did they live in? Jacob went and fetched his brother Noah's Bible, and read second and third Genesis, but couldn't find any mention of a house, so he had to concede that point to Fanshaw. His own chief point was that God created Adam in his own image, whereas snails are pretty slow and slimy, and beavers are fat and bucktoothed. They argued that point back and forth until Fanshaw conceded.

So went their debate, and both men realized that what they were actually debating was the beginning of their Great Debate: Who has the right to Stay More, the Indian or the white man? although they did not ever say so in other than metaphorical terms. When it came the usual time for Fanshaw to go back to his lady, and Jacob uttered his ritual "Stay more," Fanshaw replied, "Thank you, I believe I shall," and he stayed a long time. Jacob gave him a big hunk of stewed venison and took one for himself, and both men washed their meat down with great gulps of the Arkansas sour mash and began for the first time to get drunk together, but kept on with their Great Debate until neither man was sober enough to reason logically, at which point Fanshaw expressed an idea, a peculiar notion the exact motive of which I have never quite been able to determine:

"It is time, old lad, that you experience the one-on-top-together-fastened-between."

"Huh? How? Who?" stammered Jacob, who if sober would not have been able to utter a sound in response to such a suggestion.

"My lady," Fanshaw replied.

Jacob was still sober enough to blush, and say, "Aw, shoot. That'd be adultery."

"What is 'adultery'?"

"That's when a feller does the one-on-top business with another feller's wife."

"Your people forbid it?"

"Wal, the Bible's agin it. God punishes adulterers."

"But you do not believe in God."

"Yeah, but I dasn't ask yore woman."

"No need to ask. Often she has mentioned the thought. I have but to tell her you will."

Jacob began trembling. "But if she was even to look at me, I dasn't."

"If she looks at you, you will not see her. It will be very dark."

Jacob was in a quandary. He realized that to refuse might be taken by the Indian as an insult. But to do for the first time something he had never done before, even with the nerve of much drink, might require talent which he did not possess.

Fanshaw prompted, "There is much joy in it."

"I reckon," Jacob allowed, but he was afraid that if there was so much joy in it he might develop a hankering for it and want to do it again sometime. He remembered the first time he had taken a drink of whiskey. On the other hand, this might be the only opportunity in his life to have a woman without going through all the long bother of courting her and playing games and being embarrassed and finally working up enough nerve to ask her and then even more nerve to keep pursuing her if she turned you down the first time and then the final uncertainty of whether she would even like it or not. "Okay," Jacob whispered hoarsely.

Fanshaw clapped him on the shoulder. "Good. I will go tell her. She will be much pleased. You will enter our domicile by the west door, her door, and she will be there. There is but one consideration. A delicate matter. I apologize in advance. It must be revealed to you that, to our people, especially to the women, the body of white man has an odor which is … not altogether agreeable. Here is what I suggest. You should first wash in three waters. Wash in rainwater, then in creekwater, then in springwater. After, do not replace your buckskins, which carry the same odor. Come unadorned. She will be waiting." Fanshaw stood up then and left.

Jacob had one more drink while he built up the fire in his fireplace and hung the kettle there filled with water from his rain-barrel. He found a piece of lye soap. He took off his buckskin jacket and trousers and moccasins, and when the water was hot he finished his drink and wetted the soap and began scrubbing himself with it. While he was doing this Noah returned to the cabin.

"Shitfire," Noah said. "I thought you'd never git rid of him. He shore stayed longer than usual, and I was a-gittin powerful cold out yonder in the dark."

"You ortent to be so afeared of him. He's a good injun."

"The only good injun is a dead injun," Noah replied. Then he asked, "What you takin a bath this time of night fer?"

But Jacob just grinned and finished his bath, splashing all the soap off with hot rainwater. Then he opened the door and went naked across his fields to the creek. He tested the creekwater with his toe. It was icy cold, in this time of late winter, but he took a deep breath and plunged in. He rubbed himself all over with the creekwater, then his teeth began chattering, and he climbed out and ran up the hill toward his spring. Even the exertion of running did not keep him from being covered with gooseflesh big as small-pox. But the springwater, he discovered, was of a much higher temperature than the creekwater, and seemed almost warm by comparison. Again he washed himself all over, top to toes. The effect of all the cold and cool water was sobering him up, so after his last bath he had to return to the cabin for one more drink. Noah was asleep. Jacob drank straight from the jug, several lusty swallows, said "Ah!" and smacked his lips, then started out for the Indian's house.

It was pitch dark, there was no moon, and he couldn't find out which of the dwellings in the camp was Fanshaw's. He tried the west doors of several, groping around on his hands and knees inside without finding any woman. He began to think that Fanshaw was just playing a joke on him. But he tried one more west door, and there she was. His hand touched her fur coverlet and then her bare leg. She was lying on her back. She didn't say anything and of course he didn't either. He just climbed on top of her. She embraced him, with her arms and legs alike. Soon, soon they became fastened between. Fanshaw was right: there was much joy. The woman made murmurs and sighs of joy, and Jacob realized he was being pretty noisy himself. He wished this joy could go on all night, but there is an end to everything, and finally the woman's legs unclasped their embrace of his back and straightened out, and then the woman's whole body arched itself into a long quivering *arc*: an ark: a bow: a soft but taut arch that held him suspended up from the earth for a long moment until he fired: burst: was a lightningbolt and its thunderclap and the afterclaps rattling slowly away.

When he woke up it was daylight and he was still there, but the woman was gone.

"Shitfire, whar in tarnation have you been, and mothernaked to boot?" his brother Noah demanded, when, at long last, Jacob returned to his own bed.

Jacob decided not to hide it. "I laid with that injun's squaw last night."

"What je do thet fer?" Noah asked innocently.

"Huh? I mean, I done went and *entered* her."

"*Entered* her?"

"You eejit. We *fucked.*"

"Oh," Noah said. "What'd it feel like?"

"Lightnin and thunder."

"Gee," Noah said.

"You orter try it sometime," Jacob suggested.

"Me? Shitfire, I wouldn't go near a injun even to fuck it."

All that day, Jacob noticed an irregularity in himself, perhaps an afterclap of his afterclaps: he didn't feel like doing anything. This was the first white man's "energy shortage" in the Ozarks. Jacob spent the whole day sitting by his fire. This is the origin of the quite erroneous concept of the "shiftless hillbilly." Usually Jacob was industrious, for the hard life of the frontiersman admits of no indolence. He couldn't quite understand why he didn't feel like doing any work today, unless it had something to do with last night, although it really wasn't all that much effort to do the one-on-top-together-fastened-between, and he'd had a good night's sleep in the meantime. But suddenly Jacob realized that Fanshaw was terribly lazy, even for an Indian. He never seemed to do much: back in the summer he had puttered in his garden for maybe half an hour each day, and that was it. Even on hunts, he always took his time, and never worked up a sweat, and was ready to quit as soon as one animal had been bagged. It dawned on Jacob that there must be some direct correlation between Fanshaw's laziness and the amount of time he spent doing the one-on-top-together-fastened-between. Up until this moment, Jacob had never really felt superior to the Indian, but now he did. And it also dawned on Jacob that herein lay the real difference between their dwellings. Fanshaw's house, for all its complexity, *looked* like something that a bunch of people had thrown together in one afternoon, whereas Jacob's house *looked* like something that two men had worked from sunup to sundown for a fortnight to build.

When Fanshaw came at his usual hour that afternoon, Jacob after pouring the drinks suggested this difference as a topic of debate, probably to divert their attention from the event of the night previous.

So they harangued one another for an hour on the subject: Which looks more industrious, the red man's or the white man's domicile? "Compare a bird's nest to an anthill," Fanshaw suggested. They both avoided mentioning the event of the night previous until they had had several drinks and finished (or at least grew tired of) debating whose house looked more industrious, and the importance or unimportance of industry, but finally Fanshaw broached the event of the night previous by asking, "Well. How was it?"

"It?" said Jacob, although he knew what Fanshaw meant. "Yeah. It was hunky-dory."

"Hunky-dory?" Fanshaw said.

"Scrumdoodle," Jacob elaborated. "Galuptious. Splendiferous. Humdinger. Slopergobtious. Bardacious. Yum-yum. Swelleroo. Gumptious. Danderoo. Superbangnamious."

"But did you *like* it?" Fanshaw persisted.

"Betcha boots," Jacob said. "Shore thang. What I mean. I aint kiddin. 'Pon my word. Take it from me. I hope to tell ye. Indeedy. You're darn tootin."

Fanshaw frowned. "Say yes or no, please."

"Yeah," Jacob said.

"Good," Fanshaw said. "I said you would. Now we can debate topics which previously excluded you. I propose our first: Which would you choose, if forced to abandon the other: whiskey or woman?"

This was an interesting topic which kept them busy for another hour. Curiously enough, Jacob took the side of woman and Fanshaw took the side of whiskey. The former argued that woman was a more effective panacea, somnifacient, emollient, palliative, embrocative, demulcent and diaphoretic. The latter argued that it is better to feel importance than joy. At the end of their debate, which, again, lacking a referee, neither man won, Fanshaw intimated that Jacob was welcome to repeat this night his experience of the night previous, and Jacob was much obliged and beholden. He took another bath-in-three-waters and went again to feel the lightningbolts and thunderclaps atop the long soft but taut arc.

In the spring, early spring, Noah did all of the plowing because Jacob was just too blamed enervated to help. One day Jacob and Fanshaw were watching Noah plow, when Fanshaw asked, "What manner of animal is that which pulls the plow?"

"That's a mule," Jacob explained.

"What is a mule?"

"If a jackass serves a mare, the foal is a mule and is sterile."

"Tell me," requested Fanshaw. "What is the purpose of the mule?"

"Wal," Jacob pointed out, "a mule works harder than a horse and he don't tire out as easy."

"Because he is sterile?"

"Maybe. I never thought of it that way, but maybe you're right."

Not long afterward, still in the spring, Jacob noticed an oddity: Fanshaw's language was beginning to deteriorate. Right in the middle of one of their debates (Which is better, a round-topped door or a flat-topped door?) and apropos of nothing that Jacob could figure out, Fanshaw said, "Ho! Toward what shall my people direct their footsteps? it has been said in the house. It is toward a little valley they shall direct their footsteps. Verily, it is not a little valley that is spoken of. It is toward the bend of a river they shall direct their footsteps. Verily, it is not the bend of a river that is spoken of. It is toward a little house that they shall direct their footsteps." Jacob wondered if it was some kind of riddle or conundrum but decided it was just jibberish and maybe the Indian was losing his marbles. Yet from that day on, Fanshaw never talked good clear English anymore. "White man garden plenty big," is the way he began to talk. "Indian garden little lazy." Jacob never asked him what was happening to his speech; perhaps Jacob was afraid to.

One day in early summer Fanshaw came and simply said "Come" and led Jacob back to Fanshaw's paraboloid house. His woman was standing in front of it. It was the first time that Jacob had ever got a good look at her in the daylight, and he was embarrassed. He found it hard to keep looking at her, but he did, and saw that she was very pretty. Also he saw that her belly was bulging. Fanshaw pointed at the bulge, and then at himself. "Me mule," he declared. "Sterile. You, jackass. She mare. Jackass serve mare, make more mule."

Jacob didn't know what to say. "Wal, I'm sorry. You tole me to."

"Yo. Good? Not good?"

"It 'pends on how ye look at it," Jacob suggested.

"Yo. Good? Not good?"

Jacob meditated, and at length replied, "Good. Ever womarn orter have the right to have a baby."

"Yo. She happy." Fanshaw spoke a word to his squaw and she smiled. "I tell her smile, she smile. Now we go." Fanshaw elevated his palm above his head in the Indian "how" fashion. Jacob didn't know what else to do, so he raised his hand in the same way. When he did so, Fanshaw clasped his elevated hand and held it up there in a long tight grip which made Jacob think maybe he was trying to Indian-wrestle. Jacob was ready to break his arm off if he was, but the Indian merely held their hands together above their heads and said to him, "Farewell."

"Aw, you don't have to leave," Jacob protested. "Stay more, and we'll have us some real fine deebates."

But the Indian merely said, in his own custom, "Fuck off," and then he and his squaw, with their few possessions rolled in a blanket, began walking west. Jacob never saw them again. Sometime later, as we shall see, he removed their domicile to his backyard, where he converted it into a corncrib. Noah burned the other Indian homes in the clearing, and converted the clearing into a corn patch.

If this has been a quiet, lonely chapter, I think I must have intended it so: the moon sometimes hanging in the night sky for hour upon hour, the wind timidly on occasion rustling a few leaves, in summer the lightning bugs (even then) going off and on lazily as they had all night, or in winter morning wisps of woodsmoke rising and drifting with the morning mist. Things will pick up, as we go along.

"Funny," Jacob remarked one day to his brother Noah. "I never even learned that injun's name."

"Which?" Noah said. "Him or her?"

"Neither blessit one of 'em."

Chapter two

Let us first consider the points of resemblance between Fanshaw's domicile and the first Ingledew house, dissimilar though they may seem. Both had no windows. Both had but an earthen floor. And although the Ingledew place is foursquare, it is built of *rounded* logs. Later houses in Stay More would be built of logs hewed flat, but in their haste to clear a bit of land and put a roof over their heads, the Ingledew brothers did not take the time to hew the logs. (One early authority makes a distinction between the rounded-log dwelling and the hewed-log dwelling by referring to the former as "cabin," the latter as "house," and we shall do likewise.) Fanshaw and Jacob Ingledew were both over six feet tall, but Jacob did not have to stoop, even slightly, to go through his door, which cleared his head by several inches.

There were (the past tense is deliberate; Jacob's cabin, like Fanshaw's domicile, is gone now; it was washed away in a flood) no windows for several reasons. First, the difficulty of cutting openings in the large, heavy hardwood logs; second, the impossibility of obtaining glass for panes; third, the need to provide maximum insulation in winter and summer; and fourth, perhaps most important, what was a kind of psychological insulation against the wilderness, the possibly hostile new world, the Indians if ever they returned, etc. Just as at Deerfield, Massachusetts, and in garrison houses all over colonial New England, the first cabins and houses in the Arkansas Ozarks were a physical manifestation of the settler's desire to protect himself from unknown dangers. We can think, therefore, of the Ingledew place as a "shy" dwelling. And it is medieval; yet all of the best Ozark architecture remains essentially medieval, in the tradition of the vernacular architecture in England and Presbyterian Ireland, whence the settlers' forebears came; the classicizing tendencies of the Renaissance, baroque and rococo periods never affected the humbler architecture of those areas, and would never affect, or only slightly affect, the architecture of the Ozark highlands.

Watch this cabin leave the ground! In three upward stages, first the base: the base is of fieldstone, mostly sandstone, but rocks, of the earth, of the ground, clinging to it. The next part up is of logs, their interstices chinked with mud, not so much of the earth as rocks, but still, particularly because the logs are not hewed but left round, and because the mud was wet dirt, still of the earth. And finally the roof, rived thick boards, not shingles actually, farthest from earth, last in the ascending transition from earth to sky, split from oak logs with a frow, *worked*: most of the brothers' labor went into the roof, which they laid in the dark of the moon so the boards would not warp or crack—a superstition, but one that works. Notice how the brothers' labor increases as the house rises, except in the chimney ("chimbly" is how they say it, all of them) whose inward taper is itself a part of the ascending transition from earth to sky, rock to air.

Axe, adz, and auger were all it took. And sweat. The reasons they don't make 'em that way anymore are two: good virgin hardwood is hard to come by, and good lathering sweat seems unnecessary in an age of power machinery. If, as Jacob suspected, laziness may be correlated with sexual activity, then the Ingledew cabin was the product of years of stored-up energy. The two brothers built it, as we have seen, in a fortnight of sunup to sundown sweating. They killed two birds with one stone, however: the trees they cut to build the house cleared a field to plant in.

There is one other thing the cabin has in common with Fanshaw's place: there is not a bit of metal in it. Astonishing. No nails: the roof boards are tied to the rafters. The door hinges are made of wood. There is no iron. Where would the Ingledews find iron? Even the works of their clock were all wood.

The first "visitor" to Stay More was a young clock peddler from Connecticut, named Eli Willard. He showed up at the Ingledew cabin one evening not long after Fanshaw had permanently departed, and the Ingledew dog barked at him. This dog, whom we had little reason to notice in the previous chapter, was a hound bitch named, despite her sex, Tige or Tyge. One of the main functions of a dog was to bark at strangers and thus alert the house. But so far Tige had not barked, and Jacob wondered if she still knew how. Sometimes he would bark at her in an effort to stimulate her barking but she had simply stared at him with what might be called doggy disconcertion. So now, when the clock peddler showed up and Tige began barking, the brothers, who were inside the cabin eating their supper, were at first puzzled.

"Is that ole Tige?" Noah wondered aloud.

"Caint be," Jacob allowed, but he went to investigate, and saw the clock peddler, Eli Willard, sitting on his horse. Strapped to the saddlebag was one (1) shelf clock.

"Good evening, sir," said Eli Willard to Jacob.

"Howdy, stranger," Jacob replied. "Light down and hitch." As there was no hitching post at the Ingledew cabin this invitation must have been merely a formality, like "stay more." Nevertheless Eli Willard dismounted and found a large rock with which to weight down the ends of his horse's reins. Then he observed, "The road seems to end here."

"What road?" Jacob was curious to know.

The man pointed north. "Why, the road that I came here on. All the way from Connecticut."

Jacob had never heard of Connecticut. It sounded like some kind of Indian name, so he figured maybe it was over in Indian Territory. It was news to him that a road led from Stay More all the way over there. Jacob looked the other way, south, beyond his house, and observed, "Wal, I reckon it don't go no farther."

"A coincidence, and a good one," Eli Willard declared, "because I have only one clock left." He unstrapped the lone shelf clock from his saddlebag, and held it up for Jacob's inspection, turning it slowly around for him to admire the woodwork, and then winding it (even the key was wood) and showing Jacob that it ran properly. Since all the parts were wood, there could be no chime or gong, but this clock had a sort of rattling mechanism, so that it could "strike" the hour by making a noise that sounded like a woodpecker close up. Jacob was very impressed with this. "My last clock," Eli Willard reiterated. "I was going to keep it, out of sentimental reasons. But to honor your status as my last and final contact, I can bear to let you have it. Here." And he gave the clock into Jacob's hands.

"Wal, gosh dawg, thet's awful good of ye," Jacob said. "Caint I give ye ary thang in return?"

"Twenty dollars," Eli Willard said.

"Huh? Why, that's *money*!" Jacob exclaimed.

"Legal tender, cash, currency, coin of the realm, oil of palm," Eli Willard said. "Two sawbucks on the barrelhead."

Jacob turned the pockets on his buckskins inside out. "I aint got a cent to my name," he declared. "And neither has he"—indicating Noah, who had emerged from the cabin to witness the transaction. Noah also turned the pockets of his buckskins inside out.

Eli Willard looked from one brother to the other, and shook his head in sympathy. "Yes, it's hard to wrest a living from this rocky soil, isn't it? Be that as it may, allow me to present this clock to your wife regardless." He moved toward the door of the cabin.

"Uh, we aint got ary," Jacob pointed out.

"Allow me to place it upon your mantel then," Eli Willard said, and continued entering the cabin. Actually, this was a ruse that he, and dozens of other Connecticut clock peddlers swarming through the Ozarks, used to gain admission to the interior of the dwelling, to see if there was anything of value inside that might be traded for the clock. Eli Willard discovered there was no mantel-shelf over the fireplace. No nails in the house, he found a peg on the wall and hung the clock on it. "There!" he said. "A handsome addition to your humble home." Then he began to look around at the contents of the room.

The Ingledew cabin was, of course, only one room, unlike so many other buildings in our study. Here are the objects that Eli Willard saw: two beds "built-in," the corners of the cabin forming two of their four sides, mattresses of ticking brought from Tennessee stuffed with cornshucks grown in Arkansas, resting upon rude slats and covered with patchwork quilts (heirlooms brought from Tennessee); two ladder-back chairs which Noah carved from maple and seated with woven hickory splints; a simple table he also carved from maple; two lamps, the fuel of which was bear's oil; miscellaneous cooking utensils (which, come to think of it, were made of iron and seem to contradict what I said earlier about there being no metal in the house); Noah's Bible (which he could not read; upon his departure from Tennessee his mother had forced it upon him, having given up all hope for Jacob); on the walls things hanging: their two flintlock rifles and powder horns propped up on racks of deer antlers; two large deerskins sewed up to become vessels, one for bear's oil, the other for wild honey (these, incidentally, were the only things Eli Willard saw that interested him, but they were too large to pack off on his horse); a water bucket homefashioned of red cedar with a gourd dipper in it; from the joists of the ceiling were strung dried things, tobacco, sliced pumpkin, red pepper; and, finally, several demijohns of Arkansas sour mash (but Eli Willard was a teetotaler).

"Well," Eli Willard concluded, "I am not above accepting a note of credit." Then he explained that he would return in six months and, if the gentlemen were satisfied with their clock, they could pay him at that time. If not satisfied, they could return their clock, or, better, Eli Willard would replace it with one more satisfactory. So he got Jacob's signature on an i.o.u. for twenty dollars, shook hands with both men, and began to disappear.

"Stay more!" Jacob invited. "You caint go rushin off this time of evenin. It'll be pitch dark soon. Stay the night."

"Busy, busy," was all Eli Willard replied, and rode his horse off into the dusk. The brothers wondered where he would spend the night. Maybe he didn't spend the night. Maybe he just went to sleep on his horse and kept on going. At any rate, the brothers would not see him again for six months, when he would return for his money, and they knew they had better get to work and do something to earn twenty dollars in cash money. So they got to work.

Now that the redskin squaw was no longer there to tempt him, Jacob found that he had a lot of energy again. Both brothers rose at dawn, and after a quick breakfast (there was no coffee, not even green coffee; instead a rather palatable substitute was made from roasted corn meal and molasses) they would plunge into their work: clearing land and more land, felling trees and burning them and digging up the stumps by hitching the mule (there was only one now; a panther got the other) to the stump to pull it out: it took weeks of such labor to clear a mere acre. Each night right after supper the brothers fell into their beds, exhausted but satisfied.

Although the Ingledew cabin was medieval, we may note a few features it has in common with classical colonial buildings: the saddle-notched ends of the logs overlap one another exactly in the same manner as quoins, but whereas the quoins on most American colonial houses were false quoins made of flat boards, the quoins of the log cabin are true quoins holding not just one log to the other, but one wall to the other: they hold the whole house together. In classical Greek architecture, it is thought that the grooves in the triglyph of the frieze are a translation into marble of the grooves scored into the wooden ceiling joists of the original temples, which were made of wood instead of marble. This doesn't have anything to do, directly, with the Ingledew cabin, except to indicate that even the most elaborate classical detail has its origins in such humble structures as a log cabin's quoins.

The dimensions of the Ingledew cabin, and of space in general at Stay More, may be measured in "hats"—one hat being the distance that Jacob Ingledew could toss his coonskin headgear: approximately 16.5 feet. The Ingledew cabin is almost exactly one hat long by one hat wide, or, simply, one hat square, and also one hat in elevation, from base to gable-peak. When the brothers measured the size of a tree they had felled, or a piece of the acreage they had cleared, or the distance from their backyard to their spring, Jacob would put his coonskin cap to good use. It was a satisfying life for both of them, building and felling and clearing and pacing off, hat after hat.

Lest we get too pastoral a picture of their life and work, however, brief mention should be made of their afflictions, plagues and pests. In addition to the abovementioned panther who in the dark of night screamed at their mules, petrifying them, then attacked and killed one of them and dragged it off into the woods and devoured it, the Ingledews were constantly assailed by natural enemies, both vegetable and animal: poison ivy, poison oak, poison sumac, stinging nettles, rattlesnakes, copperheads, cottonmouths, leeches, stinging scorpions, deadly spiders, wasps, bees, yellow-jackets, hornets. One would almost believe that Nature did not want the Ingledews. Maybe She didn't.

What was worse in terms of pure torment were the ticks, the chiggers, and the frakes. Because these afflictions are not universally known but are particularly severe in the Ozarks, a word of description may be in order. Everybody gets mosquitoes, cockroaches, lice, fleas, houseflies, ants, gnats, moths, etc., and the Ingledews had more than their share of these too, but they were particularly plagued by ticks, chiggers, and frakes. Ticks (order *Acarina*, suborder *Mesostigmata*) are medium-sized to minute arachnids, coming in many shapes and colors; under a magnifying glass they are hideous, especially their mouths, with which they attach themselves to the body and suck blood until engorged and sometimes thereafter; some of them are also carriers of dreadful fevers. Chiggers (suborder *Prostigmata*, family *Thrombidiidae*) are tiny red mites, almost invisible to the naked eye, which also attach themselves to the body with a hideous mouth, and produce swelling and intense itching. Frakes (it is always plural; while a man might say he has *a* chigger or *a* tick, he always has *the* frakes), like many viruses, are not fully understood by medical science; most medical experts consider it a usually benign fungus, but others are convinced it is a variant form of herpes; all it has in common with ticks and chiggers is a predilection for the genital area; in fact, whereas ticks and chiggers may afflict any part of the body, the frakes is confined to the genital area, where it produces a rash of small blisters that eventually erupt with a discharge. Unlike ticks and chiggers too, which only come in warm weather, the frakes may strike at any time of the year. Experts are agreed that the only known predisposing cause of the frakes is hard work. It used to be thought that overwork was the cause, but now it is known that any long, sustained task, any hard and fruitful labor, is liable to bring on the frakes, as if Nature were punishing man for his puny efforts to accomplish something. This is borne out by the fact that while ticks and chiggers afflict many animals other than man, the only animals that get the frakes are horses, mules, sled dogs, beasts of burden, etc., that is, *working* animals. The itching is not quite as severe as that produced by chiggers and ticks, but the worst effect is the aftermath: that for weeks, months, possibly years after the condition has cleared up, the sufferer is left feeling that there is nothing worth doing, that all labor is vain, that life is a bad and pointless joke. The Ingledew brothers were destined to get the frakes on several occasions. The pity is, there was never anybody to tell them what caused it.

The clock which came from Connecticut was not, it must be said, a very good one. One night at midnight it struck twenty-six times. "Git up, Jake!" Noah hollered. "Shitfire, it's later than I've ever knowed it to be!" Jacob suspected that something in the inner works was amiss, for at the rate the clock was running, by his calculation, he would be a hundred and forty-three years old when the clock peddler returned. Methuselah and the other longevous old men of the Bible must have got their clocks from Connecticut. Still, Jacob dutifully wound up the clock each night before retiring. "If you got it, use it," must have been his philosophy. He was, however, required to silence the striking mechanism after the novelty of it wore off and it became annoying. After three weeks of careful investigation, Jacob found a way to open the back of the clock, and he stuffed a wadded-up vacated wasp's nest into the striking mechanism, silencing it. Jacob continued keeping time by the sun and moon and stars, but it was a diversion to watch the minute hand of his clock running around and around in the still cabin.

Not all of their land was forested; the portion that bordered the creek was flat, rich soil which was "bottom" land. But except for the clearing where the Indian camp had been, it was all covered with a dense growth of cane, bamboo, leatherwood, hazel, grapevines and large saw briars, which had to be grubbed and burned, a job which made clearing the forest seem easy. This good bottom land would be capable of producing fifty bushels of corn to the acre, but getting it cleared was the worst job the brothers had yet done, and after three weeks of clearing bottom land Noah Ingledew was "plumb beat out" and came down with the first attack of the frakes. He didn't know what it was, and neither did Jacob. Noah took off his buckskins and anointed the frakes with bear's oil, but that didn't do any good. He made a salve by boiling mullein leaves in lard, and applied that to his frakes, with negligible results. He resorted then to more drastic remedies, concocting a poultice the essential ingredient of which was panther urine, difficult to obtain. Panthers were easy enough to come by, but persuading one to urinate into a container was entirely a different matter, and since Noah was too weakened by his frakes to do the job, Jacob had to do it for him. Yet even after all the trouble that Jacob went to, the resultant panther-piss poultice had no effect whatever on Noah's frakes. Jacob offered to hitch the mule to the wagon and drive Noah back east in search of a doctor, but Noah protested that he wasn't worth it, for already the severe sense of worthlessness that comes after an attack of the frakes was beginning to affect him. He took to his bed and just lay there day after day. In time the frakes erupted and then began to heal over, but more and more did Noah feel that work is senseless, toil vain, life pointless, and he would not get up from his bed. In a way, he was unintentionally evening the score with Jacob, whose work Noah had done back during the time when Jacob didn't feel like working on account of fooling around with that Indian squaw. Now Jacob had to do all the work, but Noah mocked him.

"Hit aint no use," Noah would say. "Shitfire, yo're jist workin yore butt off fer nuthin. Earworms or worse will git all yore corn, wait and see if they or worse don't."

And yet, for all his sense of futility, Noah felt one redeeming emotion, which can only be called a sense of snugness. Lying there day after day, thinking few thoughts, having no daydreams or aspirations of any kind, he was aware only of the walls and roof of his cabin, and aware of how he was sheltered, of how his ark was a refuge, snug, cozy, restful. It was *home*. Our illustration cannot depict the site of the Ingledews' cabin, but the site contributed to the feeling of snugness, because the cabin was in a holler—by local definition, "a little hollered out place at the foot of a mountain." While the land that the cabin was on was level enough for a garden and one of their cornpatches, the land on both sides of the cabin rose abruptly up the mountainside, while behind the cabin the holler extended some three hundred feet to the Ingledews' spring, where it began an abrupt ascent of the mountain. So in his snug cabin in this snug hollow Noah aestivated. Winter came and he hibernated. Jacob never scolded him for his inactivity. He knew it could happen to himself at any time ... and it would.

In the autumn Jacob went off to look for a town where he could sell his pelts. He knew nothing of the geography of the region. He knew only a few rough basics: that civilization lay mostly toward the east, that Indian Territory was mostly in the west, that in the north it got colder and in the south it got warmer. He had no idea in which direction he would most likely find a town. His agricultural labors had produced no cash crop this season, but his spare-time trapping, for beaver, 'coon, otter and mink, had produced a few dozen pelts that ought to bring enough to pay off the clock peddler with enough left over to indulge one of Jacob's dreams: buying a cow. Next to whiskey, milk was Jacob's favorite beverage, but a year and a half had passed since he'd last had a drop of milk. Also, getting a cow was the first step toward starting a herd of beef.

But Jacob didn't know where any towns were. The last one they had passed, coming from Tennessee, must have been a hundred miles back on the White River. Still, if he could just find a small settlement where he could unload his pelts and buy a cow, he would be satisfied. He took an egg-sized rock and threw it as hard as he could, straight up into the air. Whichever direction it fell, that way Jacob would go. The rock stayed up in the air a long time, but by and by Jacob heard it coming down. He couldn't see it for all the woods, but he could hear it crashing through the trees, and the noise was coming from the south. There wasn't any road or trail at all that went south, so Jacob couldn't take the mule. He strapped as many pelts as he could carry on his back, and with his long rifle he set out on foot.

He walked for five days and four nights up mountains and down without finding a settlement, and finally was stopped by a large river too wide to swim across. This, he guessed, must be the Arkansas. He followed it downstream for just half a day, and came to a good-sized town. This, he learned, was called Spadra (it no longer exists today, or is practically a ghost town, south of Clarksville). Along the riverfront were shops, and one of these was a fur trader's. The fur trader was happy to buy Jacob Ingledew's pelts, and complimented him on the quality of them. The beaver skins fetched two dollars apiece, while the mink and otter skins brought a dollar each, and the coonskins two bits. Jacob received a total of almost a hundred dollars. He'd never had that much money in his life. But Spadra was full of establishments designed to part a man from his money: saloons, whorehouses, gambling parlors. Jacob resisted these as best he could, although his best was not good enough: he lost half his hundred dollars before getting out.

Still, he had more than enough to pay off the clock peddler and buy a cow. The latter became his next immediate objective. Looking around, he saw a large building with a sign out front: Spadra Stock Exchange. He went inside. There were a lot of men standing around tables, holding slips of paper and talking rapidly all at once. Jacob didn't see any cows, or any other stock. A man came up to him and asked if he could be of any help. Jacob told him he was in the market for cows. "Good," the man said, "swine are up, beef are down. How many?" Just one, Jacob said. The man looked at him, then said, "Wait here," and went off to confer with a group of other men standing around one of the tables. The other men cast glances at Jacob, and Jacob began to get the impression that they might be laughing at him. But at length, his man returned, and said, "All right. One cow it is. What do you bid?" Jacob said he didn't have ary idea how much to bid. How much was usual? "Six and three-eights might do it," the man said. "Can I go to seven?" Sure, Jacob told him, and the man went away again. He returned shortly, beaming. "Got it at six and five-eights," he declared. Jacob paid him six dollars and sixty-three cents, plus ten percent brokerage fee and commission, and the man started to walk away, but Jacob said Hey! Where is my cow? "In Kansas City," the man said. Jacob didn't want to show his ignorance of geography by asking how to get there, so he left the stock exchange, and stopped the first man he met on the street and asked, Which way is Kansas City? The man pointed, toward the northwest.

Jacob left Spadra, and walked for the rest of the day northwest, but he didn't come to Kansas City. He met another man and asked again, Which way is Kansas City? and the man pointed northwest. He walked on for two more days without finding any city, and met an old man and asked once more, Which way is Kansas City? and when the old man pointed northwest Jacob asked him how far it was. "What difference do it make?" the old man said. "You're a-gorn there anyhow, aint ye?" So Jacob walked on.

After several more days, he finally came out of the mountains down into a valley where there was a city, or a large-sized town. There were some loafers sitting in front of the courthouse, and he asked them if this was Kansas City. "Shore thang," one of them replied, so Jacob said he had bought a cow and wanted to find the stockyards. The loafers offered to accompany him to the stockyards; he was much obliged at their courtesy. They walked him a good distance to the other end of town, and there was the stockyards, full of cows and bulls and calves. "Jist take yore pick," one of the loafers said, so Jacob selected a good-sized Jersey heifer. One of the loafers fetched a length of rope and tied it around the heifer's neck, and then they opened the gate, and Jacob led her out. He walked her back through the town.

Looking back at one point, he saw that not just the loafers but a crowd of people were following him. When he got as far as the courthouse, he saw that a man wearing a silver star on his chest was tying a rope to a big maple tree in the courthouse yard, and on the end of the rope was a hangman's noose. Then the man wearing the star came up to Jacob and said, "Do you know what we do to cattle rustlers in this town?" No, Jacob said, he didn't know. The man pointed at the rope and said, "We hang 'em." By this time, the town square was full of people. The man wearing the star took Jacob's arm and started leading him toward the gallows. I aint rustled no cattle! Jacob protested. "Where'd you get that heifer?" the man demanded. Jacob explained that he had bought it for six dollars and sixty-three cents plus commission at the Spadra Stock Exchange and the feller there told him to come here to Kansas City to get it. "This here aint Kansas City," the man said. "It's Fayetteville, state of Arkansas. Come on," and the man led him on over to the noose.

Jacob felt just terrible. Didn't they at least give a feller a decent trial before hangin him? Take the heifer back! Jacob pled. But the man went on, and slipped the noose over Jacob's head. Just then a man in the crowd, a distinguished looking old gentleman with white hair and dressed in a suit, stepped up and said, "All right, Bradshaw. This has gone far enough." Then he said to Jacob, "I'm Judge Walker, and it just so happens I'm also the owner of the stockyard. These men have played their joke on you. Those men in Spadra also played their joke on you. But enough is enough. Take the heifer. You, Bradshaw, kindly escort this gentleman out of town and see to it that he meets no more fools along the way." So Jacob and his heifer were allowed to leave.

He didn't know how to get home, but he had a general notion that it was somewhere to the east, so he led the heifer in that direction. Although Jacob had no knowledge of geography, he had a sixth sense of direction which brought him, after a week of walking and leading the heifer, right back to Stay More. The effort and humiliation that he had been subjected to in order to obtain his cow would leave him sour on city people for the rest of his life, and for many years after this incident he preferred to remain in Stay More rather than venturing out into the world. In fact, thirty years later when he would be offered the governorship of the whole state practically on a platter, he would at first decline, out of his reluctance to have any further dealings with city people. We may thus consider one more quality of his cabin: it is insulation not alone against weather and wilderness but also against any intrusion from the more sophisticated city world, a fortress against cosmopolitans. If Jacob's cabin would look ridiculous on a city street corner, no less ridiculous would a city man look, standing here in front of his cabin.

Jacob found his brother Noah practically dead from cold and starvation during his long absence. Apparently Noah had lacked the simple will or motivation to get up and keep the fire going and eat the food that Jacob had left for him. Now Jacob had to force him to eat something. Even after eating, Noah was too weak to talk. Jacob yearned to hear him say shitfire, but Noah couldn't. So Jacob did all of the talking, telling him of his recent adventures in Spadra and Fayetteville and along the way. By the time he was finished telling it, Noah had recovered enough strength to say shitfire. And then he added, "All that bother and trouble fer nuthin. You should of stood in bed, like me."

"But allow as how we got us a cow now," Jacob replied.

"Wow," Noah said. "So let's have some milk."

But Jacob realized that the heifer would have to be serviced and have a calf before she would start giving milk. Where would they find a bull? Occasionally a small herd of buffalo wandered through the valley; Jacob wondered if a buffalo bull could service a Jersey heifer. If a jackass could service a mare and produce offspring, why not? Jacob had hoped that maybe his bitch hound Tige would get serviced by a wolf or coyote and produce dogs well-suited for wilderness living. Tige was now all swollen out around the middle but as far as Jacob knew she hadn't met up with any eligible wolves or coyotes; probably the father had been that short-tailed cur of Fanshaw's. Yes, a few weeks later, when Tige had her litter, Jacob noted that the pups seemed to resemble Fanshaw's dog. Well, we're even, in a way, now, Jacob reflected: I serviced his squaw, his dog serviced my bitch.

But where, or how, to find a bull? Winter came on, yet no more herds of buffalo wandered into the valley. Probably the Indians had wiped out all the buffalo. Jacob's Jersey heifer, who with want of imagination he named "Jerse," went into heat and bawled and bawled, but there was no relief.

Then Eli Willard the clock peddler returned after being away six months (or 143 years by his clock's reckoning). Again he had only a single clock strapped to his saddlebag. He observed, "This is *still* the end of the road. But you have survived. Many don't, you know." Then he asked, "How's the clock?"

"Blankety-blank," Jacob replied. "Goshawful. Cuss-fired. No-account. Tinhorn. Punk. Torrible. Infernal. One-gallused. Muckel-dydun. Not worth the powder to blow it up."

"But does it *run*?" Eli Willard asked.

"It's runnin fer its life," Jacob said. "It's runnin like hell was only a mile away and all the fences down."

"Well, well," said Eli Willard and coughed. "I always insist upon my customer's satisfaction. I will replace your defective clock with this superior model. The works are not made of wood but of brass. Recently in Connecticut all the clockmakers have converted from wood to brass."

"I aint so sartin that we'uns need ary kind of clock, even if it was made of gold."

"Everyone needs a clock," Eli Willard declared. "All the other people hereabouts have clocks."

"What other people? There's jist me and Noah."

"The Ozarks are filling up with people."

"I aint seed any of 'em. Did ye happen to notice if any of them people had a bull?"

"A bull?"

"Yeah, I got a heifer near 'bout two year old and she needs sarvice somethin turrible."

"I don't examine my customers' livestock," Eli Willard said. "I'm sorry."

"Wal, whar is all them folks you're talkin about?"

"That way," Eli Willard said, and pointed, the way he had come, toward the north. Jacob realized that he and Noah had come in from the east and that he had gone south and come back from the west, but they had never been north. The bulls would be to the north.

Eli Willard produced the i.o.u. that Jacob had signed six months previously. "If you will settle your account, sir, I shall be happy to leave this new clock of entirely brass works with you." Jacob realized that his primary purpose in selling the fur pelts had been to pay off the clock peddler, and he did have the twenty dollars, so he gave the money to Eli Willard, who thanked him, but added, "Of course brass being more accurate than wood and in other ways more desirable, it is also more expensive than wood, and, regretfully, we are required to charge a little extra for—"

"How much?" Jacob asked.

"Twenty dollars," Eli Willard declared.

"I'll see you in six months," Jacob said. So he signed another I.O.U., and Willard rode off the way he had come, toward the north.

The new clock compensated for the old one by being as slow as the old one was fast, and Jacob calculated that he was regaining all the years he had lost to the old clock. Also, the new clock had a metal chime to strike the hours in place of the harsh wooden pecker of the old clock. The new chime said PRONG, and since it struck only on the second Tuesday of each month, it was not at all annoying—in fact, an occasion to be looked forward to. In time the brothers turned the occasion into ritual: on the second Tuesday of each month, at the moment the clock was scheduled to chime, they would drop whatever they were doing (or Jacob would; Noah would simply rise up from his bed) and stand beside the clock. Noah would salute as the moment approached; Jacob had his rifle loaded and ready. The clock would say PRONG and the brothers would let out with whoops and Jacob would fire off his rifle (through the door, the sole opening of the house, so as not to hit anything in the cabin) and the bitch Tige and all eight of her pups would start baying and yipping and chasing their tails and the heifer Jerse would bawl at the top of her lusty lungs, and the sun would stand still for a moment. This was the origin of the custom in our own time of the Lions, Rotarians and Kiwanians meeting for lunch on the second Tuesday of each month.

One noon in the early spring, the Ingledew brothers were having their dinner. Little has been said, up to this point, about their diet; here we might relate it to the architecture of their cabin by observing that, while looking plain and simple on the surface, it actually was quite variegated, and the reason the food looked plain and simple was the result of Jacob's cooking; it would have been nearly impossible to tell from the appearance of the cooked food whether it was fish or fowl, pork or potato; but the fact was that in terms of variety, beef was the only meat that the brothers did not have.

"Meat" of course to the Ozarker meant only pork: bacon or ham or salt pork or sidemeat, and there was a superabundance of this available in the wild hogs—"razorbacks"—roaming the woods and feeding on acorn mast and providing in turn food for panthers, bobcats and bears as well as ingledews. Both Jacob and Noah seemed to prefer pork to other kinds of meat, although they were not all that particular, and had discovered that even panther meat, eschewed by most hunters, had a taste like delicate veal. Bear meat had a stronger taste.

In the beginning the brothers kept no domestic fowl since the woods were filled with pigeons and wild turkey, one of the easiest game animals to bag—Jacob wouldn't even waste powder and shot on them because he could kill them just as easily by throwing rocks at them. Likewise he wouldn't bother wasting bait to catch fish but used instead a gig, one of the few pieces of iron brought with them from Tennessee, and the stream of water that would be called Swains Creek or Little North Fork of the Little Buffalo River was teeming with bass and perch and bream and crappie and catfish, so that his fishing expeditions never lasted more than two and one-half minutes.

Jacob and Noah were also fond of "sallit," what we would call greens, but wild, the tender leaves of mustard, lamb's quarters, peppergrass, pokeweed, dock, thistle and wild lettuce, which Jacob would mix together and boil for a long time in his kettle with a bit of bacon rind and then throw in some onions and pour hot bear's oil over it and cook it and stir it until it was the same brown color as the main dish and indistinguishable from it on the plate ... and palate.

Since there was no milk—yet—the brothers washed their food down with plain spring water, occasionally diluted with a jigger of whiskey, or else their coffee substitute made of roasted corn meal and molasses. For dessert, in season, there might be a watermelon or canteloupe chilled in the spring, or simply wild honey on a corn muffin, or Jacob might try his hand at cooking fried pies which were stuffed with wild berries and were the same brown color as all the other food consumed.

Where were we? Yes: one noon in the early spring, the Ingledew brothers were having their dinner (and it is understood that "dinner"

always means the noon meal; the evening meal is always "supper")
when suddenly the population of Stay More took a dramatic leap
from two to seventeen. The bitch Tige and her eight pups started
barking and it wasn't even the second Tuesday of the month, and the
Ingledews grabbed their rifles and went outside, and there, coming
up the trail, was a caravan: a covered wagon in the vanguard, drawn
by horses, not mules, followed by pedestrians serving as drovers for
a menagerie that might have come from the Biblical Noah's Ark: a
pair, male and female, of each: two sheep, two goats, two beeves (one
a bull!), two dogs, two pigs, two house cats—and the rooster with a
harem of hens. A middle-aged woman was driving the wagon, and
the Ingledews noticed that the others, fourteen in number, were all
young people or children. There was no grown man.

"Howdy," said the woman, halting her team. "'Pears lak this
here road don't go no further."

"Hit don't, I reckon," Jacob observed.

"Reckon we'uns'll jist have to turn back a ways. Shore is purty
country 'way back around up in here. You'uns the only folks hereabouts?"

"Fur as I know, seems lak," Jacob confessed.

"I'm Lizzie Swain," the woman said. "Come from Cullowhee,
North Caroliner. This un here's my leastun, Gilbert"— she indicated
the small boy sitting beside her—"and thatun's Esther. Yonder'un's
Frank, and Nettie standin beside him. Thatun's Boyd. Next him is
Elberta and Octavia. Whar's Virgil? YOU, VIRGE! Come out so's
these fellers kin see ye. Thar he is! Thatun's Virgil. Then over yonder
is Leo, tendin the sheep. Next him is Zenobia. The one tendin the
goats is Orville. Aurora is inside the wagon here, layin down with a
stomachache. Thatun with the cow and topcow is Murray, he's my
eldest boy. And yonder's my eldest gal, Sarah, she's done past twenty.
All of ya'll kids say howdy to these here fellers."

"HOWDY!" they all said at once, with friendly, enthusiastic
smiles.

"Howdy do," responded Jacob, and Noah didn't respond at all.
In their shyness before all of these females, it never occurred to them
to introduce themselves.

"How fur back up the road does yore land go?" the woman asked.

"I don't rightly know," Jacob said. "I aint been very fur up thataways. I hear tell there's a lot of folks up around yonder some'ers, but I aint seed ary one."

"Wal, I reckon we'uns will jist git on back a ways," Lizzie Swain declared, and began turning the team of horses around.

In his discomfiture, Jacob did not even think to offer the ritual invitation, "Stay more." He just stood and watched the caravan return back up the trail. But they were scarcely out of sight when he began to hear the noise: *thock*, the unmistakable sound produced by an axe hitting a tree. It was followed rapidly by an identical sound, and then another, and then a succession of *thucks* made by a different axe, and then began a series of *thacks*, from yet another axe, followed by some thecks from yet a fourth axe, and finally the chorus was joined by a fifth axe that said *thick*, until the air was filled with a constant cannonade of *thock thuck thack theck thick*.

"Shitfire," Noah remarked. "They must be choppin the woods all to hell."

Jacob went to investigate and discovered that the family had elected to settle less than half a mile from his own place. Four of the older boys and Lizzie Swain were busy chopping at oak trees, the beginning of the structure that we shall examine in the following chapter. Jacob went up to Lizzie Swain and took the axe out of her hands.

When he did, she looked startled, and asked, "Air we too close on ye?" and the boys raised their axes to defend her, but Jacob simply took the axe and began swinging it at the tree that Lizzie Swain had been chopping. He set a pace for the other boys, but his tree was felled long before theirs were. "That's right neighborly of ye," Lizzie Swain said to him. He started in on another tree.

Mrs. Elizabeth Hansell Swain was a true courageous pioneer mother—the first white woman in Stay More. Her husband had died the year before back in Cullowhee, North Carolina, and she decided to bring her fourteen children west in order that, as she would later explain to Jacob, "they could grow up with the country." All of the

children threw their hearts into the idea, and although they had suffered a number of troubles and privations on the long journey (they
had left North Carolina over two months previously, in the dead of
winter), they were not daunted but overjoyed to have reached their
new home at last. While the older boys chopped down the virgin
oaks, the older girls and their mother busied themselves constructing a campfire and preparing a first supper that would be a feast in
celebration of arrival. Jacob was felling his eighth tree when he heard
a dinner horn blow, and, looking up, saw Lizzie Swain blowing it and
welcoming him to supper. Jacob had the first fried chicken and the
first milk that he would eat and drink in Stay More, and this was the
origin of the favorite meal of the people. He liked it so much that,
after supper, as dusk settled in the woods, it took little urging from
the children to get him to open up and tell about his adventures, and
they all sat around and listened to him tell about the Indian Fanshaw
and his strange beliefs and customs, such as maidens proposing to
braves by giving them cornbread, and he gave them a bloodcurdling
imitation of the Dawn Chant, and the children listened, awed and
entranced. Years afterward they would tell their own children of
these things, so that was the origin of the "oral tradition" which was
so strong in the Ozarks for over a hundred years, and perhaps even
today has not completely died out.

Noah Ingledew did not help the Swains build their cabin.
Jacob apologized for his brother, explaining that he had recently had
a terrible affliction from which he was still recovering. Lizzie Swain
pressed for details of the affliction, because she was an expert in
home remedies and herbal cures, but Jacob blushed and said it wasn't
"decent" to describe. Jacob also was considerably embarrassed in his
plan to get his heifer serviced by the Swains' bull. (In the Ozarks a
man would rather cut his tongue out than utter the word "bull" in
the presence of a female. There were many circumlocutions: "male,"
"topcow," "cow-critter," "surly," "gentleman-cow," "brute," "cow-brute,"
or simply "he-cow," but Jacob could not employ these euphemisms if
his object was to ask Lizzie for her bull's service. At first he tried to
get around the problem by dealing with Lizzie's oldest son, Murray,
but Murray just said, "Ask Maw.") But Jacob just couldn't. He kept

putting it off, until finally the heifer Jerse came into heat again and set up such a loud bawling that all the Swains could hear her from half a mile off. "Sounds lak somebody's heifer wants a calf," Lizzie Swain remarked. Jacob didn't say anything. "Wonder whose it is," she went on. He couldn't tell her. "You said you and yore brother was the only folks around," Lizzie observed. Jacob could only nod. "Did ye happen to notice, we'uns got a right full-blooded topcow," Lizzie informed him. Jacob gulped and nodded again. "Considerin all the help you're a-givin us a-buildin our house, the least we could do is lend ye our topcow." Jacob tried to find words to thank her, but could find no words. "Murray," she said to her oldest boy, "you and Orville and Leo take ole Horns up yonder where that heifer's a-bawlin, and see if he caint git her to hesh up."

Jacob went with them, helped them, then returned to his work, the work of building their house, and worked with a new vengeance that came both from gratitude and from his inability to express himself. Soon the Swains' house was finished. The "community effort" of over a dozen people at work on the house-raising (even the youngest children helped with the job of chinking the cracks between the logs with clay and straw) reminded Jacob of Fanshaw's description of the Indian's ritual house-raising, and he told the Swain children about it: how after the maiden had proposed to the young brave by offering him a piece of cornbread, the whole community joined together for the festival of lodge-building for the couple. Jacob brought the Swain children to his own place one day and showed them his corncrib, which was made from the two halves of Fanshaw's house reversed upon one another to form a large egg-shaped structure resting upon a cradle of stone. He explained how the house had looked in its original form. The older children touched it and peered inside, but the younger children were afraid even to touch it.

Our first chapter ended with a leaving; this one ends with a coming—appropriately in the early spring. The Swains' house is finished in a fortnight, and they can turn their attention to the land: pulling the stumps of the oaks they have cut and plowing the earth and planting it. I think of the smiling faces of the children, and Lizzie pleased with her new home, and the smell of fresh-plowed earth, and the opening of dogwood and redbud blossom, and then somehow the thought of all the pests and plagues and vermin is endurable.

Weeks and weeks were to pass before, one day, Sarah Swain, the oldest girl, past twenty, hair dark as pitch, would show up at the door of Jacob's cabin with a piece of freshbaked cornbread, which she would offer into his astonished hands.

Chapter three

At first glance it seems similar to the Ingledew cabin, but in the Ozarks, unlike other areas of the country where prepackaged houses come monotonously identical, there were no two dwellings exactly alike. We are impressed with the two most conspicuous differences: the Swain house has a porch, and its timbers are hewed rather than left round. There are other differences, subtle to notice or not visible in our illustration: a puncheon floor inside, whereas the Ingledew cabin had no floor but earth. (Puncheons are simply split logs with their flat side up, very sturdy, and over the years worn smooth and shiny by the bare feet of many children.) The Swain chimney is slightly taller than the Ingledew chimney, reducing the hazard of igniting the roof. The gable ends are shingled in the Swain house, rather fancifully, and the roof covering is true riven shingles, not boards. The chinking in the interstices between the timbers is not simply mud but more durable clay, finished off with a layer of white lime plaster. There is, as it were, a second story, which was the sleeping quarters for the seven Swain boys: a loft under the gables, reached by a ladder through a scuttle-hole. And there is a window! If we look carefully we can find it, just to the side of the chimney. Glass being unavailable, the window was "glazed" with a bobcat skin, boiled in lye and scraped and oiled, nailed over it. The bobcat skin was translucent but not transparent, letting in light but no prying eyes.

Notice that the corners, the ends of the logs, are not saddle-notched but dovetailed. This makes for a tighter fit and a more sturdy building. The hardest job in building this cabin, which fell exclusively to Jacob Ingledew and the older Swain boy, Murray, was the hewing of these logs. A chalk line was stretched the length of the log and snapped, marking it along the rounded edge; then a chopping axe was sunk into this line at intervals, and then a broadaxe (with curved handle so as to avoid hitting one's ankles) was used to hack off the rounded sides of the log. It was painstaking, grueling work—and Murray Swain, as we shall see, came down with the frakes at the end of it. But the result of this work was a house that not only looks much more "modern" than the Ingledew cabin, but is also more durable. The Swain house is the first dwelling in our study which still exists today, although, being unoccupied, its porch has collapsed and most of the shingles have blown off the roof and it is used only by young boys looking for a place to sneak a smoke or older boys with their girls looking for a place to sneak a joy. Until about twenty-five years ago, however, it had been lived in continuously by five generations of Swains.

The similarities between the Swain house and the Ingledew cabin are apparent: both have only one door and both are roughly sixteen feet (or one hat) square. The architect of the Swain house is not easy to establish; the similarities between it and the Ingledew cabin would lead some scholars to attribute it to Jacob Ingledew, but since the Swain house was essentially Lizzie Swain's house, we may assume that she had a large, if not exclusive, hand in the design of it, particularly the porch, which is like a woman's sunbonnet shading her face, and which provided extra room in temperate weather for the crowded family. Undoubtedly Jacob Ingledew and Lizzie Swain may have discussed, or even argued, several points in the design and construction of the house, just as, later, after she had become his mother-in-law, he would, as men are always doing with their moth-ers-in-law, argue: they would argue religion, they would argue folk medicine and superstition, they would argue the use of alcoholic beverages, and above all they would argue the naming of things and places in Stay More. It was Lizzie who named Swains Creek and Bantam (Banty) Creek (after one of her little fowl who drowned there) and Leapin Rock (after one of her children who would leap from it) whereas Jacob named Ingledew Mountain and its benches ("West Banch, North Banch," etc.) and various individual holes of water in the streams that Lizzie had named, Ole Bottomless in Banty Creek, Ole Beaver, Ole Crappie and Ole Stubtoe in Swains Creek. Lizzie also wanted to name the town itself—Cullowhee after her hometown—but Jacob pointed out to her that it had already been named Stay More and so it would stay.

Did Jacob accept that cornbread? The whole idea was Lizzie's, to begin with. She knew that Sarah was past marryin' age, and where else was she going to find a man? Jacob might be ten years older than Sarah, but he was ten years younger than Lizzie and besides Lizzie had already had all the children she wanted. Sarah was hard to sell on the idea, though. Like all the Swain children she idolized Jacob Ingledew and for that very reason the thought of marriage to him frightened her, almost as if it had been suggested that she go off and live with God as His wife. It would be an honor to be Mrs. God, but wouldn't it also be a terrible responsibility? When none of these arguments dissuaded her mother from trying to persuade her to take some cornbread to Jacob, Sarah argued that a man Jacob's age who had not married probably didn't care for women in the first place and would just laugh at her if she gave him some cornbread and then she would just die of mortification.

Still, Lizzie Swain kept pestering Sarah about it, in such a persistent way that Sarah thought she would lose her mind unless she yielded. Yet even after she yielded, she was reluctant. Her mother baked the cornbread and then spaced the twelve other children (Murray was in bed with the frakes) along the route to Jacob's cabin at strategic intervals in descending order of age. Then she put the cornbread into Sarah's hands and shoved her out the door with such force that Sarah kept trotting as far as where Aurora was standing, and Aurora gave her a shove that sent her trotting on to Orville, who shoved her to Zenobia, and so on, down the line, down the road to Jacob's cabin, where little Gilbert was waiting, last in line, last to push. He was only four, and pushing was a difficult feat for his small age, but his mother had patiently explained it to him, how it was necessary in order for him to have a "brother-in-law," making brother-in-law sound like something wonderful, so when Sarah came trotting up, her black hair streaming behind her, he clenched his little tongue between his teeth and got his hands on her buttocks and shoved for all he was worth, propelling her right up against Jacob's door, which she banged against, causing Jacob to open it, and her momentum was such that even though her body had stopped moving her hands kept going and thrust the cornbread into Jacob's hands.

Then she just stood there with her hands behind her and stared down at her feet and began to get very red in the face. Jacob duplicated her posture and color exactly, except that he couldn't put his hands behind his back because he had cornbread in them. He just stood there and looked down at what was in his hands and got even redder in the face than Sarah. For a long time they just stood there stiff and glowing like a pair of branding irons. Finally Jacob's brother Noah got up from his bed and came to see what it was all about. He stood there and stared back and forth at the two of them. Probably he didn't grasp the significance of the cornbread, because, being not just afraid of but uninterested in Indians, he had never been told about the customs of Fanshaw's people. But he was very concerned to see these two human beings standing in front of one another with downcast but red-hot faces. "S—tfire!" he exclaimed, and snatched the cedar water bucket off the wall and, first removing the cornbread from Jacob's hands so it wouldn't get hit, doused the heads of both of them. It is very difficult to blush with a wet head, so, since they could no longer blush, they laughed, which is also a nervous reflex. They laughed until the water on their faces was joined by their tears, and Noah looked at them like they were both crazy, and kept mumbling his favorite expletive, which, however, was somewhat cleaned up for Sarah's benefit, so that it sounded more like "shoot fair" or "sheet far."

And that was it. That was all there was to it. Jacob never said "I do," or "I will" or even "Thanks for the cornbread" or even "Aw, gosh dawg and shucks." Even today, in some of the big weddings in the Ozarks, people do not shower the bride and groom with rice but with water. At that time, of course, there was no church anywhere near Stay More, nor even a circuit rider or "saddlebag preacher," and even if there had been, he could not legitimately have married an infidel like Jacob Ingledew. So, hand in hand, Jacob and Sarah simply returned to Lizzie's house, Jacob gathering sisters-in-law and brothers-in-law right and left along the way. At Lizzie's house, Sarah announced to her mother, "Maw, we're spliced."

The month, come to think of it, was June.

"Already?" Lizzie Swain exclaimed. "What didje do, jist jump over a broomstick together?"

"No. Noah, Noah … he dumped a bucket of water on us."

"Wal, bless yore hearts, I'm so happy fer yuns," Lizzie said and embraced and kissed them both, and began sniffling. After she got control of her emotions, she said to Jacob, "But if it wouldn't be too much bother, could ye read us a little from the Bible fer the occasion?"

Elizabeth Swain, like all of her children, like, in fact, everybody in Stay More for years and years, except Jacob, was unable to read. (One must never say "illiterate" since it is so easily confused with "illegitimate," a fighting word.) In later years, when he began teaching school, Jacob wondered if his unique peculiarity, his ability to read, was perhaps a curse upon him, and for at least the length of his tenure as schoolmaster, reading was not one of the subjects in the curriculum. Lizzie did, however, have a Bible, an old heirloom, which she often touched, and whose wood-engraving illustrations she often "read," because she was a very Godfearing person. Jacob, although ungodly, did not mind reading from the Bible on this occasion of their marriage; it was the least he could do as a substitute for going hundreds of miles in search of a preacher, and maybe having to pay the man cash money, at that.

But the trouble was, he didn't know where to look, in the Bible, for an appropriate passage. He let the book fall open at random, and began reading aloud at random in the Book of Second Kings, "But Rabshakeh said unto them, Hath my master sent me to thy master, and to thee, to speak these words? hath he not sent me to the men which sit on the wall, that they may eat their own dung, and drink their own piss with you?" Jacob slammed the Bible shut, grumbling, "Blackguardy book. I don't know how to use it."

But then he remembered a passage from Genesis that he had read when debating Fanshaw on the origin of man, having to do with the marriage of Adam and Eve. He read this. "And the Lord God said, It is not good that the man should be alone; I will make him an help meet for him," and "And Adam said, This is now bone of my bones, and flesh of my flesh: she shall be called Woman, because she was taken out of Man. Therefore shall a man leave his father and his mother, and shall cleave unto his wife: and they shall be one flesh—" he would have read more, but Lizzie and Sarah, and all the female Swains, were sniveling and boohooing so loudly they drowned him out. He returned the Bible to Lizzie, and took his bride by the hand and led her back to his own place.

With a stick he gouged a groove across the dirt floor of his cabin, right down the middle, dividing the room into two halves. "That's yourn," he said to Noah. "This is ourn." But Noah got busy and built a small loft up under the gables, and moved his bed up there. It was his first activity since he had been stricken with the frakes the year before, and it was the beginning of his return to normal life.

Jacob and Sarah Ingledew did not consummate their marriage on the bridal night. As soon as it got dark, their cabin was surrounded by a horrendous din: rifles firing, drums beating, cats howling, pans banging, cowbells clanging, hands clapping, lips whistling, horns blaring, hounds bugling, it was all hell broke loose and the roof was raised an inch or two. Investigating with his lantern, Jacob discovered that it was the entire human and animal population of Stay More, serenading the newlyweds.

This was the first Stay More shivaree, or *charivari* as the French would call it, from a Latin word meaning "headache." How did this custom ever get started? What psychological motives do people have for harassing the poor couple on their first night together? If we were to interrupt young Virgil Swain while he was pulling the cat's tail to make it howl and contribute that part of noise to the racket, and interview him on this subject, he would reply, "Wal, I reckon everbody knows what folkses air *really* gittin married fer, and so we're a-teasin 'em on account of that. Hoo lordy!" Perhaps he would be right, that even the youngest among them (and maybe some of the animals too) sensed the real reason that a man and a woman would become "one flesh," and out of envy as well as out of a sense of that reason being lewd, they lewdly heckle and pester the wedded pair. I cannot help but remark upon the contrast between this behavior and that of Fanshaw's people on the wedding day: the Osage's "grunts and whoops of joy" become the white man's grunts and whoops of lewd mirth. The shivaree ends when the groom "treats": Jacob invited all of them (except the animals) into his cabin, where he gave them refreshments, sarsparilla for the younger ones, stronger stuff for the older, and Sarah's cake of cornbread smeared with wild honey and divided all around. The party ran deep into the night, and when it was over Jacob was too inebriated to find his bed. He aimed for it but missed, and spent the night sleeping on the floor (or rather the dirt, since there was no floor). The next day all of the guests came back again, for the infare (or "infair" or "enfare," as most writers misspell it). Lizzie Swain and her girls brought the food, and again it was a big blow-out with fried chicken and everything.

Only Murray Swain wasn't there, for the shivaree or the infare either. As has been mentioned, being the oldest of the Swain boys, he had worked the hardest in the construction of their house, hewing the logs with his broadaxe and lifting them into place with Jacob lifting the other end of the log, and after three weeks of this hard work he came down with the frakes. His mother tried several of her best home remedies to no avail. Jacob wanted to suggest the poultice made with panther urine, but couldn't bring himself to broach such a delicate topic to her. Lizzie resorted to a drastic cure of her own, using the warm blood of a black hen. She had Murray lie down on the ground (out back of the house so the other children wouldn't watch), then she chopped off the hen's head with an axe and let the blood dribble onto his eruptions and remain on after it had dried. This treatment seemed to be a trifle more effective than Noah's remedy, but not much, so that now, even though the shivaree and infare were weeks and weeks past and his sores had healed, he still lay abed with great feelings of futility and worthlessness. It was perhaps appropriate that he alone was absent from his sister's bridal festivities, because it was he, more than anyone else, who was responsible for the fact that Sarah Swain was unencumbered with a maidenhead at her marriage.

But Jacob did not know this, and he never would know it. Ignorant as he was of women and their ways, and having had experience only with an Indian squaw who was no maiden by a long shot, Jacob approached the debut of his bride's charms with no expectation of difficulty and therefore no disappointment or anger in having encountered none. When the infare was over and all the guests had departed and Jacob was tipsy enough for the nerve, he ran Noah out of the cabin and closed the door, darkening the interior, then he laid Sarah on the bed. That was it, he just laid her, with no more howdy-do or ceremony than the wedding itself. He was surprised, however, that her reactions during the process were not at all comparable to those of the Indian squaw; namely, she did not utter the ghost of a sigh, she did not move, she did not enfold him with arms and legs alike, and, above all, she did not make, at the end, the long taut but smooth arc: ark: bow. She was foursquare, flat; not even her gables peaked. So for him it wasn't lightning and thunder but maybe just cloudy and windy, chance of showers. Afterward he wanted to ask her if she'd had any joy in it, but he couldn't ask her things like that. They never would talk about sex...until the very last day of Jacob's life.

And these were the children of Jacob and Sarah: Benjamin, the firstborn; Isaac, born two years later; Rachel, born two years later; Christopher Columbus, born two years later; and Lucinda, the last, born two years later.

Why was it, Jacob often wondered, that when he really, truly, honest-to-God, sure-enough, straight-up-and-down *wanted* his woman, she wasn't much feeling like it, whereas the only times he ever got her was when he wasn't much feeling like it? That was a hell of a trick for Nature to play on a man...and a woman. Once, when he was upon her, she whispered in his ear, "Jake, if I go to sleep afore you git done, will ye pull down my nightgown?" It must be noted, however, that it was an excess of sexual frustration, no doubt, which caused Jacob single-handedly in a couple of weeks to build the imposing structure which we shall examine in the following chapter, leaving his cabin to Noah. He must have been aware of Noah, up there in the loft, listening, but hearing nothing except a random small grunt of Jacob's, no sounds whatever from the woman.

If that is cause for pitying Noah, there was a worse one. Sarah's next-youngest sister, Aurora, encouraged by the success of her older sister's presentation of the cornbread to Jacob, began to give thought to baking some cornbread for Noah, and her mother approved of this scheme. Noah certainly wasn't as desirable as Jacob, but Aurora was accustomed to being second to her older sister, getting her hand-me-downs and being next in line for everything. So eventually she baked the cornbread and took it to the Ingledew cabin, but Noah wasn't there; Jacob said he was out milking the cow. Aurora took the cornbread out to the cowlot and offered it to Noah. By this time Noah understood the significance of the offering and he eagerly reached to take the cornbread, but dropped it, and bending over to pick it up, he tripped and fell to the ground. Aurora couldn't help giggling. While rising up from the ground, much flustered, he snatched at the cornbread, and it broke in two. Still eager to signify his acceptance of it, he grabbed both pieces and clutched them to his bosom, where-upon they disintegrated into many fragments that showered around his feet. He was so discomposed that he turned and ran off into the woods to hide himself for a long time. Aurora decided she didn't want a husband who was so clumsy anyway, and would rather wait until the population of Stay More included some other eligible bachelor. Poor Noah was destined to remain unmarried until his death.

Early in their marriage, Jacob's wife Sarah developed a disconcerting habit which Jacob at first attributed to absent-mindedness: whenever she was outside of the cabin, working in the garden or feeding the chickens or whatever, she would not afterwards return to the cabin but instead wander down the road to her mother's house and enter it, and stay there, until Jacob came to fetch her home. Undoubtedly a psychiatrist would interpret this as a sign of her dissatisfaction with her marriage, but actually, it seems to me (as in time it dawned on Jacob), that it was a sign of her dissatisfaction with Jacob's cabin, her perhaps unconscious recognition that her mother's house was superior to it, more comfortable, less primitive. When Jacob realized this, he began to build his next house, which was as superior to the Swain house as the latter was to his first cabin.

An outsider visiting Jacob's cabin would have received the impression that Sarah was a slatternly housekeeper, but the fact was that a house with a dirt floor was very difficult to keep clean, and this discouraged Sarah from making the effort. As soon as she became pregnant for the first time, Sarah discontinued further relations with Jacob, until such time as he had completed construction of their new home, which, as we shall see, did not have a dirt floor but a puncheon floor that Jacob took the trouble to shave smooth with a drawing knife, so that Sarah would never get a splinter in her foot.

Lizzie Swain and her brood always joined the Ingledews at noon on the second Tuesday of each month to hear Jacob's clock say PRONG, and they began combining the event with the feast of fried chicken; this was the chief social occasion in Stay More for many years. Still, Jacob had never told Lizzie where he got the clock, so one day when Eli Willard showed up at the Swain house, Lizzie did not know who he was. He was just a "furriner" on horseback with bulging saddlebags.

"Ah hah," observed Mr. Willard. "Another house, and a fair one too. May the lares and penates bless you and your happy home, madam."

He talked mighty funny, Lizzie thought. "Whar ye from, stranger?" she asked him.

"Connecticut," he replied. "Willard is the name. Eli Willard. Formerly trafficker in timepieces. Now a purveyor of sundry hard goods." He patted his saddlebags. "Madam, have I got some nice things for you!"

By this time all of her children (except Murray, abed with the frakes) had gathered 'round, and they watched as Eli Willard dismounted and opened his saddlebags. To each of the boys Eli Willard gave a stick of rosewood studded with small bolts, which, he demonstrated, enclosed a knife that folded out! So that it could be carried in one's pocket without sticking one, Eli Willard explained. The boys were awed. To each of the girls he gave a pair of knives that were crossed and bolted at the cross and had rings in one end whereby, he demonstrated by inserting his thumb and forefinger through the rings, the knives could be made to move against one another, snipping, so that a straight even cut could be made through cloth, he using the hem of his own coat for a subject. The girls were lost in amazement, and their mother exclaimed, "I declare! If them aint the beatin'est things ever I saw!" Before their mother could stop them, the girls gathered up all the fabric that was in their house, namely, two muslin dishrags and a bit of linsey-woolsey, and quickly reduced this material to shreds. To Lizzie Swain Eli Willard gave an even larger pair of these scissoring knives which would cut through buckskin, the material in which all of the Swains, as well as the Ingledews, were clothed.

"Bless yore heart," said Lizzie Swain. "We'uns jist don't know how to thank you." Eli Willard explained that there *was*, in fact, a way that they could thank him. His suggestion puzzled Lizzie but after muddling it over for a while, she understood it, and protested that none of them had any of that monetary stuff, to which he assured her that her credit was good, and he would collect when he came again in a year or so. Then he inquired if the Ingledew cabin was still occupied, and, being told that it was, he remounted his horse and prepared to ride off in that direction, but Lizzie laid her hand on the horse's bridle and said, "Stranger, afore ye go, could ye tell us if they's any news out yonder." With her other hand she gestured to the north, the east, the vaguely oriental points where the world was.

"News?" said Eli Willard.

"Yeah, Connecticut must be whar lives all the gentle-peoples what made these things ye give us. Aint there any news out thar in the Nation?"

"It is all bad," Eli Willard informed her. "What do you want to hear it for?"

"Wal, we'uns is all hidden out here in the woods, y'know. It do git kinder lonesome, times. A body'd like to hear what's happenin far off and away."

Eli Willard just looked at her for a long moment, and then he announced, "*Lady of the Lake* strikes iceberg in mid-Atlantic; 215 drown. New York City fire destroys 700 buildings. Japanese earthquake kills 12,000. Worldwide cholera epidemic kills millions. Wages rise, but prices rise faster. Financial crash occurs on Van Buren's 36th day in office. Nation begins first great depression. Bank failures and closings spread like plague. 200,000 are unemployed. Business bankrupt; only pawnbrokers prosper. Van Buren declares ten-hour day on all federal jobs. There. Does that make you feel any better?"

Lizzie Swain smiled and all her children smiled, and Lizzie said, "Hit shore do. We thank ye kindly."

Shaking his head and muttering to himself, Eli Willard rode on his way. He came to the Ingledew cabin, was hailed by the bitch Tige and her now-fully-grown litter of eight, who surrounded his horse and continued barking until Jacob appeared and said, "Oh. It's you. Back already?" Then he observed, "You shore didn't stay away long, this time. Accordin to my clock, you've only been gone one day, three hours and forty-five minutes."

Eli Willard drew an envelope from his pocket, unfolded it, and read it to Jacob Ingledew. "The management deeply regrets being apprised of the alleged malfunctioning of the instrument merchandised in good faith to the customer, and under ordinary circumstances would redeem the allegedly defective instrument with one of acceptable performance, but the management must with compunction inform the customer that, since the management is at the present time no longer actively engaged in merchandising instruments of this nature, we are perforce not able to make available to the customer an alternative replacement, therefore—"

"Yeah," Jacob said. Then, "How's the weather out yore way?"

"Cold enough to freeze the tail off a brass monkey," Eli Willard reported. "Blizzards up to here—" he indicated his chin, and he was still sitting on his horse. "How about you?"

"Had one good snap long about Christmas," Jacob told him.

The two men discussed the weather for a while, one-eighth of a second by Jacob's clock, then Eli Willard opened his saddlebag and brought out a stick of ivory which enclosed a blade much sharper than those he had given the Swain boys. He unfolded it and handed it to Jacob.

"What's it fer?" Jacob asked, holding it gingerly.

"For shaving," Eli Willard explained. "Perhaps if you cut off those whiskers of yours, you might more easily find a wife."

"I've done found a wife," Jacob informed him, then he called into the cabin, "OH, SAREY! COME OUT SO'S THIS HERE PEDDLAR FELLER KIN SEE YE!"

"Congratulations," Eli Willard said to Jacob, and when Sarah appeared he amended that to, "Compliments and congratulations. A beauty. My pleasure to meet you, madam, and to present you with this." He gave her a pair of the scissoring knives like those he had given to Lizzie Swain, and explained to her how to use them. She had no cloth to cut, but took one of Jacob's beaver skins and snipped it to flinders, expressing her wonder and delight, then she offered to give him a bucket of wild raspberry preserves that she had made, but Jacob explained that this feller was blind to any barter except that issued by the federal government, of which Jacob still had a little hidden behind a loose stone in his fireplace. So he fetched his cash and paid for Sarah's scissors.

"Don't you think, madam," Eli Willard asked, "that your husband would strike a more dashing figure without his beard and mustachios?"

Sarah clipped her scissors and stared at them. "Is these good for that too?"

"Up to a point," Eli Willard replied. "But to complete the operation he would need this." He held up the straight-razor again.

"Pay him, Jake," Sarah told her husband. While Jacob had his bankroll out, Eli Willard gauged the thickness of the wad, and proceeded to sell Jacob a pocketknife, another for Noah, a hand saw, an adjustable plane, a brace and bit, and a hammer. Before he was done, Eli Willard also sold him a scythe blade and a hay fork, observing that, now that Jacob had livestock, he would need good tools for harvesting fodder. Meanwhile Sarah did not return to her cabin but, as had become her peculiar disposition, wandered off to her mother's house. Jacob took advantage of her absence to draw Eli

Willard aside and ask in a low voice, "You reckon you could lay hold of some glass to bring me, yore next trip?"

"Glass?" said Eli Willard in a hushed tone.

"Yeah," Jacob whispered. "I'm a-fixin to build me a new house, and I aim to put a couple winders in her, so I'll be needin some winder lights."

"Glass," Eli Willard susurrated hoarsely, "is frightfully hard to come by, and of course difficult to transport, and therefore frightfully expensive."

"I 'spect so," Jacob sighed, and softly inquired, "How much?"

Eli Willard whispered into his ear a preposterously exorbitant figure.

"I'll be dumbed!" Jacob croaked quietly, but then he drew himself up and declared, "Wal, you git it, and we'uns will find the money some way."

The window of the Swain house, as we have seen, being covered with boiled and scraped wildcat hide, was translucent but not transparent. It admitted light but permitted no vision, either in or out, unless at night a figure were standing between the window and the light (nocturnal illumination in the Swain house came either from the fireplace or from "lamps" which consisted of sycamore balls floating in saucers of bear's grease with the stem serving as a wick). The silhouette of a figure was standing between the light and window that night; the figure is Sarah's. Jacob has not bothered to come for her. He has discovered a wonderful use for the pocketknife he bought from Eli Willard. He can whittle a stick with it.

He is whittling the stick into shavings. Neither the stick nor the shavings have any value, but the act of pushing the knife down along the stick has a certain therapeutic value, is soothing, gives him something to do with his hands, keeps him from seeming entirely idle when in fact he is entirely idle. Henceforward generations of the men and boys of Stay More will whittle to shavings millions of cords of sticks; some of them will actually carve the sticks into totemic figures or useful objects, hatchet handles and such, but the majority of the men and boys will just keep on whittling the stick into shavings and then start on another one, as if, their houses all built and finished, they have to keep on working with wood.

Tonight Jacob sits beside his fire endlessly whittling, and Noah soon catches the contagious habit and joins him. It is Sarah whose silhouette we see passing between the light and the window of her mother's house. All the others have gone to sleep, the boys in the loft, the girls and their mother below. But Sarah's silhouette moves across our line of vision and out of it, in the direction of the ladder leading up through the scuttle-hole into the loft. We can no longer see her through the window now, but we can imagine her climbing the ladder to her brothers' quarters. We cannot easily imagine her motive, until we remember that Murray is still suffering from the after-effects of the frakes. He has no will to live. Sleeps sometimes, more often not. Lies abed, thinking no visions, hatching no plans. Feels only, if feels at all, the same feeling Noah had: of snugness, of being wrapped in the confines of this small house, of having no desire ever again to leave it. What is Sarah climbing to him for? We are not going to know.

But we should know this much, about all of those early houses in Stay More, in contrast to all of the houses that we live in today: the very architecture of "garrison"-type houses, hermetic as it was, insulating and isolating the inhabitants from extremes of hot and cold, the possibly hostile wilderness, etc., fostered because of this an atmosphere of family "togetherness" more intense than any that has ever existed since. By closing the family in on itself, the architecture forced the people of these families into a happy intimacy which we cannot comprehend because we have never known it. There were few or no secrets in these families.

In the case of the Swains, the atmosphere of togetherness was so intense that they thought of themselves not as individuals but as parts of one person. We have already seen an example in the way they cooperated as a team to propel Sarah along the route to Jacob's cabin and heart. But that was nothing. To observe the degree of their absorption one in another we would have to join them at the table, where there was never any need for anybody to ask to have something passed because everybody knew who wanted what and when and how much. They *knew*, the Swains, all of them, and nobody ever had to ask to have anything passed. When one of them was supremely happy, they were all supremely happy, and when one of them was sad, they were all sad. The only exception to this, strangely, was Murray's frakes, which seems to be the one condition whose mood is not contagious, the one condition that must be suffered alone, without empathy from those so close around one. Whatever it was, it was not empathy that caused Sarah to climb up to Murray's bed.

But Murray did not improve. In addition to his usual feeling of worthlessness, he developed a strange sensation that can only be called a kind of stationary acrophobia. The boys' sleeping loft was not all that high; just about nine feet above the floor; and indeed it was not the loft that he was afraid of falling out of. Nor his bed, which was a scant two feet high. He was simply afraid of falling out of… of… well, he was simply afraid of falling. In his dreams, when he managed to sleep, he was always falling. Not *from* anything nor *to* anything, but falling. He would wake with a cry from these dreams, and, because there were no secrets in those families, in those houses, he would tell his dream to his brothers, and they to his mother and sisters, so that when in the deep of night thereafter anyone was wakened from their sleep by Murray's cries, they would simply realize, "Murray is fallin," and turn over and go back to sleep.

Lizzie consulted Noah Ingledew, who enjoyed some esteem as the first person to catch and suffer and endure and survive the frakes, but Noah could not remember having had any sensation of falling, and thus was not able to offer any advice. Lizzie then consulted with Jacob, who, although he had not yet experienced the frakes, was looked upon as the village sage. Jacob agreed to study the problem. He got a stick and sat with it and whittled at it with his new pocket-knife. He studied and studied, whittling stick after stick. He wished Fanshaw were still around; Fanshaw might know some answers to what might help acrophobia (although Jacob, of course, did not know or use that word); whatever the condition was, it had to be related to gravity, and Fanshaw was an expert on gravity.

Jacob whittled his sticks and meditated upon how and why objects fall. At length he formulated two important premises: (1) an object must fall *from* somewhere, and (2) an object must stop falling when it gets *to* somewhere. He demonstrated and proved these concepts by throwing a rock straight up into the air as hard as he could. The rock rose and rose, but by and by Jacob heard it coming down, crashing through the trees and then making a dull thud as it hit the ground. Now the question was: where did the rock fall *from*? From the hand of Jacob who had thrown it, or from some unspecified point at which the rock could no longer rise? The latter, he believed, and suddenly realized, *Murray Swain is falling from the place at which he knows he caint rise any farther.*

He understood that much about the frakes. The next question was: when would he stop falling? When would he hit the ground? Or could somebody catch him? How? Jacob tried another experiment: he went out into his open pasture where there were no trees, and threw another rock straight up into the air and searched for it as it was coming down and ran over beneath it and cupped his hands and tried to catch it. The first few times he tried this, he missed, and the rock either hit the ground or struck him painfully on his head or shoulders. Soon Sarah and Noah and all of the Swains except Murray gathered around to watch Jacob trying to catch rocks. "S—tfire," Noah remarked to Sarah. "You ortent to have let him out of the house, Sarey." But finally Jacob succeeded in catching a rock, and then another, and still yet another—and by indirection commenced the legendary Ingledew prowess at that sport which, by fabulous coincidence, was being invented on that same day, at that same moment, by Abner Doubleday in Coopers-town, N.Y.

No element of sport, however, entered Jacob's mind; he was dead serious, and after he had succeeded in catching several rocks in succession, he stopped throwing them and came and said to the others, "I think I got it." Then he told Lizzie that they should keep a watch on Murray when he was sleeping, and if he started tossing and turning and acting like he was about to cry out, they should hold him and whisper in his ear, "I've caught ye!" That very night Lizzie took one of the lamps made from a sycamore ball floating in a saucer of bear's grease and she lit it and left it beside Murray's bed, and then in shifts she and her children kept watch on Murray until, sure enough, he began tossing and turning and acting like he was getting ready to cry out, when Orville, who was on the shift at that moment, leaned down and clutched him and whispered in his ear, "I've caught ye!" whereupon Murray smiled in his sleep and stopped tossing, stopped falling apparently, stopped having any but pleasant dreams: of tall wheat waving in the field, of the creek tumbling over shoals, of a cool dipper of spring water on a hot day, of fried chicken, of his sister Sarah's warmth and depth and damp. The Swains repeated this magic incantation whenever Murray had dreams of falling, until, eventually, he seemed to be cured. Then Lizzie Swain went to Jacob and announced, "We'uns done had a 'lection, and all voted to proclaim ye mayor of Stay More," a title that Jacob would retain for the rest of his life, even concurrently with, years later, the far grander title of governor of the whole State of Arkansas.

But Murray was not cured. Cured of dreaming dreams of falling, yes, but not of the core of his acrophobia, which festered until it erupted: one day he left his bed and dressed and went out of the house and climbed the mountain behind it until he came to a lofty projection of bluff that jutted out from the side of the mountaintop some three hundred feet (or more accurately, nineteen hats) above the mountainslope below. Young Gilbert, the Swain's least-un, had followed Murray to see where he was going, and it was he who ran home to report it to his mother, who in turn summoned Jacob, who assured her, "I'll catch him," and ran up the mountainslope, fully determined to attempt to break Murray's fall with his own arms or body, a rash resolution which, had he been able to carry it out, would have killed himself or crippled himself for life. But when he got to that area of the mountainslope directly beneath the bluff jutting out from the mountaintop, Murray was already falling, falling, and though Jacob cried out "I'll catch ye!" and "I've caught ye!" he could not, would not. Limbs of trees deflected the plummet of the body away from his grasp but did not soften the descent enough to keep Murray from slamming into that which awaits the fall of all. Jacob would never forget the sound, all of the parts of the sound: of flesh violently bruised, of lungs expelled, of bones snapping, of blood spurting. Some months later, when he himself would lie abed with the frakes and the fear of, not of falling but of getting the fear of falling, he would load his rifle and instruct Sarah to use it upon him if ever he left the house except to relieve himself out back.

Murray Swain was the founder of the Stay More cemetery. There's an old story that when the next wave of settlers came into Stay More, six families from various parts of eastern Tennessee and northern Georgia, the men were gathered at the Mayor's—Jacob's— house for the formality of requesting his permission to settle. One man declared that he would like to start a blacksmith shop. Another said that he intended to start a sheep ranch. Another declared his intention to start a trading post. Still another was going to start a gristmill. Each of the men had some intention to contribute to the establishment of the village, except for one very old man who had suffered the long trip from Georgia and was ill. "What about him?" Jacob asked the others, and they replied, "Oh. *Him.* Reckon he aims to start the cemetery." Jacob thought maybe they were trying to be funny, but he didn't laugh. He just stared them down and informed them, "We done got one." And in fact, when the old man died within a few days, and was given a proper burial, there was already another headstone in a clearing down Swains Creek a ways, a headstone quarried from slate and inscribed with the name and the too-brief dates, the last of which was the earliest in Stay More, and the inscription, "Falling no more." It was Lizzie Swain herself who, without irony or approbation or sorrow so much as plain observation, named the lofty jag of bluff "Leapin Rock," and defied all her descendants to go near it. Throughout the history of Stay More, it was always difficult for anyone to avoid seeing that landmark, looming up to the west of the village as a silent reminder that there is a place to fall from, a silent temptation to those who want to stop falling.

The six families were the Plowrights, the Coes, the Dinsmores, the Chisms, the Duckworths, and the Whitters. Collectively they increased the population of Stay More by thirty-three, as if to compensate for the decrease by one. They built cabins or houses very similar to, but carefully not identical to, those of the Ingledews and the Swains. Zachariah Dinsmore did indeed construct a primitive gristmill on

Swains Creek, and Levi Whitter erected an even more primitive building which became the village's first general store or trading post, much to the disdain of Eli Willard the next time he came.

Willard's current merchandise, the knives and scissors and razors, it must be noted, performed just a little more satisfactorily than his clocks: the jackknives could be opened only with a pair of pliers and closed only with a hammer; the screws fell out of Lizzie's scissors and Sarah's too (although they discovered that they each had two knives as a result) and Jacob's razor gave him many mornings of pure agony and bloodshed until he discovered that it worked much better if he first lathered his jowls with soap. But even beardless and fresh-shaven he found that Sarah did not appreciate him any better than she had before, at least not in bed. Once, inspired by drink, he tried again the bath-in-three-waters: rain, creek, spring, hoping it might produce some magic response in Sarah, but this had only the effect of erasing his olfactory identity. "It aint you," Sarah said, in the dark, refusing to let him into the bed. "Whoever ye air, you aint you." He slept with his dogs, whose keen noses could recognize at least a trace of whatever remained of him.

Jacob perceived eventually that the only times he had had any luck with Sarah had been after immoderate consumption of his Arkansas sour mash, but naturally this realization did nothing to curb his use of the beverage, rather the reverse. Both Sarah and her mother began to nag Jacob about his use of distilled corn. He invited them to offer one good reason why there was anything wrong with it. They could not; they could only reply that everybody knows it's "wrong," but they could not explain why anyone knows it is wrong, they could only nag him for it.

Another example, not unlike the matter of liquor, involved religion. It was no secret to Sarah or to Lizzie Swain that Jacob Ingledew felt that religion was a useless expenditure of time and thought. He was not exactly blasphemous, and took the Lord's name in vain only under severe duress, as when for example he discovered razorback shoats nursing off his cow's teats, but he did not believe, as nearly everybody else did, that our words and deeds on this earth will determine our standard of living in the hereafter. In fact, he did not believe in any sort of hereafter. For well over a hundred years, down to the present day, Ozark women would nag their men on these two subjects: whiskey and religion, instilling God knows what a fabric of guilt and evasion; and few of these men would have the solace of the knowledge that Jacob had, that since there is no logical earthly reason for not drinking, and no logical earthly reason for being religious, the nagging was invalid and therefore would be disregarded.

...But not quite. Try as he would, Jacob could not quite disregard the nagging of Sarah and her mother. He knew there was nothing he could say to turn it off. If he went outside, they would follow him. So he did more than just go outside: he left town. The nagging of Sarah and her mother may be credited for Jacob's discovery that there was indeed a people to the north.

He went north from Stay More less than six miles, down the Little Buffalo River, before coming upon a settlement that was even larger than Stay More. Larger, at least, by one house, for there were nine of them, ranging from porchless, windowless cabins more primitive than the Ingledew place to square-hewed log houses more advanced than the Swain place. Jacob approached the most elaborate of these latter, was hailed by its dogs and then greeted by its owner, John Bellah, who, Jacob learned, had come to the Ozarks even before himself. The name of the settlement was Mount Parthenon, given to it by a neighbor, Thomas K. May, "the Bible man," and for the time being the small log trading post operated by John Bellah was also the "courthouse" for the county.

"County?" said Jacob Ingledew to John Bellah.

"Yeah, we've done been declared a county," declared John Bellah. "They cut off the whole southeast part of Carroll County and let us have it."

"What's the name of this here county?" Jacob wanted to know.

"Newton," Bellah informed him. Jacob knew that this was a shortened form of "new town," and he was sorry that the new town apparently wasn't his own. But Bellah explained that it was named after, or in honor of, Thomas Willoughby Newton, who was the United States Marshal for Arkansas.

"Never heared of 'im," Jacob said.

"Whar ye from, stranger?" John Bellah wanted to know.

Jacob Ingledew was sore distressed and perplexed and agger-pervoked. To find that he lived in a county, in the first place, and then, in the second place, to be called "stranger" not six miles from his own dooryard, was a demeaning affront. His first impulse was to strike John Bellah down on the spot, but then he reflected that a wiser course of action might be to secede Stay More from the rest of the county, or perhaps, better yet, if more settlers came in and made Stay More larger than Mount Parthenon, to declare Stay More the county seat.

"I'm Mayor of Stay More," he informed John Bellah.

"Never heared of it," Bellah declared.

"Second largest town in Newton County and *you* aint heared of it?" Jacob demanded. A thought suddenly occurred to him: maybe there were more houses, by one, in Mount Parthenon than in Stay More, but that didn't necessarily mean that there were more human beings inside those houses. "What's the population of this here town, would ye kindly tell me?" he asked.

John Bellah figured, "Wal, there's me and Barbary and our four, and the Rolands with their three, and the Seabolts, no childring, but Isaac Archer and Louisa has got five, and Jim Archer and Mary Ann has got two, the Boens has got two, and Jesse Casey the blacksmith has got ten of 'em, Seburn McPherson and Bess has got three, Bill Bowin and Nancy has got four, and the Coopers, all told, Ike and Sarah Ann and his mother Nancy and their childring, six of 'em. That makes fifty-seven."

"Hah!" Jacob exclaimed and silently thanked Lizzie Swain for having been so multiparous. "Stay More has got fifty-*nine*!"

John Bellah stared woefully at him. "Whar is this city of yourn?" he asked.

Jacob pointed south.

John Bellah took a hunter's horn and blew on it three times. Soon, from all directions, fifty-six other men, women and children had assembled in Bellah's yard, standing in a circle around John Bellah and Jacob Ingledew.

"Folks," said John Bellah to the assembly, "this here feller claims they's a town up the creek a little ways has got more people in it than we'uns do."

"My stars and body!" a woman screeched.

"I'll be jimjohned!" a man roared.

"Golly Moses fishhooks!" a boy bellowed.

"It beats my grandmother!" a girl squealed.

John Bellah asked, "Air we'uns gonna take this a-layin down?"

"No sirree bob!" a woman shrieked.

"Not by a damned sight!" a man barked.

"I'll be hanged if!" a boy snarled.

"Not for the world!" a girl bleated.

"Nope, nohow," a child wailed.

John Bellah raised his arm and suggested, "Then let's go!"

"Skedaddle!" a woman yipped.

"Pull foot!" a boy snapped.

"High-tail!" a girl howled.

"Hoof it!" a child mewed.

The entire population of Mount Parthenon began moving at a brisk clip up the trail in the direction of Stay More. Jacob Ingledew could only follow along, worried and puzzled. None of these people were armed, so if they meant to fight, they would fight bare-handed.

At the northernmost end of the valley of Stay More, there was a field which had been cleared by Levi Whitter for a cow pasture, and now this field was heavy with sweet clover. It would always be called the Field of Clover after the confrontation which took place there between the people of Stay More and the people of Mount Parthenon.

One of the Swain children had seen the Parthenonians coming and had run to alert the rest of the village. All of the Stay Morons (and kindly believe me that my use of this name is meant to be neither pejorative nor facetious; if you wish to split hairs, it should be borne in mind that strictly speaking a moron is in the mental age group between seven and twelve, a time of life which, as anyone who has lived through it can tell you, is simply wonderful) left their homes and came to halt the Parthenonians' advance at Levi Whitter's clover pasture. The two communities faced one another across this field, keeping a distance of some hundred feet (or six hats) between themselves.

"Is that all of 'em, neighbor?" John Bellah asked Jacob Ingledew.

"Yeah, neighbor, I reckon," Jacob replied.

John Bellah began with his bent finger to count the Stay Morons. When he finished, he said, "Fifty-eight." Then he counted the Parthenonians and declared, "Fifty-eight."

"Huh?" Jacob said. "Here, neighbor, let me try." Also using his finger as a counter, Jacob totaled up the number of people standing over there across the field, and sure enough, it came to fifty-eight. Then he counted the number on this side of the field, and it was also fifty-eight. Something was wrong, that Stay More had lost, and Mount Parthenon gained, a person.

Soon all of the Parthenonians who knew how to count were also counting the Stay Morons, and the latter, with nothing better to do, began counting the former. Everybody who could count agreed that the two groups contained the same number of people.

"Wal, neighbor," said John Bellah to Jacob Ingledew, "seeing as how we're even…" Then he asked, "How many dwellings in your village?"

"Eight," Jacob replied.

"Seeing as how we're equal in population, neighbor," John Bellah observed, "I reckon we win, on account of we got nine dwellings." To the other Parthenonians, he announced, "We win!" and they all gave cheers of hoo raw and huzzah and then went on back home.

Jacob was left to explain to his people that Mount Parthenon had become the county seat of this here county, and that while he had contested it on the grounds of Stay More's numerical superiority, it turned out that he must have miscalculated.

Forever afterward, the rivalry between Stay More and Mount Parthenon (or simply Parthenon, as it would later be shortened to) would be intense and sensitive, if never violent. The competition between them was perhaps a factor in their growth and development, and if today Stay More is practically a ghost town then Parthenon is not much better off.

We perceive, then, one more motive that Jacob Ingledew had for building the imposing home of our next chapter: he wanted to equal the number of Parthenon's buildings. That is as good a reason as any for building a house, for sweat, for toil, for going on.

Some time later, it was Noah Ingledew, not exactly anybody's fool, who first realized and understood the error in census-taking that Jacob had made. "Shitfire!" he exclaimed to his brother. "You was countin yoreself on the wrong side!"

Chapter four

He built it all by himself, almost in secret. He meant to surprise Sarah with it, was possibly the reason, or maybe he just wanted the satisfaction of being solely responsible for it. We know what the real reason was, though he did not, could not have guessed, would have blushed and scoffed if we were to tell him. But it takes an awful lot of pent-up passion to build on this scale, alone and in just slightly over two weeks. Jacob's second home is his erection. Although that is not why, like spermaries, it is bigeminal. Consciously he may have been remembering Fanshaw's dwelling; unconsciously no doubt he was remembering one of several dreams he had the first night he slept with Fanshaw's squaw: a dream in which he saw this very structure almost exactly as he has rendered it here: two-pens-and-a-passage, a double house divided (or conjoined) by an open breezeway.

The house was (and still is) in another holler south up Ingledew Mountain from his first dwelling. He discovered it was a better holler, had a stronger spring, and was only two whoops and a holler (which is not hollow but halloo) away from his first place. Still nobody knew exactly where it was except him and his pack of dogs. Undoubtedly the neighbors, especially the Swains, would have been glad to join him and help in a speedy house-raisin', but he chose to go it alone, working from first light to last light and sometimes past light day after day for over two weeks. His pack of dogs went with him and sat around and watched; it was not until he was almost finished that they perked up and took a particular interest in the breezeway, discovering that it was a place where they could loll out of the rain and trot in the shade and breeze, a kind of doghouse almost, or at least a "dogtrot," which is what Jacob called it and which, by extension, is the most common generic name for this type of house as a whole, although there are variants: possum trot, dog run, breezeway, two-wing, open entry, etc.

Jacob Ingledew was by no means the inventor of the type, which scholars have traced all the way back to medieval Sweden, where it was called "pair-cottage," nor was Jacob's dogtrot the first in the Ozarks: there is a magnificent two-story dogtrot at Norfork which was built by Indian agent Jacob Wolfe in the first years of the century. But the Ingledew dogtrot was the first bigeminal white man's dwelling in Newton County, the first bipartition, the first conjugation, the first bifidity, the first duple.

Jacob hoped to install the glass in the windows before showing the house to pretty Sarah, but Eli Willard had not again returned, and everything else was finished, and Jacob was exhausted from his labors (and already, though he did not know it yet, infested with the frakes). So one afternoon he drove the last nail into the last shingle on the roof (the nails were the first product of Absalom Coe's blacksmith shop in Stay More) and then went back to his first place and said, "Sarey, I got a little susprise fer ye. Come on." And he led her through the woods to the clearing in the holler where their new home was erected.

She clapped her hands and oohed and ahhed and hugged his neck and carried on like that for a long time, exclaiming Did you ever! and As I live and breathe! and Fancy that! and Well hush my mouth! Jacob just blushed and said Aw shucks, but it was plain that he was very proud of himself. Then Sarah was puzzled somewhat by their new home's bifidity, that is, she wondered why there were *two* of them. She asked Jacob, "Is that un there fer Noah?"

"No," he explained, "it's fer *you*."

"Me?" She stared at him with puzzlement, and then asked anxiously, "Air we a-fixin to split up?"

He laughed. "Aw naw, darlin. That there half is fer the kitchen and fer eatin. So it's yourn. Th'other half is whar the beds will go, so it's mine."

"I caint sleep in there too?" she asked.

"Aw, shore ye kin," he said. "But don't you see? It's like if, wal, like the Bible said about a man and a woman become one flesh but they're still two people. This here is jist one house, but it's got two parts, and one part is you and th'other part is me."

Sarah still did not quite seem to grasp the philosophy of it, but she took note of the open breezeway in between, where Jacob's nine dogs were lolling about, drooling and thumping the floor with their tails. "And that part," she asked, "is it fer the dogs?"

"I didn't mean it so," he said. "It's meant fer whar we kin set in our cheers and rest, of an evenin, or maybe eat when it's hot, or whar ye kin set to shell peas and snap beans and churn the butter and such." He added: "It's our porch, sorta like. It aint you, and it aint me. It's *us*, both together."

Sarah thought that her man was a little crazy, but she was awful proud of him for building this house, which was over twice as large as any other dwelling in Stay More. Wouldn't Perilla Duckworth and Destiny Whitter, not to mention that snooty Malinda Plowright, just perish of envy when they came a-visiting? "And look at them winders!" Sarah exclaimed, taking note for the first time of the large windows in each wing of the building, even if the sash did not yet have its glass installed. She climbed the few steps to the breezeway and opened the door to "her" wing and went into it to see how bright the interior was because of the window. Only when she was inside did she notice that there was no furniture. The room was empty! There was *nothing* in it except a fireplace. It made her very uncomfortable, and she quickly came back out, saying to Jacob, "If that one is me, I'm all bare and holler."

"We'll fill ye up, quick," he assured her, and returned with her to their first house, where he said to Noah, "Wal, Brother, it's all yourn now," and then made a deal with Noah whereby Jacob and Sarah got over half of whatever furniture was portable (Noah hated to see the clock go), and also Noah's agreement to make, in the near future, a specified number of chairs, tables and bedsteads in return for Jacob's half-interest in the cabin. Noah also helped Jacob and Sarah carry their possessions and items of furniture up to the new house, where Noah too let loose with many exclamations of surprise and admiration, concluding, "Shetfare, it's the masterest house ever I seed!"

That night Jacob and Sarah spread their mattress on the puncheon floor, having no bedstead yet, in the wing of the house which was Jacob's, where he lay on his back and stared at the ceiling of his room, pleased as Punch with the work he had done, but exhausted from it, too tired to sleep. Sarah was not sleeping either. "Hit's so purty," she was sighing. "Hit's shore a fine place. Smells so clean and new. Yo're a good man, Jake." She went on admiring the house and him for a while, and then suddenly she turned to him, turned into him, turned on him, saying, "Here, Jake, let me see if I caint make that thing go fer ye." And then—it was too dark for him to see her, he had covered the window with a bearskin to keep out insects, so not even the moonlight came in to illuminate her—though she had not had any relations with him for eight months and her pregnancy was so near term that she would not now anyway—she employed one or several of her various soft clefts or clasps or crevices, or slews or furcula or nooks, to simulate hers, and stimulate his, until, sure enough, the old clouds gathered and clashed, making lightningbolt and thunderclap and afterclap rattling away.

He went into a deep and most restful sleep then. Sarah slept too, and dreamed, knowing and believing the ages-old tradition that the dream dreamt on the first night in a new house will come true. She was as excited as her great-granddaughter would be on her first visit to a motion picture theater…but she was as puzzled by the dream as her great-granddaughter would have been if she had unwittingly stumbled upon a film by Luis Buñuel.

She (Sarah) was in a large room, much larger than any she had ever been in before, where there were many people, the women dressed in fantastic silken dresses with skirts as big as haymows, the men in black woolen coats with tails like a swallow's, and Sarah was ashamed of her dusty buckskin frock, until she looked down at herself and saw that she too was dressed in a silken gown with skirt big as a haymow, the air circulating freely around her legs and loins. She saw Jacob, who was dressed in the finest of the black woolen swallowtail coats and was smoking a very large cigar, surrounded by other men who were listening to him talk and talk. He caught sight of her and blew her a kiss. Then he motioned for her to come over. She did, and he told her the names of each of the gentlemen around him, and then told them her name, and one by one they took her hand and bent sharply at the waist and placed their mouths on the back of her hand. She did not say anything. She did not know what to say. The other men then ignored her and resumed talking to Jacob. Each of them called him "Your Excellency." Some of the women came and tried to talk to Sarah, but she did not know what to say, and was not sure that she understood what the women were saying, whether they were asking questions or just making statements. She was very embarrassed.

But then the women stopped talking, because there was loud music coming from outside. Jacob came and took her hand and led her out onto the porch, and this porch was very high, there must be another house underneath it, and from this porch she could see that the yard and the road were filled with people, some of them in uniforms beating on drums and blowing bugles and fifes and all kinds of strange brass tooters and horns. Jacob waved to all the people, and they cheered "Huzzah!" He nudged her, so she waved too, and again they cheered "Huzzah!" The music-makers played louder, and the crowd cheered louder, and then, loudest of all, somebody fired off a battery of cannon, and the noise made Sarah start shaking.

When she woke up, in the early morning, she discovered that she had both hands clamped tightly over her ears. She remembered the dream and tried to puzzle it out, but all she could get from it, if it were going to come true, was that someday she and Jacob were going to be of the better sort. Quality folks. She rose and took the bearskin off the window, to let in the morning light. Jacob was still sleeping. The quilt was off him. His buckskins were piled on the floor beside the mattress. Sarah's cheeks waxed hot, seeing his bare prides, but then she noticed that his prides seemed mighty hot too, and, stooping for a closer look, saw that they, and the skin of his groin all around them, were covered with a red rash, thousands of tiny scarlet blisters, almost like chicken pox, but worse. At first she wondered if what she had done the night before might have caused it. She knew that what she had done was unnatural, not right, maybe a sin in the eyes of God. But then she remembered her brother Murray, and knew that her husband had the same terrible affliction.

She shook him awake. "Frake, look, you've got the jakes!" she exclaimed, but corrected herself, "Jake, look, you've got the frakes!" He yawned and raised himself enough to take one look, then fell back to his original position, where he would remain for months on end.

Jake's frakes became the concern of the whole community; farfetched remedies were suggested and tried, but with no effect. Lizzie Swain recommended that Sarah try the blood of a black hen, but it worked no better for Jacob than it had for Murray. Noah appeared, clawed and scratched and bloody, with a quantity of panther urine that he made into a poultice, but it worked no better for Jacob than it had for Noah. Perilla Duckworth recommended a purgative from a decoction of white walnut bark peeled downward, and then an emetic from a decoction of white walnut bark peeled upward, but these only aggravated Jacob's disposition. Destiny Whitter was certain that the frakes was just a form of erypsipelas, or "St. Anthony's Fire," which everybody knew could be easily cured with the blood of a black cat. All of the black cats of Stay More were rounded up, a total of nine, and, since it is terrible bad luck to kill a cat, particularly a black one, none were killed, but each had an ear snipped off and an inch removed from its tail, and enough black cat gore was collected to cover Jacob's frakes in three coats after first washing off all the other stuff that had been applied and caked and dried.

This bold treatment, needless to say, had absolutely no effect, and in time Jacob's frakes erupted and healed over, but he remained abed with feelings of utter worthlessness, so melancholy that not even the birth of his firstborn, Benjamin, which happened then, could rouse him from his Slough of Despond. Nor did he receive any comfort from the confines of his new house, which lacked the certain snugness of the first Ingledew cabin and the Swain house, and was a constant reminder to him of the futility of human endeavor. He could no longer understand nor remember what had motivated him to build the house. Gradually it filled up with furniture, made by Noah; and Sarah, who in the last months of her pregnancy had taken up flax-spinning and weaving, made linen curtains for the windows and other cloth decorations, so that it was indeed the most elegant home in Stay More or all of Newton County, but this brought no cheer whatever to despairing Jacob.

Almost as if Nature herself agreed with his forlorn mood, Stay More began to suffer its first severe drought. In early July, before any of the crops had been harvested except peas and spinach, the sixtieth day without rainfall occurred, and from then on it did not rain a drop for the rest of the summer. The creeks began to dry up, first Banty Creek and then Swains Creek itself, the deep holes of water remaining until last as diminishing puddles engorged with fish. If Jacob had cared, if he had not lost all sense of any purpose to life, he would have urged the people to harvest these fish and dry them as insurance against the famine ahead, but he did not, and the puddles dried until they were only mounds of dead fish. The springs from the mountainsides kept on trickling enough water for man and livestock, a few weeks after the creeks were bone dry, but then the springs began to fail, until there was no water, no trace of water of any kind, at all. By this time, the cornstalks were twisted freaks, and none of the other crops, not even the heat-loving Tah May Toh, were bearing any fruit. Great swarms of grasshoppers and locusts, apparently needing no water to survive, flew in on the hot wind and devoured all the remaining vegetation. The livestock began to die. The cows managed to find a few small tufts of brown grass and convert it into a liquid that vaguely resembled milk, which was rationed: one-half saucer of this per person per day. But soon that ration was reduced to one-quarter saucer, and then one-eighth, and then measured in drops: ten, nine, eight, seven, six, five, four, three, two, one, none, none.

The cows knelt and died. The people who felt like it (and by this time Jacob was not the only person feeling useless and helpless) loaded their oak-stave barrels and tubs and buckets and pails into their wagons, and drove off down the dry creek in search of water. Days later they returned with some murky river water. They reported that the people of Mount Parthenon were dry and suffering too; the Little Buffalo River was dry all along its length; they had followed it into the Big Buffalo, which was also dry, and followed that into the White River, which still had puddles remaining here and there, but each of these puddles was guarded day and night by fierce men with shotguns; they followed the White for miles before finding a puddle that was not guarded, and there they filled their oak-stave containers with this murky swill. They hauled it back to Stay More, strained it, and discovered that after removing all of the fish, minnows, tadpoles, crawdads, turtles, water moccasins, and a few beaver, they had only half as much water as they had started with, and then this water had to be boiled for so long to purify it that half again evaporated, so they were left with only a quarter of what they had found, and this had to be strictly rationed: a half-saucer per day per person. And then a quarter-saucer, an eighth, and so on, down, down.

These people of Stay More had come originally from eastern Tennessee, western North Carolina, and northern Georgia, an area of the country which has more consistent annual rainfall than any other, and not one of these persons, even the oldest, had ever known a drought before. Since the drought had coincided so closely with the onslaught of Jacob's frakes, the people began to wonder, naturally, if there was any connection. If Jacob Ingledew, who was their much-respected steward, shepherd, chieftain, or at least official mayor, had no hope, and couldn't care less whether it rained or not, then that might well be the reason it didn't. Many of the Stay Morons who had been performing superstitious acts to make it rain, with no luck, or praying to God for rain, with less luck, began to wonder if they had not better and more profitably direct their attentions to Jacob Ingledew instead of to God. A delegation of the menfolk was appointed, and they appeared, hats in hands, beside Jacob's bed.

Elijah Duckworth, their spokesman, spoke: "Squire Ingledew,

sir, we'uns is powerful pervoked by the lack of rain, and seein as how yore affliction come smack dab at the same time, we'uns has got to wonderin if they might be tied up some way, one with th'other."

Jacob stared at Elijah Duckworth for a while and studied the notion. "I hadn't thought of that, Lige," he declared. "I don't do much thinkin, one way or the other, lately."

"Do ye want it to rain, or not?" Elijah asked.

"Tell ye the truth, I don't honestly keer," Jacob replied.

"But you're shore to starve of thirst along with the rest of us."

"I reckon so," Jacob acknowledged.

"Do ye want yore womarn and that fine young'un to die too?" Elijah demanded. (Sarah at this time was one of the few living creatures in Stay More still producing liquid, nursing the baby Benjamin, by dint of the efforts of her mother and her many brothers and sisters, who pooled a portion of their daily ration of water for her.)

"What kin I do?" Jacob lamented morosely and rhetorically. "What kin ary man do? What's the use, nohow?"

"Mind if we set down?" Elijah Duckworth asked. Jacob gestured feebly toward the new mule-eared chairs that Noah had made, and the men drew them up beside Jacob's bed and sat in them.

Then, one by one, each man told the funniest joke he could remember. Elijah told of an old man trying to trade mules and offering to another feller a strong, lively horse mule, who, however, while being examined, ran head-on into a big tree. "'Why, that critter must be blind,' says the feller the old man was trying to trade with. 'Naw,' says the old man, 'he aint blind. He jist don't give a damn.'"

All of the men laughed and slapped their thighs and elbowed each other, but Jacob did not stir. They eyed him carefully for any sign of perhaps a twitching at the corner of his mouth or even a slight sparkle in his eye, but there was none. Maybe he had taken it too personal, they decided. So Levi Whitter told one about his oldest boy, Tim, who everybody knew was not over-bright, how Levi was rolling a load of cow manure out to his field when Tim asked him what he was going to do with it, and Levi answered "I'm going to put it on my strawberries," and Tim give a snort and says, "I put honey and cream on mine, and everybody says *I'm* a damn fool!"

Jacob didn't seem to care much for that one either, so Zachariah Dinsmore thought to play upon Jacob's disdain for religion by telling one about a preacher who stopped by to look over a farmer's spread and says, "Well, you and the Lord have sure raised some fine corn." Then when he seen the hogs, he says, "With God's help, you have got a lot of good pork." Finally they was looking at the garden next to the barn, and the preacher says, "You and God have sure growed some fine vegetables." The farmer was losing his patience, and says, "Listen, Preacher, you ought to have seen this here farm when God was a-runnin it all by Hisself!"

But this too failed to provoke any glimmer of mirth in Jacob Ingledew. The men started over, and told a round of the second-funniest jokes they could remember, and then a round of the third-funniest, and so on, and by the time they got to their ninth-funniest jokes they weren't even laughing themselves, so they gave up and went home.

The drought dragged on, the hot winds parched the flesh, the woods caught fire, and acres of virgin timber burned unchecked, leaving vast black scabs of burnt-out woodland on what had once been the beautiful countryside. Perhaps mercifully, the fires exterminated all of the woods-creatures who were dying of thirst. There would be no game to hunt during the coming famine.

A delegation of womenfolk came next to Jacob, and they stood around his bed, singing happy and pleasant inspirational songs in soprano-contralto harmony. They sang "Keep on the Sunny Side of Life" and "Home, Sweet Home" and "Burdens Are Blessings" and "Smile All the While" and "Bright Cheer Year by Year" and "Oh Happy Day" and "Juberous Times" and "Ah, Happy Heart, Light the Long Hours Ever So Gaily and Anon." Yet, even though this last was a brilliant coloratura number, Jacob's mood remained essentially unaltered. In fact, so steadfast did his mood remain that it infected the women, who began singing sad songs until Sarah shooed them off.

Then Sarah's breasts began to dry, and baby Benjamin spent long hours wailing for milk that he could not get. Was Jacob at least stricken by his small son's cries? If he was, it was hard to tell.

A delegation of young people came next to Jacob's bedside, where they performed stunts, antics, headstands, slapsticks and pratfalls, roughhouse and gymnastics, roister and fling and shindig, merrymaking to melt the heart of all but the most hopeless case... which Jacob, unfortunately, was, and remained. The summer passed, and although in September the temperature dropped slightly below 100° for the first time in weeks, there was still no rain. Nobody but the women had anything to do. The women still had to cook, whatever corn and meal remained from the year before, whatever salt pork, whatever reptiles that had not perished. The women tried to find occupation for the men and boys by putting them to work with the carding and spinning of wool shorn from the dead sheep, and scutching and swingling flax to be spun into linen thread, and even with the weaving itself. The making of *dry*goods, with ironic symbolism, became a busy industry during the drought. Come winter, even if there was no food to eat, everybody would have plenty of clothes and could shed their buckskins. If everybody died, they could at least be buried in fine raiment.

The next delegation to Jacob's bedside, the last delegation (for they alone remained to try), were the children. The children came, seventeen of them, and stood around his bed. They had no jokes to tell, nor songs to sing, nor stunts to do. They were indescribably dirty, because nobody had had a bath or a swim in three months and children naturally need washing more often anyway. They were thin too, not starving yet, but close to it. Among these children were the younger sons and daughters of Lizzie Swain, the same children who had worn such big smiles when Jacob first saw them, the same who had been so happy and excited to find a new home in a beautiful, bountiful wilderness. None of them were smiling now. They just stood around with their pinched soiled faces staring at Jacob in his bed. He became, finally, aware of them.

"What do you little squirts want?" he asked.

Nine-year-old Octavia Swain, their spokesperson, spoke. "Uncle Jake," she said, "you aint got nothin to do, and neither has we'uns. So let's us start us a school, and you be the teacher."

"Gosh all hemlock," Jacob groaned. "What would be the use?"

"So's we'uns could git the smarts, like you," she explained.

"What's the use of bein smart?" he demanded. "Class, let me see a hand! Who's the first to answer? What's the use of bein smart?"

And without realizing it, Jacob had already founded the first Stay More elementary school. The pupils sat, two by two, on the floor around Jacob's bed, and he even sat up in his bed for the first time in months. One little boy timidly raised his hand and Jacob called on him.

"If yo're smart, you kin git rich easy," offered the boy.

"That aint no answer," Jacob responded. "What's the use of bein rich? Come on, let's see if there's anybody knows the answer. Let me see another hand."

None of the children raised their hands, until finally Octavia Swain lifted hers.

"You, Tavy," Jacob said.

"Well, sir," she offered, standing up, "if I was smart, I could use my brain to answer hard questions like, 'What's the use of bein smart?'" She sat down.

Jacob thought about that for a moment, and then he did something he hadn't done in a coon's age: he laughed. Well, it wasn't exactly an all-out gutbusting hawr-de-hawr horselaugh, but at least it was a respectable straight-up-and-down chortle, and when he did, the students laughed too. "Tavy," he said, admiringly, "I 'low as how that's as good a answer as any. Okay. Now it's your turn. Axe me a question."

Octavia stood up again. "Sir, how kin we git water?"

Jacob frowned. "That's a tough one," he said. "Let me study on it a minute." His first impulse was to tell them that the only way they could get water would be to leave, abandon Stay More, go back where they all came from, where there was always a plenty of water even if an overplenty of people. But he did not suggest this. Instead he meditated on the meaning of rainfall, the circulation of waters, and the certainty of recurrence. A man could be sure of only one thing: a drought is always ended by a rainfall. But where does all the water go during the drought? He knew that the waters ran to the rivers and the rivers ran to the sea but the sea didn't run anywhere. If Swains Creek and the Buffalo River were empty, was the sea flooded? He remembered Fanshaw's theory of gravity, and the notion that the earth is round. If all the creeks and rivers were empty on this side of the earth, and the seas weren't flooded, then all the water must be over on the other side of the earth. But if that were so, and the earth really rolled around the sun as Fanshaw said it did, then it would wobble, and you'd feel it wobbling. No, the water must be someplace else. It couldn't all be evaporated up into the sky because if it were then the sky would be full of clouds that would soon rain. So if the seas had their share and couldn't hold any more, and the rivers were empty and the sky was clear, the only other place the water possibly could be was right down inside the earth.

"Dig," he answered, at length. "Tell 'em to git their shovels and find the lowest meader in Stay More and git out in the middle of it and start diggin, straight down. Don't let 'em stop 'till they find water. Class dismissed."

School met every day after that, the children bringing their lunches in little cloth sacks their mothers made for them, lunches of corn dodger or pone, frugal but filling, and soon the children came to school clean, unspotted if not immaculate, because their fathers had dug fifty feet down in Levi Whitter's Field of Clover and struck a vast subterranean pool of pure wonderful water. There was so much of it that when Jacob was told, he ordered it shared with their neighbors the Parthenonians, and for a time at least all rivalry between the two villages ceased as the Parthenonians came gratefully to fetch home water. For a time at least, a very brief time, Stay More was declared the county seat of Newton County, and Jacob's imposing double-pen dogtrot served for a while as the schoolhouse and courthouse both until Sarah complained that she couldn't fix dinner without brushing a swarm of lawyers off the table and flushing the bailiff out of the potato bin.

Jacob took no interest in the court, even though he was offered a high position there. He stayed in his own wing of the building, still bedfast, still hopeless, but determined to give an education to these children who had asked him for one. They loved school; he never had any trouble with them; he never had to get out of his bed to discipline an unruly pupil. If any one of the children, through restlessness or ennui or just pure cussedness, decided to try to disrupt the orderliness of the classroom, the other children would mob him, tie him, gag him, hoist him from the ceiling and leave him suspended there until he signaled, by frantic eyeball movements, that he was ready to behave...this whole proceeding so quick it did not interrupt the lesson that Jacob was giving.

Jacob never taught his pupils how to read. As we have seen, he was the only literate person in Stay More for a period of many years, and could not help but feel at times that his literacy was a curse upon him, or at least was something he should not infect his charges with. Deliberately then he excluded reading and writing from the curriculum, and the school was none the worse for the omission.

But what, then, did they study? Arithmetic, of course, and since all of the pupils always came barefoot to school, it was possible to do counting exercises up to and including twenty digits...or even forty, because, as in most other rural schools everywhere from time immemorial, there was a kind of buddy system, a pairing, a conjugation, a bifidity, all of them sitting and working two by two together. The curriculum also included practical matters such as how to control one's facial muscles in order to assume a "deadpan" in times of stress, challenge, insult, reproach, etc. But in the main, the curriculum was devoted to discussion and debate on purely philosophical concepts in the arts and sciences. Why does the wind blow? What makes the rain? Why must chiggers, ticks and frakes bite? Why do we scratch? Why should we live? A whole day's program could be built around any one of these questions. For example, a question such as "Why can't a person tickle himself?" would lead not only into a discussion of the psychological factors involved, but also into the anatomy and physiology of tickling, a comparison of the armpit with the underchin, with excursions even into solipsistic examination: I exist because I think, but you exist because I cannot tickle myself without you. Word got back to the families of the intense intellectual stimulation of Jacob's schoolroom, and many of the grown-ups petitioned Jacob to be allowed to attend, but this petition was not granted.

The only grown-up other than Jacob who ever came into his schoolroom was Eli Willard.

School was in session one day when the Connecticut itinerant reappeared after long absence, bringing Jacob's window glass and other merchandise. Jacob seized him and presented him to the class. "Boys and girls, this specimen here is a Peddler. You don't see them very often. They migrate, like the geese flying over. This one comes maybe once a year, like Christmas. But he aint dependable, like Christmas. He's dependable like rainfall. A Peddler is a feller who has got things you aint got, and he'll give 'em to ye, and then after you're glad you got 'em he'll tell ye how much cash money you owe him fer 'em. If you aint got cash money, he'll give credit, and collect the next time he comes 'round, and meantime you work hard to git the money someway so's ye kin pay him off. Look at his eyes. Notice how they are kinder shiftly-like. Now, class, the first question is: why is this feller's eyes shiftly-like?"

Several pupils raised their hands. Jacob called on one, who offered the possibility that it was a congenital defect; another suggested that he might have a foreign object in his eye; another wondered if the case might be that he had enemies who were following him, and he was looking out for them. Jacob was required to call upon his star pupil, Octavia Swain, in hopes of the correct answer.

"He's jist casing the joint," Octavia observed, "to see if you got anything he might want to swap ye out of."

"Kee-reck," Jacob complimented her. "Now, these here Peddler fellers is also slick talkers. They say things like—"

"I beg your pardon..." Eli Willard interrupted.

"They say things like 'I beg your pardon,'" Jacob went on, "and 'Good evening, sir' and 'Good morning, madam,' and 'Permit me to serve you in any manner I can,' and 'This is a most unexpected pleasure,' and 'I beg your acceptance of my very hearty thanks for doing me the honor to inquire if I shall have the opportunity to appreciate most cordially your extremely welcome response to my gratitude for your kindness in obliging my hope that you anticipate my wishes for—'"

"Do you want your confounded window glass, or not?" Eli Willard demanded.

"Bring it in," Jacob said to him, and while Eli Willard was

outside unloading the glass from his saddlebags, Jacob told his students, "Now directly we'll git a chance to watch how a real Peddler operates. I want you'uns to watch and listen real careful. He'll bring in them thar winder panes, which is costin me ever cent I've got to my name, and then he'll say somethin like, 'It grieves me to have to report that the current quotation on pane glass is even more frightfully dear than I had previously imagined...' and then he'll soak me for all I kin raise between now and the next time he shows up, and then he'll give me the glass, but it will turn out that the glass don't fit my winders, it's too big and has to be cut with God knows what, and he'll git this big smile on his face and whip out this little gizmo from his pocket and hold it up and say, 'Presto! A magic Acme Damascus Coal Carbon Disc Wheel Glass Cutter! In limited supply and for a short time only, ten dollars each.' And dodgast me if I don't pay. Here he comes. Watch careful, class."

Eli Willard reentered, bearing a sheaf of random-sized glass sheets packed in excelsior. He cleared his throat and began, "It grieves me to have to report—"

All seventeen of Jacob's pupils chimed in, "—THAT THE CURRENT QUOTATION ON PANE GLASS IS EVEN MORE FRIGHTFULLY DEAR THAN I HAD PREVIOUSLY IMAGINED."

Eli Willard stared at the boys and girls, then he beseeched Jacob, "Call off your dogs," and whispered into Jacob's ear the new revised exorbitant figure, and told him, "Take it or leave it."

"I aint got much choice," Jacob observed. "But look. Them there glass pieces is too big to fit my panes."

Eli Willard smiled and reached into his pocket and brought out a little gizmo which he held up. "Presto—" he began.

"OH LOOK!" chorused the class. "A MAGIC ACME DAMASCUS COAL CARBON DISC WHEEL GLASS CUTTER!"

"In limited—"

"—SUPPLY FOR A SHORT TIME ONLY, TEN CENTS EACH!"

"Ten *dollars*," Eli Willard corrected them.

"TEN CENTS," they reaffirmed.

"Dollars."

"CENTS."

"My compliments to your well-drilled academy," Eli Willard said to Jacob. "They drive a hard bargain. Very well, it is yours for the trifling sum of ten cents. Now could I interest you or any of your scholars in my latest line of merchandise?"

It turned out that on this particular visit, Eli Willard was hawking silk umbrellas for ladies and gentlemen, parasols for children, and oil slicker raincoats for all, as well as eaves trough hangers and metal spigots for rainbarrels. When neither Jacob nor his pupils expressed any interest whatever in merchandise of this nature, Eli Willard broke down and confessed that he had not been able to sell a single item of this line anywhere in the Ozarks and was now on the edge of penury. Reputable meteorologists back East had assured him that the following spring and summer promised to be very wet, but so far he was totally without luck in pushing his raingear and appurtenances.

"Buck up, feller," Jacob tried to comfort him, and then explained to his class, "By and large Peddlers don't generally cry. This is jist an exception." Then Jacob got out of bed and conducted Eli Willard across the breezeway into the other wing of his house, and told Sarah to try to scare up something to feed the poor feller. They fed him, and Jacob paid him for the glass and reminded him of how much money he still owed him, which brought some small cheer to Eli Willard as he rode on his luckless way.

It is idle to speculate whether the Stay Morons erred grievously in failing to patronize Eli Willard in his latest line of merchandise, for the rains that came the following spring and summer would have rendered umbrellas and rainwear practically useless. It was almost as if Nature, in clumsy headlong atonement for her stinginess with moisture the year before, overcompensated, went too far. Deluged. Inundated. It was terrible. If not for the proverbial forty days and nights, it rained steadily nearly every day for over a month, nobody measured or kept track but it must have been more inches than ever fell in any other month in the history of the Ozarks.

The rains began, ironically enough, on the second Tuesday of a month, right in the middle of a gala bergu that the Parthenonians threw to fete the Stay Morons for the hospitality of their waterwell.

A bergu is a kind of stew, consisting of five hundred squirrels properly cleaned and boiled to the consistency of soup in a twenty-gallon iron kettle. The Parthenonian's bergu was almost ready, while the Stay Morons stood around with their napkins tucked into their collars and their knives and spoons gripped in their hands, when the first raindrops fell, and then the cloudburst began, and in their haste to get the bergu indoors the Parthenonians dropped the kettle and spilled the five hundred stewed squirrels into the dry bed of Shop Creek, which soon began to fill with water. The Stay Morons went home hungry, and sat and watched as, day by day, Swains Creek rose higher and higher, left its banks and overflowed into fields, and Banty Creek roared through its gorges, engorging them. If the Stay Morons were angry at the Parthenonians for spilling and spoiling the bergu, the Parthenonians became angry at the Stay Morons because, being downstream from Stay More, they already had more water in the Little Buffalo than they could handle but Stay More kept sending its creeks on down to Parthenon anyway. "You're stranglin us!" John Bellah of Parthenon protested to Jacob Ingledew. "Send yore creeks somewheres else!" But there was nowhere else to send the creeks.

The Parthenonians talked about bringing a cease-and-desist action against the Stay Morons in the county court, but all the lawyers had fled to higher ground. Then the Little Buffalo River submerged the hollers along the base of Reynolds Mountain and shut Parthenon off from Stay More for the duration of the deluge, and no more was heard from them.

Until the flood became really impossible, the Stay Morons managed to keep their good sense of humor and even to make jokes about it. Their favorite jokes involved Noah Ingledew, because of his name. "Keep a watch on him," they would say, "and when he gits out his saw and hammer, start packin yore duds." Jokers would catch a pair of snakes, male and female of each, and crate them, and present them to Noah as "voyagers." Noah couldn't even indulge his favorite pastime, whittling, without somebody saying to him something like,

"Is that there the foremast or the mizzenmast?" and they would ask him things like, "Would you know an olive branch if you saw one?" and nobody ever even passed by his cabin without giving it a good kick and saying "Think she'll float?" Noah bore all of this badinage in silence, until he decided it had gone far enough, and then one day, when the rain was coming down hard and the fields were nearly all flooded, he stepped outside and yelled, "ANCHORS AWEIGH!" as loud as he could, which seems perhaps a cruel thing to do, like yelling "Fire!" in a crowded theater, and as we shall see he will soon be punished for it, but it had its effect: all of the Stay Morons came running, carrying whatever small belongings they could gather, and crowded around his cabin. Inside it, he barred the door, but yelled, from time to time, "HEAVE HO!" or "HIT THE DECK!" or "HAUL THE YARDARM!" or "SAG TO LEEWARD!" until his brother Jacob banged on the door and threatened to keelhaul him if he didn't avast this foolishness and cut off his jib.

But nobody bothered Noah after that. In fact, they wouldn't have had a chance to, even if they wanted to, because that same night, in the middle of the night, all the beaver dams in all the hills around Stay More broke and washed out, and all the ponds spilled into the already flooded streams, and Noah woke to discover that his cabin, which was the lowest dwelling in Stay More, was not floating, but that its bilge was awash. He swam to the door, raised the bar, and a wave of cold water swept the door open and sucked Noah out of it and down the now broad river that had once been gentle Swains Creek. Swept along on the roiling crest, he clutched right and clutched left, for any limb to grab, but he was carried nearly halfway to Parthenon before his fingers finally seized a branch and stopped his course. He got both hands on the limb and hauled himself up. Judging from the feel of the bark, it was a sycamore tree. He sat on the limb and rested awhile, spitting out water and getting his wind back, but the water was still rising; he climbed to a higher limb, and then again to an even higher one, where he lodged himself in the fork between limb and trunk and spent the rest of the night. He began to worry about falling asleep and tumbling into the rising waters.

Groping around in the dark, he discovered that creeping

blackjack vines snaked through the branches of the sycamore. He tore off several of these and used them in lieu of rope to lash himself firmly to the tree so that he would not fall out of it if he went to sleep. In fact, he tied himself so fast that he couldn't have got loose if he wanted to. And yet he did not fall asleep; the roaring and bubbling of the cataract beneath him kept him awake until dawn. The sun's early light revealed the whole valley under yellow-brown water. Considering the size of the big sycamore tree he was in, he judged that he must be some thirty feet (or two hats) above the ground, and yet the water was less than ten feet below him, which meant that the ground was covered with twenty feet of water. "AHOY!" he yelled several times, but there was no answer.

Meanwhile, Jacob's dogtrot house, which was situated on higher ground than any of the other dwellings, became the ark of refuge for all of the other Stay Morons. They counted heads and discovered Noah missing, and began to grieve for him, and to be sorry that they had teased him, and even to be glad for the little trick he had played on them, because they had assembled their belongings when he had called "Anchors Aweigh!" so their belongings were all ready to go when the real flood came in the middle of the night. The religious ones among them prayed for Noah's safety. Jacob had the opinion that maybe Noah was sitting on the ridgepole of his cabin, and in the morning they could construct a raft and float it down there and rescue him. As for the rest of the night, everybody was too excited to sleep, even if there were space in the two crowded pens to lie down, so they stayed awake talking and telling jokes in an effort to divert their minds from the rising water and the devastation of their fields and livestock and homes.

But then the members of the Stay More Debating Society proposed a new topic: Which is worse, a drought or a flood? Sides were drawn, and the oratory and rebuttals kept them busy until dawn. But Jacob, the referee, decreed that the match was a draw, even-Stephen, and the jug of whiskey that was to go to the winners was shared, all around. At dawn, the men began constructing a raft, which Jacob piloted, leaving his house and grounds for the first time since the frakes had got him, and beginning his return to normal life.

With Elijah Duckworth and Levi Whitter as first mate and boatswain, Jacob poled the raft down the broad yellow-brown river to the holler where his first cabin was; but it was no more. Probing with his pole for some sign of the roof or chimney, Jacob reluctantly concluded that the whole cabin must have washed away. "NO-EY!" he called, but only the roar of the river answered him. He let the raft drift aimlessly downstream, continuing to call out for his brother, until Duckworth and Whitter suggested that they would like to inspect their homesteads too. These, it turned out, were still standing, although the livestock were drowned, except for a flock of chickens on the ridgepole of Duckworth's place, and a pair of goats on Whitter's ridgepole. The other buildings, too, of Stay More had survived, except for the rude trading post, whose roof could be seen floating in an eddy off Banty Creek. What was better, the men noted, the water level seemed to be dropping rapidly, and the rain had stopped and the sun was shining marvelously in a near-cloudless sky. Before the day was over, the people could return to their homes and drag out their wet bedding to hang in the sunshine, and begin scraping mud off their floors and furniture, and start the long hard reconstruction of their lives.

But even after the floodwaters receded, Noah was still up in that tree. Not by choice; he was helplessly entangled in the black-jack vines that he had used to bind himself to the trunk. He would husband his strength for a while and then tug and tear at the vines, but to no avail. Whenever he did not feel completely exhausted, he would draw breath into his lungs and yell "AHOY!" but if anyone heard him from afar they probably took it as an echo of their own voices calling "NOAH!" or "NOEY!"

This was true in Jacob's case; since his own house did not require drying out and cleaning like the others, he could spend all of his time searching for his brother...or his brother's body...but whenever he went far enough downstream to hear the distant, faint "ahoy" he took it as only an echo of his own voice calling "NOEY!"

In time, Noah became too weak to yell very loudly. It is a marvel how he survived, but he did. Some of the details of his survival technique are not pleasant to dwell upon, but a few of the less unsavory may be mentioned: the sunshine dried his cold wet buckskins (although also drying, and tightening, the black-jack vines that bound him to the tree); there was a small saucer-shaped depression in a tree limb near his head which contained rainwater, or spunkwater as they call it, and which he, by craning his neck, could dip his tongue into and slake his thirst from time to time; his hands were still free, and he could use these to: (1) tear off leaves from the tree to chew upon; (2) unfasten his trousers in order to relieve himself; (3) seize, and pluck the feathers off of, pigeons, whose uncooked flesh was better than nothing. In this manner he managed to subsist for nearly a week, until he was found. He slept well without fear of falling into the water—or, now that the flood was gone, the ground, thirty feet below him. He was bothered by backaches occasionally, and, for two days, by constipation, but these were minor annoyances. He was troubled by thoughts of what unknown desolation the flood may have wreaked upon Stay More. One day a dove brought him an olive branch, but he did not know what it was, and ate the dove.

It was Jacob who found him. Jacob, who had nothing better to do than to search, and kept at it. The people of Stay More had begun to feel very sorry for Jacob. Every day they would hear his voice, somewhere up or down the creek, calling "NOEY!" and they would shake their heads and cast sorrowful glances at one another, and remember all over again how cruel they had been to Noah before the flood. One of the more superstitiously religious women, perhaps out of guilt, tried to justify or at least explain the loss of Noah: "Hit's God's new sign. In the last flood all perished but Noah. In this flood all survived but Noah."

In fact, Jacob himself had given up the search, and what brought him to the vicinity of Noah's sycamore tree was not the search for Noah, now abandoned, but a desire to go down to Parthenon to see if his neighbors there had survived the flood. This is how he happened to pass beneath Noah's tree, and would not have noticed Noah if the latter had not noticed him first. At first Noah thought that Jacob was just an apparition, but perhaps as a simple reflex action, he said again, one last time, "Ahoy!" and Jacob looked up and saw him high overhead.

"Heigh-ho!" Jacob exclaimed. "Whoopee! Yippity-yay! Boy oh boy! Goody gander! Hooraw! Hi-de-ho! Man alive! Hot diggety darn! Tolderollol!" Jacob jumped up and kicked his heels together twice before coming down. Then he became solicitous. "Air ye all right, Brother? You aint drownded? How's yore heartbeat? Breathin normal? Kin ye see out of both eyes? Hear out of both ears? Bowel movements reg'lar? I'll bet ye could stand a drop of good corn. Come on down."

"I'm all hung up," Noah pointed out. "This here black-jack vine has got a mighty holt on me."

"I'll git ye loose," Jacob declared, and prepared to climb the tree, but saw that the first limb was too high for him to reach. "I'll have to fetch a rope or ladder," he told Noah. "Keep cool. I'll be right back. Don't git narvous. Steady down. Easy does it. Be a man. Stay with it. Chin up." Jacob turned and ran for home. It was not a short distance, and he wasn't used to running. Pretty soon he had to stop for breath, and he told himself there wasn't any real hurry, because if Noah had been up in that tree for seven days and six nights already he could last for another hour or so.

Jacob returned home to find Sarah yelling that Baby Ben had opened the cow-pasture gate and let all the cows out, and was being chased by the bull. Jacob shooed the bull off of Ben, spanked the latter and sent him to the house, then rounded up his cows and got them back into the pasture. No sooner had he finished this when word came that the Duckworths, in trying to dry their damp belongings, had built up too large a fire in their fireplace, and the roof had caught from sparks and the house was burning. Jacob grabbed up all his empty buckets and pails and took off for the Duckworth house, and spent the next hour helping them put out the fire. Part of the roof was gone but the rest of the place was saved. Then one of the sons of Levi Whitter, who was helping fight the fire, came running to tell Levi that his wife Destiny had fallen into the well, and they didn't have rope long enough to reach her. Jacob ran home to get more rope and then down to the Field of Clover to help get Destiny out of the well. By the time they got her out and dried her off and revived her with whiskey, everybody was plumb wore out and hungry, so Jacob told Sarah to serve up a big supper for the rescue crews, and since Jacob's place had escaped the flood and their larder was still undamaged if not exactly brimming, Sarah prepared what might in such lean times be considered a sumptuous feast, and afterwards the menfolk sat around in Jacob's breezeway picking their teeth and belching in deep satisfaction. Dark came on. One of the men remarked philosophically, "Wal, boys, I reckon we've seen the worst of it." The other men nodded sagely, and got out their pocketknives and commenced whittling. The jug of corn was circulated freely among them, until, one by one, they got up and expressed their thanks for the fine supper and said they'd best be getting on down home. The last leaver clapped Jacob on the back and said, "Yeah, Jake, I reckon we've seen the worst of it. You've lost Noah, but—"

"Great Caesar's ghost!" Jacob exclaimed. "I plumb fergot all about him! Where's a ladder? Quick!" Jacob rounded up rope, a ladder, and an axe to cut the black-jack vines, and with a torch of rags soaked in bear's oil to light his way, went as fast as he could back toward the sycamore where Noah, meanwhile, having convinced himself that it really was just an apparition that he had mistaken for his brother, had supped on raw pigeon, relieved himself, and gone to sleep. Once Jacob got up into the sycamore, he had trouble waking Noah, and the still-sleepy Noah muttered to the effect that he might as well stay here. But Jacob got him down and took him home, or rather, since Noah's cabin was washed away, into his own house, where he was bedded in the loft of the kitchen.

We have essayed, in this chapter, to approach an exploration of duality, particularly as manifested in the bipartition or conjugation of Jacob Ingledew's dogtrot house, which he in his simplistic perspective considered a manifestation of the bipartition or conjugation of the sexes, but which, although he was nearly correct in that limited interpretation, has hints of extension into far larger dualities: of drought and flood, of hot and cold, of day and night, of living and not living, of sowing and reaping, of breaking down and building up. We shape our buildings, and thereafter they shape us.

"You know somethin?" Noah remarked one day to his brother. "Hit weren't nearly so bad as you'd think, up there in that tree. Naw. Why, it was kinder fun. Could ye lend me the borry of yore saw and hammer…?"

Chapter five

It was an anomaly, a freak of the Ozarks, as it were, but so was Noah Ingledew, as it were. And yet, who are we to take the measure of that man and pronounce him abnormal? There is in each of us the child who yearns to build treehouses, to return to primordial man's arboreal aerie. We don't know Noah, and never will; a man whose vocabulary of oaths was limited to a single illogical combination of feces and flame might seem to lack the imagination to design and build the original penthouse shown in our illustration; and yet not only *did* he build it, but also he made a couple of innovations in architecture, to wit: it is the first split level dwelling in the Ozarks (and bigeminal, by Jiminy!) and, perhaps owing in part to the difficulty of building up a chimney of stone to that height (two hats, or over thirty feet above the ground), it was the first dwelling in the Ozarks heated by a metal stove with tin flue—although where Noah obtained the metal and how he fashioned it into a stove, and what the stove actually looked like, I cannot say.

Noah's house and its massive sycamore tree (not the same tree he was stuck in a few pages back) were located not far from the center of Stay More, on the banks of Swains Creek, around a sharp bend of the creek as it meanders its tortuous course through the valley. The house remained stubbornly clinging to the sycamore tree for years and years after Noah's death—unoccupied even during times of housing shortage, not necessarily through reverence for Noah's memory but rather out of superstition—until well into the twentieth century, when a mixed crowd of "modern" youths, to whom the name "Noah Ingledew" meant merely the faceless cofounder of Stay More, climbed up into it for the purpose of sexual sport (a purpose to which Noah himself had put the treehouse on only one fleeting occasion), and through a combination of the ardor of their sport and the weight of their numbers (there were four boys and four girls) caused the tree house, both pens of it, to detach itself from the tree and crash to the ground. All eight of the youths were injured, none seriously, but their biggest problem was explaining to their elders the nature of the accident—the truth got out, and some of the older elders claimed they could see the ghost of Noah Ingledew nightly surveying the ruins of the treehouse.

Initial public reaction to Noah's construction of the treehouse was mixed; half of the Stay Morons declared that it confirmed their suspicion that Noah was "not over-bright," while the other half countered by saying Well as I live and breathe! and What do you know about that! and If thet aint the beatinest thang ever I seed! These people coaxed out of Noah an invitation to climb up and view the interior(s); he could admit them only one at a time; the others queued up at the base of the tree, and even some of those who had deemed Noah "not over-bright" joined the line and waited their turns to climb up and look inside his treehouse. Word quickly spread, and soon people from Parthenon and even Jasper were joining the queue, which grew longer and longer. An itinerant evangelist, or wandering "saddlebag preacher," happened by the end of the queue, which at that point was stretched out of sight of the treehouse around a bend in Swains Creek.

There was some profane cursing going on at the end of the queue, with imprecations of "Quit shovin!" and "Git in line!" and "Keep off my toes!" and the profanity, more than the queue itself, drew the preacher's attention. "Brethern and sistern," he addressed them, "how come you'uns take the Lord's Name in vain?" The people just stared at him, until one of them said, "Light down often yore goddamn horse, and take yore place in line like everybody else." This incensed the preacher, but he got down and tethered his horse to a tree, and took his place in line. The line moved slowly, and by and by the preacher tapped the shoulder of the man ahead of him and asked, "What air we a-waitin fer, anyhow?" The man, who happened to be Jacob Ingledew, looked at him. Jacob judged from the preacher's clothing, and from his remark about taking the Lord's name in vain, that he might be an ignorant preacher who had just stumbled by, and he asked him, "Air ye a preacher, Reverend?"

"Some has been known to say so," the preacher replied.

"Wal, Reverend," Jacob said, "you're jist in time. It's the Jedgment Day, and up yonder God has set Hisself a booth up in a tree, and we're all a-waitin to be jedged."

The preacher began to sweat, and while he continued to wait patiently in the queue, he gave himself over to silent prayer. After a while his place in line had moved around the bend of Swains Creek, and he came in view of the big sycamore tree with Noah's treehouse thirty feet off the ground, and people climbing up the ladder to it. His knees trembled and he stumbled against Jacob, who said, "Quit shovin, Reverend. God has got all day." Jacob meanwhile had quietly passed along to the others the news of the joke that was being played on the poor preacher, and the others gave him amused looks and tried hard not to laugh. One woman said to the preacher, "You aint skairt, air ye, Reverend? Don't the Lord place the preachers on His right hand?" "Yeah," the preacher replied, "but there was a few sins in my past that air still a-troublin me."

By the time the preacher reached the head of the queue at the base of the big sycamore tree, he was lathered with sweat and trembling as if with the palsy. Jacob took his turn climbing up to view the interior(s) of his brother's treehouse, but decided against telling Noah that his next visitor would be a dumb preacher expecting to meet God. When Jacob climbed down, he had to assist the preacher in climbing the rude rungs up the tree, and to give him a final shove to propel him through the door of the treehouse, where the preacher fell down on his knees before the astonished Noah, crying, "LORD, I REPENT EVER BIT OF IT!" Noah, who had been sitting in his chair welcoming each visitor with the same mild words: "Howdy. Make yerself pleasant" (that is, "Make yourself at home"), and had repeated this so many times by now that it was automatic, now said to the prostrate preacher, "Howdy. Make yerself pleasant." The preacher looked around him and saw that there was an empty chair in the room, and managed to hoist himself into it, where he sat with clenched hands between his knees and gazed in awe at Noah. Noah at that time was about thirty-four years old, and he sure didn't look like anybody's conventional conception of God, but the preacher had never seen God before, and you couldn't never tell. Maybe he was just Saint Peter, the preacher thought, but either way the preacher was in for a hot time of it, on account of his past sins. "Fergive us our trespasses," he beseeched, "as we fergive them that trespass against us."

Noah, for his part, was more than a little discomfited. Although he had said to each visitor, "Howdy. Make yerself pleasant," this had been a mere formality, and not one of the people had taken him at his word and sat down in the other chair, until this feller came along. The feller seemed tetched in the head someway. He was dressed kind of funny, too, in a black suit and hat and necktie. And now he was asking to be forgiven for trespassing. "Aint no trespass," Noah reassured him. "If all them other folks could come up here, reckon ye got as much right as any."

God—or Saint Peter—talked kind of funny, the preacher thought. He talked just like he looked: just plain folks. Well, sure, the preacher realized, God would want to make Himself appear like one of His people. "You fergive me, then?" he timidly asked.

"Why, shore," Noah declared. "Come again sometime."

"You mean that's *all?*" the preacher asked. "That's all there is to it? I kin git to go to heaven, now?"

Noah was a little annoyed by this feller's silliness, but he wanted to make light of it. "Shitfire," he remarked, "you kin git to go to hell, fer all I care."

The preacher fainted. When he came to, he was no longer in

God's treehouse, but flat out on a sandbar by a riverbank surrounded by a vast mob of howling fiends who were pointing their fingers at him and cackling fit to bust. He fainted again at the sight of these denizens of hell, and when he revived the second time there were not so many of them and they were not cackling but just chuckling, and a woman among them who felt sorry for him took the trouble to explain the trick that had been played upon him.

He grew exceedingly angry, as well as mortified. Strangely enough, the brunt of his anger became focused upon Noah, as if Noah had been responsible for the trick, and the preacher became determined to "git even, someway." He began to preach against men living in trees. His gatherings were small, because most people were still laughing at him too much to be able to sit and listen to him seriously. But to whatever gathering he could assemble, in the name of God, in brush arbors constructed in Stay More, Parthenon and Jasper, he ranted against the unnaturalness of men living in trees.

By purest coincidence only, this was just two years after Darwin had published the findings of his voyage on the H.M.S. Beagle, and we may be sure that the preacher had never heard of Darwin, and in any case the conflict between religion and the theory of evolution was still years in the future, but the preacher accused Noah Ingledew of being a monkey. "What other reason would a creature have fer livin up in a tree?" he would demand of his audiences, and quote Scripture to prove that man was meant to walk on the ground and dwell on the ground, and a man living up in a tree was bound to bring the wrath of God upon all the people.

Little by little, the preacher converted a few of the people to his position against Noah, but he could persuade none of them to join him in his plan, which was to take an axe and chop down the sycamore, so in the end he had to go it all alone. But as soon as he began swinging the axe against the tree, in the light of the moon one night, Noah stepped to the edge of his dogtrot (or rather birdtrot, because no dogs ever got up there) and urinated down upon the preacher's head. The preacher retreated, yelling, "I'll git ye, yet!" and he went away and preached to the people for several more days and nights, without succeeding in persuading any of them to help him chop down the tree. He went again with his axe late at night, when he was sure Noah would be asleep, but at the first THOCK of the axe Noah woke up, and squatted backwards at the edge of his bird-trot. Enraged, the preacher hurled his axe at Noah. The axe missed Noah, but imbedded itself in the side of the treehouse, where Noah allowed it to remain as an ornament, and where it may be minutely detected in our illustration. His brother Jacob, visiting the next day, noticed it and asked Noah about it and then declared, "Wal, that preacher has done went too far." So Jacob assembled the menfolk of Stay More and they took a split rail off a fence and carried it to the preacher and Jacob said, "Climb up. Or do you need a saddle?" and, to use the expression that would be employed whenever this ceremony was duplicated in the future, they "rode him out of town on a rail." He protested, "If it weren't fer the honor, I'd jist as soon walk." He was never seen again. Nor, for that matter, were any other preachers, saddlebag or otherwise, seen in Stay More for years thereafter.

Except for one instance, to be scrutinized in moderate detail later, Noah lived the life of a celibate bachelor. But he was not a recluse. Over the years people visited him in his treehouse, not just out of curiosity, and he was especially popular with his nephews and nieces; it was said that each of Jacob Ingledew's five children had "come of age" when he or she was old enough to climb unassisted up the ladder into Noah's treehouse. Little Benjamin made the first ascent at the age of four, Isaac bested him by going up at three-and-a-half, Rachel was nearly five before she got up, and neither Lum nor Lucinda could do much better than Benjamin. Noah cultivated a knack for making candy apples (he had his own orchard, established with the help of a passing "furriner" named John Chapman, better known as Johnny Appleseed), and these candy apples were the reward for the ascent to his treehouse of his nephews and nieces. But that was not the reason they climbed up to visit him; they climbed because they liked him.

We do not know exactly why. We know so pitifully little about the true workings of Noah's mind and heart. The one clue we have, if such it be, was that Noah had a wide-eyed sense of wonder which was perhaps childlike or with which the children empathized.

Everything either fascinated him or (like Indians) terrified him. He felt constantly confronted with the unknown. Sometimes he would sit idly in his treehouse, just listening to the beating of his heart or to the slow wafting of air in and out of his nostrils, and these things, circulation, respiration, would captivate him with wonder. He never took anything for granted. The sun might so easily choose not to come up some morning, and Noah would not be surprised, he would be just as fascinated as he was with the fact that the sun came up and went down every day.

Noah understood nothing; he only witnessed it. The intricate growth and tasseling and pollination of a stalk of corn was endlessly absorbing to him, but he did not comprehend the sexuality of plants any better than he did the sexuality of animals. Like any rural person, he was exposed daily to the varied spectacle of one animal affixing itself to another animal for the purpose of perpetuating its species and experiencing pleasure into the bargain. Noah watched these spectacles entranced. We cannot know to what extent he felt excluded from Nature's grand saturnalia, nor are we going to learn how much or how little appetite he personally possessed, much less how, if ever, he gratified it, but we can discern this much: that Noah, knowing nothing and understanding less, knew at least the fundamental difference between man and the other animals in regard to the ritual of mating: that for all animals it required merely a casual exchange of glances or of scents, or perhaps a little posturing, preening and circling, whereas for man it is a protracted business of gallantry, courting and coaxing and caressing, proposing and promoting and preparing, that costs literally millions of words, of which animals are not capable. Nor was Noah.

Why, then, was his treehouse bigeminal? Merely in emulation of his brother's dogtrot? If, as we have conclusively demonstrated, bigeminality is symbolic of the division of the sexes, was the second half of Noah's house merely wishful thinking or subconscious yearning? A symbol of his absent "better half"? Perhaps. It could well be that he never gave up hope that some girl would again bring him a piece of cornbread which he could accept without clumsiness. But if any visitor to his treehouse remarked upon its bigeminality, Noah would simply point out that one half was where he slept and the other half was where he cooked and ate and sat, not necessarily in that order. It is only purest coincidence, of no significance whatever, that Noah's first two years in his tree-house were the same two years that Thoreau lived at Walden, but like Thoreau, Noah had one chair for solitude, two for friendship, and three for society—although that society usually consisted only of his nephews and nieces.

In our pitiful ignorance of the man, we do not even know how he managed to entertain them, apart from presenting them with candy apples. Did he tell them stories, or did they just sit and munch their apples in silence? Little Benjamin, at least, must have been silent, for it is told about him that he was eight years old before uttering his first words, which were, "Watch it, Paw!" at the moment the latter was about to be charged from behind by a bull while in the pasture, whereupon Jacob, after jumping out of the bull's path, exclaimed to Benjamin, "How come you never said nary a word afore now?" to which Benjamin replied, "I never had nothin 'portant to say."

If this legend is true (and I have no reason to doubt it), then Benjamin must have sat silently munching his candy apple while Noah talked, but what did Noah say? He does not seem the storytelling type, even less the joke-cracking type. Did he verbalize his wonder at the mystery of the pollination of corn, or of the sun's diurnal appearance? Quite possibly he did not talk at all, but it is disquieting to visualize the two of them sitting there silently, eerie in that aerie, for over four years, until Noah remarked, "Yore pap tells me ye kin talk right easy," and Benjamin allowed, "Yep," and Noah shook his head in commiseration and said, "A durn shame." Thereafter, Benjamin felt obliged to say something, so he began, from the age of nine onwards, to ask Noah questions. It never mattered that Noah was unable to answer a single one of Benjamin's questions, or at least to answer one accurately; Benjamin went on asking them, and Noah went on trying and failing to answer them. There were things Benjamin could not discuss with his parents. We know that he slept, until his twelfth year, in a "truckle," or trundle bed, at the foot of his parents' own bed, and that in that proximity he was suffered to eavesdrop upon their occasional (infrequent; once a month, on the average, usually the night of the Second Tuesday of the Month) exchanges of words that meant nothing to him. (Could it be that he had never talked because he associated words with nothingness, or, worse, dark unfathomable deeds connected with the words his father and mother spoke to each other in their bed at night?)

"How's that?" Benjamin would hear one of them say to the other in the dark in their bed.

"Wal, I reckon," he would hear the other reply. He could not tell their voices apart; his mother's voice at such times was low and husky. Benjamin could not tell if these were his father or his mother:

"Yore nose is cold."

"There."

"Move down."

"Yore knee is in my monkey."

"Seems lak we caint git it through."

"Here I go."

"Don't do that."

"Why not?"

"I said."

"Now."

"Where?"

"Holy hop-toads!"

"Done?"

"Um."

His parents never talked like this during the daytime, and it puzzled Benjamin to the extent that, when he was nine years old and began to ask Noah questions, he would repeat what his parents had said in bed to Noah and ask Noah what it meant. Even assuming Noah actually knew the meaning of the various utterances, doubtless he would not have been able to discuss it with a mere lad of nine. So his "answers" were inaccurate. He would, for example, interpret "Seems lak we caint git it through" as meaning that Sarah was trying to help Jacob put his pants on and couldn't get one leg into them. "Monkey," he would define, is the base of the spine, where a monkey's tail would go, so "Yore knee is in my monkey"…Benjamin seemed satisfied with these explanations, but by the time he was twelve years old and pubescent himself, and had witnessed sufficient numbers of animals wild and domestic pairing themselves together with a strange mixture both of apparent pain and intense pleasure, it dawned on him that the voices he heard in the night once a month on the average had some connection with this business of one animal having a hole which another animal would wish to probe with his dood, and although Benjamin would not have wished to suspect that his very own dear mother ever did that sort of thing with his father, at length he persuaded himself that it was inevitable, so that the time came when in the night he heard one of his parents saying to the other:

"Seems as 'ough we caint fasten our thangs together no more."

Benjamin was moved to suggest, audibly, "Try a rope."

Whereupon his father trundled the trundle bed out of the door, across the breezeway into the other wing, where Benjamin slept thereafter until he was fifteen, when he left home.

Noah has been accused, unjustly I think, of being partly responsible for Benjamin's leaving home. Benjamin, like any resident of Stay More, male or female, had been obliged, from the age of seven onward, to work as hard as he possibly could, starting at sunrise and keeping on until sunset, the year around, Sundays not excepted. Since Benjamin was Jacob's oldest son, and since at the age of fifteen he was full-grown, he was obliged to do a man's work somewhat prematurely, with the predictable result that he came down with the frakes, which kept him in bed for most of his fifteenth year, and left him with, not so much a sense of futility or the vainness of labor, but rather with a conviction that if a man (or boy) had to work, there ought to be some kind of work somewhere that wasn't so goshdarned *hard*. But when he asked his father about this, when he asked his father if there weren't places in the world somewhere where people didn't have to toil from sunup to sundown, his father merely gave him a lecture on how Stay More was the center of the universe, as it were, and of the necessity for a man (or boy) to do the most labor of which he was capable, to "do his damnedest," as Jacob put it. So Benjamin went to Noah. "Uncle Noah," he inquired, "I been wonderin: aint there anyplace out yonder in the world where a body'd not have to slave the livelong day jist to do what was 'spected of him?"

Noah could not tell him of cities, having never seen one himself, unless you count Memphis, which at the time Noah had briefly passed through it on his way to the Ozarks was scarcely more than a large town. Noah could tell him of certain shiftless persons who managed to eke out a subsistence with a modicum of effort, but Noah chose wisely not to tell him of these types. All Noah could tell him was what little he himself had heard rumored about a distant Promised Land way off in the west, which was called in the Spanish "Hot Oven," or Californy, where gold had recently been discovered, and where, it was said, a man could spend a few hours searching for gold and then take the rest of the week off. Benjamin asked Noah to explain what "gold" was, and why it was so valuable, and Noah did the best he could.

"How come you never wanted to go there?" Benjamin asked him. Noah explained that it was a long ways off and besides you had to pass through a lot of Indian country to get there and Noah would be just as happy if he never saw another Indian in his life. But Benjamin, having never seen an Indian and having none of his uncle's irrational fear of them, began to consider, increasingly and seriously, the idea of going to California to, if not make his fortune, avoid a life of hard labor. He kept his intention a secret from no one, but no one took him seriously. A person never left Stay More except to go to the county seat or to go to rest in the Stay More cemetery.

One summer Saturday afternoon, when all the Ingledews were enjoying one of their annual shopping or swapping trips into Jasper, Benjamin saw a little crowd assembled on a corner of the courthouse square, and, joining them, saw them clustered around a man whom we might refer to as Newton County's first and only itinerant "travel agent." This man, Charlie Fancher, was offering, for the rather lavish sum of $50, to "book passage" on a wagon train that was departing soon for Californy. He painted a more glowing picture of Californy than Uncle Noah had, extolling its excellent climate and its picturesque mountains and its view of the ocean. No one in Newton County had ever seen an ocean or could even imagine seeing that much water in one place. They listened in awe to the travel agent, but when he got around to mentioning the price, $50, they began, one by one, to drift away, until only Benjamin was left standing with the travel agent.

"Shitepoke town," the agent grumbled, not necessarily to Benjamin. "I shoulda knowed better than git lost way back up here in these hills." Then he noticed Benjamin and said, "Kid, you aint happenin to have fifty dollars layin around loose, have ye?"

"Nossir," Benjamin declared. "Fifteen, twenty, is the most I could ever hope to lay hands on. But I'd be right glad to work it off. I could drive a wagon and help tend the teams."

"Hmmm," the agent said, and sized him up. "You any good with a rifle?"

"I kin knock a squirrel off a tree limb from ten hats off."

"Hats?" the agent said.

Benjamin explained that unit of measure to the agent, who calculated it and then said, "Well, okay, kid. You're on. Let's go. Let's git out of this shitepoke town."

"Let me say goodbye to my folks," Benjamin requested.

"Cut it short," the agent said.

Benjamin's folks were scattered around the village. He had to hunt them up individually, and explain to each of them what he was going to do, and deafen himself to their protests and tears. His younger brother Isaac begged to go with him, but Benjamin told him he would send for him in a couple of years when Isaac was older. His little sisters Rachel and Lucinda grabbed his arms and said they wouldn't let him go, and he had to tear his shirt getting loose from them. His mother reminded him that his sixteenth birthday was coming up soon, and she had wanted to make it special for him. He said he was powerful sorry. His father Jacob said, "What if I was to say you caint go?" "You'd have to tie me up," Benjamin averred. Jacob drew back his fist as if to smite Benjamin, but Benjamin did not cower nor flinch. Jacob dropped his arm. "Paw," Benjamin protested, "I'll come home soon as I git rich." Jacob snorted and said, "There aint no place for a rich man in this country." But when Jacob saw that he could not dissuade Benjamin, he gave Benjamin his horse and then shook hands with him and wished him luck.

Noah was the last of his folks that Benjamin could find, and when Benjamin told him what he was doing, Noah moaned and faulted himself for having mentioned Californy to him in the first place. Benjamin pointed out that even if Noah hadn't mentioned it, he would still have heard about it from this man Charlie Fancher that he was going with. "Shitfire, let Fancher show hisself," Noah declared. "I'll shred him up with my bare hands." But Benjamin clapped his uncle on the shoulder and said, "Goodbye, Uncle Noey. And thanks fer all them candy apples," and then he mounted the horse his father had given him and went to rejoin Charlie Fancher. They rode north to the town of Harrison, and from there west to the town of Berryville, where the wagon train was assembled, and the people that Fancher had "recruited" from all over the Ozarks, over 140 of them, got into the wagons. Charlie Fancher started the wagon train moving west, Benjamin driving one of the lead wagons with eight people in it, westward out of Arkansas and across the national boundary line into Indian territory, where occasionally they saw parties or even camps of Indians, but had no conflicts with any of them, until, weeks later, in a valley called Mountain Meadows, in a place called Utah, they were suddenly surrounded by a large band of mounted Indians in war paint who began shooting at them, not with bows and arrows but with rifles.

Charlie Fancher ordered the wagons to form into a circle and everybody got behind the wagons and Benjamin and all the other men who could handle a rifle returned the fire of the Indians, killing many of them, and keeping them at bay for hours into the night, then all of the following day, and the one after that, three days in all, until a white flag appeared among the enemy, a flag of truce under which approached a group of men. These were not Indians but white men, whose leader introduced himself as John D. Lee and told Charlie Fancher that his wagon train must turn back and that he and his fellow white men would protect their retreat from the Indians as far back as Cedar City. But the man insisted that Fancher and all his party must go on foot and unarmed in order to allay the suspicions of the Indians, a condition which Fancher was reluctant to accept, yet a condition which had no alternative except to stay and fight, which few of the Fancher party wanted to do, among those few Benjamin, who smelled something suspicious in the whole business, but had no liberty to disobey his leader, Fancher. At length Fancher ordered his party to yield to the retreat order, to leave their wagons and weapons and begin the march toward Cedar City. They never reached it, because as soon as they were out of sight of their wagons the Indians came again, along with those treacherous white men, and slaughtered every last single one of them, sparing only the youngest children.

Benjamin, as he felt the searing bullet tearing life out of his breast, was sorry that he had ever left home.

There was no survivor to return the news to Arkansas, but sometime later Eli Willard from Connecticut, hawking musical instruments this time, happened to bring with him a copy of a New York newspaper, to leave with Lizzie Swain and her family, who had such a hankering for occasional news from the outside world, although they could not read, and nobody could read except Jacob, who didn't mind reading to Lizzie and her brood the newspaper Eli Willard had dropped off (and his business was pretty good this time around; to the populace of Stay More he sold three banjos, a piano, a parlor organ, and other instruments, including a fiddle that Jacob bought for his son Isaac, and a Jew's harp that Noah bought for himself). Lizzie and her children assembled in Jacob's dogtrot and he began reading them the newspaper. He hadn't read very far, however, before he came to a big headline, "MOUNTAIN MEADOWS MASSACRE" with a sub-headline "140 Arkansans Slain in Utah Valley" and a sub-headline "Suspect Mormon Plot." Jacob's voice quavered as he read the text of the item, and his voice broke when he came to the name of Charles Fancher, because that was the name of the man Benjamin had told him he was going with. Jacob stopped altogether when he came to the words, "...not one single survivor, except a few children under the age of seven who have been discovered to be in the custody of the Mormons in Salt Lake City." He read the rest of the item silently to himself, as Lizzie and her children stared at him. It had been charged that Mormons had incited and directed the attack, to keep the Fancher party out of Utah, although the wagon train was merely passing through Utah on its way to California. The investigation was continuing (but it would not be, we know, until exactly ten years later that John D. Lee, a fanatical Mormon settler, would be tried, found guilty, excommunicated by his Church, and put to death on the site of the massacre).

"What's a Mormon?" Jacob said to Lizzie.

But Lizzie could only shake her head, and ask, "Is the news pretty bad?"

Jacob declared, "My boy Benjamin is dead."

Everyone in Stay More assembled in the yard of Jacob's dogtrot to offer their condolences to Jacob and Sarah, and to discuss the news of the atrocity. Jacob asked them if any of them knew what a Mormon was, but none of them had ever heard of such a creature. Jacob addressed the gathering briefly, in conclusion, expressing his sorrow at the loss of his eldest son, and more particularly his sorrow that his son had been misguided and deluded into leaving home. Jacob's voice rose. "But jist let me say this. Fer all of you folks, and fer all of yore generations after ye, from this day forward, ferevermore, I, Jacob Ingledew, do hereby solemnly place a curse upon any person who leaves Stay More to go west. Amen."

So it was that Isaac took his brother's place as the oldest son, just as earlier he had taken his brother's place sleeping at the foot of the parents' bed, where he remained until manhood, wisely keeping his mouth shut when he heard his father or mother saying unfathomable words in the dark once a month. Isaac Ingledew was never much given to talk anyway, and it is said of him that he earned his nickname, "Coon," because, like a raccoon, he never opened his mouth except to eat or to cuss.

To appreciate his nickname, we would have to have heard a raccoon cussing, and many of us have not. Isaac, as we shall see (or hear), was the greatest cusser of all the Ingledews. Unlike Benjamin, who allegedly never spoke until he was eight, Isaac said his first word at eleven months, the word being "shitfire," which he must have learned from one of his relatives, but by the age of six he had broadened his stock of oaths to include all that were known (and some unknown) in Stay More. When his father bought for him a fiddle from Eli Willard, he quickly learned how to play it, and became eventually a champion fiddler who was capable, on occasion, of making the fiddle cuss. We are going to see and hear a lot of Isaac "Coon" Ingledew, for it was he who fought beside his father in the War.

The War. The first anybody (other than Jacob Ingledew, who kept it to himself) heard of war, heard that the whole nation had split itself right in two and was fighting itself, was when coffee, tea, pepper and such, which were always imported, became at first short in supply, and then impossible to obtain, at which point Eli Willard, who had been supplying these items, confessed that he could no longer obtain them. Then he held aloft the particular item that he was selling this year: a Sharps rifle.

"Stop!" Jacob Ingledew exclaimed. "Turn yore wagon and git the hell back whar ye came from!"

The people stared at Jacob, wondering why he was being suddenly hostile to his old friend from Connecticut.

"But you're going to need these," Eli Willard protested, still holding the Sharps rifle aloft. "No man should be without one. As a weapon it is vastly superior to your old breechloaders and flintlocks."

"Fer shootin folks, you mean," Jacob said. "Git back down the road, I say."

But the other men of Stay More were curious to examine the new hardware (Eli Willard was also carrying a line of side-arms), and they protested to Jacob, as respectfully as they could, stopping short of telling him outright to shut up, but making it clear that they couldn't understand why they shouldn't buy a new shootin iron if they felt like it.

"Yeah," Noah chimed in, "shitfire, let me see thet thang," and he took the Sharps rifle from Eli Willard and began examining it appreciatively.

Jacob sighed. It was a small sigh, as sighs go, but we should try to understand it: two years previously, the people of Newton County had been asked to send a delegate to a special state convention at the state capital, Little Rock. The delegate, they were told, need not be a politician, lawyer or county official; there were only two qualifications: one, that he be wise, and two, that he be typical. The people thought of all the wise men of Newton County, but none of them were typical. Then they thought of all the typical men of Newton County, but the only wise one among those was Jacob Ingledew, so the people prevailed upon him to become their delegate. Jacob didn't want anything to do with any city, or even a big town. But the people pointed out that the convention was only supposed to last a few days. Jacob protested that he didn't have any idea of what he was supposed to do when he got there, and none of the people did either, but they told him that he was the only one of them who was *both* typical and wise.

Pride was not one of Jacob's sins, but he couldn't help feeling flattered when they told him that, so he accepted, and at the appointed time, mid-March, he saddled his horse, donned a fine nut-brown suit of clothes that Sarah had woven and sewn special for the occasion, and rode off down to Little Rock, a distance of some 150 miles. He reported for duty at the capitol, a large building made entirely out of white marble; it was the biggest building he'd ever seen. He was assigned a seat at a desk in a big room, the biggest room he'd ever been in, with dozens of other desks. The men sitting at the other desks looked well-fixed and most of them were smoking cigars. Jacob decided he would keep his mouth shut and his ears open and not let anybody put anything over on him. So when the well-fixedest-looking man of them all came into the room, and all the men stood up, Jacob stayed in his seat. Somebody announced, "His Excellency, Governor Rector!" and everybody but Jacob clapped their hands, and the well-fixedest-looking man stepped up on a platform in the front of the room and made a long speech. Jacob listened carefully.

The governor began by saying, "Gentlemen, it is assumed by most that this convention was called in response to the election, last month, of Jefferson Davis as provisional president of the Confederacy. President Lincoln, who received not one single Arkansas vote in the recent election, apparently likes to think of us as a safe Border State, along with Missouri. But, gentlemen, Arkansas is *south* of Missouri!" Jacob realized that, if nothing else, he was going to learn a few things about geography. The governor went on to say, "Many of you gentlemen are pioneers. *I* am a pioneer. Many of you gentlemen are also slaveowners. *I* am a slaveowner. The Confederacy is made up of pioneers and slaveowners. Shall we join them, or not? That is the issue of this convention!"

The governor's speech lasted for over an hour, and Jacob had to admit that the man was the fanciest speaker he'd ever listened to. Then several other less-fancy speakers took turns giving one-hour speeches. They didn't all sound the same. The ones that talked just like folks back up home were the ones who didn't want to join the Confederacy. The ones that wanted to join the Confederacy, like the governor, talked real slow and lazy-like. At first Jacob didn't have any idea what the Confederacy was, but gradually he got a picture of it, yet he still couldn't understand that the only reason they were confederated was because they didn't want to give up their slaves.

Jacob had seen slaves, back in Tennessee, where just about anybody with a lot of land that wasn't too hilly would have some niggers around the place. And there was even one family he knew of, up in Newton County not too far from Stay More, who kept a couple of niggers. Jacob had met them. He had never given a thought to having a slave himself, because, the way he saw it, a man shouldn't have more land than him and his sons could take care of. And he had never been able to understand why slaves all had to be dark-complected. He'd never heard of a light-complected slave. But apparently what he was supposed to do in this convention was listen to all these men talk about joining the Confederacy, and then vote on it. Hell, if some of those states wanted to confederate theirself, he didn't personally have any objection, but if Arkansas joined up with them, that would mean all of the people of Arkansas supported slavery. Jacob didn't actually support slavery, but on the other hand he didn't see anything wrong with it except that all the slaves were dark-complected, and it stands to reason that there ought to be equality and have just as many light-complected slaves.

Then too, there were a lot of things being said in those speeches that Jacob didn't understand at all. He didn't know who "John Brown" was. He didn't know what was meant by "emancipation" and "secession" and "state sovereignty" and "Fugitive Slave Law." Finally somebody said, "Today's session is adjourned. You gentlemen will please collect your remuneration at the door." Jacob didn't know what "remuneration" was either, but he got in line with the rest of the fellows, and when his turn came a man at the door gave him three dollars cash money, which was a pleasant surprise, and meant that he wouldn't have to sleep with his horse at the livery stable but could get a bed in a house somewhere. But outside the capitol, there was a fancy-dressed black man hollering, "This way, gemmens and sirs!" and pointing down the street at a big building with a sign on it that said Anthony House. All the other delegates were heading that way, so Jacob tagged along, and when he got there he found that they weren't even going to charge him anything for his room, and he got a big room all to himself, and they put out a fine big supper downstairs and afterward most of the delegates sat around smoking cigars, and somebody gave Jacob a handful of cigars, and they poured honest-to-God *pure* whiskey, and drank and swapped yarns and cussed Lincoln and stayed up nearly all night.

Jacob discovered that the Presiding Delegate, David Walker, was the son of the Judge Walker who had "pardoned" Jacob years before when he "stole" his heifer at Fayetteville. Jacob told this yarn to Walker, told it *on* himself, and they both had a good laugh over it. Then Jacob got chummy with a distinguished-looking old white-haired gent who was the delegate from Ashley County down in the southeast part of the state, and owned a twenty-room house and 340 slaves. Jacob confessed that he wasn't nothing but a ignorant hillbilly, and he got the old gent to tell him the meaning of "secession," "emancipation," "state sovereignty," "Fugitive Slave Law," and who "John Brown" was. The old gent was right proud to harangue Jacob's ear until nearly dawn, and Jacob went to bed thinking that the secessionists sure had a good case for their cause.

Back at the capitol the next day he listened to speeches all day long, and that night at the hotel he asked the old gent from Ashley

County to explain anything that he hadn't understood. This went on for three days, and on the third day the head delegate David Walker stood up and said, "Would the delegate from Newton County care to express his views?" Jacob wondered who the delegate from Newton County was, and after a minute of silence he noticed that several men were staring at him, and then he remembered who the delegate from Newton County was, and he coughed and bobbed his Adam's apple, and mumbled, "I reckon not." "Are we ready to vote, then?" asked the head delegate. "AYE!" they all hollered, and David Walker said, "Those in favor of secession, please stand." Thirty-five men stood up. "Those opposed?" Jacob found himself rising up from his chair, and his chum the old gent from Ashley County was glowering ferociously at him. But thirty-eight other men were also standing. And outside, on the banks of the river, thirty-nine Federal guns were fired in salute of those who had kept Arkansas in the Union. Jacob collected his last remuneration and went back home to Stay More. When any of the Stay Morons asked him, "What was that all about?" he would shake his head and say, "Durn if I know."

March passed, and then April, and when May came a messenger brought word to Jacob that the convention was reconvening at Little Rock. This time he told Sarah what the other men's suits had looked like, and she stayed up all night making him one that was fairly like theirs, and the next day he put it on and rode off to Little Rock again. There, Governor Rector gave another fancy one-hour speech, talking about the bombing of a fort called Sumter, and Lincoln's call for seventy-five thousand volunteers. "I have told him," Rector said, "that no troops from Arkansas will be furnished. His demand is only adding insult to injury. The people of this commonwealth are freemen, not slaves, and will defend to the last extremity our honor, lives, and property against Northern mendacity and usurpation!" The hall and the gallery up above were packed with spectators, almost all of them hollering "SECEDE!" every time the governor paused for breath. Jacob's former chum the old gent from Ashley County passed a note to him which said, "You have a nerve to show your head here. I doubt you will leave alive."

After the governor's speech, almost all the other speeches were strongly in favor of secession. The only one speaking against it was the head delegate, David Walker of Fayetteville, and his speech was apologetic and half-hearted. When he finished he said, "Well, are we ready to vote, or would the delegate from Newton County care to express his views this time?" Jacob coughed and bobbed his Adam's apple, and then discovered that he was standing up. He tried to sit back down, but couldn't. He stuffed his hands into his pockets, then took them out and stuffed them back in. Everybody was staring at him. Then he heard himself asking a question: "How many of you fellers has ever been to Newton County?" Only four or five of them raised their hands. "Wal, you know Newton County is so fur off in the mountains we have to wipe the owl shit off the clock to tell what time it is." All of the delegates laughed, and Jacob heard some tittering up in the gallery; looking up, he noticed there were women there, and he got very red in the face and mumbled, "Sorry, ladies." Then he went on. "But the folks up yonder have picked me out to represent 'em at this here convention. I reckon they picked me on account of I feel the same way about most things that they do. And here is what I feel. If you fellers that owns slaves wants to secede, that's yore right and yore privilege, but I could count all the slaves of Newton County on one hand and still have maybe a couple of fingers still standin, and Newton County is stayin in the Union!" There was applause from a small few of the delegates and from somebody up in the gallery. Jacob tried to go on, but the words wouldn't come, so he sat down.

The governor stood up and said, "May I comment upon that? If Newton County stays in the Union after Arkansas secedes, there will be worse than owl droppings on your clocks!" The delegates laughed, and the governor said, "Let us vote!"

The vote was taken, and there were only four men besides Jacob who stood up to vote "No," and those four were also from the Ozarks. One of them, David Walker of Fayetteville, said, "If it is inevitable that Arkansas secede, let the wires carry the news to all the world that Arkansas stands as a unit! May we request that you gentlemen withdraw your votes, to make the result unanimous? I will withdraw mine. All right, we shall take the vote again. All in favor of secession, please stand." Everybody stood up... except Jacob. "All opposed?" Jacob stood, and stood there alone, in awkward silence, while delegates around him cursed him, and a woman up in the gallery flung a bouquet of flowers which fell at Jacob's feet, and he looked up and smiled at her, and she blew a kiss to him. The head delegate said to him, "For the last time, sir, will you not withdraw your vote, to make the result unanimous?" "I will not," Jacob said, still standing, and the head delegate said, "Very well. The final tabulation is sixty-nine in favor, one opposed. The convention is adjourned until tomorrow, at which time we will begin the drafting of a new Constitution. May I suggest that the delegate from Newton County might honorably resign his seat before then."

But Jacob did not resign his seat. When he left the capitol that afternoon, the woman who had thrown the bouquet of flowers at his feet was waiting for him. This woman, whose name we cannot know because she was a member of one of Little Rock's finest families, a family still prominent socially and politically today, took Jacob home with her to her very fine house, which had no slaves, and fed him supper, and gave him to drink, and took him to bed. In the morning she fed him breakfast and sent him off to the capitol, where he claimed his seat and his right to vote for Newton County, and participated in the day's session. He supported the convention in its work, and voted "No" only on those issues related to slavery and secession.

The convention remained in session until the close of the month, and each night Jacob went to the woman's house for supper and bed and pleasure. Once she told him that she thought the real reason for the War was not slavery itself but the ungratified sexual appetites of the men involved. It was always men who made war. Jacob felt no desire to fight anybody, but he went on voting "No" at the convention; he voted "No" against the raising of an "Arkansas Army," he voted "No" against a two-million-dollar "Arkansas War Loan," he voted "No" against the confiscation of all public lands and money in the state, and finally he voted "No" against a motion to hang Jacob Ingledew for treason and sedition. The motion narrowly passed, however, and might have been carried out if they could have found him, not knowing that he was staying at the house of the woman. That night he lay with her a final time, then took his trousers off the bedpost and announced that he had better get on out of town. She hated to let him go, but knew it was for the best. "My darling backwoodsman," she said in parting, kissing him and letting him ride off home to his backwoods, where he told nobody that Arkansas was out of the Union, nor that the Union was torn, nor that men were killing one another.

That was, as I say, two years before Eli Willard showed up again carrying a line of Sharps rifles and sidearms, and still nobody but Jacob knew that the country had been at war for two years, except for the scarcity of coffee, tea, black pepper and such, a shortage which, like all shortages, was difficult if not impossible to understand, and so no attempt was made to understand it, rather only to get around it, by using substitutes: parched okra seeds and chicory for coffee, ordinary sassafras for tea, and ground garden pepper for pepper.

Now Eli Willard was selling firearms right and left, in defiance of Jacob, who was fuming and on the verge of demolishing Eli Willard and his wagon. His own brother Noah had been the first to buy a Sharps rifle, and was already demonstrating how he could shoot the eye out of a squirrel from eight hats off.

Jacob couldn't stand it. Finally he demanded of Eli Willard, "Don't you know there's a War on?"

"All the more reason," Eli Willard retorted.

"War?" Noah said. "What war?"

"Yeah, what war?" the other men joined in.

Jacob wondered how to explain it, or even whether or not to try. What they didn't know wouldn't hurt them; that had been his policy for two years. But how much longer could he protect his people from the strife of the nation?

"Why don't *you* tell them?" he said to Eli Willard. "You're a Yankee."

"Are you a Rebel?" Eli Willard asked him.

"Hell no," Jacob declared, "but I aint exactly a Yankee either."

"Well, then," Eli Willard began, "you see, gentlemen, it's like this…"

That night Noah sat in his treehouse, fondling his new Sharps rifle and puzzling over what Eli Willard had said. From what we know of Noah, by now, we can assume that he was struck with wonder, no, that he was positively dumbfounded, at the idea of the whole country splitting in two, and of men killing each other. We would not be going too far to imagine that his gaze fell upon the opposite wing of his treehouse and his mind dwelt fleetingly on a different kind of bigeminality: of disjunction, separation, disunion.

Jacob too, in his dogtrot, was taking note of the bigeminality of his dwelling and thinking about how even countries can be divided. His trouble was that he was caught in the wrong wing of the House. And like Noah too, he was fondling a new Sharps rifle.

Chapter six

The prairie schooner, or conestoga wagon, which our example clearly is not, was the prototypical mobile home, although it was less a home than a vehicle to those who used it, and those were all heading west. Conestoga wagons may have been built in the Ozarks, but were not used there, save in passing. The Ozark's first true mobile home, in the modern sense of that term, *i.e.*, a vehicle more often immobile than mobile although capable of the latter, is illustrated to the left. We do not know who built it, nor whether it was actually built in the Ozarks proper, although that was where it traveled. The driver was an immature youth called Moon Satterfield. He was silent and humorless; we know very little about him, except that he did not like Stay More, and was eager to move on. The wagon was parked at Stay More for less than two weeks.

The occupant of the other of the two interior chambers of this mobile home (yes, it too was apparently bigeminal) was a barely post-adolescent damsel named Viridiana Boatright, called "Virdie." We know much more about her than about Moon Satterfield, but still we do not know exactly who her employers were. When she first arrived in Stay More, it was "norated" around town that a cat wagon had fetched up just outside the village, but two peculiarities were soon noted about this cat wagon: (1) there was only one cat in it, and (2) she wasn't charging anything. She dispensed her voluptuous favors to any and all willing and able Stay More men, and most of the hot-blooded boys of the town wanted in too, but she wasn't taking anyone under eighteen, although some of the bolder lads lied about their age to get in. The reason Virdie wasn't taking anyone under eighteen wasn't known, but presently it was rumored that she was recruiting, or trying to recruit, soldiers to the cause of the Confederate States of America. When Jacob Ingledew heard this rumor, he went to her at once, waited a minute until her current prospect came out of the wagon, then barged in on her. "Now lookee here, young lady..." he began, wagging his finger in her face, but she threw her soft arms around his neck and buried her full lips beneath his earlobe. He tried to separate himself from her, but she gyrated her hips against his, pressing and stroking and fluttering, and darting her tongue into his ear, which caused his legs to fail him, so that she quite easily pulled him down to her bed.

When she was finished with him, she asked, "Now weren't thet a heap o' fun?" Jacob had to allow that it was, that by his three standards of measure, Fanshaw's squaw, Sarah his wife, and the lady in Little Rock, Virdie Boatright was the best of them all. "Yeah, but I don't aim to jine up with the Rebels, and I don't want the menfolks of this here town to jine up neither, so you'd better jist get on back to wherever ye come from." Virdie laughed. She had a right pleasant and womanly laugh, Jacob had to allow.

"Who," she asked, "are you to be talkin so big?" "I'm the mayor of this here town," Jacob informed her, "and what I say gener'ly goes." "Air ye now?" Virdie exclaimed, her face lighting up right winsomely, Jacob had to allow. "The mayor! Wal, I declare! I never had me a mayor afore. In thet case, let's do it again!" and before Jacob could protest she spread him out on her bed and employed her full stock of novel therapies to revive and temper his root, whereupon she clambered atop him. He'd never had a woman on top of him before and at first he resented her usurpation of his rightful position, as if, by taking over from him, she symbolized her intention of taking over the town from him. But as she churned and squirmed, rising and falling gently and then less gently and then much less gently, Jacob reflected that this wasn't such a bad idea after all, that there was no earthly reason why a man and a woman shouldn't take turns, trade places ever now and again, and equalize the work, if, as in the case, the woman enjoyed it as much as the man. Virdie cried out, a long low groan, but she didn't stop, and Jacob realized that if she kept on going like that he might very well cry out himself. But just then a voice outside the wagon called "JAKE! AIR YE IN THAR?" and he knew it was Sarah. "ANSWER ME!" she requested, so he did. "Yeah, I'm in here, but I'll be right out." He was bucking beneath the weight of Virdie in an effort to finish. "WHAT'RE YE DOIN IN THAR, JAKE?" Sarah wanted to know. "I'm havin words—" he panted "—with this here Rebel foe." He was nearly there, although he realized that the wagon must be visibly shaking. Virdie suddenly stuffed her dress into her mouth, but it was not enough to keep another one of her long groans from coming out. "JAKE!" Sarah hollered. "YOU AINT A-HURTING HER, AIR YE?" "Jist a little," he answered, "to teach her a lesson." And then he got there, rapturously, reflecting, *Godalmighty, if I could git this reg'lar, maybe I'd jine the Rebels after all.* Virdie climbed off him, smiling, and while he was buttoning his pants she kept her arms around him and her lips on his face and neck. He moved away from her to the door, opened it, and turned back to say to her, so Sarah could hear: "And jist remember what I said: no menfolks of Stay More air fightin on the Rebel side!" He meant it too.

But soon he heard a rumor that most of the men in Limestone Valley, to the south of Stay More, which had been Virdie Boatright's previous "stand" (or "recline") before coming to Stay More, had joined the Confederate army, or at least were preparing to fight as guerrillas on the Southern side. When he heard this, he issued an order of assembly for all men of Stay More, who dutifully gathered at the appointed time in the yard of Jacob's dogtrot. Some of the men brought their wives and children, but he sent these away, declaring that the meeting was for men only. Then he addressed them, saying, "Nearly all you fellers bought new shootin arns from Eli Willard, and so did I. You heared what he said about all the rest o' the country splittin off to fight. Now there's that 'ere loose womarn come to town, Virdie Boatright, tryin to git you fellers to jine the Rebels. Most of you fellers have sampled what she's givin away free—" Here he was interrupted by a general clamor of hand-clapping, hip-slapping, lip-smacking, finger-snapping, whistling, and grunts of pleasure.

"Maybe you've heared," he went on, "that her perticular campaign, or whatever you'd call it, has converted Limestone Valley to the Rebels. That means we've got the enemy numberin up right over yon mountain—" He gestured to the south. "Unless—" and his eyes moved slowly from man to man "—unless some of you fellers don't consider the Rebels enemies no more." He paused, then demanded, "Wal? How many of you has she recruited?" To his astonishment, every man jack of them raised their hands, including, to his dismay and disbelief, his own brother Noah. "Noey?!" he exclaimed, turning to him. "Godalmighty, you wouldn't be funnin me, would ye? Don't give me that! Says who? Tell me another. Hooey! Can you tie that? Don't make me laugh! I wasn't born yestiddy. Git along with ye. My foot. What do you mean, anyhow? I won't buy that. Like hell you did. Where do you get that stuff? You're full of beans. Noey, fer cryin out loud, air ye shore ye heared my question right?"

"What does 'recruit' mean?" Noah asked.

"That means she has got ye to pledge or promise to jine the Rebel army."

"Aw, naw!" Noah protested. "She never done that to me."

"Me neither," chorused several of the others.

"Wal, then," Jacob asked, "how many of you has she made pledge or promise to jine the Rebel army?" Not a single man raised his hand. "Wal, what in thunderation did y'all *think* I meant by 'recruit'?" He addressed this question to the men at large, but his eyes were on Noah, and Noah only blushed and hemmed and hawed. Jacob turned to Gilbert Swain. "What did *you* think I meant?"

"Aw, heck," Gilbert said, "like you jist said, most of us fellers has sampled what she's givin away free. Boy howdy, she's done recruited me four times already!"

"But don't she say nothin 'bout the Rebel army?" Jacob wanted to know.

"Not a word to me," Gilbert claimed.

"Nor me neither," chorused the others.

"Hmm," uttered Jacob, shaking his head. "Wal, supposin she does. Any of you fellers want to fight fer the Rebels?"

They all shook their heads, declaring, "Not me!" and "Nor me neither!"

"Wal, then, the question is: do we want to remain neutral or do we want to fight for the Union if those boys down in Limestone Valley try to start somethin?" A lively and formal debate was organized, which lasted for the rest of the afternoon. At the end a vote was taken, and the majority favored neutrality. Jacob dismissed the gathering, but took Noah aside and said to him, "Noey, honest injun, no buts about it, shore-nuff, really-truly, straight-up-and-down, tell me the pint-blank truth: did thet thar Virdie Boatright actually git ye inter her wagon?"

"Naw," said Noah.

"I didn't think so. But you said she 'recruited' you…"

"I never got inter her wagon," Noah declared, "but she clumb up inter my house."

"Did she now?" Jacob said. "And then what?"

"Wal…" Noah hesitated. "She tole me her name, and I tole her mine."

"Is that so?" Jacob said. "And then what?"

"She ast me did I live all alone by myself up in thet tree."

"Do tell?" Jacob said. "And then what?"

"She ast me did I keer to git a little lovin."

"Golly moses," Jacob said. "And then what?"

"I tole her I never had none afore."

"Indeedy," Jacob said. "And then what?"

"Aw…" Noah protested. "*You* know."

"Naw, I caint imagine," Jacob declared. "Tell me."

So Noah told him, in some hesitant detail, which we may omit here, how Virdie Boatright succeeded in an undertaking which any woman other than she could never have accomplished. It was not easy, and it was not quick. But Noah's half-century of virginity was sacrificed, or, if that is not the word, expropriated, or, if that is not the word, it was dispossessed; in any case, for that one time in his life at least, he didn't have it anymore.

"What'd it feel like?" Jacob wanted to know.

"Shitfire," Noah said.

"Wal?" Jacob persisted. "What *did* it feel like?"

"That's it," Noah said. "Shitfire. It felt like shitfire."

"Oh," Jacob said.

In the days following, bits of war news trickled into Stay More: the Confederate Army of Arkansas had boldly invaded Missouri and defeated the Federal Army at Wilson's Creek, but had retreated back into Arkansas, where, in the hills and valleys of Pea Ridge in northwestern Arkansas, it met again a regrouped and larger Federal Army, and, after several days of fierce fighting, was beaten, although it was rumored that the Rebels still considered themselves in full control of Arkansas. A few men from Limestone Valley claimed to have been involved on the Rebel side at Pea Ridge. So far as Jacob could tell, none of the men of Stay More were showing any signs of joining the Rebels. Not then, anyway. But they were clearly restless, particularly the younger men. Jacob felt pretty restless himself, and wondered if he was too old to enlist in the army.

The men of Stay More, including Jacob, began to exhibit open signs of their restlessness: they could be seen kicking fence posts, dogs, and even occasionally a small child. They each developed a nervous tic of smashing one fist into the palm of the other hand. They swore more often than usual. Whittling was no longer therapeutic enough, although they denuded the forests with their whittling. Soon the younger men began fighting one another with their hands and teeth. Jacob's sense of community responsibility never deserted him, and he attempted to organize energetic games of Base Ball to channel the aggressive energy of the men, but, as referee of the games, he often found himself losing his temper and kicking somebody. If only, Jacob thought, if only he could *talk* to Sarah and get her to realize that if she would let him have her more often then he would be all right. Better yet, if he could persuade Sarah to talk to the womenfolk of Stay More and convince them to be more yielding to their husbands, then all of the men of Stay More would be all right. But Jacob had never been able to talk to Sarah about sex, and never would, until the last day of his life. He considered, briefly, talking instead to Lizzie Swain, who, now in her sixties, was virtually the matriarch of the village. Lizzie could easily call a meeting of all the womenfolk and perhaps persuade them to open their thighs more often for their husbands.

But Jacob realized that he could no more broach such a topic with Lizzie than he could have asked her, years earlier, to have her bull service his cow. So instead he organized a Public Works Project: all of the men were to take their sledgehammers and smash boulders into gravel, and pave the road from Stay More to Jasper with crushed gravel. This project kept them busy for a while, but when they had graveled the road as far as Jasper they discovered that Virdie Boatright's wagon was parked off the courthouse square. When they tried to get in, she wouldn't let them, not even Jacob. There were just too many men in Jasper, she told him. She couldn't "accommodate" any more.

The Stay Morons cursed and smacked their fists into their palms and went on back to Stay More, where they resumed kicking posts and dogs with a vengeance, and Jacob exercised his brains to think of something else for them to do, but then he got angry with himself for wasting so much of his good thought on those worthless clods, and, being angry with himself, he kicked a post so hard he broke his foot. The foot was slow to heal, and he couldn't walk at all, but it didn't matter anyway, because he, along with every last man who had worked so hard crushing rocks for the road to Jasper, suddenly came down with the frakes. The entire able-bodied male population of Stay More (numbering in that year approximately forty-six) came down with the frakes!

Most of them were of the opinion that it was a venereal disease contracted from Virdie Boatright, and in some parts of the Ozarks even today there are people who stubbornly persist in believing that the frakes is a venereal disease, but Noah Ingledew, who had had the frakes before while still a virgin, knew that it was not, and tried to assure his fellows that it was not, but most of them went on believing (or rather lay bedridden convinced) that Virdie Boatright was responsible. It was commonly, even if atrociously, believed in the Ozarks that the only cure for a venereal disease is to transmit it to a person of the opposite sex, and the men of Stay More yearned desperately for this cure, which could not be had for two reasons: (1) no female was willing to lie with a man infested with the frakes, and (2) no male infested with the frakes was potent while he had the frakes.

One would think—one would *like* to think—that the extreme lassitude and sense of utter futility which come as the aftermath of the frakes would have disencumbered these men of their aggressions, their restless incipient martiality. But it did not happen that way. True, all of the men did feel weak and futile, but they still felt restless and belligerent. A dangerous combination. Since they were all bedridden and could no longer kick posts and dogs (although they could still smash one fist into the palm of the other hand, and frequently did) they were reduced to such acts as tearing their bedcovers and gnashing the bedposts. Naturally the womenfolk were dismayed and, although the frakes had cleared up and the men were potent again, the women all refused to sleep with the men, which made the men rend their bedcovers all the harder and chomp the bedposts all the fiercer, and this vicious cycle continued until there was not one whole quilt or blanket in Stay More, nor one bedpost still standing.

The day came at last when the men could leave their beds and move about, whereupon, although they still felt weak and futile, they resumed kicking posts and dogs and an occasional child, and fighting one another with hands and teeth. The women sulked and held many quilting bees at which they complained everlastingly to one another of what monsters their husbands were, and took a collective vow to have no further relations with their husbands until the men stopped being so mean, which made the men all the meaner, and so on.

Word came from Jasper, where Virdie Boatright had gone after leaving Stay More, that the sheriff himself, John Cecil, one of the most popular and revered men in the county, had joined the Confederates and had been appointed captain in charge of Newton County. When Jacob Ingledew heard that, he felt more weak and futile than ever; he also felt more restless and belligerent than ever, and he caught his wife Sarah and raped her. It was the only time in his life that he ever raped her, and for a little while afterwards he felt contrite, and begged her forgiveness, which she withheld, taking her younger children and moving back to her mother's house, and telling her older son, Isaac, what his father had done to her. Isaac, who was a young man of twenty at this time and already well over six feet tall (and who, of course, along with all the other men of Stay More, had been infected with the frakes and was sharing their suffering and weakness and futility and restlessness and belligerence), put down the fiddle that he was sawing to pieces and sought out his father and said tersely, "Gon whup ye, Paw." Jacob snorted with derisive laughter, and rolled up his sleeves and prepared to demolish his son. Undoubtedly Isaac, who was several inches taller and many pounds heavier than his father, not to mention being thirty-odd years younger and quicker, would easily have won the contest, might possibly even have killed his father, if they had not been interrupted by Gilbert Swain, bringing news from Jasper that one of the Stay Morons had joined Capt. John Cecil's Rebels.

"NO!" Jacob thundered. "It caint be. Who was the dawg?"

"I hate to tell ye," Gilbert demurred.

Jacob grabbed Gilbert Swain by his collar and hauled his face close to his own, and angrily hissed, "You're jist a-funnin me, boy, and it aint so funny."

"H-h-honest to God," Gilbert protested. "I seen him myself."

Jacob tightened his grip and twisted it, then hollered into Gilbert's face, "THEN TELL ME WHO IT WAS!"

"Don't hole it agin me, Uncle Jake, please," Gilbert begged. "It weren't my fault."

"Son," Jacob said as calmly as he could, "if you don't tell me who it was, right now, I am fixin to bash yore haid down yore throat."

"Let go of me, and I will," Gilbert said.

Jacob released him. Gilbert stepped back, half-turning as if to flee, and nearly whispered. "It was Noey."

"Huh?" Jacob said. "Noey *who?*"

"Uncle Noey," Gilbert said. "Yore brother. Noah Ingledew."

We will leave Jacob standing there overwhelmed in silent immobility for a very long moment while we meditate upon this situation. It should be remembered that Noah Ingledew was a bachelor, a frustrated virgin until Virdie Boatright came briefly into his life and his treehouse. It should be considered that her strategy or therapy or *primum mobile* or whatever we may call it, if it worked at all, would most likely work upon a man like Noah. We do not know how many hours he spent in his lonely treehouse reminiscing about the fleeting fulfillment that Virdie Boatright had given him, nor what intensified longings he was left with. We do know that he kicked as many posts and dogs as any other man in Stay More, and that he crushed more rock than most, and that his bout with the frakes was severe and compounded by having no woman to attend his bedfastness. Therefore it is reasonable to conclude that while his weakness and futility were greater than any other man's, so were his restlessness and belligerence. Admittedly it is difficult to think of mild, shy, bland Noah Ingledew as belligerent; even more difficult is it to picture him in uniform; even more difficult, well-nigh impossible, to imagine him in uniform shooting at his fellowmen. But war itself, I think, is more difficult to understand.

Jacob went at once to Noah's treehouse and called up to it, "Oh, Brother dear. Come out." But there was no answer, so he climbed up into the treehouse, and found both wings empty. He returned to his own house and saddled his horse and rode at a fast gallop into Jasper, where he inquired at the courthouse for John Cecil, but was told that Cecil was no longer sheriff since becoming captain of the county Confederates. He asked where Cecil could be found, and was told that the Rebels had no fixed headquarters but were roaming freely over the county, and, indeed, all over the Ozarks. Jacob asked where the Union headquarters were, and was told that the nearest fixed Federal headquarters were up in Springfield, Missouri.

Instead of returning to Stay More, Jacob rode his horse northward toward Springfield. The journey took him only two days, he was that impatient. In Springfield he found the Union headquarters and told the recruiting sergeant that he wanted to enlist forty-five men in the Union Army. The recruiting sergeant was experienced only with individuals, not with masses of men, so the sergeant passed him on up to a lieutenant, who sent him to a captain, who directed him to a major, who introduced him to a colonel, who delivered him to Gen. James A. Melton, commander of the Union Army at Springfield.

Gen. Melton was a meticulous diarist, whose writings survive. Here is an excerpt from the entry in his journal for that day:

> I had the honor to receive to-day one Jacob Engledieu, who hails from the excessively bucolic wilds of Newton County down in Arkansas. Although Arkansas is one of the Confederated States, Newton County, I have it on the good report of my brother, Major John Melton, has thus far resisted being swallowed into the Confederacy, although there are scattered bands of Rebels operating there, and a somewhat crude and brazen recruitment effort conducted by a hired wanton named Verdy Boughtrite. Thus I welcomed the appearance of Mr. (now Capt.) Engledieu, all the more so because I had already known of his notoriety as the only delegate to the Arkansas Secession Convention who steadfastly refused to vote with the majority (although in the beginning of our interview, I refrained from telling Capt. Engledieu that I already knew he was a Union hero).
>
> Capt. Engledieu is tall, lean but sinewy, and has eyes so blue that they seem always watering. He is a man of the soil and of the woods, and makes no pretensions to gentility or sophistication, in speech, manner or appearance. But I am persuaded he is keen of wit, a natural leader of men, and like all of his fellow Ozarkers most probably a deadly marksman. Every one of those boys can hit a squirrel in the eye at eighty yards. His first question to me was whether or not a man of his years (58) was too old to volunteer for the army. I asked if he had previous military experience, to which he replied in the negative. I said I did not think a man of his years would be happy as a mere foot soldier. To which he replied that he had a mighty fine horse, and, drawing me to the window, gestured at the animal tethered outside; indeed, a fine horse, but I said I did doubt as well whether he would be happy as a mere cavalry private. It was at this point he informed me that, if I

would accept him, he would donate 45 additional men from his settlement of Staymore in the abovementioned County, each of whom also had a horse or riding animal (albeit not as mighty fine as his own, he intimated). In that case, I said, I could appoint him lieutenant in charge of a cavalry platoon. He let me know by his grin that this pleased him, and then he said he also intended to recruit as many men as possible from the communities of Parthenon, Jasper and elswhere in the County. In that case, I replied, I could appoint him captain in charge of a cavalry troop, which I did, on the spot, and then, because he was totally without any knowledge of military structure, I explained to him that a platoon is divided into four squads, and four platoons plus Headquarters section make up a troop or company, and so many companies make a battalion and so many battalions a regiment, and so forth. I also instructed him briefly on the conduct of war, and I believe he was a good listener.

Concluding the interview, I told him to muster his men, drill them at length, then, if they passed an inspection, which my brother, Major Melton, would perform, I would commence regular orders for their detachment. Capt. Engledieu saluted me, but, his salute being somewhat irregular, I demonstrated the proper form until he had mastered it, and took his leave, supplied with a requisition to the quartermaster for three dozen black cavalry hats and cavalry sabers. I was left optimistic that he will be useful in dealing with Rebel forays in that quarter.

Upon his return to Stay More, Jacob found that the men were still kicking dogs and posts, and slamming their fists into their palms, and for the first time this pleased him. He went into his house and hollered, "Sarey! Make me a uniform!" But Sarah was not there, and he remembered why she was not there. He went to Lizzie Swain's cabin and asked to speak to Sarah, but Lizzie would not let him. A fine kettle of fish: him a captain in the United States Army cavalry, and no way to get a uniform. Well, there were forty or more other women in town who might make him a uniform. He ordered an assembly of all the men, distributed the cavalry hats and sabers among them, and offered a lieutenancy to the first man whose wife would make a uniform for Jacob. The womenfolk of Stay More got busy, weaving wool and dyeing it blue with indigo, and cutting and sewing it into Federal uniforms. Sarah was quick to hear of this activity, and, not to be outdone, she sneaked back to her spinning wheel and loom and worked through the night by oil light for two nights and two days, and won the contest to be the first to provide Captain Ingledew with a uniform.

Try as he might, Jacob couldn't very well appoint himself lieutenant, since he was already captain, so in the end he gave the lieutenancy to his son Isaac, and appointed four sergeants and eight corporals, and then the forty-six of them donned their new uniforms and climbed on their horses or mules or whatever riding animals they had (one donkey, two oxen, a large ram, and a tame buck), and Jacob began to drill them.

They raised a lot of dust. Women and children covered their faces with wet handkerchiefs, and all the green leaves turned tan, and the porches and roofs had inch-deep coats of dust. A favorable wind came and lifted the dust into an enormous dust cloud that hovered high in the sky over Stay More, visible for miles and miles, and people came from all over Newton County to see what was causing the cloud of dust, and to marvel at Jacob Ingledew's cavalry parading, mounting, dismounting, shooting at targets while in full gallop, and generally raising dust. When a sizable audience had gathered, Jacob halted his men in formation, and, sitting atop his own horse at their front, made a speech, inviting all of the menfolk in the audience to join his cavalry and all the womenfolk to make uniforms for the men. The women seemed just as eager as the men, if not more so, and within a few days Jacob's cavalry had swollen to slightly over a hundred. The cloud of dust covered the whole county, and people from neighboring counties, Madison and Searcy and Boone, came to watch Jacob's cavalry, and some of these men joined too.

When Major Melton, the general's brother, arrived eventually to inspect Jacob's troops and assess their fitness for war, he discovered that the first thing he would have to do would be to promote Jacob

Ingledew from captain to major because of the size of his cavalry. Then Major Ingledew paraded his men for Major Melton. The latter's only serious criticism was of some of the irregular animals that were being ridden; he did not feel that there was any place in the United States Cavalry for oxen, donkeys, rams or bucks, and he offered a shipment of horses from Springfield to replace them. Otherwise he was greatly impressed with both the horsemanship and marksmanship of Jacob's men, and conveyed to him from General Melton his first orders: pursue and destroy Captain John Cecil and his Rebels.

This was what Jacob was waiting for, but as soon as Major Melton had gone, he addressed his men, saying, "Boys, now listen to me good. I don't want there to be no killin. You know what I mean? Okay, let's go!" and he led his men out in search of John Cecil's Rebels. For three months Jacob's cavalry scoured the wilderness of Newton County, hunting and finding Rebels. Such was their marksmanship that they could fire at a Rebel and knock his weapon from his hands, or chip a boulder near his head to nick him with, or break a tree branch to fall upon him, or splatter mud in his face, or shoot his horse out from under him, or in various other ways annoy, harrass and slightly injure him. Of course the Rebels were equally good marksmen themselves, and they too had no desire to kill but only to make noise and annoy, harrass and slightly injure the Federals.

For three months the opposing forces fought one another all over Newton County, and only one man was killed—when he foolishly tried to yank his opponent's weapon out of his hands, causing it accidentally to discharge. Most all of these men, Rebel and Federal, were cousins or in-laws or even, like Jacob and Noah, brothers. One of Jacob's sergeants, Sam Cecil, was the younger brother of the Rebel leader himself. Sam Cecil had no more interest in killing John Cecil than Jacob in killing Noah. But when General Melton in Springfield learned that three months of fighting had produced only one fatal casualty, he was sorely displeased, and he dispatched his brother Major Melton with a shipment of heavy artillery. Major Melton remained long enough with Jacob's men to instruct them in the deployment of cannon, and left Jacob with the general's stern command: shoot to kill.

It is difficult to fire a cannon without killing or grievously injuring the enemy, but Jacob's artillerymen practiced diligently and in time learned how to fire a cannon so that it would cause a tree limb to fall upon the enemy or splatter mud all over him, or at least make him wet his pants in fear. The best thing about cannon was the noise they made, and it was the noise of war, rather than killing, which the men enjoyed, and which relieved them of their need to kick posts or dogs or slam their fists into their palms. There were many men and boys who wanted to join Jacob's army but had no horse or suitable riding animal, so Jacob created a regiment of Infantry Volunteers and promoted his son Isaac to captain and placed him in charge of the infantry. With both cavalry and infantry, Jacob could engage the enemy in a pitched battle instead of mere raids and skirmishes, and the only Newton County battle that made the history books was the Battle of Whiteley's Mill, near Boxley in the western part of the county.

Capt. Cecil's spies learned of the planned attack in advance, and his Rebels were reinforced by other guerrilla bands from neighboring counties, so that the Confederate strength was nearly 250 men, the same number that Jacob commanded. Jacob's artillerymen rolled their cannon up onto a ridge overlooking the valley in which the Confederates formed their battle line, and, at a signal from Jacob, began firing their cannon in such a way as to splatter the enemy with mud and make him wet his pants in fear. Then Jacob charged the line with his cavalry from one side while Isaac brought up his infantry regiment from the other. For more than two hours the battle raged, tooth and nail. Jacob's artillerymen blasted every tree in the valley, and the battle would have gone on longer except that the valley became overcast with a dark veil of gunpowder and smoke that blotted out the sun, and the men were choking from the heavy odor of it. Jacob assessed the situation and the casualties: one of his men had his horse shot out from under him and broke his leg and was captured; one of Capt. Cecil's guerrillas had been accidentally wounded while attempting to remove his wet pants. Jacob ordered a retreat; his ammunition was used up. Throughout the battle he had searched everywhere for his brother Noah but had been unable to spot him, until, as he and his men were retreating, he saw Noah standing amidst a crowd of Rebels who were shouting their notorious "Rebel Yell," the bloodcurdling victory whoop that reminded Jacob somewhat of Fanshaw's dawn chant. Noah was hollering it as loudly as the others, and Jacob felt taunted and humiliated in his retreat.

As was expected of him, he filed a report of the battle and sent it to headquarters, and received from General Melton this reply:

> Major: you have the honor to report that the numbers of men now under your command qualifies you for promotion to colonel. But you ask me to believe that your regiments assaulted Rebel forces in a pitched battle of over *two hours* duration, all the while steadily employing the heavy field pieces recently shipped to you, *without one single battle death on either side*. Sir, that is not warfare. That is *fraternization with the enemy*! Fraternization with the enemy is a serious dereliction of duty, punishable by death. But I am loath to have you and your entire command hanged. Therefore I am demoting you to captain and placing my brother, Major Melton, in command of your regiments, with instructions to improve their abilities to spill blood, maim, and, I hope, deprive the enemy of life. You will answer to him, and, I hope, render him every assistance in dispersing and exterminating the Confederate forces in Newton County.

The bearer of this letter was Major Melton himself, who said to Jacob, "Just out of curiosity, could you tell me how five hundred men could mobilize and fight for over two hours without a single one getting killed?"

"It weren't easy," Jacob admitted.

"Don't your men aim their weapons in the general direction of the enemy?" Major Melton wanted to know.

"Shore," Jacob replied, "we shoot *at* 'em."

"And the enemy, I assume, shoot *at* you. Might I ask how much ammunition was used at Whiteley's Mill?"

Jacob calculated. "Wal, we started out with a thousand rounds of cannon shot and ten thousand of rifle shot, and when it was all over we were near 'bout shotless. That's the main reason I had to retreat."

"And not a single one of those rounds hit anybody?"

"Wal, there was this one Reb who was tryin to take off his bepissed pants, and he tripped, and…"

"I heard about that," Major Melton interrupted, impatiently. "Sir, you make a joke of war."

"War is a purty sorry joke," Jacob opined.

"My fear is that you and your men, as well as the enemy, will eventually persuade yourselves that this conflict is all a lot of foolishness and simply call it off without consulting higher echelons."

"That is your fear," said Jacob, "and my hope."

"Would you prefer," Major Melton asked, "that your regiments be transferred to a theater of operations where the enemy are not cousins and brothers?"

"I'd a heap sight prefer that to this," Jacob declared.

"All right. I'll recommend it to Headquarters. But first," Major Melton held up his index finger, "we have a job to do."

Major Melton took over command of Jacob's cavalry and infantry regiments, and Jacob was demoted to the captaincy of Company A of the cavalry regiment; this company was composed mainly of the original Stay More men. Major Melton assembled all of the troops and made a long speech to them, explaining the necessity of killing, and pointing out that a refusal to kill amounted to fraternization with the enemy, a dereliction of duty punishable by death. The men listened sullenly and suspiciously, and when Major Melton was finished with them they reverted to their old habits of smashing their fists into their palms, and, because the movements of the armies had knocked down every post and there were no posts to kick, and all the dogs in the county had learned to hide at the sight of man, they kicked each other. Jacob wondered if Virdie Boatright would ever come back. Even if she did, she might not have anything to do with a soldier dressed in blue. Or mightn't she? Even if she might, she couldn't take on a whole regiment of them. Or couldn't she? Even if she could, the benefits would only be temporary. Or wouldn't they? Even if they weren't…but Jacob began to realize that what was done could not be undone. For a while he gave serious thought to secretly sending a messenger to Capt. Cecil warning him that Major Melton now intended to shoot to kill. But that would be treason. Or at least fraternization with the enemy. The best that Jacob could hope for would be that if Major Melton started killing he might be killed in return, and then for a while the Federals and Confederates of Newton County could go back to their old safe way of fighting. These thoughts were interrupted by the sight and sound of Major Melton riding up and down the lines brandishing his saber and yelling, "Forward, ho!"

For weeks they searched for Capt. Cecil without finding a single Rebel. Their rations were low, and Jacob didn't like Major Melton's idea of "expropriating" rations from the civilian population of the county. Even in peacetime these people had a hard enough task living from hand to mouth. Now they were being victimized not just by the Federal troops but also by roving bands of bushwhackers and jayhawkers.

The people always suffer the brunt of war, Jacob realized, and he yearned to slip away to Stay More to see if his own people were enduring their hardships. He suggested to Major Melton that Capt. Cecil's troops might have left the county to join Confederate engagements elsewhere. But Major Melton was determined to continue the search, until every holler of Newton County had been explored. Finally Major Melton asked Jacob, "Which of your men would know Cecil best?" and Jacob replied that would be Sergeant Sam Cecil, his own brother. Sam Cecil was called up, and Major Melton asked him if he had any idea where his brother might be hiding. Sam did, but was reluctant to say. Major Melton lost his temper and busted Sam to private, then assembled all the troops and gave them a long lecture on the superiority of patriotism over brotherhood, concluding rhetorically, "If your brother pointed his weapon at you and prepared to fire, would you not return his fire?" Afterward Sam Cecil came to Jacob and said he had decided to go ahead and tell the major where he thought his brother was hiding, but, he asked Jacob, would it be all right to send a secret messenger to John Cecil, warning him that

Major Melton now intended to shoot to kill? Jacob had to explain to Sam that that would be treason or at least fraternization with the enemy, and Jacob in clear conscience could not give Sam permission to do so. Even if he did warn his brother, Jacob pointed out, what good would it do? It would just mean that the Rebels would be waiting and ready to shoot to kill, themselves. Yeah, Sam admitted, if somebody's gonna git kilt, it mout as well be *them* 'stead of *us*. So he went to Major Melton and told him that his brother was probably hiding in Limestone Valley, that hotbed of Confederate sympathizers. Major Melton restored Sam to sergeant, and promoted him to chief scout for the expedition to invade Limestone Valley.

The attack was carefully planned, and kept secret from all but the higher officers, but still, when the Federals swept down into Limestone Valley at the crack of dawn, they discovered that John Cecil had been tipped off and was already in full flight with his band of some 180 men. Major Melton ordered a cavalry charge in pursuit and rode at the head of it himself, and was the first to overtake and kill one of the fleeing Rebels. At the far end of Limestone Valley, Capt. John Cecil halted his flight and tried to rally his men to form a line of defense, but when the Rebels saw that the Federals were shooting to kill, saw dozens of their comrades falling, they ran for their lives, scattering all over the mountain. Still Major Melton pursued them, killing many and capturing several. Jacob dutifully followed, but still could not bring himself to kill anyone, although, when he was forced to, he would shoot to wound rather than kill, and he wounded several.

The pursuing cavalry were as scattered as their quarry, and Jacob found himself separated from the others, alone in a holler of Big Piney Creek, where he was chasing a Rebel soldier. The soldier was on foot, and Jacob soon caught up with him. The soldier turned to face him and to fire at him, and Jacob discovered that it was Noah.

Before Noah could fire, Jacob yelled, "Hey, Noey! It's me, Jake!"

Noah did not lower his rifle. "Shit," he said, "fire."

Instinctively Jacob brought his rifle up and sighted, to protect himself, but he went on talking, "This is foolish, Noah. This is crazy."

"Shit," said Noah again, "fire," and squeezed the trigger.

In the same instant Jacob returned his fire. These brothers, like all the Ozark mountain men, were sharpshooters. Each had aimed precisely at the other's left eye, the sighting eye. Thus, their bullets met midway between them, collided and fused into a lump of lead, and dropped to the earth. They fired again, and again their bullets collided between them.

"SHIT!" Noah hollered. "FIRE!"

His voice startled Jacob's horse, and the horse's sudden movement spoiled his aim. Their third bullets, instead of colliding in midair, missed each other. Noah's bullet hit Jacob in the shoulder. Jacob's bullet hit Noah in the heart.

Major Melton granted a one-week furlough to Jacob so that he could return to Stay More for his brother's funeral. Noah was buried near Murray Swain in the cemetery on Swains Creek. His tombstone, which even today somebody always covers with flowers on the anniversary of his death, says simply "Corp. Noah L. Ingledew, c.s.a.," followed by his dates of birth and death, and the simple inscription, "Who was right." Undoubtedly, *unquestionably*, a question mark was intended to follow these words, but perhaps the stonecutter did not know how to cut one, with the resultant ambiguity suggesting that Noah might have been right. Or perhaps he was; I am just guessing.

The people of Stay More felt such great sorrow for Jacob Ingledew that they could not possibly conceive of a single adequate word of condolence that might be spoken to him; consequently no one spoke to Jacob, and he mistakenly interpreted this as a sign of their scorn or derision, which he felt he justly deserved. Not even his own wife Sarah could think of any words adequate to express her sorrow and her pity for him. All she could do, by way of solace, was to make herself freely available in bed, but Jacob did not think that copulation was appropriate in a time of bereavement, so he rejected her offering. He spent much of his time standing by Swains Creek beneath the sycamore tree in which Noah's treehouse was perched, staring up at it. Over and over again in his mind he relived the last moments of Noah's life, trying to figure out what was going through

Noah's mind. He realized that Noah must have seen many of his fellow soldiers killed by Major Melton's troops (altogether, in the skirmish of Limestone Valley, thirty Rebels were killed, forty-three were wounded, and eight taken prisoner) and that Noah suddenly knew that the game of war was no longer a game, that it was now: kill or be killed. But his own brother? Had Noah really believed that Jacob would kill him? But Jacob knew that he himself was thinking along similar lines during those tense moments.

In time he reached the point where he realized that thinking was useless, and took a vow to quit thinking. Then he seriously considered shooting himself, but realized that in order to do that he would have to think about it, and if he had taken a vow to quit thinking he couldn't do it. So he didn't. For the rest of his furlough he did not think a single thought, and thus when his furlough was over he did not know it. Major Melton had to come and get him. Major Melton was impressed that his speech on the superiority of patriotism over brotherhood had had such a dramatic effect in Jacob's case, and he had reported favorably to his own brother, General Melton, at Headquarters, who had sent an order restoring Jacob to major and transferring him and his cavalry regiments to the command of General Frederick Steele, who was in eastern Arkansas preparing to march upon Little Rock. Jacob still wasn't thinking, but one of his aides helped him put on his boots and saddle his horse and mount it, then the aide pointed the horse eastward and said "Giddyup" to it and kicked it, then summoned the rest of Jacob's cavalry to follow, and they began their long ride to Helena on the Mississippi River, where they were welcomed by the Federal garrison there.

General Steele himself welcomed Jacob, and was especially delighted to have in his command the person who was reputed to be not only the lone Arkansas delegate opposing secession at the state convention but also the lone soldier who had killed his own brother. All the newspapers were in the habit of referring to the War as a great clash of "brother against brother" but so far General Steele had never heard of any man who had actually killed his brother, so he was ineffably glad to meet Jacob and have him and his cavalry join the assault on Little Rock, and on the spot he promoted Jacob to colonel.

Jacob thought nothing of it, because he still wasn't thinking. But soon, when he had shot and killed his first Rebel in eastern Arkansas, he was forced to think: he thought that this man he had killed was a southern slaveowner of the type who had fomented the rebellion and deserved to die. Thinking, Jacob realized that there was nothing wrong in killing this type of person. In fact, this type of person was indirectly responsible for starting a war which had resulted in the death of his brother Noah. It would be revenge to kill them, and Jacob took his revenge, killing them wherever he found them.

By the time General Steele's army reached Little Rock, Jacob's marksmanship and anger had become a legend among the troops of both sides, and it is said that the real reason the Confederates gave up the city without any resistance was their fear of being mowed down like dogs by Jacob Ingledew. In any case, General Steele occupied the capital without the loss of a single man, and breveted Jacob brigadier general, and sent him out to harass the retreating Rebels south and west of the city. Those he did not annihilate were driven so far away they never came back. Jacob returned to Little Rock and went to the house of the lady whom we have seen before, the lady who must remain nameless because her family name is a revered one in Little Rock society today. He took off his boots and hung his trousers on the bedpost, and afterwards he and lady lay together talking for a long time, about war, and death, and duty, and, yes, love or whatever it might be called.

That was in September. The following January, delegates from twenty-three loyalist counties converged on Little Rock and voted to choose General Jacob Ingledew as provisional governor. The following March, the people of the state elected him governor, and he was inaugurated in April. Arkansas was the first of the seceded states to secede from the Secession.

Chapter seven

No, our illustration this time around is not the governor's mansion in Little Rock. That city, after all, is not in the Ozarks, missing by at least eight miles, so the dwelling that Jacob occupied there does not rightfully belong in a study of Ozark architecture. Our illustration is of the house that Jacob built in Stay More *after* he returned from his four-year term as governor; thus we will have to wait until the end of this chapter to learn why it is trigeminal rather than bigeminal, in fact one of the few trigeminal structures in the Ozarks, as well as the single most impressive building in Stay More. This was the third and last house that Jacob Ingledew built in Stay More, although being third is not the reason why it was trigeminal. We may guess or anticipate the real reason, but we would do better to wait until the end of the chapter.

Although this house was (and still is) the most impressive dwelling of Stay More, it is relatively modest by comparison with the house Jacob occupied in Little Rock, which we cannot illustrate here. Confederate Governor Flanagin abandoned it quickly in the face of the advance of General Steele's army, taking only a few personal possessions and mementos and some of his wife's best silver. So it was fully and rather opulently furnished when Jacob moved into it. As long as he was only provisional governor, he did not send for his wife Sarah and his children. He thought of writing them and telling them that he had been chosen provisional governor, but, remembering that no one in Stay More could read, he dispatched instead a messenger to carry the news orally. Not far outside of Little Rock this messenger was ambushed by bushwhackers and killed. The people of Stay More would have to wait for some time to learn of the high position attained by one of their own. Meanwhile the Little Rock lady (whom we cannot name) came clandestinely each night to the governor's mansion to keep Jacob's company in bed, and to share his burden as helmsman for the ship of state.

This burden, as long as he was only provisional governor, was not a heavy one. Most important matters, both military and civil, remained in the care of the military governor, General Steele, and Jacob did not seem to mind that all of the messages from President Lincoln during this period were addressed not to him but to Steele. The lady explained to Jacob what a "figurehead" is, as distinct from a "puppet," which he was not. He took more interest in supervising the drafting of a new state constitution. He made few speeches, and these were carefully corrected and rehearsed in advance with the help of his ladyfriend. He avoided coarse language, especially in the presence of women. A reporter from the New York *Tribune* interviewed him at that time and wrote a long piece which was both condescending toward his back-country appearance and deportment and warmly approving of his platform, expressed, as he was quoted, "to git this here state back into the Union and keep'er thar till hell freezes over."

For a long time, his ladyfriend made a timid, half-hearted attempt to refine his diction, and at least succeeded to the point where his speech no longer betrayed his true intelligence, but still there were many loyal Unionists in the state who were embarrassed by his image, and indeed, the reason that Jacob's name appears so sporadically in histories of Arkansas is that historians are still somewhat discomfited, if not embarrassed, by his image. There was not, however, any man willing to run against him in the election. The election offered only a pair of alternatives: ratification of a new constitution, or not; and

Jacob Ingledew for governor, or not. In the actual election, Jacob polled more votes than the constitution did, a circumstance that was not pleasing to President Lincoln, although Lincoln finally wrote directly to him to congratulate him, a brief letter that was always afterwards one of Jacob's few prized possessions: "Governor Engledew: I am much gratified that you got out so large a vote, so nearly all the right way, at the late election; and not less so that your state government, including the legislature, is organized and in good working order. Whatever I can I will do to protect you; meanwhile you must do your utmost to protect yourselves. A. Lincoln."

Lincoln's cautionary conclusion was warranted; many parts of Arkansas, especially the southwest, were still under Confederate control, and bands of bushwhackers roamed the whole state, right up to the gates of Little Rock; no citizen or soldier of that city dared to go more than a mile outside of it without heavy protection. When he was elected, Jacob sent another messenger to Stay More to ask his family to come to Little Rock in time for the inauguration, but this messenger too was ambushed and killed by bushwhackers before reaching his destination. The nervousness that Jacob exhibited during his inaugural address was not so much from speaking to a large crowd of people as from his anxiety about his family. Except for that nervousness, his address was forthright if not eloquent, solemn if not ponderous, and dignified if not majestic. The Arkansas *Gazette* commented: "For a man so little versed in the arts of the public forum, Gov. Ingledew acquitted himself handily. His personal views against the institution of slavery were made unassailable. He inspired confidence in a rich future for Arkansas." Jacob's ladyfriend, of course, had written the address, although the sentiments expressed in it were his own.

We may with good reason wonder: why, if Jacob achieved office by popular election, did nobody in Newton County know about it? Didn't they have the election in Newton County? Probably not, because the departure of Jacob's cavalry had brought Cecil's Rebels out of hiding, and Newton County was temporarily under Confederate control at the time of the election. But surely, we might ask, didn't a single one of Jacob's cavalrymen get furloughed or discharged after Little Rock fell to them, and return home to Newton County to spread the news of Jacob's success? Apparently not, for General Steele intended to keep as large a force as possible on duty in Little Rock. Still, we might reasonably argue, Newton County wasn't so isolated that no news of Jacob's governorship would somehow trickle into it. But obviously it must have been. Because it was nearly a month after Jacob's inauguration before Eli Willard brought the news. He had read about it in a Connecticut newspaper. Now, selling a line of elixirs, balms and unguents, which few people had the money to pay for, he came again to Stay More and was somewhat surprised to find Sarah Ingledew and her younger children still living, or trying to, at the old dogtrot.

"My congratulations, madam," he said to her. "Or should I offer my sympathies? Have you and your husband come to a parting of the ways?"

"Naw, he's jist off some'ers a-fightin that infernal War," she informed Eli Willard.

Eli Willard wondered if there might be some other Jacob Ingledew, but it was not a common name, and the newspaper item had clearly implied that the new governor was from an isolated settlement in the Ozarks.

"You aren't divor—" he started to ask her, but changed this to: "You are still married?"

"Why, shore," she replied.

Suddenly Eli Willard understood, and was moved. If Jacob Ingledew despite his humble origins had attained the governorship of the state, he would not want to display his ragtag family in the marble halls of the capitol, so he had deliberately refrained from sending for them.

"I feel for you," Eli Willard said to Sarah.

She drew back. "You'd jist better not, Eli Willard."

"I mean—" he said, "that I understand how you must feel, and I am touched."

He sure was talking as if he was touched, Sarah decided. How must she feel? she wondered.

"But looking at the more positive side of it," Eli Willard remarked, "I suppose it is more comfortable to abide in the tranquillity of these sylvan mountains than cope with the myriad concerns and distractions of the urban hurly-burly."

Sarah decided that he must be building up some new sales pitch, and she said, "Whatever yo're sellin this time, Mister Willard, I'm sorry to tell ye, but we'uns couldn't find a red cent around this place if it was ransom fer our life."

"You know your credit is always good with me," he reminded her. "But doesn't he even send you any of his salary?"

"Who?"

"The governor."

Sarah was convinced now that Eli Willard didn't have all his buttons. Probably it was the result of being out in the hot broiling sun all day long. The poor feller was sunstruck. She invited him into the shade of the breezeway while she fetched him a dipper of cold water. If that didn't help, she would have to make him a tea of jimsonweed leaves.

Eli Willard, while he drank the water, began to wonder if Jacob Ingledew had chosen not only to keep his family at home but also to withhold from them the news of his gubernatoriality. If that were true, then Jacob Ingledew was a heartless man, and Eli Willard had never thought of him as being heartless.

He asked her directly, "You don't know where your husband is?"

"Last I heared tell," she replied, "he was headin fer the Missippi River for to fight fer Gen'l Steele."

"Ah hah," Eli Willard was moved to murmur, marveling at the difficulty of communications in Arkansas. "Madam, I have the honor to be the first informant to report to you the wonderful news that your estimable husband has been elected to the governorship of the State of Arkansas."

Sarah went into her kitchen and began decocting an infusion of jimsonweed leaves. If that didn't help, she might have to try a purgative of slippery-elm bark.

The narcotic in jimsonweed is similar to that of belladonna, or deadly nightshade, but the dose in Eli Willard's drink was only enough to make him slightly intoxicated. After selling Sarah a few of his balms and unguents on credit, and failing further in his attempts to convince her that her husband was governor, he went on his way, visiting the other dwellings of Stay More, each in its turn, and the news was widely norated around the village that Eli Willard, whom everyone had always assumed to be a teetotaler, had turned up drunk, and in his drunkenness was telling everybody that Jacob Ingledew was governor of Arkansas. Sarah was boiling her slippery-elm bark as fast as she could, but still it would take several hours before it would be ready to use, and by that time Eli Willard's case of sunstroke might have reached final coma.

Captain Isaac Ingledew of the Federal Infantry, pausing in Stay More to rest from his constant pursuit of John Cecil, learned of Eli Willard's latest visit. He was a great admirer of Eli Willard, having spent his "growing-up" years looking forward to each reappearance of the peddler, who had usually given him a piece of candy. He knew that Eli Willard never drank. Now he did not want to believe that a nice man like Eli Willard was drunk and saying crazy things about his father, so he sought out Eli Willard himself. Being, as we have observed, the most taciturn of all the Ingledews (whence came his nickname "Coon") as well as the most profane, Isaac said to him simply, "Shit. Governor?"

"Yes indeed," Eli Willard replied. "And congratulations to you too, for being captain. No doubt your father will promote you to major, or even colonel."

"Where'd ye git that?" Isaac wanted to know.

"Which?"

"That Paw is governor."

"I read it in a newspaper," Eli Willard declared.

"Lak hell."

"I did, believe me. I considered that it might have been a mistake, but how many men in small Ozark villages would be named Jacob Ingledew?"

"Nary a goddamn one."

"Then your father is governor, no doubt about it, and again my congratulations to you. Now, may I interest you in this bottle of new, sure-fire, all-purpose..."

After much thought, Isaac decided that Eli Willard might conceivably be right, even if he were obviously drunk for the first time. Isaac *wanted* to believe him. Still, he did not protest when his mother and a group of Stay Morons grabbed Eli Willard and held him down and made him take a large dose of slippery-elm bark. This powerful purgative gave the poor peddler such a bad case of the canters (more severe than the trots but less severe than the gallops) that he was unable to leave Stay More for three days. Sarah gave him a bed, from which, however, he frequently had to canter. On the third day, after the canter had slowed to a trot, and the trot had slowed to a walk, Sarah said to him, "Now then, what did ye say the name of the governor is?"

"John Johnson," Eli Willard replied, and Sarah let him go on his way.

Isaac Ingledew realized that the only way to find out if his father were actually governor would be to go and find his father and make him deny it or admit it. Isaac—or any man—*should* have been reluctant to go off alone through bushwhacker country, but he wasn't afraid. He decided, however, to change from his uniform into civvies, and not to carry a rifle but only a pistol concealed under his belt. This showed his wisdom, for during the two weeks that it took him to walk to Little Rock (all of the riding animals had been taken by Jacob's cavalry), he was ambushed by bushwhackers on seventeen separate occasions.

Isaac, we may have noticed, was a big man, one might almost say a giant of a man, six feet seven inches in height, 230 pounds in weight, shoes size fourteen. Dressed as a farmer, he should have been able to talk his way out of several of the ambushes, but, being taciturn, he was unable to talk his way out of any of them. He fought his way bare-handed out of nine and was required to use his pistol in the remaining eight ambushes, in which he killed thirteen bushwhackers and wounded the same number. At the onset of each ambush, he uttered a single obscene expletive, employing a different one each time, making a total of seventeen distinct obscene expletives. He was somewhat fatigued by the time he reached Little Rock late one afternoon, but he began at once to search for the governor's mansion.

Being taciturn he didn't want to ask anyone for directions, but Little Rock was not a very large town in those days, and he knew that if he just kept looking he would find the governor's house. He *did*, too, somehow, but when he found it he realized that he would feel like a goddamn fool if it turned out that the occupant of the mansion was not his father. He couldn't very well just go up and holler the goddamn house and disappear if the man wasn't his father. Back home you didn't need to holler a house because everybody had dogs and the dogs hollered the house for you. But here in the city, the governor, whoever he was, didn't seem to have any goddamn dogs around the place, and Isaac would have to holler the house, and if the man wasn't his father he would be embarrassed as hell or maybe even put in the goddamn jail. No, he couldn't do it. He went away and wandered around through the town, thinking. He couldn't just stop somebody on the street and ask them who the governor was. If he could read, he could have bought any one of Little Rock's three daily newspapers and have found some mention of the governor in it, but he couldn't read.

After much thought, he decided that the best thing would be to wait until dark, and sneak around the governor's house peeking into windows, and if he saw that the man really was his father then he wouldn't be reluctant to holler the house. So he did that: he waited until it was full dark and went back to the governor's house, which had a lot of lights burning inside. But there was a soldier on the porch standing guard by the door. Isaac sneaked around to the back, but there was another soldier back there guarding the rear door. At least the two sides of the house weren't guarded, and the bushes were fairly thick at the sides. Crawling on his belly, Isaac wormed through the side yard and the bushes and up to the side of the house, where he raised his head up to the windowsill and peered into a room. There wasn't anybody in it. But Jesus jumping Christ, Isaac said to himself, what fancy furniture and stuff! He couldn't conceive of his father living in a place like that, and once again, for the thousandth time, he wondered if Eli Willard actually was a goddamn drunken liar. He crept along the side of the house and peered into another window, another room. Nobody in there either, just more fancy furniture.

Wait a minute. Yonder through the door comes a woman. She is dressed in silk to the floor. She is laughing and tossing her head. The governor's wife, you'd reckon. So Eli Willard is a drunken goddamn liar, after all. Wait a minute. Yonder through the door comes a man. He is dressed in a fancy suit with vest and tie, but that doesn't fool Isaac. Isaac would know that face anywhere. The governor is laughing too, and holding in each hand a fancy tulip-shaped glass with amber liquid in it. What does he need *two* of them for? No, he is handing one to the woman. Then he and the woman bang their glasses together, and each takes a drink, and the woman gives the governor a big kiss on his cheek, and they sit down real close together in one of those fancy settees, and the governor puts his arm…

Isaac felt a sting in his shoulder, and swatted at it. His swat touched cold steel and he turned to see that it was the bayonet of one of the soldier-guards.

"Just what do you think you're doing?" the guard demanded.

Even if Isaac hadn't been the most taciturn of all the Ingledews, he wouldn't have known what to say.

They took him off and locked him up. The other prisoners were Rebel soldiers from south Arkansas, and Isaac didn't like the way they talked or the things they said, but there wasn't much he could do about it because they outnumbered him by dozens. He could have avoided prison if he had tried to persuade the soldiers that he was the governor's son, but he didn't want to embarrass the governor, and already he was himself deeply embarrassed if not mortified to have discovered that his father had a sweetheart. So *that* was the reason nobody in Stay More had been told that he was the governor! Isaac decided just to keep his mouth shut, an easy decision for him since he rarely opened it except to eat and cuss, and when he got out of prison he would just go on back home to Stay More and keep his mouth shut there too and be nice to his mother and never tell her.

But he didn't get out of prison. Early the following morning he was taken before a military court and tried as a Confederate spy. He gave his name as "John Johnson." The guard who had captured him went on the stand to testify. Then Isaac went on the stand, and the prosecutor asked him what he was doing looking in the window of the governor's mansion. Isaac replied, "Nothing." The prosecutor with much sarcasm speculated about several facetious motives that John Johnson might have had, then declared what the true motive was: that John Johnson was spying upon the governor. "Do you deny it?" the prosecutor demanded. No, Isaac admitted. "Then what was the motive of your spying? Did you intend to assassinate the governor?" Here the prosecutor held up Exhibit A: Isaac's pistol. "Naw," Isaac said. The prosecutor tried for several hours, with one brief recess, to find out John Johnson's motive, and finally made a speech to the officers of the tribunal in which the motive was claimed to be assassination. The officers agreed, and sentenced Isaac to hang at dawn of the following day. Back in his cell, awaiting his end, Isaac tried to feel sorry for himself, but that was an emotion to which he was a stranger.

At dawn he was taken out to a public gallows, riding to it atop his own coffin, staring coolly at the spectators who were jeering him. The gallows was surrounded by troops; he couldn't run away if he wanted to. He was hustled up the steps to the gallows, and the noose was thrown like a lariat over his head, then tightened. The provost-marshal prepared a blindfold, but waited. He waited a long time, holding the blindfold.

Bored, Isaac demanded, "What're ye waitin fer?"

"The governor," the man replied. "He aint et his breakfast yet."

"Tie on the #@%*&#@* blindfold!" Isaac insisted.

"Not till the governor gets a look at your traitorous mug."

Another half-hour passed before a carriage finally arrived with the governor. The governor was ill-humored and complaining about having to leave his coffee and watch spies git hung. Then he looked up at the spy. The spy had his eyes closed. Scared shitless, no doubt, the governor reflected. But then the governor decided he didn't actually look scared, apart from the closed eyes. He was standing tall and proud, awaiting his dread fate manfully. A big and handsome man. Why did he have his eyes closed? "Tell him to pop open them peepers," the governor ordered an aide. This command was conveyed to the spy, who obeyed. His eyes were blue. Just like mine, the governor thought, and then he recognized the spy.

"*Isaac*??" he croaked.

"Howdy, Paw," Isaac returned mildly.

"*What in tarnation* air ye a-standin up there for, boy?"

"They're a-fixin for to hang me, Paw," Isaac said.

Jacob grabbed the nearest general by the collar and demanded, "What's the charge, buster?"

"Attempted assassination, sir," the general replied.

"Who was he 'temptin to 'assinate?" Jacob asked.

"You, sir," the general replied.

Jacob looked up at Isaac. "That true, son?"

"Aw, naw, Paw," Isaac said.

"He was caught peering into a window of your house, sir," the general said, "with a pistol in his possession. He was duly tried by a military tribunal, and convicted."

"That's terrible," Jacob declared. "My own boy. General, that there is my own flesh and blood. I've knowed him since the day he was born. He's a chip off the old block. Isaac Ingledew is my son, sir."

"That's terrible," the general agreed.

"I don't aim to jist stand here and watch him git hung," Jacob declared.

"I don't think you're required by law to watch, sir," the general offered, somewhat lamely.

"But don't the law give me the right to grant him a pardon?" Jacob asked.

"I believe it does, sir."

"Okay. Isaac boy, you are done hereby pardoned, per executive order. Come go home with me and eat you some victuals." Jacob led his son down from the scaffold and took him to the governor's mansion and fed him a large breakfast, during which he questioned Isaac about his motives for peering in the window with a pistol in his possession. Isaac was just as taciturn with his father as he was with anybody else, but he was able to nod or shake his head in response to simple yes-or-no questions, and in this manner Jacob was able to determine that his son had not meant to assassinate him, and also that his son had seen Jacob in the company of his ladyfriend, who, Jacob tried unconvincingly to persuade Isaac, was the secretary of state. Jacob learned that the messengers he had sent to Stay More had never arrived. Bushwhackers were thicker than flies, Isaac told him, not mentioning that he himself had been ambushed seventeen times. After breakfast, Jacob took Isaac over to a Main Street tailor and had him fitted out with a good suit, which was sewn on the spot and altered to fit Isaac's six-seven frame, then Jacob gave Isaac a tour of the state capitol building and showed him his own large and lavish office, where he gave Isaac a cigar, his first, and a drink of honest-to-God *pure* whiskey, likewise his first, and asked him if he wouldn't like to live here in Little Rock. Isaac shook his head, and Jacob understood. In that case, Jacob said, he would make Isaac a present of the Ingledew dogtrot in Stay More, and eighty acres of land. Isaac was choked with gratitude, and didn't know what to say even if he hadn't been unable to say anything anyway. Jacob told him that he was going to dispatch a cavalry platoon to escort Isaac back up to Stay More and escort Sarah and the other children back down to Little Rock. Then he questioned Isaac at some length about the progress of the fighting in Newton County, promoted him to colonel, shook hands, and sent him on his way.

Jacob worried about what "arrangement" to make with his ladyfriend once Sarah arrived in Little Rock. He and his ladyfriend had already discussed the inevitable. It had never been a secret to the ladyfriend that Jacob was married. The ladyfriend herself had been married at one time to one of the most prominent citizens of Little Rock. Jacob tried to understand his own feelings. Without using the word "love," which is a deeply embarrassing term to all Ozarks men, or simply denotes sex for its own sake, Jacob realized that Sarah still occupied the prime position in his affections, and indeed, since absence makes the heart grow fonder and he hadn't seen her for almost a year, he was very eager to have her with him again, and knew that when she came to Little Rock she would be "First Lady" in more than one respect.

Arriving back in Stay More, Isaac began the arduous task of persuading his mother that she was First Lady of Arkansas and that the First Gentleman of Arkansas desired to have her join him in Little Rock. Being taciturn, Isaac was not able to talk her into believing it.

She wanted to dose him with slippery-elm bark, but he told her that if she did, she would also have to dose the entire cavalry platoon that had escorted him from Little Rock and was waiting to escort her to Little Rock, and while she was at it she might as well dose their horses too, and then maybe the sight of all those horses with the trots and canters and gallops would convince her that she was the First Lady of Arkansas, but that would delay the trip to Little Rock. It was the longest speech he had ever made in his life, and it exhausted him, but it convinced his mother, whose first response, however, was, "But I don't have a blessit thing to wear." Isaac, who was wearing the new suit his father had had tailored for him, indicated it, and told her that his father would most likely "fix her up" too when she got there. So she put on her best black dress, and dressed the girls Rachel and Lucinda in the only dresses they had, and told Lum to put on his best britches and wash good behind the ears, but Lum wasn't going, he declared. He said he didn't care if his father was elected king of England, he didn't want nothing to do with no cities. Isaac told him that his father had given Isaac the house and eighty acres, and Lum could stay and keep the farm while Isaac rejoined his Federal infantry in pursuit of Cecil's Rebels. Sarah stuffed a few belongings into a gunnysack and she and her daughters waved goodbye to Isaac and Lum, and rode off with the cavalry platoon to Little Rock.

Sarah's dream, which she had dreamt years earlier on the occasion of their first night in the dogtrot, came exactly true. The dream had been about the perhaps excessively highfalutin reception that Jacob now hosted in her honor, after he had taken her and their daughters out to the town's best dressmaker and had them fitted out with hoops. Most of the younger girls of that day did not wear hoops, but Jacob was determined to have all three of his "gals," including Sarah, in hoops. Rachel was almost twenty, and looked quite ladylike in hers, but Lucinda was only fifteen, and looked uncomfortable, and felt uncomfortable, and was not able to move about in her hoops, nor sit, so during the reception she remained parked inside her hoops in one corner, where no one spoke to her, although I doubt that this experience was sufficiently traumatic to account for the fact that many years later she went insane.

The part of the reception that Sarah did not like at all was when the other ladies tried to talk to her and she couldn't understand them, couldn't tell whether they were asking questions or just making statements. "It is so festive?" a woman would say to her, and she didn't know if this was a question or not. "The price of crinoline is outrageous?" another woman would say. "I am Senator Fishback's wife?" another would say. "The militia makes one feel more secure?" "The price of coffee is ridiculous?" "The band will be playing soon?" "Your daughters are exquisite?" Some of these words, like "exquisite," Sarah did not even understand, and to the lady who asked this particular question, if it was a question, she mumbled in reply, "Not as fur as I know, yet."

She was very glad when Jacob came and took her hand and led her away from the ladies and out onto the balcony to watch the band playing, and to see the crowd waving and cheering, and to hear the cannon firing their salutes. The Arkansas *Gazette's* society editor commented the following day: "For a woman so little familiarized with the amenities of the drawing room, the governor's lady acquitted herself handily." Jacob read this item to her, but was required to explain, as best he could, "amenities," "drawing room," and "acquitted." Still Sarah wondered if they weren't poking fun at her, and her next words to Jacob were: "Jake, how long do you have to be governor?" When he told her four years, she sighed.

She was to do a lot of sighing during those four years. She would sigh when the *Gazette* wrote, in reference to a habit of Jacob's: "For a man who prefers to receive visiting dignitaries with his coonskin cap atop his head, the governor acquitted himself handily." When the Little Rock *National Democrat*, commenting on a dinner ("luncheon" they called it) that Sarah held for the legislators' wives, wrote: "For a woman whose culinary accomplishment is limited to porcine dishes, the governor's lady acquitted herself handily," Sarah sighed. Sarah sighed when the Arkansas Advocate, commenting on Jacob's conciliation of a feud between the legislature and the Little Rock Ministerial Alliance, wrote, "For a professedly unregenerate disbeliever, the governor acquitted himself handily." Finally the New York *Tribune*, in a long "profile" on the Arkansas governor and his family, commented about Sarah: "For a lady of such high standing and comforts, Mrs. Ingledew sighs handily."

Jacob Ingledew was not a great governor, but he was a good one. His administration began without a dollar in the treasury, yet by the end of his term every cent of expenses had been paid, with a surplus of $270,000 in the vaults. His strong suit was a near-genius for raising revenue. He taxed everything that could be taxed, and many things that could not. He was the inventor of highway taxes: for the upkeeping of streets and roadways the provost-marshal was ordered to collect a highway tax of two weeks' labor or fifty dollars from every citizen between the ages of eighteen and fifty years, actual government employees excepted. Most people preferred working for the government at low wages to gain this exemption, and there was no dearth of cheap government labor. At one time, Jacob had working at the governor's mansion alone three majordomos, six butlers, seven coachmen, nine maids, eleven cooks, thirteen valets, and thirty-two yardmen. The grounds were immaculate, but the yardmen began fighting among themselves with their shears and spades, and Sarah sighed.

Jacob also managed, adequately if not adroitly, the orchestration of the three separate branches of government. It has been pointed out (or if it hasn't, it has been now) that the three branches of government may be compared to the three levels of personality as seen by Freud: the legislative body is the id, the executive body is the ego, and the judicial body is the superego. Jacob got along splendidly with his legislature, who were for the most part simple country men like himself, some of them uncouth, many of them illiterate, all of them loud and hard-drinking and tobacco-chewing. Superciliously the Little Rock *Daily Republican* observed that Jacob's legislature was composed of "at least a few worthies who, we may assure our readers, are able to sign their names without running out their tongues or distorting their countenances in the effort, and thus acquit themselves handily." The judiciary branch, on the other hand, was composed mainly of city men, or citified men, sedate, grave, and disapproving. They disapproved of most of Jacob's taxes, declaring the taxes unconstitutional.

Jacob did not get along very well at all with his supreme court. He did not like city men to begin with, as we have seen. City men who were also justices were as intolerable to him as our superegos are to our egos. But the superego, I think, is gullible, and Jacob gulled his justices. He would invite them into his office, and take a gallon stone jug from a barrel filled with straw, and offer them "whiskey so good you kin smell the feet of the boys who plowed the corn." The justices would sniff their noses and at first decline, but he would urge his real mountain dew upon them and, while they became progressively intoxicated, he would tell them tall tales, wild stories, fish stories, which they believed. He would tell them of having caught a four-hundred-pound catfish which he hadn't been able to drag out of the water. "Yes," one of the justices would remark, "I suppose it's difficult to land those big ones." Jacob would explain how he tickled the catfish's whiskers, and stroked its head, causing it to leap out of the water and follow him around like a dog. The justices would nod, declaring that they had heard that catfish are easily tamed. Jacob would say, "I jist throwed a bridle on her, and rid her plumb home." When none of the justices expressed any incredulity at that, he would raise his voice and declare, "I tied her to my strawstack, and bedded her down with the cattle all winter." The justices would solemnly nod. Finally, Jacob would desperately declare that he bred the catfish to a mule, and foaled two horse colts! At this point, one of the justices would remark, "I do not believe that part of it. Everybody knows that mules are not fertile."

Then, Jacob would know, he had them right where he wanted them, and he could proceed to explain to them why, for example, the air of Arkansas, being, as anybody knows, the sweetest and purest air to breathe anywhere, is therefore taxable, and it is perfectly justifiable to put a tax on breathing. In the end, the justices yielded, but were so drunk they had to be carried from Jacob's office. Government labor being cheap, Jacob retained twelve men for the purpose of carrying drunk justices out of his office.

Jacob's successive successes in the office of governor meant nothing to Sarah; he did not discuss affairs of state with her; to her he was just the same old Jake, and she did not defer to him any more than she would have "back home." Obviously she missed "back home," and it was Sarah Ingledew who is credited with the coinage of the adjective "old-timey" in reference to the lost past. Increasingly, for the rest of that century and down through our own century, mass nostalgia would employ this expression that Sarah invented… although nostalgia isn't what it used to be. Today we are even speaking of "old-timey" television, and tomorrow we shall be speaking of "old-timey" gasoline and electricity, but it was Sarah Ingledew who first said, "Jake, I shore do miss them old-timey days back home." And the governor got a bit misty-eyed himself (although it was hard to tell, because the blueness of his eyes made them seem always watering) and replied, "Yeah, Sarey, them were the days." (This expression, grammatically corrected, also entered our language.)

Nor was this merely a fleeting mood on both their parts. It lingered, and it infected those around them, who in turn infected those around them, until all of the people were in the grips of epidemic nostalgia. Although the French had identified the disease early in that century, *nostalgie* had not been identified or named in America at this time, and it would be a few more years before a Missourian, Sydney Smith, having discovered its spread from Arkansas to Missouri, would write his seminal article, "What a Dreadful Disease Is Nostalgia on the Banks of the Missouri!" and still more years before the first English dictionary would define it. But it began with Sarah's casual remark to Jacob, and soon everyone had it, and because it had no name yet and no one could name it, they simply referred to it as *it*, and noted that there was a lot of it going around in those days. People would stop one another and ask, "Do you have it yet?" and admit "Yes, I caught it last night, I think," and all of the Little Rock newspapers ran editorials with titles like "It Does Not Acquit Itself Handily."

The war was not over, bushwhackers and jayhawkers still roamed and pillaged, but people were tired of it all. Everybody yearned for the old-timey prewar days, but everybody knew that the old-timey prewar days would never—no, never—come again, and because they would not come again people could only wish for them, and because wishing for something that can never be had is wishful thinking, and because wishful thinking is erroneous identification of one's wishes with reality, then reality is warped into a melancholy dream. In this dream that was life, all the people developed sheep's eyes, which enhanced their looks at the expense of their vision.

There was only one person in Little Rock who did not catch "it," and that was Jacob's ladyfriend (whom we cannot name). Probably the reason that she did not catch nostalgia was that there had been little or nothing in the old-timey prewar days that she had enjoyed; she lived for the future, not in languishing longing for the past. All around her people, including her lover, *especially* her lover, were afflicted with the aches of pining for the past, but she remained oriented to the future. Undoubtedly she would have looked all the more beautiful with sheep's eyes (I have seen a daguerreotype of her), but she did not get them. We do not know her; not even her name; of all the many persons in our story she will remain the most mysterious; but we know this much about her, that she alone was afflicted with longing for the future, and that she had come to the point where she could not conceive of a future without Jacob, and yet she knew that when his term expired he would leave Little Rock. He could, if he wished, run for another term, but he was stricken deeply with nostalgia, and the people, also stricken, were longing for the governors of the past, men like Izard and Conway and Yell, all aristocrats compared to Jacob Ingledew (and the man they would elect to replace him, Powell Clayton, would be the most aristocratic of them all). So if Jacob's lady-friend wanted to hang onto him, she would have to scheme.

So she schemed. She told Jacob that she wanted to become Sarah's social secretary. Jacob pointed out that, government labor being cheap, Sarah already had eight social secretaries. Whom We Cannot Name responded to that by pointing out that that would make it all the easier to "slip her in" among the others. Jacob wondered why she needed the salary, which wasn't much, one dollar a day. She said she did not need the money, of course; she only wanted to be "closer" to Jacob. Jacob pointed out that as far as being "close" was concerned, it wouldn't do them any good to be "close" in the governor's mansion, because every room was so full of people, servants and secretaries and such, that they would never have a moment's privacy. But Jacob's ladyfriend persisted, and he hired her as Sarah's ninth social secretary. The other secretaries, she soon discovered, were not, like herself, products of Little Rock's finer society, and she quickly learned to dominate them.

Sarah had very little to do with her social secretaries; she went where they told her to when they told her to, but Sarah did not give them orders, nor spend any time in idle conversation with them, nor seek their advice. Nor did they curry her favor. But her new ninth social secretary, Sarah discovered, was somehow different from the others. A very friendly person. A refined lady, too, and yet the woman did not look down upon Sarah nor make her feel uncomfortable. And on top of that, the woman was a very attractive person, who made a handsome decoration for the governor's mansion. Soon Sarah found that she and her ninth social secretary had become good friends. When Sarah was invited to give a speech to the Little Rock Beaux Arts Club, the woman offered to write it for her. Sarah was so close to the woman by this time that she was able to confide in her the well-kept secret that she could not read. The woman did not look down upon her for it. Instead the woman offered to help her rehearse the speech over a period of several days, and the woman also spoke many words of encouragement, so that when Sarah finally delivered the speech to the Beaux Arts Club, the Arkansas *Advocate* commented, "For a lady of somewhat limited elocution and enunciation, the governor's wife acquitted herself handily."

One day Sarah remarked to her ninth social secretary, "Honey, I just don't know what I'd do without you." Sarah bragged to Jacob about what a great fine beautiful person her ninth social secretary was, but Jacob pretended lack of interest. Sarah tried to persuade Jacob to meet her, but Jacob said he was too busy. But Sarah kept after him about it, dogging his heels, until finally she caught him in the hall-way of the mansion and presented her ninth social secretary to him. "This is her, Jake," Sarah said. "That I've been tellin ye about. This is the lady that keeps the world together fer me." Jacob said, "Howdy do, ma'am," and offered his hand. The woman took it, and, smiling, said, "It is a pleasure to make your acquaintance, Your Excellency."

Jacob excused himself, and went on. Sarah apologized to the woman, saying, "If you got to know him, you'd see he's a real fine man." "I'm sure he is," said the ninth social secretary.

When Jacob came to her house and her bed that night, she and Jacob had a gentle little laugh over that. But Jacob felt guilty, and often he had a temptation to confess to Sarah. Sometimes he would think about saying something to Sarah, forming the words in his mind, but would stop just short of speaking, whereupon Sarah, disconcertingly, would say "What?" This would continue for the rest of their lives, at times unnerving him. He would *know* that he had not actually spoken, that he had only been thinking about speaking, but still Sarah would say "What?" Was she reading his mind? Whatever the case, he never actually spoke to her, but for the rest of their lives he went on thinking about speaking to her, and each time he thought about it, she would say "What?" We have seen, much earlier on, how at one time the young Sarah revered Jacob as if he were God, and did not want to marry him for that reason, and it seems to me that we stand for the rest of our lives in the same relation to God, always asking that "What?" which has no answer. Perhaps we should feel no greater pity for Sarah than we should feel for ourselves.

One thing-of-the-past that the people of Arkansas in their excruciating nostalgia yearned for most was a return to statehood. For although Arkansas had been the first state to leave the Confederacy, she had not yet been reaccepted into the Union. The Congress of the United States would not let her come home. Nostalgia in its deepest sense is a yearning for home. But the Congress, dominated by Thaddeus Stevens and his radical Republicans, had not only refused to allow any of the seceded states back into the Union but also passed the dread Reconstruction Act, which would throw the South into seven long and lean years of carpetbaggery. Jacob disliked the carpetbaggers even more than he disliked the Confederates, but he was caught between them and could do nothing. Both sides began to blame him for the failure of Arkansas to reenter the Union. They began to call him "Old Imbecility," and to openly mock his country ways. He lost control of his legislature to them. He could no longer handle the supreme court justices, who ceased coming to his office to drink his mountain dew and listen to his tall tales. The supreme court declared unconstitutional his law that Arkansawyers who had borne arms against the United States were not eligible to vote, and this allowed the ex-Confederates to sweep back into government. But the carpet-baggers, or Republicans as they called themselves, gained control, and nominated one of their own, Powell Clayton, an ex-Pennsylvanian, to run for governor. Jacob could not have beaten him even if he were not infected with hopeless nostalgia and longing for Stay More. Shortly after the election in which Clayton took the governorship, Congress restored Arkansas to the Union.

One of the few utterances of Jacob Ingledew that found its way into recorded history was by virtue of Powell Clayton's memoirs, written in his eighties after a distinguished career as governor and later U.S. Senator from Arkansas. Clayton reminisced about the day of his inauguration in midsummer, waiting in his carriage, seated beside the outgoing governor. He described the outgoing governor: mild blue eyes, tangled beard, long wavy locks of the mountaineer, wearing a suit of plain homespun. Clayton was wearing, by contrast, a suit of full broadcloth, with frock coat and wide wing collar; and he was wearing fine kid gloves. As the outgoing governor got into the carriage, he took a long look at the gloves, and then, Clayton recalled, Jacob Ingledew remarked, "Well, I reckon I never saw anyone but you wearing gloves in July! Only dudes do that!" To which Clayton, by his account, retorted, "Governor, it's not the garb that makes the man; but in deference to you and especially in view of the character of the work I am about to enter upon today, which will require handling without gloves, I will now remove mine." Clayton also wrote of being invited to Jacob's office after the inauguration, where the ex-governor fished a gallon stone jug out of a barrel of straw and offered Clayton a drink of mountain dew. Clayton had good cause to recall the incident, because it was the only expression of goodwill the mountaineers ever gave him.

Jacob hired a carriage to take him home to Stay More. When he entered it, he found Sarah and his daughters already there. He also found his ladyfriend there, dressed for travel and holding her hat-box in her lap.

"Where do ye think you're a-headin?" he asked her.

"She's goin with us, Jake!" Sarah exclaimed. "I ast her to, and she said she would! I jist couldn't never git along without her!"

Jacob took his seat. It was crowded, five of them in a carriage meant for four, and it was a long way to Stay More. "Hhmmph," he was moved to comment. But as the carriage pulled away from the governor's mansion and moved north out of the city of Little Rock, he began to chuckle, and then to laugh.

"What's so funny, Jake?" Sarah asked.

He gained control of himself and replied, "Nothin. I'm jist right glad to git out of that town."

"Me too," said Sarah.

"Me too," chorused their daughters.

And, "Me too," said the ladyfriend. It is one of the few things we have heard her say; it is all we will.

Our illustration for this chapter is of a house which is, therefore, trigeminal rather than bigeminal, a treble rather than a duple, although I doubt if anybody ever consciously thought of the symbolism of it: that the left door, as we face the house, is Sarah's, the center door, Jacob's, the right door, Whom We Cannot Name's. There were interior connecting doors between the center and both sides. A later occupant, in our century, removed the partition between the left and center chambers, making one large living room, and that is the way it may be seen today. Jacob, in concession to the amenities of his ladyfriend's former environment, constructed the first "outhouse" or privy in Stay More. Heretofore, everybody in Stay More had simply "gone out" and used the woods or bushes, or the open, and children were taught not to foul a path lest they get a "sty" on their bottoms or cause the death of their sisters. The expression "go out" was so clearly understood that one might even remark of an incontinent child or drunken man, "He went out in his britches." But now, on a little knoll behind his house, Jacob built Stay More's first privy, which was also trigeminal, in a way: it had three holes, the possible significance of which I must leave to the speculation of my students. The people of Stay More thought that Jacob was "puttin on airs" by constructing a privy, but they did not think anything unseemly about his ladyfriend. To all of them, forever, she was only "Sarey's friend," or "Aunt Sarey's friend," or "Grammaw Sarey's friend," or "Great-Grammaw Sarey's friend." Indeed, the only words on her tombstone are "Sarah's Friend." But she was not to die until well into our own century. Jacob himself lived until the first year of our century, and Sarah survived him by one day. The words on Jacob's tombstone are: "He done his damndest." Harry Truman, the only Ozarker ever to make it all the way to the Presidency, liked to quote those words, and requested that they be put on his own tombstone, although for some reason they were not.

The buildings in our study thus far have been medieval, with gable roofs; Jacob's trigeminal house is a hip-roofed Victorian example of "steamboat gothic." Facing the main road in the exact center of downtown Stay More, it is...

But we have had enough, for now, of the generation of Jacob; if generations generate, we must move on.

Chapter eight

Being taciturn, Isaac Ingledew (called—never to his face—
"Colonel Coon" for the rest of his life), became a miller, and here
we see his mill. A miller didn't have to talk if he didn't feel like it,
although most millers did. Isaac's customers chatted and gossiped
freely with one another, while he ground their grain and meal in
silence. Whenever something went wrong with the machinery in
his mill, he would cuss profusely and obscenely, but otherwise he
kept his mouth shut. People came from miles in every direction to
Isaac's mill, but everyone knew that Colonel Coon did not enjoy
speech, and no one tried to draw him out. Still they could not help
wondering whether he ever spoke at least to his wife. It is something
of a miracle that Isaac Ingledew had a wife. But he did. Her name
was Salina Denton, naturally pronounced "Sleeny," and she was a
real "looker," as they said of her. Isaac Ingledew came across her,
or chanced upon her, or stumbled into her life, toward the end of
the War, when he and his men (or rather *man*, a lone major who
remained the last infantryman in Colonel Coon's command at that
late juncture) were pursuing the remnants of the Confederate army
in Newton County, a band of three bushwhackers.

Although small in numbers, this band was still wreaking havoc from one end of the county to the other, terrorizing helpless women and children and old men, and Isaac and his one-man army were determined, although outnumbered, to wipe them out. They caught and killed one of the three after the band had raided the Denton cabin, thereby equalizing the two armies, and while his major went off in pursuit of the other two, Isaac inspected the damage to the Denton cabin, and found Salina Denton cowering there, alone, in ranting hysterics. He wanted to calm her down, but, being taciturn, he didn't know what to say. He tried to pat her on the back, but when he did so, she began to climb him. He set her down gently but she climbed him again. Again he set her down, but again she climbed him, and by this time he became aroused, to put it mildly. So the third time she climbed him, he did not set her down, although she went on raving. He was, we should remember, a giant of a man, and while there was nothing exactly small about Salina Denton, he supported her easily. Apparently the act or deed brought her to her senses, for afterward she said calmly, "Whar am I?" and then she looked at him and said, "Who are you? And what's thet out fer?" Hastily he buttoned himself and fled.

He and his major spent the next year tracking down and killing the two remnants of the Confederate Army, and then they declared the War won and went home. Isaac planted most of the eighty acres his father had given him in wheat and corn, and began the construction of his mill, assisted by his brother Lum and his Swain uncles. He had finished one door of the mill when a girl appeared, on foot, barefoot, holding an infant in her arms. It took him a moment to recognize and remember her, but still he did not even say "Howdy." She did, however, and then she held out the infant to him and asked, "Do ye wanter take a gander at yore son?" Isaac took a gander at the baby, and even chucked it under the chin; he tried to mumble "Cootchy-coo," but the words would not come. And then he said to Salina the only thing that anybody ever heard him say to her publicly. Gesturing across the valley at the distant knoll where the dogtrot house his father had given him was located, he declared, "That's my place up yonder." Salina and her baby moved in. The infant boy was named

Denton Ingledew, after his mother's last name. Turning back to his work, Isaac built another door on the mill, and thus we might think of the mill as being also bigeminal in symbolism of the new union, but in this particular case we know that the bigeminality was strictly functional: one door was for people going into the mill, the other door was for people coming out.

Isaac worked that day until well past dark, deliberately postponing going home to his woman, to whom he did not know what else to say. But inevitably he had to go home, where Salina was waiting with a pretty fine supper she had fixed. While he ate it, Isaac couldn't think of a blessed thing to say, but that was all right, because Salina, by contrast with her husband, was just about the most talkative person who ever lived in Stay More. That night she began: "My name's Sleeny Denton, and I'm seventeen year old, and I've got two older brothers and three older sisters that have all done flew the roost, and we lived up Right Prong Holler all our life, my daddy and mom were gone visitin kinfolks in Demijohn that day ye came, that's how come ye didn't meet 'em, and I'd jist had the everlastin wits skeered out o' me by them bushwhackers that lit far to the house, 'till you come and run 'em off, and then done what ye done, which I have to say I didn't mind a bit, it was the most fun, I'm tellin ye, and I wouldn't care if ye did it again soon as ye git done eatin, although not in the same room with the baby, because I'm strict about that, you'll find, but aint he the cutest little spadger ever ye saw, looks jist lak ye, same eyes and all, 'though I think his nose kinder favors my daddy's, and he's got Mom's ears, but you kin jist tell by lookin at him that he'll grow up to be big and strong lak you, why, my, I never seed ary man in my life as big and strong as you, it's a sin to Moses how big and strong, and I tole my daddy what yore uniform looked lak, and ast my daddy what did them bars on yore collar mean, and my daddy said them bars meant ye were a colonel! and my sakes alive! if I haven't always wanted to marry me a colonel! why, when I was jist a little chicky I used to tell my playmates I was a-fixin to marry me a colonel when I got growed up, and now jist look at me! I've done went and done it!"

After Isaac had finished eating, he stood up, belched to signify his satisfaction with the meal, and began stretching. While he was stretching, Salina, first putting the baby into the other house of the dogtrot, climbed him. She was not hysterical now, but she went on talking, a blue streak, the whole time he did her, although her words were interlaced with coos and burbles and were terminated by a squeal. Thus their second-born, Monroe Ingledew, was conceived. In fact, one of the few things of distinction about John Ingledew, their third son, apart from his being the father of the next great wave of Ingledews in our ongoing saga, was that he was the first of Isaac's and Salina's children to be conceived when his parents were in a horizontal rather than a vertical position, for it took them that long to discover, albeit accidentally, that it was possible to do it while lying down. It may be noted in passing that Isaac Ingledew was the only Ingledew male who never again got the frakes. He worked hard, but not hard enough to get the frakes, or, if he did work hard enough to get the frakes, Salina's hearty, refreshing sensuality gave him immunity.

He was, as I say, a miller. He was not the first; we may have glimpsed, chapters back, the rude gristmill of Zachariah Dinsmore, which was a primitive "tub wheel" mill, on Swains Creek. Isaac's mill was on Banty Creek, near its mouth where it empties into Swains Creek, where it was swiftest, swift enough to power the large undershot wheel that powered the grindstone. But soon after he had built the mill, Banty Creek went dry. Rather than turn the whole mill structure around so that its wheel would be in Swains Creek (which wouldn't have worked anyway—or, rather, it would have turned the wheel in the opposite direction, and, Isaac realized, unground the meal), he decided to convert to steam power. A boiler and an engine and the necessary machinery would cost him a thousand dollars, which he did not have. Reticently he asked his father, recently retired from the governorship, for a loan, but Jacob claimed that he had spent all his money building his trigeminal house, a lame excuse, but Isaac, being taciturn, did not argue.

Learning that the cities suffered a scarcity of bacon, Isaac took his gun into the woods and slaughtered five hundred razorback hogs, dressed them with the help of his wife and brother, and carted them off to Springfield, Missouri, where he easily sold them for more than enough to purchase the boiler and engine and machinery, which he purchased there and carted back to Stay More and installed in the smaller building which may be seen in the rear of our illustration. It was the first engine in Newton County, one of the first engines in all of the Arkansas Ozarks. He brought with him from Springfield a fireman, named Toliver Cole, or Cole Toliver (it is not certain which), to operate the engine. There was still enough water in Banty Creek to fuel the boiler.

Everyone in Stay More, and half the populaces of Parthenon and Jasper, gathered at The Ingledew Grist Co. to watch the first firing of the engine. Toliver Cole (or Cole Toliver) was impressed with the size of his audience, and for the occasion he wore a top hat, cutaway, and spats, although in place of a tie he wore his usual red bandana. Fifteen girls fell in love with him, so he could take his pick, and afterwards picked Rachel Ingledew, Isaac's young sister, who became Mrs. Cole, or Mrs. Toliver. But the ceremony of the firing was awesome, horrifying, well worth the trip to those who had come from a distance. Lum Ingledew, Isaac's brother, was given the concession, and did a brisk business in sassafrasade, jujubes, and folding fans. As the engine started up, women fanned themselves, and prayed, or fainted. Grown men trembled and wiped their sweating palms on their shirtfronts. Children screamed, dogs howled, birds flew away. It was the Second Tuesday of the Month, and up the hill at the Ingledew dogtrot, the old Eli Willard clock said PRONG, unnoticed, unheard.

Strange to relate, Isaac's business fell off. People reverted to laboriously pounding their grain in stone mortars, Indian-fashion. Being taciturn, Isaac could not go around asking people why they would not patronize his mill. Were they actually afraid of his engine? At any rate, he had to lay off his new brother-in-law, who went back to Springfield, taking Rachel with him. For days, weeks, Isaac sat in his captain's chair on the porch of his mill, waiting for customers. He would go home late in the evening, and Salina would climb him and make him feel better, momentarily, but she never asked him, "How's business?" and even if she had, he could not have told her. He kept a fire lighted under his boiler, and checked the pressure gauge now and then, but never threw the switch to start the engine.

Gradually, the people, although they did not want to patronize his mill, began to miss the chatting and gossip that they had indulged in while waiting for Colonel Coon to grind their grain, and one by one, sackless or with their gunnysacks empty, they began coming back to his mill and sitting on his porch and chatting and gossiping with one another. Isaac sat among them, listening, yearning to open his mouth and ask them why they did not patronize his mill any longer. Were they afraid of his engine? Would they bring their grain to him if he threw out the engine and moved the mill around so that its wheel was in Swains Creek? What about earplugs? Or what if he offered to pick up and deliver their grain so that they did not have to see, let alone hear, the engine? But he could not ask these things. And because he never spoke, the people began to take his presence for granted, they began to feel that he was only an inanimate fixture, and they began to talk about him as if he were not there.

It is amazing how much a man can learn about himself in this fashion. Isaac learned that he was well-belovèd to them all. He learned how much the men envied him because of his beautiful wife Salina, and how much the women envied Salina because she had "caught" a big, strong, handsome man like Isaac. He learned that there was not a man in Newton County who was willing to fight him, on a dare, or for any amount of money. He learned that all of the men had dreams, nearly every night, involving amatory sport with Salina, and that the women had dreams involving the same with Isaac. But he did not learn why neither the men nor the women, nor the children, would bring their grain to be ground in his mill.

In time, his own fields of wheat and corn were ripe for harvest, and he harvested them, and hauled the grain to his mill, and built up the fire under his boiler, and hooked up his engine, and ground his grain and meal. The people left the porch of the mill and drifted off, and did not come back until he had shut down the engine. Birds, rats and mice infested his mill and ate through the gunny-sacks and devoured his grain and meal and flour, but fled when he started the engine again. It was a choice: no pests but no people, or people and pests. He opted for the latter, and let the birds, rats and mice have his grain. By and by, he became almost content, sitting among the people, listening to them talk about him. The seasons passed, seedtime, grain and harvest. But after another harvest, the people began to complain among themselves about the back breaking job of grinding their grain in stone mortars, Indian-fashion. Isaac listened to their grumblings for as long as he could stand it, and then he reviewed in his mind his stock of choice profanities until he had picked the one that seemed to him choicest and most profane. He stood up and uttered it, loudly. Then he asked,

"How come y'all don't bring yore #@%&*# grain to my #@%&*# mill?"

The people grew silent, staring at one another and at Isaac. All of them suddenly realized that he was *there*, where they had forgotten that he had been. This embarrassed them greatly, and they remembered all the things they had said about him, and they all began to get very red in the face, and to slink down in their chairs, and one by one they put their tails between their legs and crept away. Soon each of them returned, carrying upon their backs or their mules' backs gunnysacks filled with grain. Isaac fired his engine and ground their grain, and grew prosperous over the years, running the mill day and night; he had to hire two helpers and train a new fireman. It was not until his old age, in our own century, after Stay More had seen the coming of a newer and commoner kind of self-propelled engine, that Isaac Ingledew finally learned the reason why people had ever been reluctant to come to his mill: not that they were afraid of the sight or sound of his engine, but rather, as his middle-aged daughter Drussie expressed it to him one day, "I reckon folks back in them old-timey days just couldn't stand fer no kind of PROG RESS."

Indeed, she was right, not alone about *that* instance of resistance to progress, but to the entire history of Stay More, nay, the entire history of the Ozarks. Everything new, everything progressive or forward-looking, was anathema to those people, and who are we to fault them for it? "Stay More" is synonymous with "Status Quo"; in fact, there are people who believe, or who like to believe, that the name of the town was intended as an entreaty, beseeching the past to remain present. Today, Colonel Coon's newfangled engine is an antique; after his death, it was transferred to Oren Duckworth's tomato canning factory, where it powered the conveyor belt for a generation, but has been out of use and rusting for half of my lifetime.

It was in the generation of Isaac, also, that Stay More and the Ozarks experienced the first serious fuel shortage, called the First Spell of Darkness. All of the lamps, as we have seen, were fueled with bear's oil, but as the human population increased the population of bears decreased. Isaac himself shot the last bear of Stay More, and when that bruin's lard was all used up, the people experienced their first blackout. It was very dark, and the moon wasn't scheduled to reappear for two weeks, and it was the hottest part of summer, so that fireplace light was uncomfortable. Most people simply went to bed, but this indirectly caused a population explosion which in turn would lead to a future depletion of fuel. Isaac's oldest sons, Denton and Monroe, ran around in the dark yard of the dogtrot catching lightning bugs and putting them into a glass jar, but this kind of lamp was feeble and temporary, since the boys didn't know what the bugs ate and didn't feed them, and they died. In an emergency, someone could always make a torch from sap-rich pine, but otherwise most people just went to bed... except Isaac Ingledew and his two helpers and his fireman, who had to stay up 'way past dark to finish the grinding of the day's flour and meal. By leaving the boiler room door open, some light came into the mill, scarcely enough to work by but enough to keep the men from being entirely blind, and they lit a pine torch from time to time for delicate operations.

It was during this first Spell of Darkness that lawlessness first came to Stay More (unless we consider, as we should, the War lawless); and note that I say it *came* to Stay More; it did not originate there. Isaac's mill had been running night and day for several weeks, and it was rumored that he kept a large sum of money at the mill. This was not true; he kept only enough to make change; the rest of his small fortune was kept in a location which even I do not know. But after dark the men working inside the mill bolted the doors, as any businesses do when they have closed to the public but are still working.

One night after the doors had been bolted, Isaac was standing near one of the big oak doors at the main entrance, trying to adjust a faulty elevator by pine-torch light, when there came a knocking at the door. Isaac hesitated for only a moment, deciding that it must be some customer coming in late, perhaps after a breakdown, and then he opened the door. A man slipped inside, breathing hard. Isaac gave him the once over and guessed that the man had been riding long and hard. Because of his own experience riding horses, Isaac could even guess how long the man had been in the saddle, at what speed he was traveling, and therefore how far he had come, and from which direction…Missouri. In the dim light only the man's eyeballs could be seen clearly: his eyes were taking in everything. The man sized up Isaac, who stood a good foot taller, and asked, "You own this here mill?" Isaac nodded. The man began walking around, inspecting the machinery. Not knowing that Isaac was taciturn, he began asking Isaac a lot of questions about his business. How wide an area of the county did the mill serve? From how far away did customers come? How many employees did Isaac have? Isaac answered, if he answered at all, in monosyllables. Meanwhile, the fireman had come up from the engine room with the iron rod that he used to stir his fire, and got in back of the man without being noticed and held the iron bar above the back of his head. The two helpers had rebolted the doors and the side door leading to the engine room. Isaac felt no fear: even if he had been alone with the man, he would have felt no fear, although the dark shadow of a bulge of a gun was obvious inside the man's shirt. After a few minutes the man asked the price of cracked corn. Isaac told him. The man said, "I'll take two bushel. There's eight more fellers out there with me, and their horses aint been fed." Isaac gave him two bushels of cracked corn, and the man took out a large roll of bills and peeled one of them off and gave it to Isaac. Then they unbolted a door for him and he vanished into the darkness. They could not see any other men or horses out there, but it was very dark.

As soon as the door was bolted again, the fireman burst out excitedly, "Don't ye know who that was?" Isaac shook his head. "Hit was Jesse James hisself!" exclaimed the fireman. "He'll be back, no doubt about it, and he'll rob ye! Or try to." Isaac grinned. He did have some money that night, but it would have been small pickin for the likes of Jesse James. The fireman and the two helpers were looking at Isaac as if waiting for his instructions or for permission to return to the safety of their homes. Being taciturn, Isaac did not know quite what to say, even to his own employees. There was still work to be done in the mill that night, but Isaac figured it could wait until morning. "Fire out," he said, which was his traditional nightly terseness signaling that the engine could be shut off and the men could go home (and which to our modern ears would sound like "Far out," possibly a comment on the situation). They lost no time in closing up shop. But Isaac remained behind, alone, after each of them had said to him, "G'night, Colonel. Take keer."

After extinguishing the lone pine torch that had provided illumination inside the mill, Isaac bolted the doors again and then, from beneath the high desk where he kept his accounts, he took out his fiddle-case and opened it, and tucked the fiddle under his chin, and began to play.

As we have remarked, and will continue to remark, Isaac might have been taciturn with words, but not with notes of music, and there were some people, particularly old-timers, who claimed that they could understand perfectly well what Isaac's fiddle was saying. No, they couldn't quite put it into *words*, but they could still understand it. Children, especially girls, were never allowed to listen while Isaac was fiddling. None of the houses of Stay More were close enough to the mill for the sound of this fiddling to carry to them tonight. If Jacob Ingledew had gone out onto his porch and strained his ears… but no, the ex-governor's hearing was failing in his later years. So there was nobody to hear Isaac's fiddle, except himself…and a band of nine men sitting on their horses in the woods behind the mill. We can only imagine what thoughts they might have been having, or what words they were speaking to one another, as they listened to the fiddling.

Most biographers of Jesse James refrain from mentioning the Stay More episode, and in others it is reduced to a mere footnote or the trailing edge of a paragraph. But the James gang itself was made up largely of Ozarkers, albeit Ozark desperadoes who were clearly determined, tonight, to part Isaac from his small fortune. So these Ozarkers in the James gang must have understood part of what Isaac's fiddle was saying to them, and they knew for the most part that it was cussing them to high heaven and daring them to enter his mill at their own peril. We may even suppose that if Frank James was there that night, which he was, he tried his best to dissuade Jesse from proceeding. Unquestionably, one or more of the James gang must have remarked to their leader that a back woods gristmill was hardly in the same class with a bank or a train, and undoubtedly Jesse himself could not shake loose his impression of what a giant of a man Isaac was. But the James gang never backed away from an enterprise, so they didn't. Jesse himself mounted the mill porch and banged on the door, hollering, "Open up! Cut out that goddumb fiddlin and open the godburn door!" But Isaac went on fiddling, if anything, faster, louder, more obscene. Some of the gang began heaving their shoulders against the door, trying to break it down.

As we have seen, the bigeminality of Isaac's mill was because one door was for entering, the other for leaving, to create traffic flow and avoid confusion. Now these gangsters in their ignorance were trying to enter the exit door, and this incensed Isaac all the more, and his fiddle music became really animated and profane. But the gangsters succeeded in busting the door loose from its hinges and entered, whereupon the fiddle music abruptly stopped. "You, Luke," the ringleader ordered one of his men, "guard this here door. Bob and Cole guard the other doors." Then he hollered into the dark interior, "Okay, mister millerman, give up, or die!"

Now Isaac's mill, being three-and-a-half stories in height, was a labyrinth of nooks and crannies, passages, stairs, catwalks, traps, hoppers, cribs, coves, lofts, galleries and stoops. Isaac could have been in, or on, any of these; he knew them all by heart, in the pitch dark. One advantage of dark times, even though they bring desperadoes bent on crime, is that they make seeing difficult for the desperadoes. "Strike a light," the gangleader ordered, and one of the men lighted a torch. Huddling close together, with their revolvers cocked and pointed in every direction, the men prowled the mill, searching for Isaac. They probed all over the first level, then ascended to the second, and then to the third. On the third-and-a-half level, they were inching along a catwalk when suddenly two of them tripped—or were pushed—and plummeted all the way back to the first level, where they broke several bones and began howling in pain. The remaining four men decided that Isaac was not to be found in the ceiling of the mill, and began to descend; by the time they got to the first level they discovered that they were not four but two: Jesse and Frank alone. They called for their comrades but received no answer. "Luke? Bob? Cole?" Jesse called to the men he had left posted at the doors, but he received no answer.

One may imagine that at this point the intrepid Jesse James felt an involuntary shudder; none of the biographies mention it, although an unfavorable biography of Frank James declares that at this point Frank "spontaneously defecated into one leg of his trousers." "Let's get out of here," Frank suggested to his brother, and his brother wisely agreed. The two men quickly left the mill, remounted their horses and rode off. They had not ridden far, however, when Jesse said, "Frank, I wonder if we should jist ride off and leave 'em behind like that. Frank? FRANK??" He discovered the horse beside him was riderless, and he spurred his own horse as hard as he could, and did not even slow down until he was outside of Newton County. It would be weeks later before all of his gang would rejoin him; none of them killed, but each with various bones broken, and it would be years before the James gang went back into criminal action...never again in the state of Arkansas. Working in the mill the next day, one of Isaac's helpers asked him, "Have any trouble last night, Colonel?" "Some," Isaac replied, but, being taciturn, did not elaborate.

There really wasn't much need for light after dark during the First Spell of Darkness, since no one could read, except Jacob (and, now, his ladyfriend—and they used candles). The only need for light after dark was to find one's way to "go out." That was a problem on a dark night. But the problem was solved when Eli Willard, making his usual timely reappearance, brought a wagon-load of chamberpots, which he facetiously called "thundermugs" and which the people of Stay More eventually referred to as "slop jars." Ownership of a chamberpot, they felt, was not "puttin on airs" like the construction of a privy, nor was it necessarily PROG RESS; it was merely a convenient way to remain in while going out, or to go out without going out. Children were given the task of emptying and cleaning the chamberpots each morning, and were warned not to empty them into a path, lest the pots become permanently stuck to the child's fingers. Nobody ever knew of any child whose pot stuck to his fingers, but no child was ever known to empty a pot into a path, so the superstition was just as efficacious as all their other superstitions.

Eli Willard, while selling the chamberpots to every house, happened to hear of the shortage of bear's oil which had caused a shortage of light which had caused the boom in chamberpots, and, having sold his last chamberpot, he promised to bring relief for the fuel shortage on his next trip. True to his word, when he came again, a year later, he was driving a large wagon filled with barrels. The barrels, he said, contained "whale" oil. Since no one in Stay More had ever seen the ocean or could even imagine it, Eli Willard had to explain to them that a "whale" is a kind of big fish that lived in the ocean. Had they never read about Jonah in the Bible? Apparently not, because they did not read. They were suspicious of fish oil; they thought it would smell fishy. It did, but not like any of the fish of Stay More. Eli Willard used his pitchmanship to promote his product, and made a killing. He was also offering a line of special new lamps to burn the whale oil in, and made a further killing with these. Verily, Eli Willard made so much money selling whale oil and lamps that he retired from the game, and was not seen in Stay More again for ten years.

Those ten years were called the Decade of Light. There would be another Spell of Darkness after them, but for ten years there was a plenty of light. The last of Isaac's children, Perlina and Drussie, had been conceived when Salina climbed him in the dark of the First Spell of Darkness. During the Decade of Light, she no longer climbed him, for, as we may have noticed, she was over-fastidious about not being seen by her children, and it was at the beginning of the Decade of Light when John, her third son, happened to spot his mother climbing his father by the light of whale oil. He was about five years old at the time. Far from suffering any "primal scene" trauma from the experience, he thought it looked like some wonderful game, and as soon as his mother was finished, he climbed his father and said, "Do me." Salina was shocked, and never again climbed Isaac during the Decade of Light. But little John frequently climbed Isaac and said, "Do me," to which Isaac, being taciturn, could only reply "Not now, son," which did not deter John from later climbing his father and saying "Do me" again. This was how John got his nickname, "Doomy," which he had so much trouble outliving in later life. Most people always thought that the nickname derived from the air of doom that seemed to surround John throughout his adult life, but that is not the fact of the case.

Because Salina would not climb Isaac during the Decade of Light, he became restless. One day he spoke to himself. Being taciturn, Isaac did not like to talk, even to himself. But now he announced to himself, "I'm gonna git me a new jug, and drink till the goddamn world looks little." Isaac, like many silent men, was a connoisseur of fine liquor. His father Jacob had once spoken of "whiskey so good you kin smell the feet of the boys who plowed the corn." Isaac not only could smell their feet but also could identify them and tell what they had had for breakfast. He could distinguish corn whiskey by regions as ably as any French wine taster could distinguish the vineyards of France. Abler. And in the case of metheglin—variously pronounced "mathiglum" or "mothiglum"—which is a spiced variety of mead, he could not only distinguish between that made from honey and that made from sorghum, but also identify each of the spices. So, having determined to drink until the world looked little, he was determined to do it in style, and after reflection he selected Seth Chism's sour mash, which was, perhaps, one might say, the Château Lafitte Rothschild of Newton County.

Seth Chism had ground his grain at Isaac's mill, and Isaac had ground it with especial care because he knew the care with which Seth Chism would distill it. Being taciturn, Isaac could not very well ask Seth Chism for a jug of it, but Seth understood the only possible meaning of a palm full of coins, and wordlessly made the sale. Isaac took his jug into his mill, barred the door, and began to diminish the size of the world. Because he was such a big man, it required half of the jug to reduce the world to half its size. He wanted to continue, but realized that if he drank all the jug the world would be reduced to nothing, so he stopped, and began to test the half-world. There was a barrel of flour in the mill which he knew weighed two hundred pounds; he hoisted it and then held it overhead, convinced it weighed only one hundred pounds. Then he went outside on the porch of his mill and looked around. The trees were half as high, the creek half as full and wide, the blue dome of heaven half as far away. He started down from the high porch, but the top step seemed half as far as it was, and, stepping only halfway, he went over into a somersault and landed flat on his back on the hard ground below. The fall would have killed a man half his size, or broken half his bones, but all it did to Isaac was knock half his breath out of him. He lay there for a while, getting that half back, and while he was lying there a rider rode up, a stranger, a man not three foot tall on a stallion not eight hands high. The little man on the tiny stallion did not know that Isaac was taciturn, and asked him a question:

"Howdy. Whar at is yore post office?"

The only office Isaac had ever heard tell on was his father Jacob's office, where the ex-governor claimed he was writing his memoirs, but was not. Isaac remained silent, but at length got up from the ground, dusted himself off, and looked down at the little rider. "What's a post office?" he said.

"Whar at do you'uns git yore mail?"

Near 'bout ever farmer in Stay More valley had one or more males around the place, if this feller was referrin to topcows, but since he was ridin a stallion there weren't no sense in his lookin fer a cow-critter male. Isaac remained silent.

The stranger turned to his saddlebags, opened them, and drew out a small card, which he offered to Isaac. "This here postcard is addressed to 'The Good People of Stay More, Arkansas.' I reckon this here is Stay More, aint it?"

Isaac nodded.

"Then take it," the stranger requested, and Isaac took it. Thus, in the beginning of the Decade of Light, in, coincidentally, the same year postcards were invented, Stay More became a post office.

The stranger turned his horse and prepared to ride off, but paused. He stared at Isaac for a moment and then asked, "Jist out of curiosity, what war you a-laying thar on the ground fer, when I rid up?"

Isaac studied the postcard, which he could not read, then gave the stranger a look that was not exactly hostile, but not cordial either. "Layin low fer moles," he answered, and the rider stared at him for only an instant longer before spurring his horse and riding off. Isaac decided to deliver the postcard to his father, who could read it. His father's house was only half as far as it used to be, and Isaac reached it in half the time. His father too, he discovered, was shrunk to half his size, sitting in his tiny office pretending to write his half-baked memoirs. Isaac gave him the little card. Jacob took the card and read both sides of it, was at first puzzled, then chuckled.

"It's from ole Eli Willard," Jacob told his son. "He must've got so all-fired rich sellin his whale oil that he's done took off for a tour of the world. Sent this'un here from some'ers called 'Stone-hinge,' in Old England, clear across the sea. Says, 'Having marvelous time. Wish you were here. Onward to London t'morrow. My fondest regards to all of you. Eli Willard.'" Jacob chuckled again, and observed, "Right thoughty of him, weren't it?" He poked the postcard into a pigeonhole of his desk, and resumed pretending to write his memoirs, not noticing, or not commenting upon, the fact that his son Isaac positively reeked of Seth Chism's aqua vitae. Isaac left, vaguely troubled with the thought that Eli Willard was expanding the world that Isaac was trying to contract. For several years following, throughout the Decade of Light, postcards kept coming from Eli Willard in Paris, Geneva, Venice, Rome, Naples, Athens, Istanbul, Sevastopol, Tehran, Bombay, Rangoon, Singapore, Shanghai, Osaka, Honolulu, and, the last one, San Francisco.

Every day, Isaac drank half a jug of corn whiskey to keep the world to half its size, but nobody seemed to notice that he was constantly half seas o'er, not even his better half, Salina, who, however, continued not to climb him. Seth Chism raised his price to half a dollar a jug, but this did not strain Isaac's finances, because he continued to run his mill, half for corn, half for wheat, troubled only by having to double each measure to get it right, and vaguely troubled by postcards that came from halfway around the world. Stay More was officially declared a United States Post Office, and the postmastership was appointed to Isaac's younger brother, Christopher Columbus "Lum" Ingledew, who, however, like everybody else except Jacob and his ladyfriend, could neither read nor write, a considerable handicap for a postmaster. It was decided to start a school, the first since Jacob's little academy of many years previous, and everybody pitched in to build the schoolhouse, which we shall examine in the next chapter. Jacob declined the schoolmastership on the grounds of being past the retirement age. A subscription was got up, and a young man from Harrison up in neighboring Boone County, by the name of Boone Harrison, was hired, at $75 per term plus room and board, to teach the school. Boone Harrison was just barely literate himself, but he could, and did, teach people how to read and write, and thus it was that during the Decade of Light the people of Stay More acquired not only a post office but a means of patronizing both ends of it, sending and receiving, and once they became literate they spent all their spare time writing letters, a worthless enterprise.

The post office in its early years was not a separate structure, but occupied one small corner of Isaac's mill, where, twice weekly, Lum Ingledew would sort and distribute mail, what little there was of it, until the people discovered how to write off for catalogs and to circulate chain letters. One of the first catalogs to arrive in Stay More was a seed catalog, and the recipients discovered to their amazement that the Tah May Toh, which grew wild on fifteen-foot vines all over Stay More, and which they had always thought poisonous, was considered edible, so immediately everybody began harvesting and eating 'maters, as they called them, and suffering no effects other than the heady (and body) sense of voluptuousness that gave the 'mater its nickname, "love apple." It is not exactly an aphrodisiac, because no frigid woman nor impotent man has ever been cured by eating one, but in the case of persons already healthily disposed toward sex, it enriches the disposition. Hence, the numbers of people who comprised Stay More's maximum population during the last part of that century were conceived and born during the Decade of Light.

But Isaac's wife Salina, even though she acquired just as fond a taste for 'maters as anybody else, still would not climb Isaac during the Decade of Light. After eating a 'mater, she might remark to him, "I'd like to climb a tree," but she wouldn't climb him. In time, she spoke of "climbing the walls," but she never again climbed Isaac until the Decade of Light was over. And he went on drinking, so that she looked to him too small, less than three feet high, to climb him anyway.

Oddly enough, all of the energy or voluptuousness or libido or lubricity generated by the love apple cannot be discharged through sex alone. There is a generous residue that seeks other outlets, so during the peak of 'mater-pickin time the women commenced frenzies of quilting bees, and the men devoted all their spare time to the game they called Base Ball, originated by Jacob Ingledew years before. The equipment remained unrefined: a hickory stake for a bat, a round chunk of sandstone for a ball, gunnysacks for bases; but the men spent so much time playing it during 'mater-pickin time that they perfected it in many ways: some players were so strong they could knock the rock clear out of the field, which constituted a "free run home," while the pitchers, in order to thwart this type of batter, learned how to make the rock actually "curve" instead of going in a straight line, and some pitchers, by applying their tobacco juice to the rock, could really confuse and harass the batter. Isaac Ingledew, once the greatest batter and pitcher of all, was still in his thirties, and tried to play, but could not: he would swing at the rock before it was halfway to him.

Every five years during the Decade of Light, that is, twice, Stay More hosted a gala reunion of the G.A.R., the veterans who had fought with Jacob and Isaac during the War. These men would come, with their families, from all over Newton and adjoining counties, and hundreds of primitive tents would be pitched in the Field of Clover, and a great time would be had by all. The women of Stay More would spend days in their kitchens preparing banquets. The menfolk kept the stills running night and day, and shot all the game out of all the woods. The reunion began on a Second Tuesday of the Month and lasted only three days, but that was long enough to eat up all the food and drink all the liquor and listen to a speech by Jacob Ingledew. The first reunion was such a big success that when time came five years later for the second one, even some of John Cecil's Rebels tried to sneak in with their families, but they were spotted and driven away. The second reunion happened by accident to occur during the peak of 'mater-pickin time. The womenfolk not only served loads of fresh whole 'maters cooled in springwater, but also they prepared and served baked stuffed 'mater, fried 'mater, broiled 'mater, sautéed crumbed 'mater, as well as 'mater juice, 'mater gazpacho, 'mater compote, 'mater aspic, ketchup, puree, relish, 'mater salad, 'mater jam and 'mater pie, this last, however, being made with green 'maters, which do not have the potency of red ones. Most of the out-of-town reunionists were skeptical of 'maters, until the Stay Morons assured them that they had been eating them for several years now without being p'izened, whereupon they, and everybody, tucked their napkins in their collars and did their duty.

The banquet was again scheduled to run three days, but nobody slept the first night, either making sounds or listening to them. The tent camp in the Field of Clover was a ruckus of amatory sounds, and the various residences of town were not exactly silent, either, except for Isaac Ingledew's. Isaac got out of bed, allowing as how he had better go and see what could be done to quieten things down. On the dark road to the Field of Clover, he was climbed eight times, so when he arrived at the tent camp he was grateful to accept the drink that somebody offered him and to rest awhile. Returning home, he was only climbed twice, so he figured that things were beginning to quieten down. Once asleep, in deep, deep sleep, he did not notice the noises going on through the night. In the morning it was absolutely silent, until the creak of the first wagonwheel as, one by one, the out-of-town reunionists began returning homeward. By noon the tent camp was abandoned, and the people of Stay More did not come out of their houses for all that day. There would be another G.A.R. reunion in five more years, but it would be scheduled at a time of year other than 'mater-pickin. And that year would be beyond the Decade of Light.

The Decade of Light, like most decades, lasted only ten years. And then it was over. The barrels of whale oil went dry, were empty.

The Second Spell of Darkness was ushered in. By daylight, people sat on their porches watching the road for the reappearance of Eli Willard. By night, untired, they went to bed and lay awake with insomnia. The chamberpots were hauled out from under the beds and dusted off, and a new generation of children was warned that the pots would stick to their fingers if they emptied them into a path. Realizing their insomnia was hopeless, the people sat up in the dark, telling to one another terrifying ghost stories, which did nothing for their insomnia but gave them something to do in the dark. Women and children were more suggestible, and both more susceptible to, and addicted to, the shivers brought on by these tales of "boogers" and "haints." One enterprising group of women, in an effort to kick the habit, attempted to have a quilting bee in the dark, but the product, which somebody referred to as a "crazy quilt," was a source of mirth to everybody else. The men tried to whittle in the dark, and a number of fingers were lost before this practice was abandoned. When all the ghost stories that everybody knew had been told and retold several times, the more imaginative (and more insomniac) Stay Morons began to create new stories, fantastic tales that stretched credulity beyond bounds. But having nothing else to do, the people began to believe these stories, and the Second Period of Darkness that followed the Decade of Light was not real, that is, it was mostly fictitious or illusory, all in the mind. Isaac Ingledew sobered up, because now that it was dark again Salina was climbing him all the time, every time she caught him standing, and sometimes even when he was sitting, but, being sober, he believed that he was only imagining it, that it was not real. The world was full-sized again for him, nothing was halved, but the full-sized world was dark and fanciful.

In time, among all the other dark chimeras and phantasms that were conceived in this world, there appeared the unmistakable specter of Eli Willard, driving another large wagon laden with barrels. He was older, and his trip around the world had broadened him about the middle, but, no doubt about it, he was Eli Willard. The barrels he had this time, he said, contained a fuel which did not smell fishy. It smelled powerful strong, all right, but it did not smell fishy. It was made from coal, a kind of rock, a pitch black rock deep in the earth. It was called kerosine, he said. There were grown people in Stay More who had been too young during Eli Willard's previous visit to remember him, although they had heard his name many times, but this feller trying to hoax them into believing that oil could be squeezed out of a rock could not possibly be Eli Willard, but an imposter. Everybody knows that rocks are the driest things that are. No, whale oil was good enough for them, any time. But this person pretending to be Eli Willard claimed that all the whales had been killed; there was no more whale oil. Nothing but kerosine. The Stay Morons, especially the younger ones, were suspicious of him. The sun went down, darkness fell, Eli Willard lighted one of his kerosine lamps as a demonstration. His patience was ebbing. "Take it or leave it," he said. So they left it. Whether or not they believed that oil could be squeezed out of a black rock, they equated such an artificial product with PROG RESS, and wanted none of it.

PROG RESS is always at the expense of pain and sacrifice and expense, and even if the Stay Morons did not know of the men who had toiled and died to mine the coal and make the oil, they guessed rightly that kerosine is the product of pain and sacrifice and expense. Darkness might tend to obscure and even confuse the world, but in darkness there was little pain or sacrifice or expense. Eli Willard sold not a drop of kerosine in the Ozarks, not that year anyway, and lost his shirt. Now, at Stay More, he was more dispirited than he had been years earlier when he had failed to sell raincoats and umbrellas during the drought. He turned off his demonstration lamp and sat with his head in his hands in the darkness. He hoped somebody would offer him a bed for the night, but nobody did, because with their insomnia they no longer went to bed but stayed up telling wild and fanciful stories.

Eli Willard listened to these stories, and was amazed. He had thought he understood the Ozark mind and heart as well as any outsider could, but these stories dumbfounded him. They were either incredibly fabulous or impossibly inconceivable. At any rate, he was captivated, so that when daylight came and the people stopped telling stories and went to work, he decided to stay for another night to hear more stories. But throughout the long day, with nothing to do because nobody was buying kerosine, he felt a growing ennui that left him utterly weary and miserable by late afternoon. Salina Ingledew found him in this condition and asked what was ailing him. He replied simply, "I'm bored."

Now, to any Stay Moron, any Ozarker, the word "bored" had nothing to do with boredom, but meant humiliated or chagrined. Salina spread the word to her neighbors, and everyone assumed that Eli Willard was humiliated because of his failure to sell kerosine, but this did not change their attitude toward purchasing coal oil. Had they known what he really meant by being "bored," they would have been puzzled, for at that time nobody in the Ozarks had ever been bored in the sense that Eli Willard meant. "Boredom" was a word, and an emotion, like "nostalgia," that had to be learned and acquired, and fortunately Eli Willard's boredom was not yet contagious, although he was severely afflicted with it. Anyone who has contracted acute boredom knows that it doesn't easily go away; hence, when the people began telling their stories again after darkness, Eli Willard listened to them but was no longer amazed. He was bored. What had seemed fabulous and fanciful in the stories now struck him merely as long-windedness. What had seemed clever and imaginative now seemed only silly. In the middle of an exceptionally long and silly story, he left town, using his kerosine lamps to light his way.

Both the post office and the school remained closed during the Second Spell of Darkness, but nobody seemed to miss either one of them. Most of what came through the post office had been what we would today refer to as "junk mail" and it was a relief not to get any. As for the school, the people began to realize that Jacob Ingledew had had a good reason for excluding reading and writing from his old academy. The more one read or wrote, the less one talked. At any rate, Boone Harrison the schoolmaster returned home to the county and town he was named after, and the schoolhouse was converted, as we shall soon see, to other purposes. When everybody told, or had heard, every possible tale and fiction that could be told or heard, and the most inventive of the yarn spinners had exhausted their imaginations, the Stay Morons turned for diversion to the singing of songs. Modern folklorists have tabulated and recorded 2,349 distinct "folk songs" heard in the Ozarks, all but 847 of which have been traced to ancient England, Scotland, Wales, or Ireland; 176 of the latter were invented and composed in Stay More at one time or another, but all 2,349 of the songs were known by heart to one or more Stay Morons, so the dark and starless nights were filled with song, and Isaac Ingledew would furnish accompaniment with his fiddle, at least after the children had gone to bed.

Song is poetry, of a kind, and the night is the most poetic of times, so the people of Stay More were no longer oppressed by the darkness, and most all of them were able to sleep again after a night of singing. Most all of them, that is, except Isaac Ingledew, who had discovered during his months of insomnia that sleep is an extravagant and useless pastime, and who never slept again, to the end of his days. We do not know, and can scarcely imagine, how he passed the many hours of life that others give over to slumber, but he was never idle, except when Salina was climbing him, which she continued to do, every chance she got, until…. But that is another story, another chapter, another edifice.

Chapter nine

I t was built as a schoolhouse, and so it remained during the Decade of Light, Boone Harrison holding sway as literacy-giver to the young and old of Stay More, many of whom would walk three or four miles in all kinds of weather just to "git a little schoolin." The schoolhouse was both a house of learning and the community center. Its bigeminality (we have hinted unsubtly and often that architectural bigeminality is sexual) was definitely and overtly sexist: the left door was for females, the right door for males, without exception (although an occasional "tomboy" among the girls would boldly use the right door...but no boy ever used the left door, because there was never the equivalent of a "queen," "nancy," "molly," or "betty" anywhere in the Ozarks). Since both doors led to the same one-room interior, we may assume that the reason for two of them was to facilitate egress at recess, lunch and dismissal, which, when indicated by Boone Harrison, cleared the room in 3.6 seconds. Any door, of course, is for both entering and leaving. Some doors are more pleasurable to enter, while others are more pleasurable to exit, but in any case one must usually always enter before exiting. The study of architecture is a fine thing.

Boone Harrison never discussed the doors with his pupils; tacitly they understood what the doors were for, and which to use, according to sex. The signal to enter was the ringing of the bell, housed in the small cupola atop the ridgepole; the signal to exit was Boone Harrison sitting down. When he sat down, he would take out his pocketknife and whittle goose-feathers into quill pens for his pupils to write with. He manufactured his own ink from the "ink balls" that grow on oak trees, boiling them in a little water and setting the liquid with copperas. The pupils always licked their pens as an aid to concentration before commencing to write, and this caused their lips to turn the blue-green color of the ink. It was easy to distinguish the literate from the illiterate Stay Morons: the latter did not have blue-green lips. During the Decade of Light, there arose almost a caste system based upon lip color, with those of deep blue-green lips at the upper caste, and those with natural lips at the bottom. It was possible to cross caste lines by kissing, and kissing became very popular, until in time the color of one's lips was meaningless, and the caste system fell apart, and the Decade of Light came to an end, and Boone Harrison sat down for the last time, then stood up and went home to the county and town he was named after, and those who could read and write forgot how.

The schoolhouse was empty during the first years of the Second Spell of Darkness. Vandals broke its windows one by one, and some-one stole the picture of George Washington that was its sole interior decoration. The pages of the McGuffey's Readers, Ray's Arithmetics and the Blue Back Spellers were employed as "asswipes" until they were used up. Bats and owls roosted in the ceiling of the schoolhouse, and were nocturnal. Everything was nocturnal. It was dark and often starless and even the moon was missing as often as not. Because all women are beautiful in the dark, all the girls and women of Stay More were ravishing, and were ravished. And because the darkness makes one invisible to one's enemies, nobody had any enemies. It was a dark and peaceful and licentious time.

Then, one day (or night), for the first time since the coming of the "saddlebag preacher" who had pestered Noah Ingledew because of his treehouse and had been ridden out of town on a rail, an itinerant evangelist showed up in town. He discovered the schoolhouse empty and unused, and decided to convert it to a church. The hour of his first service was norated around the village, but when the hour came nobody showed up, except old Elijah Duckworth, who took a seat on the front bench, and waited. The preacher waited too, and when nobody else showed up, he asked Lige if he thought he should go ahead with the service. "Wal, Reverend," Lige observed, "if I put some hay in the wagon and take it down to the pasture to feed the cows and only one cow shows up, I feed her." So the preacher went ahead and gave his service, with a rousing full-length sermon. Afterwards he asked Lige what he had thought of it. "Wal, Reverend, I'll tell ye," said Lige. "If I put some hay in the wagon and go down to the pasture to feed the cows and only one cow shows up, I don't give her the whole damn load."

Later Lige spread word to the other Stay Morons that the preacher was a "Presbyterian." The old-timers had a vague memory of the saddlebag preacher of Noah's time, and they had vague associations of unpleasantness with him. The new-timers had never heard of a preacher, and this "Presbyterian" seemed very suspicious. So they stayed away from his services. Failing to get any further audiences, he began pastoring them individually, door to door. Presbyterians, he explained to them, were strong believers in predestination, but the Stay Morons couldn't understand predestination any better than Presbyterianism. Trying to simplify it, the minister would shout, "What is to be, will be!" "Why, shore," his listeners were apt to respond, "any durn fool knows that."

The Presbyterian began to claim that, as evidence of his message, the world was predestined to be plunged into darkness during the daylight on a certain day soon approaching. Nobody believed him; nobody wanted to believe him, because the world was dark enough already. But on the day appointed (which the Presbyterian had previously learned about from astronomers in the East) there occurred a total eclipse of the sun which darkened the earth for a while, long enough for the preacher to convert everybody except the Ingledews to Presbyterianism. Thereafter he managed to fill the schoolhouse (now churchhouse) every Sunday morning, until one day, when another preacher, who called himself a "Methodist," came into the church-house and challenged the Presbyterian to a debate on the subject of predestination, which the Methodist was against. The debate lasted for three days, then the Methodist challenged the Presbyterian to prove predestination, which the Presbyterian could not do, there being no other eclipses scheduled for the immediate future. The congregation was allowed to put the matter to a vote, and since the majority of them liked the idea of free salvation better than predestination, they gave the pastorate to the Methodist, who conducted services for some time thereafter, until the day another preacher, calling himself a "Baptist," came and challenged the Methodist to a debate over the issue of baptism by sprinkling or immersion.

Most Stay Morons readily agreed that immersion is certainly a lot more fun and probably cleaner than sprinkling, and they became Baptists in denomination until a "Campbellite" minister appeared and argued against denominationalism, pointing out that there is nothing in the Bible authorizing anybody to call themselves Baptists, Methodists, Presbyterians or anything else. If, he said, there had to be a name over the door of the church, then let it be simply "Church of Christ." This made eminent sense to everybody, and they dismissed the Baptist preacher and installed the Campbellite, but he was not a very interesting, let alone exciting, personality. The Dinsmores, who gave him a place to sleep his first Saturday in town, said he wouldn't eat his supper. They said he had remarked, "You folks sure do set a good table, but I don't never eat much when I'm a-fixin to give a sarmon." Then on Sunday morning the Dinsmores set out a fine breakfast of ham and eggs, but the preacher wouldn't touch it. "Earthly food seems to hinder a true feast of the spirit," he said. "My finest sarmons has all been preached on a empty stomach." So he had just one cup of coffee and went off to the churchhouse. After listening to his sermon, one of the Dinsmores remarked, "Why, that there preacher might just as well have et."

The Campbellite was supplanted by a colorful preacher of the "Holiness" faith, who amazed the Stay Morons by handling poison-ous snakes without being bitten and running his hand through fire without being burned. For several months the Stay More church was a Holiness church, until the novelty of the snakes and fire wore off. Subsequently, other ministers converted the church to Assembly of God, Gospel Tabernacle, Seventh-Day Adventist and Pentecostal. One Sunday, even a Roman Catholic priest wandered into Stay More and was permitted to celebrate a mass at the church, but afterwards the stares that he received from the Stay Morons unnerved him, and he wandered on out of town. Stay More had run the gamut of gentile religions without deciding upon any one of them.

Then Eli Willard returned. His hair was nearly all white now, and he was wearing a different kind of suit. He had no whale oil or kerosine; he had nothing. Each person who saw him noticed this, and asked him, "What're ye sellin this time?" but Eli Willard just smiled. He tethered his horse to a post at Isaac's mill, then sat in a chair on the porch. Isaac, being taciturn, didn't ask him any questions. After most of the population of Stay More had assembled around the porch, Eli Willard stood up and cleared his throat and said, "Friends and Good People. I hawk no goods, vend no wares. A higher calling brings me to you, and I offer you free of charge this wonderful message. Others will tell you that God is divided into three: the Father, the Son, and the Holy Ghost. I do not hold with that. I believe that there is, at most, one God. Hence I am now pleased to call myself a Unitarian. Unitarians do not believe in heaven or hell, except in the spirit, in the *now* rather than the hereafter. Unitarians believe—"

He was interrupted and drowned out by a chorus of protests. *No heaven? No hell?* Fiddle-faddle! If there is no hereafter, why live? If there had been one thing that all the other preachers had agreed upon, it was that we must conduct our lives in such a way as to be rewarded after death and avoid punishment in the hereafter. The men began shaking their fists at Eli Willard, the women spat at him, and the younger people began throwing rocks at him. He had to duck inside the mill for protection. He stayed there until everyone had left, except Isaac. He said to Isaac, in parting, "Well, I tried." Isaac, who did not believe in the hereafter but had no use for Unitarianism either, did not comment.

None of the Ingledew males were ever converted to any religion, perhaps a heritage from Jacob, who had originally left Tennessee because, as he had told Fanshaw, "the preachers was so thick a feller couldn't say 'heck' without gittin a sermon fer it." Isaac, if anything, was even less of a believer than his father had been, and his sons would be less than he, and their sons less than they, and so on, until the last Ingledew, who…but he is the last chapter, and we are only halfway there. What little light there was during the Second Spell of Darkness came in the form of lightning; Isaac would shake his fist at the lightning and silently dare God to strike him down. God never did. God killed many an animal with lightning, and blasted many a tree, and from time to time destroyed a human being or two, but God never hit Isaac.

Isaac's wife Salina "caught religion" when the Presbyterian produced an eclipse of the sun, and although she was most partial to the Baptist, she attended all the church services in Stay More, and Isaac sometimes accompanied her out of curiosity, which is the bottom rung on the ladder of motives for going to church, the other rungs being, in ascending hierarchy: 2, being too timid to refuse, 3, a sense of duty, 4, a desire to mingle with others, 5, a desire to learn the means of salvation, 6, a desire to be saved, 7, lust for paradise in the hereafter, 8, schizophrenic need to need, 9, insanity, and 10, sainthood. There were very few Stay Morons who ascended to the top of this ladder. Isaac remained on the bottom rung, and Salina got about as far as the sixth. As far as anybody could tell, she never asked him what he thought of the sermons, or never asked him anything about religion, although she talked to him freely, for hours on end, expressing her own views and opinions. One of the preachers had gone so far as to hint that sexual intercourse, even between lawfully wed husband and wife, was not in the best interests of attaining heaven, and once again Salina ceased climbing Isaac, even though it was dark and no one could see them, and once again Isaac turned to strong beverages for solace.

Nearly all the preachers, in particular the Methodist, abhorred alcohol, and preached frequently against it, and consequently Seth Chism had "caught religion" and given up the making of his superior sour mash, so Isaac was required to patronize Caleb Duckworth's inferior brand of rotgut. This stuff was just as capable of reducing the world to half its size, but it also reduced time to half its length, which was terribly confusing to Isaac, who in compensation for it began to double everything: each day was forty-eight hours in length, or rather Monday came twice a week, and the Second Tuesday of the Month was also the Third; spring and summer came twice a year, and so did autumn, which wasn't so bad, but two winters in one year was awful.

Actually, the Year that Winter Came Twice was perceived not alone by Isaac but also by everyone in Stay More. It was the coldest and longest winter that anyone had ever known. Isaac could have warned them of its coming, because he knew that the first frost always occurred six weeks after the first chirp of a katydid, and he had heard the first katydid's chirp twelve weeks before, which, even by his double reckoning, meant that a heavy frost was coming any minute now, but, being taciturn, he didn't warn anybody, and sure enough the terrible winter came and caught them by surprise. All the birds flew south, but a large flock of mallards flying over was caught in freak currents of frozen air, and, frozen solid as stones, plummeted to the earth, breaking through roofs all over Stay More, or landing upon a random farm animal, dog, or cat, who were killed. The people gathered up all the frozen ducks and stacked them in a pile, where they remained frozen throughout the winter. Whenever anybody had a hankering for duckmeat, they would just grab one off the pile and throw it into the fire.

But it was so cold that winter that keeping the fires going night and day was a major effort. The youngsters were required to keep the fires going at night, and, as one of the survivors of that winter expressed it to me in his old age, "We had to put wood on the fire all night with one hand, and sleep with the other!" This might be an exaggeration, but we may imagine what he meant. In order to obtain enough wood for the fires, the Stay Morons practically denuded the forests during the course of the Winter that Came Twice, cutting all the second-growth timber that had started growing after the great fire which had occurred during the great drought. Before Christmas, it began to snow heavily in Stay More; snow rarely fell in the Ozarks, and never before Christmas, but now there were blizzards. By Christmas, as my informant quoted above expressed it, "the snow was so all-fired deep we had to shit standing up!" Again he might be exaggerating, but we may picture the practice.

The barns of that era were rather ramshackle, and offered little protection to the livestock, who froze; chickens saved themselves by roosting on the chimney shoulders and absorbing some warmth from the stones. The leather belts and pulleys in Isaac's mill would not run because they were frozen, and even if he thawed them out he couldn't make a fire hot enough to boil the frozen water in his boiler. It was too blamed cold to work in the mill anyway, and his helpers and fireman had already quit on him, so halfway through the winter, or rather between the two winters that came that year, he quit and went home to sit by the fire, which was what everybody else was already doing. With not even the chore of milking to do, since the cows were frozen, there was no work for anybody except women, except chopping wood for the fires. Everybody had runny noses, and some people had runny eyes, and some coughed badly, and several developed chest complaints, and a few, despite herbal remedies, died, but could not be buried until the ground thawed in the spring, so were left frozen in Isaac's unused mill. Isaac's family was more fortunate than most; the son John had a bad cough, but only Salina was sick enough to go to bed, and the girls Perlina and Drussie were old enough to assume their mother's duties.

Although, architecturally speaking, the houses of that time were built well, the fireplaces were not of optimum efficiency: most of the heat went up the chimney. And simply sitting beside the fire was not sufficient to keep warm on the coldest days of that winter. But there was nothing else to do, and consequently the Stay Morons discovered by accident that condition which we call boredom, which had been unknown to them before. Since the word "bored" meant "humiliated" to them, they would have a problem finding a name for their condition. It was Denton Ingledew, Isaac's oldest boy, who first identified and attempted to name the condition. He was past marryin' age, and so was the second oldest boy, Monroe, but they, like so many Ingledews, were too shy to approach women with romance or even matrimony in mind, so they still lived at home in Isaac's dogtrot house. One day in the coldest part of the winter, all the Ingledews of Isaac's household were crowded together around the fire, trying to keep warm. They had been sitting there for five hours, not moving much except to throw another log on the fire. Denton yawned, and said, "I feel so kinda like…" but no word would come to him. He could not name his condition. Half an hour later Monroe yawned too, and said, "Yeah, I know what ye mean." But he couldn't name it either. Some time later, John, the third boy, yawned, and remarked, "Me, too," but was unable to expand upon that. After a while, Willis, the last son, remarked, "Same here," but he too was at a loss for names.

The condition, whatever it was, had affected the girls too by this time; although they weren't yawning, tears were trickling slowly down their cheeks. "I've got the wearies," remarked Perlina, and Drussie, some time later, put in, "It's jist so teejus," but neither of these words would quite do. After further reflection, Denton observed of his condition, "I aint interested in a damn thing. It's sorter like after I had the frakes." Monroe, who had also had the frakes, said, "Yeah, that's sorter it," and John, veteran of the frakes too, added, "I reckon." The girls, who like all females had not had the frakes, did not quite understand. Isaac, their father, did not know what his children were talking about, because he wasn't bored and never would be. A man who can stay awake all night long without ever going to sleep for the rest of his life is the least likely person to get bored. Willis, who had also had the frakes, remarked, "Naw, when a feller's a-gittin over the frakes, he jist don't give a damn about nothin, but this here that we'uns have caught, it's somethin else. I feel like I'd *like* to give a damn about somethin, but there jist aint nothin around right at the moment to latch onto." "Yeah," his sisters chimed in. "That's more like it." Some time later, Denton observed, "But we still aint got a word fer it." As the hours drifted by, one or the other of them would make a suggestion. Again Perlina offered "wearies." They debated it, concluding it wasn't quite right. "Teejusments," suggested Drussie. "Mopes," offered Willis. "Ho-hums," suggested John. Monroe came up with "timesick." They liked that one, but thought it was kind of highfallutin.

Finally Denton snapped his fingers and said, "sour hours." The way he pronounced it was almost identical to the way they pronounce "sorrows," which means not grief but regrets, and the resemblance, with the suggestion that sour hours produce sorrows, won the votes of his brothers and sisters. They were so excited over finding a word for their condition that their condition no longer obtained, and they couldn't wait to spread the word through the village, which they promptly did, finding dozens of people sitting beside their fireplaces afflicted with the sourhours. As soon as they were told this new word for their condition, they rapidly grew interested in it, and before long nobody had the sourhours anymore, at least not for another hour or two. Pronunciation of the noun, sourhour, and of the passive verb, sourhoured, if vociferous enough, also resembles the barking of a certain breed of dog, and for the next hour or two everybody in Stay More went around barking at one another, and their dogs tilted their heads to one side and gave their masters puzzled looks. But after an hour or two, the people grew sourhoured of barking at one another, and gave it up, and resumed passing the sour hours by the fire, day after day, shivering with cold, yawning, rubbing their arms, thinking no thoughts, none at all.

They were discovered there thus, late in the winter, by the first preacher to come to Stay More since the winter began. Most preachers seemed to have such a fondness for hellfire that cold weather was abominable to them, and not one had been seen since summer, until this one came. This one was a big man, almost as tall as Isaac Ingledew, and he was dressed up in furs, bearskins and coonskins and beaver skins, which made him look even bigger, positively mammoth, and the horse he was riding on was the biggest horse anyone had ever seen, big enough to support not only the mammoth preacher but also the girl, or young woman, riding behind him, also dressed all over in animal skins. The very sight of this couple and their horse was enough to banish the sourhours for the rest of the day. Beneath the preacher's otterskin hat protruded bushy tufts of red hair surrounding a pink freckled face reddened by the cold, a large red mustache dripping with icicles: it was a surpassingly gentle face, not jolly, but capable of compassion and animation. He seemed to be close to forty, but not beyond it, while his companion was only a teenager. Her hair was the same color as his, which made people surmise that she was his daughter. He went from door to door in the village, speaking in a soft, almost inaudible voice, inviting everyone to join him at the meeting house on the following morning, which was Sunday. He and the girl, or young woman, were given beds for the night at the Dinsmores, who had boarded the unhungry Campbellite, and they noted that he, in contrast to the former, had a prodigious appetite. They offered him a second helping, and then a third, a fourth, and a fifth; they believed he would have accepted a sixth, if they had offered it, which they could not. His name, they learned, was Long Jack Stapleton. *Brother* Long Jack Stapleton, he said, although nobody ever learned which denomination, if any, he belonged to. No, the young woman was not his daughter; she was his "baby sister," name of Sirena.

After supper the Dinsmores were treated to a preview of his powers of narration, when he told them the story of Samson and Delilah, creating such powerful word pictures that his audience could actually "see" the whole dramatic love story unfolding before their eyes. If the modern mobile home may be traced back to Viridiana Boatright's "cat wagon," if the monthly luncheon of Lions and Rotarians may be traced to Jacob and Noah Ingledew's ceremony of the clock on the Second Tuesday of the Month, if the oral tradition may be traced to Jacob's entertaining Lizzie Swain and her large brood with stories about Indians, then surely it would be no exaggeration to trace the motion picture, and by extension television, to Brother Long Jack Stapleton. Before his service on Sunday morning, the Dinsmores had spread word of his powers throughout the village, and all the men and boys crowded through the right door and all the women and girls through the left door, and the meeting house was packed to the rafters, so that body heat alone was sufficient to warm the room, which had been below freezing moments earlier. Brother Stapleton mounted the pulpit; without all his furs he did not look quite so imposing, but still he was the most striking figure ever to stand on that platform. He surveyed the "amen corner," where the most prominent men of the church were sitting, spotted his host Clyde Dinsmore among them, and asked, "Brother Dinsmore, 'sposin ye could lead us sing a hymn or two?"

Brother Dinsmore rose from his bench, shifted his cud of

tobacco from one cheek to the other, and faced the congregation. "Brethern and sistern, let's us sing one of them old'uns that we'uns all know—'Warshed in the Blood.'" Then he cleared his throat loudly and gave out the key: "DO MI SOL DO! DO SOL MI DO!" and began swinging his arms vigorously as every voice sang at its top… every voice, that is, except Brother Long Jack Stapleton's. Maybe he didn't know the words. Then Brother Dinsmore requested that they sing "Lead, Kindly Light," followed by "Abide with Me." After that, Brother Stapleton asked for a volunteer to lead them in prayer, and Seth Chism stood up and thanked God for sending them a parson in the coldest winter ever known to man and beast, and asked God to grant the parson power to banish their sourhours and save their souls, in the Name of Jesus Christ, Amen. Then he sat down and Brother Stapleton began his sermon.

"Brethering and sistering," he addressed them in his gentle voice that could barely be heard in the back of the room, "I take as my text this mornin the eleventh and twelfth verses of the second chapter of Solomon's song, 'For lo, the winter is past, the snow is over and gone, the flowers appear on the earth; the time of the singin of birds is come, and the voice of the turtle is heared in our land.'"

"Hold on, Parson!" said Brother Chism, rising to his feet. "Turtles aint got no voices!"

"It means turtle*dove*," Brother Stapleton explained, and described one, and held out his hand, and a real, or seemingly real turtledove flew down and alighted upon his hand, and everyone's mouth gaped open…everyone's but his sister Sirena, who had seen him do this trick many times before. Then the preacher's gentle voice lifted and quickened, and he pounded his Bible and said, "That's what it says here, friends, '*For lo*,' it says, 'the winter is *past*,' it says, 'the snow is *over and gone*,' it says!" And the rhythms of his voice lulled his audience, hypnotized them, their eyes glazed over as he painted pictures of springtime and bloom and the renewal of the verdant earth.

The chief difference between Brother Stapleton's magic and that of the motion picture and television is that while the latter are only *visual*, the former was not only visual but also tactile, olfactory, and gustatory. His audience could feel the spring breeze blowing through their hair, smell the blossom of dogwood, taste the first-harvested sprout of sparrowgrass. For the length of his sermon, which lasted two and one-half hours, the winter actually was over and gone. The main body of his sermon he devoted to the story of Solomon, dwelling upon the legendary love between the wise King and the Dark Girl of the Song. He did not use the word "love," which was an embarrassment, but everybody knew exactly what he was talking about, and everybody could see vividly depicted on the "screen" of the mind the exact lineaments of the dazzling Solomon in all his glory and the exquisite exotic beauty of the girl, and they could see as clearly as if they were there the nut orchards and fruit orchards and shepherds' tents where the lovers met. We may appreciate the suitability of Stapleton's selection of the subject matter, for Solomon himself (or whoever wrote his Song) was a master of description who gave us a vivid image of his beloved, step by step from her eyes to her toes. Brother Stapleton's "projection" or "showing" or "screening" concluded after two-and-a-half hours with the words, "And so, my friends, we may think that God keers fer each of us jist like King Solomon keered fer that purty gal, and we air comforted by it." Then he ceased.

His audience, like an audience at a movie theater when the house lights come on after a gripping film, sat motionless and unseeing for several minutes. Then most of them smiled and looked very entertained and satisfied, but a few of them looked perplexed, and one of these, Seth Chism, rose and asked, "Aint there to be no call to the mourner's bench?"

Brother Stapleton stared for a moment at that front bench, empty, reserved for sinners seeking salvation. He shook his head.

Clyde Dinsmore rose and asked, "Aint there to be no communion? We done brung the grape juice and sody crackers."

Brother Stapleton replied, "No, Brother Dinsmore, but mightn't ye lead us in the closin prayer?"

Brother Dinsmore made a short prayer, thanking God for the "show" and apologizing to Him for the absence of the call for sinners and communion, in Jesus' Name, Amen. Everybody had their heads bowed, except the male Ingledews, who noticed that Brother Stapleton crossed his fingers at the moment Jesus' name was invoked.

Then the service was over.

Salina Ingledew invited Brother Stapleton and his sister Sirena to Sunday dinner, and everybody went home, marveling to one another about how real that "show" had been, everybody, that is, except the deacons of the "amen corner," Brothers Chism, Dinsmore, Plowright, Coe and Whitter, who remained behind in the meeting house to discuss their new minister and his unorthodox ways of conducting a service. They granted that he sure spoke a right powerful sermon, they even admitted that they had seen those images plain as day, but some of those images seemed a mite too bold; for instance, in that part toward the end, what was the King and that girlfriend of his doing out there in that orchard as night was coming on? The deacons might be mistaken, but it sure looked to them like that King and his girlfriend were actually fornicating! Right there in full view of everybody, even the women and children. The rest of the show was all right, real pretty in fact, but that part was scandalous! The deacons agreed that they should speak with Brother Stapleton, and find out if the King and his girlfriend were really doing what it looked like they were doing, and, if so, how come Brother Stapleton allowed it to be shown right there in front of the women and children?

Meanwhile, the new minister was enjoying himself at the Ingledew's table, where he had six helpings of spit-roasted mallard with all the trimmings. Salina and her daughters held Brother Stapleton in absolute awe, not alone for his fabulous sermon but also for his appetite. It was the custom, then and for many years afterward, for the women and girls to wait until the men and boys had finished eating before serving themselves, but Salina and her daughters couldn't help hanging around the table and watching Brother Stapleton eat. Sirena Stapleton, who usually tried *not* watching her brother eat, hung around too, because she was falling in love with all four of the Ingledew brothers. At the table, Brother Stapleton tried to engage Isaac in conversation, but quickly discovered that Isaac was taciturn, so he talked instead with the "boys" (even though the boys were as grown as they would ever be, Ingledew brothers would always be known as "the boys," even in their old age). The boys did not hold Brother Stapleton in such awe as their mother and sisters did, but still they sure had enjoyed watching that show, they said, and hoped he would put on some more shows for them to watch. He replied that he wasn't in any great hurry to move on. Denton Ingledew, the oldest brother, was brave enough to ask, "How come, durin the prayer, you crossed yore fingers at the end?"

Brother Stapleton choked on a bite of mallard wing, but composed himself and eyed Denton coolly. "How'd ye know I had my fingers crossed?"

"I was watchin," Denton declared. He looked to his brothers, who nodded in affirmation. "We'uns all saw ye."

"Why weren't yore haids bowed durin the prayer?" Brother Stapleton asked.

"We don't bow our haids," Denton said. "Aint ary one of us believes in God, 'ceptin Maw and them gals."

"Too bad," said Brother Stapleton. "How kin ye believe in Jesus iffen ye don't believe in God?"

"I reckon we'uns don't believe in Him neither," Denton said.

"Me neither," said Brother Stapleton. "Which is why I crossed my fingers when His name was taken."

Salina Ingledew was unable to restrain herself from rushing this news to the other ladies of Stay More, and her daughters passed it on to their friends, and soon the talk of the town was about the heterodox beliefs of Brother Stapleton. The deacons of the meeting house decided that he must be a Jew and ought to be hanged or better yet burned. Meanwhile, Sirena Stapleton was trying unsuccessfully to draw the attention of the four Ingledew brothers; not one of them would even look at her. Their sister Perlina took her aside and explained, "It aint no use. Ingledews is always shy toward gals."

Salina Ingledew felt a little uncomfortable having in her house a minister who did not believe in Jesus, but since it was always customary to urge the parting guest to remain, when Salina said to Brother Stapleton, "Stay more. Stay and eat you some supper with us," he replied, "Why, thank you," and stayed to eat six helpings of scrambled eggs. Again, after supper, Salina was obliged to say, "Stay more. Better jist spend the night with us," and Brother Stapleton replied, "Why, thank you." There weren't any spare beds, but Salina prepared a pallet on the floor of the boys' sleeping loft for him, and one on the floor of the girls' sleeping loft for his sister Sirena. In the middle of the night, Sirena, sleepless on the thin pallet, and very cold despite the heap of quilts covering her, and doubtless feeling frustrated over her failure to get any of the Ingledew boys to notice her, climbed down from the girls' loft and climbed up to the boys' loft, where the four boys were all sleeping in one bed. She managed to crowd in beside them without waking them, and was warmed, and slept, rising before dawn to return to her own pallet.

Brother Stapleton and his sister remained with the Ingledews thereafter, because it was unheard of for anybody not to say "Stay more," and Salina went on saying it. Each night Sirena crept into bed with the Ingledew boys without waking them; each day they went on ignoring her existence. Although the deacons were talking about burning Brother Stapleton, everybody else was impatient to view another of his movies, and their impatience made their sourhours ever sourer, so that in the end they prevailed, and prevailed upon Brother Stapleton the following Sabbath to give them another picture show. This time he told them the passionate and touching story of the prophet Hosea and his marriage to the prostitute Gomer, whom he continued to love despite her infidelities, and whom he sold into bondage and then redeemed from bondage and carried away to the desert to remove her from temptation and have her for his own. The deacons were convinced that there was one scene toward the end, where Hosea and Gomer were lying together behind a sand dune in the desert, when the intercourse was so explicit you could even see their genitals, but the deacons were so enthralled that they did not protest, until the sermon was over and the rest of the congregation had departed, when they accosted Brother Stapleton, and one of the deacons, Seth Chism, said to him, "Pastor, was I jist imaginin things, or didn't that there Hosea actually commence to shaggin his wife in that part toward the end in the desert?"

"A man sees what he wants to see," Brother Stapleton replied.

"A man, yeah," Brother Chism said, "but what about all the womenfolk and childreng? It aint fitten to show things like that to their innocent eyes."

"No eyes is innocent," the minister replied.

Through the rest of that bitterly cold winter, the people of Stay More lived from one Sunday to the next, suffering intolerable sourhours in between, just to go to Brother Stapleton's cinema. He showed the romantic stories of Abraham and Sarah, of David and Bathsheba, of Jacob and Rachel, of Ruth and Boaz, even the incestuous story of Amnon and his half-sister Tamar. Each of the Ingledew brothers was aroused by these shows, and each of them had private daydreams of being able to do that with that pretty redhead Sirena, but each of them knew that it was impossible because they couldn't even get up the nerve to look at her. Sirena continued, unbeknownst, sleeping with them. One morning she awakened before daylight to discover that the brother next to her had a risen root, although he was still asleep and mildly snoring. She thought that was amazing: getting a serviceable dinger while sleeping. She also thought it was exciting. She lifted his nightshirt and her nightdress, and climbed aboard. He never woke. She wondered which one of the four brothers he was; she couldn't see a thing. She wondered what he would think if he woke. She wondered how vigorous she could be without waking him. She was very vigorous, and at the end she stuffed her fist into her mouth to stifle her sound. Before leaving the room she gave his shoulder a gentle shake and whispered into his ear, "Which one are you? What's your name?" "Nmpth," he responded. "What's your name?" she said again. "John," he said without ever fully waking.

Before the start of each of Brother Stapleton's shows, one of the deacons would request, "Show us a pitcher of heaven, Preacher!" or one of the other deacons would request, "Show us pitchers of hell!" but Brother Stapleton could not show them heaven or hell because he did not believe in them. He could, however, show them paradise, and he told them the exquisitely connubial story of Adam and Eve, depicting Eden as the setting for their dramatic romance and temptation and fall. The congregation viewed the enchanting scenery of Eden with delight, until one of them observed and exclaimed: "Why, it aint no different than Stay More in the middle of summer in a good year!"

All the others nodded their heads and chimed in with: "It's a fact!" "That's the Gospel truth!" "Sure thing!"

Brother Stapleton smiled and went on with the show. Adam came on the screen, naked as a jaybird, and all the women blushed and covered their eyes. Then Eve appeared, and she wasn't wearing a stitch either; some of the men whistled, panted or clapped. The deacons rose as one from the amen corner and stalked out of the meeting house, but most of them could later be seen peeking in the windows. When Adam and Eve looked at each other, they didn't seem to mind that they didn't have any clothes; in fact, they didn't seem to notice, and pretty soon the congregation took it for granted too, because although Adam and Eve were naked they weren't fooling around with each other or anything, they were just talking about the fruit that Eve wanted to eat, and then they were eating it, when all of a sudden they got embarrassed about not having clothes, so they made some skirts out of fig leaves, with which they made do, until God gave them some buckskins to wear. Adam and Eve never did sleep with one another as long as they were in the Garden, but as soon as they were driven out of Eden they began doing it all the time, usually behind bushes and large rocks, but eventually they were so desperate to couple that they didn't care whether they were seen or not, and they were doing it so often that all the women and children had to leave the meeting house, and even the men were finally forced to follow the women because of their excitation. One of the deacons took a lump of charcoal and scrawled a large "X" on the front of the meeting house, and the deacons decreed that the people could watch no more of those shows.

The Ingledews were somewhat relieved, not because they hadn't enjoyed watching the shows, but because Brother Stapleton and his sister had continued to lodge and dine at Isaac's and Salina's house, and the preacher had almost eaten them out of house and home. He had also, unbeknownst to them, been banishing the sourhours of Perlina and Drussie by giving the girls private screenings of some of his short subjects and previews of coming attractions, although these were all "decent," that is, presentable. Perlina and Drussie both loved him madly, and they had walked out of the Adam and Eve show not because they were offended but because all the other women and girls were walking out and they figured it was expected of them. In truth they had been fascinated, but couldn't admit it, even to each other. Each of them wanted to ask Brother Stapleton privately to show them the part they had missed after walking out, but neither of them could quite muster the nerve. Ingledew girls were never afflicted with man-shyness in the way that all Ingledews boys were afflicted with woman-shyness, but all the same there were limits to what a girl could ask a preacher to do.

And yet when they heard that the deacons had decreed there would be no more shows at the meeting house, they feared that Brother Stapleton would leave them for good and go somewhere else, and then the sourhours would come back again and bog them down forevermore. Perlina, at least, the older of the two sisters, would do anything to avoid that. So she washed her hair with sassafras-bark shampoo and drank a quart of tea made from butterfly weed, both of which are good for nerve, then she sought and found Brother Stapleton when he was alone and requested, "Show me the rest of that show."

"Where did you leave?" he wanted to know.

"The part where she'd done birthed Cain and they were fixin to make Abel."

"It gits awful free and fast, there," he warned her.

"I don't keer. I want to see it," she insisted.

Long Jack Stapleton threaded his projector and allowed Perlina to view a re-run of the end of the Adam and Eve story, when the amatory couple were giving themselves up to their urges with such frequency and force and noise that even their animals watched them with great curiosity. It was almost more than Perlina could bear, but she watched it all, to the end, and realized that unless this man would have her right then and there she would start howling like a heifer in heat. Yet when she embraced him he gently separated himself from her. "Fer the love of God!" she entreated, trying unsuccessfully to attach herself to him, "I'm burnin up!"

"I caint," he said ruefully. "I aint able."

"You're a man, aint ye?" she protested.

He shook his head. "Not exactly."

"Huh?" she said. "What does *that* mean?"

"I caint tell ye," he said, and took his leave of her.

But Perlina could not give up. The next time she saw Long Jack's sister, Sirena, she asked her why, or how, or where, her brother was not a man. Sirena blushed, and whispered into Perlina's ear the details of an "accident" that had befallen Long Jack in his young manhood, an accident related to his nickname, in a reverse sort of way. Perlina was saddened by this news, but also felt such a great wave of compassion for Long Jack, as well as a desire to keep him and his shows in Stay More, that she went to him and told him she wanted to marry him despite his "shortcoming." Her proposal moved him to tears. In the woods, the first bud of springtime opened, as the temperature climbed above freezing for the first time in months.

Meanwhile, in the kitchen of the Ingledew house, Sirena Stapleton walked boldly up to the table where the four brothers were sitting and boldly asked, "Which one of you is named John?" All four of them avoided her eyes, but the one named John managed to put his index finger on his Adam's apple.

"I gotta talk to you," she said to him.

"I caint," he said ruefully. "I aint able."

"You're a man, aint ye?" she protested.

"That's why I caint," he observed.

She grabbed his arm and pulled him to his feet and dragged him out of the kitchen and across the breezeway into the privacy of the other wing of the dogtrot, where she informed him, "I'm in the family way."

"Yeah, but you're leavin, aint ye?"

"I mean, I'm knocked up."

"Huh?"

"I'm with child," she said, patting her abdomen.

"Do tell? Wal, I'll lend my shotgun to yore brother, and he'll make the feller marry ye, if ye want."

"The feller was you."

"*Huh*? Why, I never!"

She explained. John was blushing furiously, and as she described what had transpired, he nearly burst with embarrassment. How could she say such things to him? Worse, how could a girl have done such a thing to him? It sure was a good thing he had been asleep, or else he would have been powerfully mortified. He daydreamed all the time about laying with this pretty redhead Sirena, but the thought that he had actually done it, or that she had done it to him without his knowing it, made him want to go and dig a deep hole and jump in it and cover himself up. He wished she would hush up. He wished she would let him alone and not even look at him again, but he knew that a feller has to live up to his responsibilities, and if he was the baby's father then he would just have to *be* the baby's father.

It was a double wedding. Brother Stapleton granted his sister's hand in marriage to John Ingledew, then he asked Isaac Ingledew for Perlina's hand. Isaac, being taciturn, managed to nod. There being no ministers in Stay More other than himself, he officiated at his own nuptials and those of his sister and brother-in-law. The day of the wedding was full springtime; it would not be cold for another year. The weddings were duly attended by all the other Ingledews but no one else, because the deacons forbade it. The deacons were going to be in for a surprise.

Perlina never did tell a soul about her husband's shortcoming, which wasn't so short that she didn't conceive and bear a large family over the years. Since Long Jack Stapleton was now living his own love story, he didn't feel any need whatever to preach the love stories of the Bible, although he still had the power to speak word pictures more graphic than movies, and when he promised the deacons never to show any "undecent" pictures anymore they reluctantly let him use the meeting house again, and he began showing stories of the great battles in the Bible, scenes of bloodshed and gore, flashing swords and decapitation, torture and pillage and scourging and mutilation. He packed the people in, and even the deacons themselves returned to his services, where they sat at their select bench with their eyes glued to the images, and one or the other of them would urge on the action with "Praise the Lord!" and "Amen!" and "Gawd git 'em!" As summertime wiped out the last trace of the long bitter winter, people came from all over Newton County to see Brother Stapleton's shows; the meeting house wouldn't hold them all, so he had to give matinées in the afternoon and candlelit productions at night. He even began the practice of passing a plate for free will offering, and gleaned enough coins to support Perlina and himself in fairly good style.

They lived happily ever after.

Chapter ten

The first general merchandise store in Stay More was the work and the business of Isaac's younger brother, Christopher Columbus "Lum" Ingledew. We have caught only glimpses of him—his refusing to go with his mother to Little Rock, his helping Isaac build the mill and then handling the concession during the ceremony of the engine-firing, his serving as postmaster during the Decade of Light—he has not been conspicuous, perhaps because he was not marked with any specific characteristic comparable to Isaac's taciturnity; Lum was not very talkative, but neither was he reticent: he said what had to be said, and did what had to be done, and one thing that had to be done was to build and operate a general merchandise store, because the population of Stay More was exploding. During the Second Spell of Darkness, fondness for 'maters and the concealing dark were a potent combination of factors fostering conception. Old Jacob Ingledew decreed that no more settlers would be allowed to immigrate into Stay More because it was so crowded already, and his decree remained the law, but even without further immigration the population went on exploding. A high incidence of inbreeding naturally resulted in the birth of a more than common number of defectives, usually idiots.

The people of Stay More did not know that the origin of the word *idiot*, pronounced "idjit" or "eejit," is the Greek *idios*, meaning private. The idiots of Stay More were not private; they were very public; they were allowed to come and go as they pleased.

Lum Ingledew's general merchandise store was erected on the main road, near the mill, in front of the mill (shown in the rear of our illustration), but even after he finished it the people continued to use the mill as their communal gathering place, out of habit and out of respect for Isaac, although the porch and yard of the mill were now so crowded that a person couldn't sit down. So, because idiots usually prefer to sit, or squat, or kneel, or recline in various postures, and because there was no room for them at the mill, they began to use the porch of Lum's store. Our illustration does not show them there, but that is where they were. Lum didn't mind, so long as they did not wander into the store and tamper with the merchandise. They were speechless and made no talk to distract him while he was waiting on customers. Although they were speechless and lacked full control of their faces and limbs, they nevertheless possessed curiosity, and liked to loll on the store porch watching the world go by. Lum had a barrel of black walnuts, and when he wasn't busy waiting on customers, he would crack the walnuts, pick their meats, and distribute them among the idiots, because it was popularly believed that the black walnut, whose shell resembles the human skull and whose meat resembles the human brain, is a good cure for mental deficiency. For years Lum fed black walnuts to the idiots who frequented his store porch, but it never seemed to do any good.

Sportsmen from the cities, St. Louis and Kansas City and even Chicago, began coming to Stay More to hunt and fish (nobody knows who betrayed to the cities the secret that the waters of Stay More were teeming with easy-to-catch fish, and that the air was full of fine game birds, but at any rate the sportsmen came) and they patronized Lum Ingledew's store, buying their tackle and ammunition from him, and buying tins of sardines and Vienna sausages to eat on crackers for their lunch; he also sold them whiskey. The sportsmen could not help noticing the idiots on the porch, and, unaware that the normal population was congregating at the mill behind the store, they mis-

takenly assumed that the idiots were typical, and they carried back
to their cities a gross misrepresentation of the Ozark people, which is
undoubtedly the origin of all of the spurious humor, not to mention
the ridicule, that has been perpetuated ever since. In fact the idiots
represented only a very small percentage of the populace. The sportsmen also depleted the reserves of fish and game, but nobody protested,
either because they didn't know what was happening or because, like
Lum, they needed the money that the sportsmen brought with them
and spent. An occasional sportsman would invite one or two of the
idiots to accompany him fishing or hunting, although he would soon
discover that idiots are useless for practically anything.

The idiots of Stay More never got the sourhours; they sometimes attended, but could not understand, Brother Stapleton's Magic
Bible Shows; but they were never afflicted with the sourhours, nor,
indeed, any emotion or feeling: they neither grieved over deaths nor
exulted over pleasures. If they especially enjoyed eating, it was not
possible to tell. They slept because it came natural to them. The only
thing that they apparently *wanted* to do, and which they did all the
time, was to loll and squat on the porch of Lum's store. They were
loitering there thus one afternoon when Eli Willard next returned
to Stay More.

Eli Willard was distressed, on two accounts: 1, he was sorry
to see that Stay More now had a full-fledged general store, to com-
pete with his peddling; and 2, he was sorry to see that the younger
generation of Stay Morons were such sorry specimens; some of them
looked like the Mongolians he had seen on his trip around the world.
Maybe, he thought, these were the same uncouth youngsters who
had thrown rocks at him when he had brought his rejected message
of Unitarianism. He was not now carrying that message; he had
returned to traffic in material goods, particularly, this time around,
grooming aids, which these youths on the store porch could obviously
put to good use. In addition to a line of toothbrushes, ear cleaners,
hair tonics, body braces and trusses and other grooming aids, he had
rebottled (and perfumed) his unsold kerosine and was now marketing
it as "Willard's Miracle All-Purpose Hand Cleaner and Lubricant."

He began with a demonstration of this latter. He dipped his

hands into the dust of the road and covered his hands thoroughly with dirt, rubbing and smearing the dirt all over his hands. The idiots watched him closely. Then from a container in his wagon, he took out handfuls of soot and blacked his hands. "Now, watch," he said, needlessly, since all eyes hung on his every move. He uncapped a bottle of his miracle all-purpose hand cleaner, poured some into one palm, and rubbed his hands together. Presto! All the dirt and soot were loosened and he wiped it off on a towel. "Two bits a bottle," he said, and held three bottles in each hand, offering them, but there were no takers. Perhaps, he reflected, there was no future whatever in kerosine, as far as Stay More was concerned.

Then he demonstrated the toothbrush. The idiots stared at him. He next demonstrated the ear cleaner, which had a tiny scoop at one end and a sponge at the other end of an ornate ivory handle. The idiots not only stared at him but also at one another. He next demonstrated the hair tonic. Since his own hair was mostly gone, he selected a bushy-headed boy from his audience. As he sprinkled the tonic on the boy's hair the boy began whimpering and kicking.

"But doesn't it instantly make your scalp feel better?" Eli Willard asked. The boy continued whimpering; the others began edging away from him; they all scuttled hurriedly into the store. Lum Ingledew looked up from his account book and was puzzled to see all of the idiots rushing into his store. He went out to investigate.

"What's a-gorn on?" he demanded of Eli Willard, but then recognized him and exclaimed, "Why, if it aint ole Eli Willard!" He noticed the items of merchandise and said, "Preachin didn't make ye no money, did it?"

"I'm afraid it didn't," Eli Willard admitted.

"Reckon me and you is sorta rivals, then," Lum observed. "I'm the propriorater of this here store. What-all you got thar?" Eli Willard showed him the various grooming aids. "I don't carry none a them," Lum observed, "so maybe we aint rivals atter all."

"My luck hasn't turned," Eli Willard observed. "Even though all of these are cheaply priced, I failed to sell a single one of them to those young people."

Lum Ingledew laughed. "Them young people is idjits. Put all their brains in one pile, you'd have maybe a cupful."

Eli Willard meditated upon that curious circumstance. "In all of the rest of the world," he declared, "idiots are placed in institutions."

"Is that a fack? Wal, I reckon folks hereabouts couldn't afford it."

"The government pays for it. I'm sure the good state of Arkansas has an asylum somewhere that would take them in, free of charge."

"Wal, heck, they aint done no harm," Lum said in their defense. "We jist let 'em alone and they keep to theirself and don't bother a soul. If you want to hug one, it'll hug ye right back."

Eli Willard shuddered at the thought. The idiots were crowded into the doorway of the store, peering out at him.

We may note that although the Ingledew General Store was not bigeminal in the strictest sense of having two separate parts or doors, it had three *double* doors, which almost amounts to the same thing, except that there was no distinction as to which side of the double door was used by which sex: male and female alike used either side. Huddled close together, all of the idiots of Stay More could crowd into the center doorway and peer out at Eli Willard. Since he was no longer rubbing dirt on his hands or sticking things in his ear or threatening to pour liquid on their heads, they lost their fear of him and gradually returned to the porch, where they resumed sitting or squatting or kneeling or reclining, and continued staring at him. He was disconcerted, and drove his wagon on over to the mill, where people with minds were, and sold them toothbrushes, liquid and powder dentifrices, ear cleaners, trusses, and other grooming aids, including many, many bottles of his Miracle All-purpose Hand Cleaner. A year later, Sirena Ingledew, happening to light her cob pipe right after using the hand cleaner, discovered that the liquid was inflammable, and, after chanting a secret saying to draw the fire out of her burns, she poured some of the hand cleaner into an old lamp and made the further discovery that it could serve as a fuel. The Second Spell of Darkness was over.

But while the Spell of Darkness came to an end, and the school and post office were restored, the population explosion went on. The forests on the steepest hillsides were girdled and turned into pasture, and large quantities of Willard's Miracle All-purpose Hand Cleaner were deliberately poured onto the forest floor to ignite it and burn the forest and create more pastures and fields. Any piece of ground that could be cultivated was plowed up. The farmed plots became progressively steeper, up the sheer mountainsides, until the farmers began falling out of their fields, but that did not stop them; their sons carried on. Isaac's mill ran twenty-four hours a day; since he never slept, he worked always, stopping only to eat. Lum Ingledew hired both John and Willis to clerk full time in his store, but still business was so brisk that another general merchandise store was opened at the other end of what had now become Main Street, and in between there were established offices of physicians and dentists.

Until that point, all illnesses had been treated with herbal cures or incantations, and all toothaches were simply cured by extraction, but now ambitious young men among the families of Plowright, Swain, Chism and Whitter, who had been taught by Boone Harrison in their childhood to read and still remembered how, sent off to St. Louis for correspondence courses in medicine and dentistry, studied their lessons diligently, practiced on the idiots until they had ironed out the kinks in their practice, then hung out their shingles on small new white-painted buildings up and down Main Street. The idiots' other problem was that because of the population explosion they were crowded off of Lum's store porch and lost their favorite gathering place. Restless, they wandered, and discovered an orchard, and ate green apples, and had to be taken back to the doctors.

There were so many people in Stay More that nobody could keep track of them all. A few got lost, and nobody noticed. John Ingledew, if pressed, could not tell how many brothers and sisters he had, nor, in fact, how many children he had. (He had ten, all told, each conceived in his sleep, except for one, who was, as we will learn, conceived in the sleep of his brother Willis.) There were times when he could not even find his wife, Sirena. He would hear her, in some other room, humming to herself, or sneezing, or just breathing, but he could not find her. This contributed to his constant expression of foreboding, which people associated with the childhood nickname he had never outgrown, "Doomy." As his sister Perlina expressed it to her husband, Brother Stapleton, "Doomy allus looks like the world's comin to a end any minute now." This air made him the less effective of the two brothers who clerked at their Uncle Lum's store; in fact, anybody coming to the store would always rather have Willis wait upon them, and would turn to John only if Willis and Lum were both very busy. John was sensitive about this, and it further affected his facial expression. No doubt John had a good heart and was a good husband (when he could find her) and a reasonably good father, but in appearance, although he was just as handsome as any other Ingledew, he was the most disagreeable of them all, and for this reason I am, and always have been, prejudiced against him.

When Lum Ingledew died, he willed his store to Willis, not even mentioning John, and this further affected John's mien. Lum Ingledew died during an epidemic of typhoid fever, the first corrective measure that Nature took against the overpopulation. This is not to suggest that Nature singled out Lum Ingledew, but that he was haplessly one of many random persons who were put beneath the earth in order to make more room on top of it. Before Stay More got its doctors, the worst afflictions that anyone got were pneumonia and the frakes, neither of which is contagious, and nobody ever died of the latter. But after the doctors hung their shingles, there were epidemics of, successively: typhoid fever, shingles, tuberculosis, influenza, meningitis, poliomyelitis, and yellow fever. The doctors were able to identify each one of these, but they were not able to cure any of them. They prescribed and sold an esoteric pharmacopoeia that was of no earthly use. The lucky persons were those whose grandmothers insisted on administering the old remedies: slippery-elm bark tonic, chicken blood and cat blood, ground roots and herbs. The unlucky ones, or those who did not have grandmothers, like Lum Ingledew, perished. Even some who had grandmothers perished. John and Sirena Ingledew lost two of their children. Perlina and Long Jack Stapleton lost three of theirs. Denton and Monroe Ingledew gave up farming and turned to gravedigging and were employed so steadily they both got the frakes. The doctors too were working so hard they both got the frakes, and treated one another, without success. One by one the idiots died and could not grieve for each other, until there was only one left, and he, in his last hours, seemed suddenly to realize that all of his companions had preceded him out of this life, but, instead of weeping, he laughed and cheered.

And then the Century died. The whole Century itself, which had lasted for an even hundred years, was dead. It would be no more. Those who had been born during it, as all of them had, grieved for its passing. Old Jacob Ingledew especially, who had lived through more of it than anybody else, mourned its irrevocable demise, and took to his bed, never to rise again. It was some small consolation to him that during the first year of the new Century the people of Arkansas elected another Ozarks mountaineer, Jeff Davis, as their governor, but even that good news was not enough to give him something to live for, and he expired. He said to his wife, seated at his bedside, "Sarey, feel my pulse." She felt for it, could find none, and told him so: "You aint got ary pulse, Jake." He then said, "That's what I figgered. Wal, afore I go, Sarey, promise to tell me somethin." She promised. "Tell me, Sarey, how come, all our life long since you and me was hitched, we never…did…get our things together more often than once a month at the mostest." Sarah blushed, swallowed, and, because she had promised, but because her "friend" who was also Jacob's ladyfriend was present in the room, she bent down and whispered the somewhat lengthy answer into Jacob's ear, and he smiled and closed his eyes and died. While he was lying in state, the next day, Sarah lay down beside him and followed him out of existence.

Everybody else who had not died came to their joint funeral, which was the grandest funeral ever given in Stay More, despite a constant rainstorm. Brother Long Jack Stapleton gave the eulogy: a five-hour show of Jacob's entire life condensed, and considerably censored. Everyone present realized that there could never be another life like that, and because they already realized that there could never be another Century like the one late lamented, they were inconsolable and lachrymose. For weeks after the funeral no one was able to do anything. It was as if everybody was temporarily recovering from the frakes. John Ingledew in particular, who already had such a doomy air, was plunged into gloom over the loss of his grandparents and the loss of the Century. We too should pause here for a minute of silent meditation.

Death cheapens the value of life. As dying becomes commonplace, grieving is rarer, shallower. So many people had died in Stay More that nobody cared anymore who was living or not. Death was a fact of life. Some people did not get sick at all, and felt guilty, and committed suicide, leapt from Leapin Rock. There were incidents of poisoning, arson, shooting, lynching, all unheard-of before. More unheard-of were the incidents of rampant ruffianism. Nearly all Stay Morons had been noted for their simple gentleness, but now several of them turned mean and rowdy. If there had been one distinguishing difference between the mountaineer of the Ozarks and his kinsmen the mountaineers of Kentucky and Tennessee, it was that the latter were noted for bloody feuding while the former, even if just as impulsive, was not quarrelsome. But now men began beating and shooting one another in earnest. Take, for example, Ike Whitter, who was possibly the worst rowdy in Stay More. He was a rugged six-footer, barrel-chested, brawny, hard as nails. When sober he was merely ill-humored; when drunk, as he was every Saturday, he became ferocious. Any man bold enough to fight him had to agree to his rule that the taking of eyeballs was permitted. Three men each had an eye gouged out before everyone conceded that Ike Whitter was the toughest customer in the village...next, of course, to Isaac Ingledew, whose strength was so legendary that Ike Whitter never even gave a thought to challenging him, even though Isaac was getting pretty close to sixty. The people always knew that there was *one* man who could always lick Ike Whitter, so they let Ike have his fun, and even enjoyed the spectacle of his gouging out an eyeball here and there. But nobody wanted to invite Ike Whitter to anything; he was never invited to the house-raisin's, barn-raisin's, shootin matches, cornhuskin's, games of Base Ball, square dances or Brother Staple-ton's Magic Bible Shows. He was indignant at these slights, but he did not object, until he was not even invited to his own sister's weddin, and when that happened he showed up anyway, picked a fight with the groom, and killed him. They sent to Jasper for the sheriff. Sheriff Barker came with a sworn warrant, and two revolvers, which he cocked and pointed simultaneously at Ike Whitter.

"Ike Whitter," said the sheriff. "You are a prisoner, under suspicion of murder. Come along peaceable."

"Haw," snorted Ike Whitter. "The devil ye say. You'd better jist slope away from here, sheriff, cause I'm liable to git dangerous toward ary man that would point pistols at me."

"I'm only doin my duty," the sheriff said, somewhat apologetically. "The people of this here county have appointed me to keep order. You have did a crime. Grubbin out a eyeball here and there is one thing, but murder is a hoss of a different feather. It is my bounden duty to remit ye to the county jail."

Ike Whitter leered. "Wal, reckon ye got the drap on me." He held out his wrists. "Put on the handcuffs."

The sheriff, in order to fish out his handcuffs, had to return one of his two revolvers to its holster, and as he did so, Ike Whitter slapped the other one out of his hand, then hit the sheriff a swipe on his ear that laid him out, then extracted one of his eyeballs. The sheriff, screaming "Oh, Ike, Lordy, don't kill me!" made a hasty retreat. When the sheriff returned to Jasper and reported what had happened to him, it aroused so much interest and was considered so newsworthy that a printing press was brought from Harrison and Newton County's first newspaper, the Jasper *Disaster,* was established, with a banner headline on its first issue: SHERIFF HALF-BLINDED BY STAY MORE MALEFACTOR.

Other items reported were scattered incidents of poisoning, arson, shooting, lynching, prostitution and insanity, as well as a few wedding and birthday announcements, and the meeting of the Grange. Copies of the first issue reached Stay More, and one of Ike Whitter's few cronies read the front page to Ike, who could not read, and Ike was considerably impressed that there was such a thing as a newspaper and even more impressed, and immensely flattered, that he dominated the first issue of it. He took the front page and nailed it to the front of the Ingledew General Merchandise Store, for all eyes to see, but the eyes were not seeing it because they were staying home out of fear of him. He had the town to himself. Willis Ingledew turned the store over to John and went off to see the St. Louis World's Fair. John Ingledew managed the store for only a few days until Ike Whitter came in and began helping himself to Vienna sausages and crackers and anything else he desired. John went to his father, Isaac, and complained, "Paw, somethin's got to be done about Ike Whitter."

Isaac, as taciturn in his late fifties as he ever was, suggested laconically, "Lynch him."

John went around the village, talking to all the men. Most of them did not wish to meddle with Ike Whitter, but John succeeded in recruiting, in addition to his older brothers Denton and Monroe, one Dinsmore, one Chism, one Coe, one Plowright, and one Swain. These eight men took their rifles and coils of rope and marched upon the Ingledew General Store, where they found Ike Whitter and two of his cronies sitting on the porch, eating can after can of confiscated sardines. Ike Whitter had his rifle in his lap, and at the approach of the lynch mob he raised it and began firing at them, wounding one Coe and one Dinsmore. The only place the lynch mob could take cover was Jacob Ingledew's house, where Jacob's ladyfriend now lived alone, severely frightened by the sound of gunfire. They told her to take cover in a back room; then they manned the windows of the three front rooms, breaking out the panes and firing across the road at the three doors of the General Store, where Ike and his two cronies lurked and returned the fire. For an hour they fusilladed one another, without any apparent effect on either side, except the shattering of every window in the Ingledew house and in the Ingledew store. Glass was a lot cheaper in those days than it had been when Jacob Ingledew installed the first panes of Stay More, but still it wasn't so cheap that this wasn't a terrible waste, and there was one man at least who was mindful of it.

As John and his lynch mob watched, one of Ike Whitter's cronies, the one in the left door, came tumbling out through the door of the store, down the steps, and crashed into the dirt of the road, where he lay jumbled and inert. John and his lynch mob stopped firing. After another instant, the other crony in the right door repeated the movements of the first. Then, after a longer pause, Ike Whitter himself came tumbling out through the center door and collapsed into the road. John and his lynch mob rushed to investigate, found Ike Whitter breathing, but just barely, and entered the store just in time to see Isaac Ingledew closing the rear door behind him.

"Gawdamighty," each of the eight said quietly. Then they revived and bound Ike Whitter and his cronies, and lynched them. The new Jasper *Disaster* headlined the event: STAY MORE VIGILANTES PUT NOOSE ON VILLAINS. There would not be any more ruffians in Stay More for years and years.

But the sheriff, One-eyed Barker, appeared with a warrant for the arrest of John Ingledew and the other vigilantes.

"What in tarnation *for*?" John demanded.

"Violation of the lynch law," said One-eyed Barker. "It's a-gin the law to take the law into yore own hands."

John and his lynch mob surrendered, were jailed in Jasper, and brought before a judge and jury in the County courthouse. They were represented by Jim Tom Duckworth, a Stay Moron, who, some months previously, had mailed off to St. Louis to purchase the twelve-volume *Whitestone's Easy Jurisprudence and Forensic Medicine Self-Taught.* Jim Tom argued before the court that Ike Whitter and his cronies were already half-dead when Isaac Ingledew got through with them, and therefore his clients had not killed them but only half-killed them. Isaac Ingledew was subpoenaed to depone. Since the judge, like the jury and everybody else, knew that Isaac Ingledew was too taciturn to depone, the judge conducted Isaac to his chambers along with the prosecuting attorney and Jim Tom Duckworth, and there he explained that the examination and cross-examination were to be arranged in such a way that Isaac could depone simply by nodding or shaking his head in response to yes-or-no questions. The trial then proceeded. Did Isaac Ingledew enter upon the premises of the Ingledew General Merchandise Store in Stay More, county of Newton, state of Arkansas at the time of the incident hitherto described, gaining entry by means of the rear door of said premises? Isaac nodded. Was Isaac Ingledew's sole motive or intent the cessation, interruption, or termination of the hostilities, armed conflict, altercation, or contentiousness then in progress? He nodded. Did Isaac Ingledew approach each of the adversaries, combatants or victims, each in turn, each and severally from the rear, catching each by surprise? Isaac shook his head. Then if each was not caught by surprise, was the first one caught by surprise? A nod. The first one, as well as the subsequent two, were seen by the defendants to emerge, come forth, or burst out of their respective doorways in extremely rapid manner, not under their own volition; might it be assumed that Isaac Ingledew had thrown, flang, heaved or chunked each man bodily out through their respective doorways? He nodded. And yet, we may assume, that even being thrown, flang, heaved or chunked out through their respective doorways, and thence downward off the high porch and into the road, would not account for the alleged unconsciousness or alleged half-death of each of the three adversaries, combatants or victims; so is it to be surmised that Isaac Ingledew, before throwing, flinging, heaving or chunking each and several of the aforementioned adversaries, combatants or victims, did first bash in their heads?

"Objection!" cried Jim Tom Duckworth, leaping to his feet. "The prosecutor is asking the witness a leadin question."

"Overruled," decreed the judge. "Prosecution's jist tryin to fine out what ole Coon—Mr. Ingledew—actually done to them varmints afore he throwed 'em out. Witness must respond."

Isaac nodded.

Did Isaac Ingledew do other to the adversaries, combatants or victims, than merely bash in their heads? Isaac nodded. Did Isaac perhaps break their arms? Isaac nodded. Furthermore, did Isaac possibly stomp on their toes? Isaac nodded. Furthermore, did Isaac, by any chance, punch, sock, slug or whop the abdomens or regions of the midriffs in such a way as to deflate the lungs and conceivably cause internal injury? Isaac nodded. Was the motive of this sequence of bashing, stomping, breaking, and whopping to deprive the adversaries, combatants or victims of life, or merely to disable them?

"Objection!" said Jim Tom Duckworth. "The prosecutor is askin two separate questions."

"Sustained," said the judge. "Prosecution will ask one question at a time."

Was it to deprive them of life? Isaac shook his head. Was it to merely disable them? Isaac nodded.

Your witness, the prosecutor said to Jim Tom, and Jim Tom stood before Isaac and asked, "Did ye expect them fellers to git up and lead normal lifes after all what you'd done to 'em?" Isaac shook his head. "Wal, did ye expect 'em to git up by and by or at least be carried off to bed to get well, or part well, and then maybe lead jist sorta normal lifes, maybe walkin on crutches, or carryin a cane, for the rest of their lifes?" Isaac nodded. "How long did ye expect 'em to live, thataway? Aw heck, I fergot I aint suppose to ask questions that caint be answered yes or no. Wal, did ye expect 'em to live to be a hundred?" Isaac shook his head. "Eighty?" Isaac shook his head. "Fifty, at least?" Isaac nodded. Jim Tom turned to the judge. "Yore Honor, as everbody knows, fifty is jist one half of a hundred, so I have done proved my point, namely and likewise, that my clients removed only half of the life of them fellers and this ole gent took the other half." Jim Tom turned to the jury. "Fine gents of the jury," he addressed them. "Half is half, as you can plainly see. You kin either both half-punish my clients and Isaac Ingledew, or else only punish half of my clients, and as there is eight of them, you'll have to decide which four. The defense rests."

The jury deliberated for three weeks and a day. They returned a verdict that the lynch law was unconstitutional and was therefore invalid. The judge instructed them that such a decision was not for them to make, or in any case was not their charge. Their charge was to determine whether the defendants were innocent, guilty, or half-guilty, and, if the latter, whether all eight of them were guilty or half-guilty, or whether four of them were guilty and four innocent, and if so, which four. The jury retired once more. They were never seen again. Some folks claimed that three of them had been seen fishing on the Buffalo River, and another one was thought to be living alone in an isolated cabin on Mount Sherman, but this was only hearsay and not admissible. The judge declared a mistrial and everybody went home.

It was peaceful everywhere after that. Willis Ingledew came home from the St. Louis World's Fair and resumed managing his general store. To anyone who would listen, Willis could loquaciously boast for hours on end of the wonders he had seen at the fair: the buildings themselves, great palaces of white marble, any one of which was larger than all the buildings of Stay More put together. No one believed this. Willis insisted that there were a thousand white marble statues of people and animals ten times life-size. The Stay Morons shook their heads and looked at Willis out of the corners of their eyes. Willis claimed that on one day of the fair, there were over a million people on the grounds. Everybody knew that there weren't that many people in the whole world, and they wondered if Willis had taken to strong drink, or perhaps even had become a dope fiend. Willis tried to convince them that there had been an enormous bird cage, covering over an acre, which contained exotic birds of all sizes and colors, but the people told one another that that one was for the birds, and they wondered why Willis was sawing off such whoppers. Willis's business began to fall off; most people preferred patronizing one of the other general stores rather than listen to Willis tell tall tales about the St. Louis World's Fair. Even after he shut up about the subject, weeks later, his business was still bad, and he had to lay off his clerk and brother, John.

Laid off, John had nothing better to do than take his children and go off to see for himself what the St. Louis World's Fair looked like. He loaded his wife and eight kids into the wagon and drove off up to Springfield, and they took the train from there. They had never seen a train before. Newton County is the only one of Arkansas' seventy-five counties in which not one mile of railroad track has ever been laid, which perhaps more than any other statistic gives a good idea of how isolated it has always been. At the sight of the train, the children's jaws dropped open and remained that way for the rest of the trip, which became increasingly awe-inspiring.

The World's Fair, sure enough, was everything and more that Willis had said it was. "Uncle Willis didn't tell the half of it," remarked one of the boys. But John Ingledew, whatever his shortcomings, was smart. "Now listen to me, younguns," he told his children on the return trip home. "Don't breathe a word about that place to nobody, or I'll whop the whey outen ye." They had to wait at Jasper for a few days, until the children could close their jaws, before they went on home to Stay More. Whenever anyone asked John about St. Louis, he would reply that it was just like Stay More, except there was more of it. Folks lived in the same kind of houses, he said, but they had a couple of extry general stores, and a bridge across their creek. John won the respect of the town for his truthfulness, whereas Willis was practically disgraced.

This did not exactly change the expression of doom that was a permanent fixture of John's face, but it made him feel superior to his younger brother for the first time, and, feeling superior, he established Stay More's first fraternal organization, Ingledewville Lodge, No. 642, of the Free and Accepted Masonic Order. He could not persuade his father to join, but he signed up all his brothers, plus several Plowrights, Swains, Goes, Dinsmores, Chisms, Duckworths and Whitters, twenty-eight of them in all. None of them protested that the lodge was called Ingledewville Lodge, because that was customary. Everything about Masonry was customary, and some of the customs went all the way back to the knights of the Dark Ages.

The main custom of Masonry is secrecy, and that was what they liked best about it. The trappings of Masonry might not have been worth much to them, but they were secret, and the secret knowledge of them placed a man above his neighbors. Only the best men of Stay More belonged to the Masons; that was why there were only twenty-eight of them. At first John didn't even want to invite Willis to join, because Willis was so inferior to him, but they needed a large private room for their Lodge, and the only one available was the back room of Willis's store, and also they needed a "tiler," who is the officer standing outside the door during meetings to guard the secrecy of the meetings, so John appointed Willis as tiler. He appointed himself Worshipful Master. The other offices were by election: Denton Ingledew was Senior Warden, Monroe Ingledew was Junior Warden, Long Jack Stapleton was Chaplain, Jim Tom Duckworth was Senior Steward, and so on. There was an office for every man—for example, Deputy Junior Deacon and Adjunct Associate Deputy Junior Steward—and each man had a badge of office which he proudly wore suspended from a ribbon around his neck. They were not so proud of their little lambskin aprons, but that was an essential and sacred garment of Masonry, and besides, they only wore their little aprons during meetings, and the meetings were strictly secret, so none of the womenfolk or the children could see them in their little aprons and laugh at them or point at them. Willis stood outside the door of the back room of his store when the meetings were held, and brandished his ceremonial mace. Nobody ever tried to break in to any of the meetings, but if they had, Willis was supposed to brain them with his ceremonial mace.

Once the Lodge was established, John wrote off to the national headquarters in Washington asking to be supplied with enough secrets to keep them busy for a year or so. In reply he received a request for a tithe of the dues. He did not know what a tithe was, and none of the other members did either. They figured it was one of the secret words. He answered to headquarters by protesting that he couldn't very well send a tithe if they wouldn't send him the secrets first so he could find out what a tithe was and send it to them. This brought a rather sarcastic reply intimating that if John and his Lodge brethren did not know the meaning of tithe, they were perhaps not intelligent enough to be Masons. Stung by this, John rode off to Jasper and asked the county judge what a tithe is. The judge referred him to the county clerk, who suggested that he ask the sheriff. One-eyed Barker referred him to the county surveyor, who recommended the coroner. The county coroner didn't know but was pretty sure that the treasurer would know, and sure enough Curgus Young the county treasurer told him what a tithe is. He returned home and conveyed this information to his Lodge brethren. "Men," he declared, "we've solved half the problem. Now if we can just find out what 'dues' are." He was only kidding, of course, because he already knew what dues are, but he did not know how much he should assess. It seemed reasonable that if the national headquarters got ten percent of their dues, then the dues ought to be ten percent of the members' income. But no member except Willis Ingledew had ever sat down and figured out what his income was, and even Willis's figures were based on gross rather than net. So John just took off his hat and passed it around among the members, counted up the proceeds, divided that by ten, and sent ten percent, which was $2.15, to Washington. In return he received a protest against his parsimony, but he also received an official kit full of secret words to play with.

None of the words, however, was parsimony, so he still didn't know what that meant. The words were, in alphabetical order: ashlar, brazen pilar, circumambulation, discalceation, esoteric, floor cloth, gauntlet, hele, indented tassel, joined hands, low twelve, northeast corner, omnific, pectoral, quorum, rite, symbol, trowel, unaffiliate, vouching, winding stairs, xenophobe, and zeugma.

The brethren of the Lodge were summoned, Willis was posted outside the door with his mace and a blank look, they donned their little lambskin aprons, discalceated themselves, spread a floor cloth with indented tassel, vouched for one another, holding a trowel in one hand and placing their other hand on their pectorals, joined hands and began to circumambulate from the northeast corner. It was all very esoteric, and lasted until low twelve.

They did that on the Second Tuesday of every Month for over a year, until the novelty began to pall, and John Ingledew passed the hat once more. It had been a drought year, so the tithe of the collection came to only $1.68, which he sent off to headquarters, requesting a new supply of secrets. In return he received another kit with a covering letter execrating his niggardliness, but the kit contained neither "execrating" nor "niggardliness"; in fact, this kit did not contain secret words but secret abbreviations, and headquarters had neglected to include any definitions or explanations of them. The brethren of the Lodge gathered and entertained themselves until low twelve by trying to figure out the meanings.

"F. & A. M." was easy: "Free and Accepted Masons." So was "A.D." for year of the Lord, and "W.M." for Worshipful Master. They solved "S.T.M.," Second Tuesday of the Month, and they even solved "M.O.V.P.E.R.," Mystic Order Veiled Prophets of the Enchanted Realm, but they were stumped by "T.G.A.O.T.U." For hours they considered several possibilities: The Goddamn Alliance of Tear-Uppers, The Gentleman's Association Opposed to Usury, The Greasy As Oil

Tonic Unguent, Timid Geese Always Open Their Umbrellas, Tom's Goat Ate Oliver's Turnips Up, The Grinning and Ogling Tipplers' Union—on into the night the steadfast brethren labored, so obsessed with their object that even when they conversed among themselves their sentences could be abbreviated in the same letters. "They got all our thoughts unstrung," complained one. "To guess abbreviations often takes understandin," observed another. "Try givin another one to unravel," another requested.

The following day John Ingledew wrote to headquarters complaining that the abbreviations had come without any explanation, and he, for one, would sure like to know what the hell T.G.A.O.T.U. stood for. The reply was curt and consisted only of the words themselves: The Grand Architect of the Universe. This struck the brethren of the Lodge as an anticlimactic comedown from some of the more fanciful meanings they had imagined; they liked The Grinning and Ogling Tipplers' Union a lot better. Some of them wished that John had not bothered to find out the meaning, and now that he had, what was the use of it?

What was the Grand Architect of the Universe? What was an "architect"? For the first time in the history of our study of Ozarks architecture, the Stay Morons began to discuss architects. One of the Masons was certain that an architect is an assemblage of musicians. Another was just as convinced that an architect is a place where weapons and ammunition are stored. A third man scoffed at them and said that to architect means to speak clearly and expressively. A fourth thought that architect is a poison. Another was certain that architect was just a fancy word for mathematics. Another who had done well in geography in school explained that the Architect is the name for the region around the north pole; the region around the south pole is the Antarchitect. Willis Ingledew recalled having seen an architect in the giant bird cage at the World's Fair in St. Louis; he described its colors and plumage and wingspread, but nobody listened because nobody believed Willis anymore.

Once again, John Ingledew went off to Jasper to seek an answer, but the county treasurer thought an architect was just a member of the architocracy, or upper class; the county coroner discreetly explained than an architect is a portion of the rectum that has slipped out of place; the county surveyor was certain that Architect was a town over in Madison County, but he couldn't find it on the map; the sheriff had the honesty to admit that he didn't know, although it sounded like it probably came off of a hay baling machine; the county clerk declared that the architect is the place where archives are kept, and he showed John the architect in the courthouse basement; the county judge knew that "arch" was an indication of highest rank, as in arch-duke or archbishop, so an architect was the highest ranking itect, and an itect is a kind of itch mite that causes scabies.

There was only one thing John could do. Reluctant as he was, he returned to Stay More and knocked on the door of his grandfather's house, where the woman Whom We Cannot Name now lived alone, on Jacob's legacy, which had easily borne the expense of replacing all the windows shattered by the ruffians and the lynch mob. John knew the woman only as "Grammaw's friend," but he had never before spoken to her. It was known that she had been a city woman and was educated, but that alone made her strange and remote to John. Now she came to the door, and opened it. She was in her eighties, yet still pretty. John asked her what an architect is. She told him. He thanked her, and left.

"Fellers," John told the next meeting of the Lodge, "it's just a man who draws up plans for buildings." They stared at him and at one another. John looked up at the ceiling over their heads. "Who drew up the plans for this building?" He opened the door and spoke to Willis, who was guarding the meeting with his mace. "Willis, did Uncle Lum draw up the plans for this here store?" Willis thought about it, but could not recall having seen any plans. "He was good at figgers," Willis said, "but he couldn't draw worth a damn. I reckon he jist built it." "It aint got no plan to it," John observed. That is not precisely true, we may protest. But there is a point: who, indeed, *planned* any of the buildings in this book? Who decided that a door goes here, a window there? How was the pitch of the roof determined? Was the construction totally spontaneous? If not, then perhaps there is a Grand Architect of the Universe. John decided that this was what was meant by the name, or person, or whatever it was. He explained it to his fellow Masons, but they snorted their disapproval and said they liked The Grinning and Ogling Tipplers' Union a lot better.

One day a postcard came from Masonic headquarters. It asked simply: "Do you believe in The Grand Architect of the Universe?"

John replied with a postcard: "Who is it?"

Back came the answer: "God, or whatever you choose to call Him."

John assembled the Lodge. "Fellers, reckon we'll have to take a vote. I don't believe in God, and I know Denton and Monroe don't neither, nor Willis, so that makes four of us. How many of the rest of you'uns do?" The vote was taken and came out 11 For, 17 Against. John conveyed this tabulation to headquarters.

Headquarters responded: "Then you may no longer call yourselves Masons."

The members of Lodge No. 642, F. & A. M., were at first indignant, then saddened, and finally defiant: they would not give up their little lambskin aprons and other ceremonial regalia; they would continue to meet; they would continue their secrecy and their playing with secrets; they would not call themselves Masons.

In my possession is a group photograph of all twenty-eight of them, in two rows, the front row kneeling, the back row standing. It is almost impossible to tell them apart: each man, except John, has a handlebar mustache; all of them, including John, are wearing identical broad-brimmed, flat-topped hats; each man is also wearing his little lambskin apron. Written on the back of the photograph is the date and the legend, "The Grinning and Ogling Tipplers' Union," although not one of the men in the photograph is either grinning or ogling; all of them are absolutely deadpan. Also written on the back of the photograph is the name of the photographer: "Willard Studios."

When Eli Willard arrived in Stay More for the umpteenth time, bringing a big camera and a portable lab, everybody noticed something mighty peculiar about his wagon, but it took them a while to figure it out: there weren't any horses pulling the wagon.

Chapter eleven

I t suddenly occurs to me, at the sight of Eli Willard driving up in the first horseless carriage to appear in Stay More, that our investigation has been essentially pastoral and yet we have not dwelt upon very many pastures, let alone the architecture for storing pasturage, namely, the barn. Hence, to remedy that oversight, the illustration to the left. There were many barns in Stay More in the last Century, but they were rather flimsy affairs. The barn of Denton and Monroe Ingledew belongs to our Century, although the design of it is possibly ancient. Denton and Monroe were not the architects; they were only the builders. Who gave them the design?

This barn stood (and still stands) on the sophisticated structural principle known as the cantilever; it is cantilevered all around, front, back, sides. This is as "modern" as Frank Lloyd Wright's "Falling Water" house, but while the cantilevering of the latter is mostly for appearance's sake, the cantilevering of this humble barn is purely functional: it provides additional protection from the rain and sun for the livestock. Who taught the principle of the cantilever to Denton and Monroe? There were not, at this time, any other cantilevered structures in Stay More, or in Newton County.

From a distance, this barn has some resemblance to the Ingledew dogtrot, which might possibly have inspired it, but that building was not cantilevered. The "dogtrot" here is a horsetrot, or rather a horsewalk, high enough for a wagonload of hay to be pulled into it and transferred to the lofts of the two cribs, yes, *two*, bigeminal not necessarily as male and female, although it was not merely coincidence that all of the cows kept in the left crib happened to be females while all of the horses stabled in the right crib were males. According to family tradition, quite possibly apocryphal, there was one of the horses, once upon a time, who carried on a sustained affair with one of the cows. Who told Denton and Monroe about bigeminality? Their grandfather, Jacob? I doubt it. Man naturally knows how to build good and true buildings, honest and unselfconscious. Or perhaps there is a Grand Architect of the Universe, after all.

But what does this barn have to do with Eli Willard's horseless carriage? Well, on a more practical level, it was the place where he parked the carriage during a sudden heavy rainstorm, because the carriage, an early Oldsmobile, had no top—and thus converting the barn temporarily into Stay More's first garage. On a heavy-handed symbolic level, the barn is the most pastoral of structures, and the coming of the automobile signaled the decline of the pastoral age. Indeed, when Eli Willard drove into the barn between the two cribs for horses and cows, the horses reared up whinnying and snorting and broke the gates of their stalls, and the cows gave sour milk for a week afterwards. But this reaction was as nothing compared with the first appearance of his automobile in the center of town, where tethered horses broke their reins and ran away, horses and mules hitched to wagons stampeded, all of the dogs of Stay More howled until they were hoarse, children screamed, women fainted, and the brass clock, which Eli Willard had sold sixty-odd years before, said PRONG.

Eli Willard must have been in his eighties now; a man of that age would be denied a driver's license today, but he still had two good eyes and two good ears and a strong pair of hands to hold the wheel with which he steered the machine. He came to a stop in front of the Ingledew General Merchandise Store, and everybody who had not fainted or was not tending to those who had, crowded into the road, keeping a safe distance from the vehicle, except for the bravest of the Ingledews, Swains, Plowrights, Coes, Dinsmores, Chisms, Duckworths and Whitters, one man of each, who approached the machine warily after Eli Willard had cut off its engine, and who got down on their knees and stuck their heads under it to see how it was put together. Eli Willard gave a squeeze to a large rubber bulb attached to a brass horn pointing downward, and the resultant sound produced eight bruised heads, one each to an Ingledew, Swain, Plowright, Coe, Dinsmore, Chism, Duckworth and Whitter. Each of them rose and shouted his favorite epithet at Eli Willard.

"Sorry, gentlemen," said the octogenarian from Connecticut. "I couldn't resist. Where I come from, it is considered the height of rudeness to examine the mechanisms of another's motorcar."

"Gawdeverallmighty!" exclaimed a Swain, "hit aint a man nor a beast, hit's a *thang*!"

"Whatever on earth is the world a-comin to?" asked a Dinsmore.

"Hit aint even got a bridle on it!" observed a Coe.

"Is that *all* of it?" wondered a Plowright. "Aint there any *more* to it?"

"Lookit them thar tars," said a Chism, and kicked one. "*Rubber* tars! What's inside 'em? Straw?"

"Air," said Eli Willard.

"*Air!*" exclaimed all eight of them incredulously, and one demanded, "How d'ye git the air *in* 'em?"

Eli Willard demonstrated his tire pump.

"If that aint the beatinest thang ever I seed!" one exclaimed, and each man had to try it for himself, squirting air into his eyes, mouth and ears.

An Ingledew put his ear to the hood. "She was rattlin and runnin. But she's quiet as daybreak now. Is she dead?"

Eli Willard took off his coat, retarded the spark, inserted the crank and spun it. The engine leaped to life. The men backed away, and the ring of the crowd keeping its distance expanded to more distance. The exertion of spinning the crank wearied the old man, and he sat down on the running board to rest for a few moments. Then he stood up slowly and addressed the crowd, delivering his spiel for the taking of their photographs. "Fifty cents for one person or a couple, a dollar for a group. Step right this way."

No one stepped. He took from the rear of his vehicle the large camera and tripod, and began setting them up. Once more he appealed to the crowd, "Doesn't anybody have fifty cents to get photographed?" No one responded. "Sharp and clear pictures, card mounted," he said. "None of your fuzzy tintypes. Developed on the spot." He gestured at his portable developing laboratory. But no one came forward. "All right," he said, "twenty-five cents. Two bits. I don't make any profit at that price, but I'm not going to just give them away." Still no one moved, until, edging her way through the crowd, came the figure of an old but pretty woman. She went up to Eli Willard and placed a half dollar in his hand.

"Ah," Eli Willard said, smiling and recognizing her. "Sarah's friend." Step right over here." He positioned her, then put his head under the hood of his camera, made adjustments, and took her picture. While he was developing it, he asked her, "And how is Sarah?" She did not answer, but from the look in her eyes he understood that Sarah was not. "And Jacob too?" The woman gave the ghost of a nod. Eli Willard brushed away a tear while he finished developing the picture. He mounted it on a stiff card and showed it to her. She was satisfied with it. As she was returning to her home, the crowd closed in on her and insisted on seeing the photograph. She gave it to them, and they passed it from hand to hand, smudging it with their fingers, so that by the time it had circulated among all of them and had come back to her, it was defaced. She returned it to Eli Willard. "Let me make you another one, without charge," he offered, and while he was making it, he noticed that the others no longer formed a crowd but were getting into a queue; many of them dashed to their homes to don their best clothes and rushed right back.

The Masons—or, now, The Grinning and Ogling Tipplers' Union—were already dressed for their monthly meeting, so after photographing Sarah's friend again, he made the group photograph which I have mentioned of T.G.A.O.T.U., at their request moving his tripod around to the rear of the Ingledew store, where they could put on their little lambskin aprons in relative privacy. "Mason!" Eli Willard exclaimed, but John Ingledew explained to him that they were miscreant or reprobate Masons who now called themselves by another name. That name was not revealed to Eli Willard, but even so he tried all his tricks to get them to grin or ogle at the instant he took their picture. He made comical faces at them, told a couple of hilarious jokes, and even related what the farmer's daughter said to the traveling salesman, all without avail: the twenty-eight men are expressionless in that photograph.

All day he made photographs. He offered a choice of fake backdrops, painted on canvas: one was of Niagara Falls, with a real barrel in front of it that the subject could sit in and appear to have gone over the falls in; another featured a stampede of buffalo bearing down on the subject from behind; another featured an automobile that the subject appeared to be driving; another showed a lavish mansion and acres of gardened estate that the subject could appear to be the owner of; the last—not very popular at Stay More—was the interior of the White House office of the President of the United States. Eli Willard photographed all of the Ingledews, except Isaac, who was unwilling, so we do not know what that patriarch looked like; we can only guess, by subtracting the looks of Salina, who was photographed, from those of all their children, all of whom were photographed, Perlina in a double shot with Long Jack Stapleton, and John in a group photograph with Sirena and all of their children. Since Eli Willard's camera was portable, he was able, at their request, to photograph the Ladies' Quilting Bee Society at work on one of their spectacular star pattern quilts, the two dentists at work with patients in their chairs, the two doctors at work with patients on their tables, Willis at work as postmaster, and other "candid" images which form a valuable documentary record of life in Stay More early in our Century.

The photographing session was terminated, late that afternoon, by a sudden heavy shower. The line of customers broke up and ran for shelter on the porches of the store or mill. Old Eli Willard, working as fast as he could, tried to drape his equipment and his automobile with the canvases that he used as backdrops for his photographs, when suddenly his eye caught sight of Denton's and Monroe's unusual barn in a nearby field. "Whose barn is that?" he asked the people taking refuge from the rain on the store porch. "Mine and Denton's," said Monroe, who was there. "Might I ask permission to park there out of the rain?" asked Eli Willard. "Park?" said Monroe, who had never heard the word before. "I'd like to remove my motorcar there," Eli Willard said rapidly, because the rain was coming down in torrents now. Monroe had, of course, heard of the word "remove," as in remove one's hat, but, whereas a hat is pretty light-weight and easy to remove, it would take a mighty stout feller to remove a whole motorcar, unless…it suddenly occured to Monroe that perhaps what Ole Eli Willard wanted to do was *drive* the motorcar up to the barn and into the passageway, or maybe, if he wanted to remove it there, it meant he wanted to drive it there and remove it, take it apart, or whatever. "Wal—" Monroe said, but faltered. He didn't particularly care one way or the other himself, but maybe he ought to go find Denton and talk it over with his brother to see if Denton didn't mind.

"I've got to get my motorcar out of the rain!" Eli Willard beseeched. "Aw, yeah, shore," Monroe said. "Go right ahead." Eli Willard cranked his engine, hopped in, and drove quickly to the Ingledew barn. He had to get out and unlatch the barnyard gate and drive through it and get out again and relatch the gate, and by the time he was sheltered in the passageway, frightening the cows and horses, he might just as well have stayed out in the rain because he and his car were soaked. He took a tin can from his tool box and began to bail the water out of the car.

Denton Ingledew had meanwhile been inside the cow crib milking one of the cows. When the Oldsmobile pulled into the passageway, Demon's cow put her hind foot in the milk pail and kicked it over, lashed the side of his face with her tail, commenced bellowing along with her sisters, and turned completely around, mashing Denton against the wall. He got out alive, and began cussing Eli Willard, who protested, "Your brother said I could park here." "Park?" said Denton, who had never heard the word before.

"It's raining cats and dogs," Eli Willard pointed out. "I had to get my motorcar out of the rain."

Denton noticed how wet Eli Willard and his motorcar were, and observed, "Didn't do ye much good, did it? My cows is havin conniption fits. And lookee at them hosses in thar, a-bustin up their stalls. You have done went too far, Mr. Willard. I am a-gorn to have to law ye."

"Law me?" said Eli Willard.

"Sue ye in court," Denton explained, and he went off to confer with his attorney, Jim Tom Duckworth, who counseled him that it stood to reason, even if it didn't stand in the books, that damages and nuisances caused by animals' reactions to the sight and sound of self-propelled conveyances ought to be actionable, and Jim Tom straightway took the matter to court at Jasper.

Eli Willard was summonsed, to appear as soon as the rain stopped. But the rain lasted for several days before stopping, and by then the dirt road was a morass of mud. The motorcar was mired hopelessly before it had gone fifty feet from the barn. Laughing, Monroe Ingledew offered, for a small consideration, to hitch a team of his horses to the motorcar and get it out. The horses performed this task contemptuously but successfully. Eli Willard paid Monroe the small consideration, and drove on. He had not gone far, however, when he got stuck again, up to the hubs. One of the Swain men hitched a team to him and pulled him out, for a slight fee. In front of the Plowrights' house, another team extricated him from the ooze, in return for a freewill donation. The Dinsmores accepted a trifling premium. The Chisms required only a scant compensation. The Duckworths' bill was insignificant. But Eli Willard realized that at his present rate of travel he would take weeks to reach Jasper, so he persuaded the Whitters, after they had hauled his motorcar out of the mud for a pittance, to accept a substantial reward in return for pulling him all the way to the Jasper courthouse, which they did, people pointing and laughing all along the route. Eli Willard hired one of the lawyers hanging around the courthouse to represent him.

There was no jury; the judge alone heard the case. "Yore

Honor," Jim Tom began, "my client the plaintiff here, with the help of his brother a-sittin over thar, built a mighty fine barn up to Stay More, with a sorta open passway right through the middle of it for the purpose of drivin a team and wagon into the barn under cover to unload the hay and put it up in the two lofts either side of the passway. The defendant, thar, on the date mentioned, did unlaw-fully operate a self-propelled vee hickle, or hossless kerridge, that's it yonder a-settin right out thar through the winder, in such a manner as to enter the aforementioned passway, with the intent to, or fer the purpose of, gittin in out a the rain, and by so doing, did aggerper-voke the plaintiff's cows and hosses, which caused the former to give sour milk ever since, and caused the latter to rare up and strike the gates of their stalls in such a way as to shatter same, not to mention it has lately been discovered one of 'em has got a lame fetlock. We ask real damages of one hundred smackers plus punitive damages of one hundred."

Eli Willard's attorney said, "If hit please the Court, I'd like to ask Yore Honor to find whar it says, anywhar in the statues, that hit's a-gin the law to drive a hossless kerridge into a barn."

The judge recessed the court while he consulted the books, which said nothing whatever about hossless kerridges. He reconvened the court, informed the plaintiff and defendant of this fact, and declared, "Since I caint rule *ipso jure*, reckon I'll jist have to rule *ipso facto*. Proceed, gents."

Eli Willard's attorney argued that the defendant had received permission from the plaintiff's brother, co-builder of the barn, to deposit his vee hickle there. The defendant did not know that the barn was inhabited by cows and horses at that moment, and the defendant had no intention of causing any damage, and furthermore the defendant, as you can plainly see, is very old and probably senile and probably didn't even know what he was doing.

Be that as it may, argued Jim Tom Duckworth, a senile old man had no business operating a dangerous machine. "Yore Honor," he asked the judge, "do you know what makes that hossless kerridge go?"

"Court perfesses ignorance," replied the judge.

"Infernal *combustion!*" declared Jim Tom. "That thar senile ole defendant has been combustin all over creation, and it's all that combustin what skeers the cows and hosses and gener'ly raises up hell."

Eli Willard was not feeling well. He did not enjoy hearing references to his advanced age, and he did not like the thought that he was senile. He told his attorney, "Rest our case, and let's get it over with."

"Yore Honor," the attorney began his summation, "jist let me say this. My client is innocent. As you well know, all my clients is innocent, but *this here* client, I'm a-tellin ye, is straight-up-and-down innocent, which means that he caint possibly be guilty noway. Why, he's the tore-downdest innocentest feller they ever was. To look at it another way, he is blameless. The fault, if thar ever was one, aint his'n. May hit please the Court, I do hereby pronounce this pore ole senile Yankee peddler feller, whose hands is clean as a hound-dog's tooth, pure of crime and in the clear! Defense rests."

"Yore Honor," countered Jim Tom Duckworth, "I shore wouldn't swaller that line, iffen I was you. The defendant's hands aint clean; they're red! Look at 'em! Why, that feller is guilty. He is the guiltiest defendant ever I saw; in fact, he is the *most* guiltiest defendant ever I saw. It's *all* his fault, ever bit of it, right down the line. He has transgressed! He has trespassed! He has offended! He has damaged! Judge, listen to me, if he aint guilty, I'm a monkey's uncle. If he aint guilty, black is white and up is down and hot is cold and dry is wet and God knows what all! I swear up and down and all over the place that he is guilty. He don't know what innocent is. He has done wrong and must pay for it. I stand here with proud haid bared afore the bar of justice and I p'int my finger at that rascal and I declare that he is, without the slightest doubt in the least, to blame. He is GEE EYE DOUBLE-ELL TEE WHY!"

The judge listened thoughtfully to both of these summations, and decided that Jim Tom's was the more eloquent of the two, and thus he found against the defendant. Eli Willard paid up, and left town.

The Jasper *Disaster* gave the case brief mention under the headline MOTORIST CONVICTED OF SPOOKING LIVESTOCK. The years went by, one by one, and Eli Willard did not come back to Stay More again. The people wondered if he was just sulking, or if he had died. Either way, they were very sorry to see him go, or, rather, very sorry to see him not come back. Denton Ingledew himself wanted to write a letter to Eli Willard and apologize and invite him to come back, but he did not know where to address it. At any rate, no more hossless kerridges were seen in Stay More for several years, and the Ingledew barn remained pastoral.

These were the Ingledew children, John's sons, conceived at night while he slept, and his assumed daughter: Elhannon Harvey, who never could speak his own name, and was called "E.H."; he had an excess of yellow bile, and was generally irascible. Odell Hueston, called variously "Ode," "Dell" and "Odd," had an excess of black bile, and was thus the son who most resembled his father: gloomy and doomy. Bevis Handy, called "Beef" or sometimes "Bevis," destined to become the father of the next (and penultimate) wave of Ingledews, had an excess of blood, and was, depending on how you interpreted it, excitable, passionate or maniacal. Tearle Harley, called always "Tearle," which is pronounced "Tull," had an excess of sweat and was industrious, too much so, which made him frakes-prone, so that in his thirties he acquired an excess of alcohol, which rendered him good natured and witty, because alcohol is the most humorous of the humors. Lola Hannah, called "Lola," pronounced "Lowly," the only daughter, who was not really John's daughter but Willis's, although none of them knew that, not even her mother, who was sleepwalking when she entered Willis's room, and not Willis, who slept through it all; Lola had an excess of menses, and was untouchable. Stanfield Henry, called, for some reason, "Stay," as in Stay More, or sometimes "Flem" because he had an excess of phlegm and was sluggish, or self-possessed. And the last-born, Raymond Hugh, called "Ray," who had an excess of semen, and was lustful. Raymond was just reaching puberty when his older brothers and his half-sister turned the hayloft of the barn into a clubhouse, but he could tell a joke just as ribald as anyone's.

The boys tried to exclude Lola from these hayloft gatherings, but she insisted on attending, and threatened to tell on them if they didn't let her, although she never participated in their activities but remained an interested kibitzer. They said and did things in her presence that they would never have dreamed of saying or doing in the presence of any other female, but after all she was their sister; if they had known she was only their half-sister, they would have said and done only half the things. Lola remained a spinster all her life, and one cannot help but wonder if the fact that she was the only girl among six brothers had anything to do with it, or whether her watching and listening to the goings-on of the hayloft clubhouse gave her a negative attitude toward the opposite sex.

During the pastoral age symbolized by our barn, there was an influx of new homesteaders, not farmers but people from the cities, mostly single women. A smart land lawyer in Jasper got rich by challenging in court Jacob Ingledew's decree against further immigration, on the grounds that it violated the Homestead Act, and winning the case, and selling his services to people suffering from "city fever" who wanted to get back to the land. These people had spent all their lives in the cities, laboring in business and industry, saving their pennies, and dreaming of a better life. There appeared on the newsstands of the cities a rash of new magazines: *Country Life in America, America Outdoors, Rural Digest, Arcadian Times, Hill and Dale, Silvan Weekly, Ladies' Bucolic Companion, Back-country Journal, Pastoral Pictures,* extolling the healthful benefits of a return to the soil.

The only possible real return to the soil is to the grave, but the magazines did not believe it. They sent their reporters out across the land. One of them, a young woman from *Arcadian Times,* published in Chicago, got lost in the backcountry and stumbled upon Stay More. She walked down the Main Street, slowly, with her notebook in hand, pausing now and then to write "impressions." The Stay Morons watched her. She was wearing a skirt that came down to a pair of high button shoes, and a ruffled blouse that revealed most of her shoulders; beneath these garments she wore a corset which constricted her waistline to, as one observer put it, "not no more thick than my thigh." She entered Willis Ingledew's General Store and browsed around, mumbling from time to time, "How quaint," and pausing to write impressions in her notebook.

"Could I be of some hep to ye, ma'am?" Willis asked her.

She stared at him, then smiled with delight, and requested, "Say that again, please."

"Could I be of some hep to ye, ma'am?" he repeated patiently.

She wrote these words down in her notebook, then asked, "What is the name of this place?" Willis pointed at the post office in one corner of the store, where a sign clearly said, "U.S. Post Office, Stay More, Ark." She wrote this down, then said, "Oh! Is *that* your post office?"

"Nome," said Willis, "it's the undertaker's."

The young woman was moved to remark, "Ha, ha." Then she wrote this down in her notebook.

"Was you wantin to buy anything, lady?" Willis asked.

After writing this down, the woman said, "No, thank you. I'm simply gathering gleanings. What is your name?"

"Willis Ingledew, ma'am," he replied.

"How quaint," she said, and wrote this down, then wandered on out of the store. She strolled along to the gristmill, and walked all the way around it to the creek. It was in busy operation, but over the noise of the machinery she approached Isaac Ingledew and asked him, "Does it really run?" Isaac slowly shook his head. "How tall are you, by the way?" she asked. Isaac held out his hand at the level of his headtop, to indicate how tall he was. This tactic provoked her to comment, "Hee, hee." Then she scribbled in her notebook. She asked him, "And what is your name, sir?"

One of the other men at the mill said to her, "Hit's Isaac Ingledew, lady, and he don't like to talk none, so you'd best not be askin him no questions."

"How quaint. Are you related to Willis Ingledew?" she asked Isaac. He shook his head. "You look as if you might be his father," she observed. "Why is it that you don't like to talk?" He did not answer. "Perhaps you have a congenital speech impediment that medical science could cure? Or possibly it's psychological. Do you understand psychology?" He made no response. "It could be that when you were a child something frightened you speechless and you've never been able to talk since."

"Lady," said one of the other men, "he aint never been frightened by man nor beast in his whole life long, so you're jist a-wastin yore time. He don't like to talk because—"

"Not so fast," said the young woman, taking notes as rapidly as she could. "I can't keep up with you."

"He don't like to talk because he don't like to talk. Now why don't you ask me somethin, and leave him alone?"

"Very well. What is your name, sir?"

"Puddin Tame," he replied.

"How do you spell that last name?"

"I caint spell, ma'am."

"How quaint. Have you lived here all your life?"

He felt his pulse. "No. Not yet."

"Hi, hi," she commented. "What work do you do?"

"I keep the 'skeeters out of the mill."

"Mosquitoes? How do you keep them out?"

"With my shotgun."

"My. Are they that big?"

"You aint seen any Stay More 'skeeters yet? Wal, iffen ye do, don't swat at one. Jist makes it mad. Fling rocks at it as fast as ye kin."

"I believe you are having me on, sir," she said, closing her notebook and leaving the mill. But as she strolled further about the village she kept her eyes open, and at one point she bent down and picked up a rock which she carried in her hand. She caught sight of the unusual Ingledew barn and walked all around it, noting that it had no windows and was dramatically cantilevered. She walked into the passageway that ran through it, where she heard voices coming from the loft above. She listened, hearing an off-color joke. Then she climbed to the top of the ladder, with difficulty on account of her ankle-length dress. The young Ingledews were surprised to see this elegant young lady holding a notebook in one hand and a rock in the other. Hastily they buttoned themselves. "How quaint," the elegant young lady was moved to comment. "What is this?" None of them answered. "Is this your house?" They looked at one another and then nodded in unison. "What is all the dried grass for?" she asked. "Oh, is it to sleep on?" They nodded. She looked at Lola. "Are you the lady of the house?" Lola nodded. "Which of them is your husband?" "All of 'em," declared Lola solemnly. "How quaint. Even him?" she said, indicating thirteen-year-old Raymond. Lola nodded. "What are your names?" "Ingledew." "All of you?" They nodded. The elegant young lady climbed down the ladder.

She noticed the two cribs, which were empty; the horses and cows were out to pasture. One of the horses, she noticed, was mounted upon one of the cows. To herself she remarked, "How quaint." Then somehow she found the road to Jasper. As she walked along it, a turkey buzzard flew out of a tree in her direction. She screamed and threw the rock she was carrying at it. The rock missed, but the turkey buzzard did not come and sting her. At Jasper she caught a coach which took her to Harrison, where she caught a train back to Chicago. Not long afterwards, an issue of *Arcadian Times* carried her article, "A Most Quaint Village Deep in the Ozarks," with wood engravings by the staff artist illustrating a typical home filled with dried grass, a giant mosquito, and a seven-foot inhabitant who never spoke. All of the inhabitants, said the article, were named Hinkledew, with the exception of a Mr. Tame, who had told her how to deal with the giant mosquitoes. The region was an utterly enchanting and enchanted one. The people ground their own flour and meal in an enormous mill powered by a steam engine. The post office was in the general store. The only painted buildings in town were the small offices of two doctors and two dentists. The people were polyandrous, one woman having as many as six husbands; there was probably a shortage of women. Their pastimes were sensual. The pastimes of the horses and cows were sensual. Everything, except for the giant mosquitoes, was utterly enchanting.

As a direct or indirect result of this article, people from the cities, particularly women, who had slaved as clerks and secretaries and millworkers, saving their money and dreaming of a better life, withdrew their deposits, packed their bags, and took the train to Harrison, where a coach took them to Jasper, where they hired the land lawyer to drive them to Stay More, and homesteaded every tract of land that had not been claimed. The men of Stay More were hired to build their houses for them; at first, the women insisted on a house that resembled the Ingledew barn, but, being assured that the barn was a barn, they accepted log cabins. For fifty dollars cash, a Stay Moron would build them a simple and quite habitable log cabin. These cabins are not illustrated here because they were anachronisms. They looked like Jacob Ingledew's first cabin, but the door was in the gable end and the windows on the sides. Today the ruins and skeletons of these cabins are mistaken for early settlers' houses.

The women homesteaders were flirtatious with their builders, and the building went slow, interrupted by many a roll in the bushes. Even though these women enjoyed and were undoubtedly grateful for these rendezvous, they were condescending toward the Stay Morons, openly referring to them as "blue-eyed monkeys." Once the cabins were built, these women enlisted the Stay More menfolk to the cause of their rural education: how to plant a garden, how to tell the difference between a large mosquito and a turkey buzzard. During "nature study" hikes in the woods, they would pause frequently for further gratification of the flesh. A Stay More woman, suspicious because her husband was no longer making any demands on her, followed him into the woods one day and caught him at it, and spread the word to the other women of Stay More, who also suddenly realized that their husbands were no longer making demands on them, and were outraged at the boldness of these city women; the women of Stay More determined that they would not allow their husbands into their beds again until their husbands gave up philandering the city women; this stratagem had the reverse of the intended effect. For a long time the women of Stay More were unhappy and jealous. But everyone else was happy. The newcomers were good for the economy. The money they spent to have their cabins built went into the pockets of the natives. They bought their groceries from Willis Ingledew or the other general store, and bought their flour from the mill. They were not good at gardening, not the first year anyway, and were required to buy their produce from the local people. The first year too they had not acquired immunity to the twenty-three Stay More viruses, and they often patronized the two local doctors. Everybody, except the wives of Stay More, agreed that the city women were the best thing that ever happened to Stay More.

One day one of the city women suggested to her paramour, "Why don't you leave your wife to her other husbands and come and be mine?" Her paramour laughed and said, "Where'd ye git the idee my old womarn had another man?" And then the awful truth was out. One by one, the city women learned that Stay Morons were not polyandrous after all, that, in fact, there was a slight surplus of females in the population, which the city women had increased. But it was too late. They had invested their life savings to have the cabins built and to establish roots in the enchanted backcountry. They loved the fresh air and the sunshine, and the smell of wildflowers and weeds and the creekwater. They loved their blue-eyed monkey lovers, even if they could never marry them. They could not go back to the cities. So they tried as best as they could to adapt themselves to Stay More life. The many snakes and reptiles of Stay More frightened them, and their general nervousness caused all of them to smoke a lot of cigarettes, in the privacy of their cabins. Their Stay More lovers discovered that cigarettes aren't as much bother as a pipe, and can also be inhaled, and the Stay More men took up the smoking of cigarettes, in public as well as in private, and were nagged by the womenfolk, who warned them that the cigarettes, no less than the city women, would be their undoing.

One night the whole sky seemed to explode with gigantic sparks, in what was one of the rare reappearances of the comet known as Halley's but unknown to the Stay Morons, who interpreted it as a cosmic caution to give up their sinful ways. Although they did not give up the smoking of cigarettes, they gave up philandering with the city women. The city women were required to turn their attention to unmarried men. But all of the unmarried men were Ingledews, who, the city women were dismayed to discover, were too shy even to notice them, except Willis Ingledew, who waited on them in his general merchandise store but who, if he talked at all, talked endlessly about his experiences at the St. Louis World's Fair some years before, which bored the city women, since they had all been to the fair.

Searching for men, the city women began to attend the games of Base Ball and the shooting matches where the men and boys of Stay More, having taken down their grandfathers' muzzle-loaders from over the doors of their houses, competed for a beef calf by firing, from four hats away, at a slip of paper tacked to a tree. The women were amazed at the marksmanship, particularly of the Ingledews, who always won, but the women failed utterly to attract the notice of any of the Ingledews…except the youngest, Raymond, who was only fourteen years old. Raymond, having an excess of the humor of semen in his system, couldn't wait until he was old enough to philander one of the city women, not realizing that when he was old enough to court one of them, they would be too old for him. Whenever they were watching the games of Base Ball or the shooting matches, Raymond always did things to call attention to himself, making diving catches of the ball, shooting from the hip with Jacob's muzzle-loader. "What a cute boy," the city women would exclaim, but they wouldn't flirt with him. At the meetings of the hayloft clubhouse, Raymond would boast to his older brothers of what he intended to do to the city women, but his older brothers, although they themselves constantly talked of precisely what they would *like* to do to the city women if only they weren't too shy to approach them, laughed at Raymond and told him he was too young, and double-dog-dared him to find a hole for his pole.

This became a constant obsession for Raymond. He would stop at a city woman's cabin and say to her, "I was on my way to the store and jist a-wonderin iffen I could bring ye anythang." "Why, bless your heart," she would reply. "I need a spool of white thread." He would bring it to her, and hang around, waiting to see if she would flirt with him, but she would not. He would try another woman, offering to mow the weeds around her cabin, and when he was finished the woman would ask, "What can I give you?" "Aw," Raymond would say, "…you know…" "Twenty-five cents enough?" she would ask, and fetch him a quarter. There was one very pretty woman who had obtained a cow but did not know how to milk it. Raymond offered to show her. After she had mastered the practice, and was stroking the cow's teats firmly, Raymond boldly asked her, "What does that make you think of?" After a moment's reflection, the woman replied, "Butter. I'm going to get me a churn and make my own butter." There was another woman who was noted for her devotion to nature study, and had been known to tour the woods with several different men before the exploding night sky had frightened them out of the practice. "By golly," Raymond said to her, "I know jist as much about the woods as e'er a man alive." "You sweet boy," the woman replied. "Let's see if you do." They went into the woods, and Raymond demonstrated that he could name every tree and every flower. But the woman showed no intention of flirting with him. "Aint we gonna lay down?" he asked her. "I'm not tired," she replied and thanked him for the tour and went back to her cabin, leaving him less satisfied than ever.

Raymond decided he would have to commit rape. There was one woman whose cabin was way off up on Ledbetter Mountain, too far for the nearest neighbor to hear her if she hollered. Raymond made a disguise out of a pillowcase with two slits for his eyes, and went to the cabin. The woman hollered. "Won't do ye no good," he told her. "Nobody kin hear ye. You know what I'm after, and I aim to git it." She asked, "Aren't you that cute Raymond Ingledew boy who shows off at Base Ball and shooting matches?" "Nome, I'm one a his older brothers," he replied. She reproved him, "I never thought an Ingledew would be a robber." "I aint a robber, ma'am, I'm a rapist." The woman broke up with laughter; she couldn't stop. Raymond tried to hold her still so that he could rape her, but he couldn't hold her; she went on rocking with laughter. Raymond went home and buried his disguise, and decided he would wait until he was fifteen and see what happened.

Chapter twelve

Willis Ingledew made so much money from the operation of his General Merchandise Store, particularly after the city women became his customers, that he didn't know what to do with it. He had no family to support, and he was nervous about having so much money, which he kept in a locked drawer of the post office, but he knew that this was a misuse of U.S. government property. He decided he would have to buy something. What was the most expensive article that he could use?

After considerable thought, he decided that a hossless kerridge probably cost a right smart of cash, so he ran off to Springfield, Missouri, where the nearest Ford agency was located, and bought himself a Model T Ford and brought it home, but the people of Stay More, having learned long since not to believe Willis Ingledew, did not believe he had a hossless kerridge, and ignored it. He drove up and down every dry road in the village, tooting his horn and waving, but nobody believed it, and nobody returned his waves. He offered rides to his nephews and his niece Lola who was his secret daughter, but all of them said, "Aw, you're jist a-funnin us" and "Quit yore kiddin, Uncle Will."

There was one person in the town, however, who did believe that Willis had acquired a Model T Ford, who could not ignore him, and that was his brother John. As we have seen, it was very important to John to be able to feel superior to Willis. Even though Willis owned the General Store, John was the respected leader of the lynch mob and the Worshipful Master of the Masons, or Top Tippler of T.G.A.O.T.U., but he did not own, and could ill afford to own, a hossless kerridge.

Consumed with envy, he began a systematic campaign to persuade the other Stay Morons that Willis was a villain because hossless kerridges were the worst form of PROG RESS and dangerous and they spooked the livestock and polluted the air and ought to be permanently banished from Stay More, but nobody listened to John because nobody believed that Willis really had one. It was very frustrating to John, trying to convince the people that Willis actually did possess an automobile, in order to persuade them that his possession of the automobile was deleterious. "Don't carry on so, Doomy," his older brothers Denton and Monroe said to him. "There's nothin to worry about. Hit's all only in yore haid. Fergit it. We aint interested."

He appealed to Brother Long Jack Stapleton to make a picture show of Willis's automobile, so that the people could see it, but Long Jack just stared at him and said, "*What* automobile?"

In time, John's envy of Willis's Model T Ford revealed itself to him for what it really was: envy. He came to realize that he would never be content until he had a Model T Ford for his very own, or, better yet, a Model U, V, W, X, Y or Z. Yet he had no money. He asked his father for a loan, but Isaac did not reply. The only other person who had money was Willis, and John couldn't very well ask Willis for a loan to go out and buy a car to best him with. Like all of us who have at one time or another been short of cash, he dreamed of robbing the bank. He hatched elaborate plans for holding up the bank, in disguise. He considered many different types of disguise, and even tried out several. Then he suddenly realized that there wasn't any bank. Stay More didn't have one. In that case, he decided, somebody had better start one, and it might as well be him.

He made elaborate mental plans for his bank and its building, which adorns this chapter. In the first place, he determined, a bank building had to be a stronghold, so it couldn't be robbed. He knew he must build his bank of heavy stones and cement. There were plenty of heavy stones lying around loose, but he would have to buy the cement, and he didn't have the money. "Willis," he said to his brother, "aint you a little bit skeered that somethin might happen to all the money you got stashed away some'ers?"

"If you're tryin to git me to tell whar it's hid, it won't do you no good," Willis said.

"Naw, naw, I aint interested in whar it's hid. I just got to wonderin if you'd ever give a thought to whether somebody might find it and take it from ye?"

"That'll be the day."

"A furriner or a stranger or a tourist might come a-passin through, and when he sees that thar Model T he'll know you got lots of money hid some'ers, and he might start sneakin around lookin fer it."

"*What* Model T?"

John snorted. "Aw, I aint fooled. That's it a-settin yonder, plain as day, even if nobody else believes it. Now look, here's what I got in mind: I'm aimin to start me a bank. All I need is the cash to pay fer the see-ment, if you'd be so kind as to loan it to me and take it out of my wages."

"Hmmm," Willis said, and pondered his brother's venture. "Whar you aim to find a steel door with combination lock fer yore vault?"

"Hadn't thought of that," John confessed. "Do ye reckon Sears, Roebuck would carry them things?"

"I misdoubt it," Willis said. "But I got some equipment catalogs that might have 'em." He dragged out his catalogs, and the brothers pored through them, until they had found a steel door with combination lock manufactured in St. Louis. The price of it, John was dismayed to learn, was almost enough to pay for an automobile. But whereas he couldn't ask Willis for a loan to buy a car, he could, and did, ask Willis to help him get set up in his bank, pointing out the advantage to Willis, and to their father, and to their brothers and sisters and everybody, of having a safe place to keep their money. Willis thought a bank would just be an extra temptation to rob it, but John said he was going to make his bank out of heavy stone and put bars on the windows and with that steel door with combination lock for the vault, the only way any robber could get the money would be to hold up John, and as everybody knew John was the fastest trigger east of Indian Territory, which wasn't Indian Territory anymore because Oklahoma had been granted statehood and Arkansas was no longer the western frontier.

After much persuasion, Willis considered the fact that if John left his employ and went into business for himself Willis would be getting rid of a clerk whom many customers didn't like on account of his gloomy, doomy expression, and he also realized that while a gloomy-doomy expression is not an asset for a store clerk, it would be just perfect for a banker. So he loaned John the money for his cement, and sent off to St. Louis for a steel door with combination lock. It was summer, the creeks were dry, and the bed of Swains Creek was cluttered with an abundance of large stones; John selected among these and hauled them up Main Street to the north end, and began building his bank on the east side of the street. He named it the Swains Creek Bank and Trust Company, appropriately, for the creek had furnished the building materials. While he was building it, he attracted much curiosity, particularly among the younger generation, who wanted to know what kind of shop he was building. When he told them it was a bank, they asked what he was going to sell, and when he told them that he was not going to sell anything but just take in money, they went home and told their parents that John Ingledew was playing with rocks and some of the rocks had gotten into his head. But all six of John's sons helped him with the masonry, and from time to time a lodgebrother from T.G.A.O.T.U. would stop by to help out, and the building was finished just in time to install the steel door with combination lock shipped from St. Louis. The vault was constructed of the same masonry as the building itself, and was bonded to it; it took six men to lift the steel door and hold it in place while it was bolted to the vault. Then John went to Jasper, where a job printing outfit was operated as a sideline to the Jasper

Disaster, and ordered the printing of his deposit slips, checks, savings books and other forms.

The printer was also the editor of the *Disaster,* and he interviewed John and ran a front page story under the headline, NEW FINANCIAL EMPORIUM TO DEBUT AT STAY MORE. The article mentioned that a gala ribbon cutting and grand opening would feature refreshments on the house to all comers. John went all the way to Harrison just to get the lemons to make lemonade with, to serve to the womenfolk and children; to the men, of course, he would serve the best corn that could be found. Sirena and her daughter Lola were kept busy for a week baking pies and cakes.

The festivities lasted all day on the Second Tuesday of the Month, and were enjoyed by all present in downtown Stay More. John wished that Eli Willard was there to photograph the whole shebang. He waited until late afternoon, when most of the men were pleasantly plastered, to make his speech. Then he stood on the porch of his bank and addressed his townsmen, with an air of civic pride, telling them how glad he was to be able to contribute this handsome stone edifice to the Main Street skyline, a rugged building that would last forever, that all of us gathered here together can boast of to our great-great-grandchildren that we were present on the day it was first opened, a building solemnly dedicated to the preservation and protection of our hard-earned pennies and nickels, so that we may sleep better at night secure in the knowledge our riches are sealed away in a vault behind a door that took six men to lift, dedicated to the proposition that this great land of ours is a society of free enterprise wherein a man may work to earn capital and possess his capital in the form of cash and coins, and deposit his capital into the firm and powerful safekeeping of the Swains Creek Bank and Trust Company and hold up his head before all other men, the line forms right over here.

The line did not form. The men and women looked at one another, waiting to see who would go first, but nobody went. The city women had all brought their savings with them to deposit, but they would not move until the natives did. John Ingledew overheard a Swain woman saying to her husband, "Homer, d'ye reckon that loose stone in the chimley-hearth is the best place to keep it?" "Sshh, hush, old woman," he replied, but it was too late; the people around them had heard her. In another part of the crowd, a Plowright woman remarked to her husband, "It does kinder make a lump under the mattress," while a Chism woman said to hers, "The rats might chew it if you keep on leavin it under the barn," while a Duckworth woman said to hers, "I don't mind ye stashin it in the peeanner, but it keeps some a the notes from soundin." Before long, just about everybody had an idea of where everybody else was keeping their money, so they all went home and lifted rocks and mattresses and reached under barns and into pianos, and brought their money to deposit in John Ingledew's bank, and the city women deposited their savings.

John collected almost five thousand dollars. His hands shook just from touching that much money, but he gathered it all up and carried it to his vault. The steel door on the vault, however, would not open. It had a little dial set into it with numbers from 0 to 9 running around it. That was the combination lock, he knew, but he did not know the combination. He fiddled with it for a while, turning it this way and that, but realized that it was hopeless. He was very nervous, and decided he had better return the money to the depositors until he could find out what the combination number was. He went from house to house, seeking to return the money, but he was rebuffed at every door; the people had revealed their money hiding places, and entrusted their money to John's bank; it was up to John to keep his side of the bargain. He took the money home and ate supper with it in his lap; he put it under his pillow before going to bed; he kept his revolver loaded and in his hand while he tried to sleep, but he couldn't sleep. He remembered that his father never slept, so he took the money down to the mill and asked Isaac if he would mind keeping an eye on the money for him. Isaac nodded. John reflected, and decided that since he had asked his father if he would mind, and his father nodded, that meant that he *would* mind. "You mean you won't?" John said. Isaac nodded. John took the money home again and lay sleepless all night with it under his pillow. Early on the following morn, he sought out his brother Willis and asked him to drive his Model T up to St. Louis and find the vault-door manufacturer and find out what the combination was. Willis declined, suggesting that

John send a first class special delivery letter; as postmaster, he sold the stamps to John.

John mailed his letter and went sleepless for four nights waiting for the reply, which said: "Before we can give you this information, you must furnish proof that you are indeed the owner of the bank." How could he furnish proof? He drew up a petition, which said, "We, the undersigned, citizens of Stay More, county of Newton, state of Arkansas, do solemnly swear that John Ingledew is well known to us as John Ingledew, and is the owner of the Swains Creek Bank and Trust Company." He took this petition around to everybody he could find; most of them signed it, although many of them could not write and had to sign an "X." The petition was covered with a great variety of X's. But he mailed it off, and went sleepless four more nights waiting for the reply, which said: "You will find the combination engraved in small figures in the lower left corner on the reverse of the door." John thought about that for a while, then fired off another letter. "Goddamn it all to hell, how can I see the reverse of the goddamn door if the door is locked?" He waited another four days for the reply: "Please do not use profanity. If you will furnish us the serial number of your door, we can supply the combination from our files." John couldn't find any serial number, and wrote to tell them so. They replied: "The serial number is located in the upper right corner on the reverse of the door." If John had not gone for so many nights without sleep, he would have lost his temper in the worst way, but he had no temper left to lose. He tried to curse, but it came out, "Ghdfm."

He wrote another letter. "Dearest Sirs. I sure do hate to keep on bothering you good people like this, and I just know all of you fellers have much more important things to do than waste your time on a dumb old hillbilly like me, but I have to call your attention to the fact that there is no possible way I could send you the serial number of my door if the serial number is on the back side of it and the door is locked. On bended knee I beg of you, good gentlemen, to scratch your heads and think of something else." He posted this, went home and fell asleep and slept for four days and nights with the money under his pillow and his revolver in his hand. The reply came, enclosing the combination number, which had been located by tracing the shipping invoice number to the list of serial numbers. John ran all the way up Main Street to the bank with his money and tried the combination on the vault door; tumblers clicked, but nothing happened. John noticed that there was a handle on the door, and he discovered that the handle would turn, and when it was turned the door opened; he foreverafter wondered if it would have opened in the first place if he had simply turned the handle. He put the money into the vault and locked it. Then he sat down at his desk and hid the combination number in the bottom drawer.

He was in business. The business of a bank is to take folks' money and keep it safe and pay interest on it by loaning it out at a higher rate of interest to other folks. Whom did John know who would like to borrow some money? Well, there was a feller who wanted very much to take out an automobile loan so he could get him a Model T, or better. Feller named John Ingledew. "John, how much do you need for this loan?" John asked him. John told him. "That's quite a lot. Are you a upstandin citizen of the community, and a good family man?" John asked him. "Some has been known to say so," John modestly replied. "What is your occupation?" John wanted to know. "Why, I'm the pressydunt and cheerman of the board of the Swains Creek Bank and Trust Company," John replied. "Do tell? Sir, it's an honor to do business with such a tycoon. Your credit with us is always good. But I ought to point out, sir, that a Model T is the common man's vee hickle, and a gentleman of your position ought to git hisself a better car." "Is that so? Well, I will certainly have to give thought to that. Thank you for your advice. And thank you for the loan." "You're welcome. Come again, sir." John opened the vault and took out the money for John's automobile loan, and John put it in his pocket, closed the bank, and went off to Springfield and bought himself an Overland six-cylinder sedan, took an hour of driving lessons, and drove it home.

The people of Stay More believed it when they saw it, and were very much impressed. Willis was not impressed. John hoped that Willis would turn green with envy, since the Overland was such a better automobile than the Ford Model T. But since nobody believed that Willis had a Model T, he felt there wasn't any point in his being envious of an automobile that was better than one that did not exist. Denton Ingledew said to his brother Monroe, "Wonder whar ole Doomy got the money?" Monroe replied, "Aw, bankers is all rich, don't ye know that?" John parked his Overland in front of the bank, where it remained a symbol of affluence and an object of admiration. The doctors and dentists of Stay More felt that they too ought to have Overlands, and they applied to the bank for automobile loans, but John would not loan them enough for Overlands, and they had to settle for lesser cars, the financing of which emptied John's vault, so that when Willis came to the bank and said to John, "How 'bout payin me back the money I lent ye fer the steel door and see-ment?" John had to put him off until another day.

John decided that he had better get out into the hills and go to work on some of the misers. Stay More had a number of these. They did not hide their money in the piano or under the mattress; they buried it. John drove his Overland right up to their dooryards, if they could be reached; if not, he tried to leave the car within distant view, so the misers could be impressed by the sight of it. He intimated that if the misers would deposit their money in his bank and let it accumulate interest, the misers too could afford an automobile some day. But the misers did not like the thought of having their coins and bills all mixed together with everybody else's; they didn't like the thought of exchanging their savings for a slip of scribbled paper. Only *they* knew where their money was buried, not even their wives and children, so it was safe.

"Maybe it's safe, yeah," John agreed. "But don't you know that the cost of everthing is goin up, and when prices rise, the value of the money goes down. So you might think you got a hunerd dollars buried out yonder behind the corncrib, but when you go to dig it up and spend it, you might discover it's only fifty dollars." Some of the misers could not resist this logic, and they yielded, grabbing their spades and going off and coming back with earth-caked casks and rusty iron coffers containing silver and gold pieces and a few greenbacks. They gave their money to John in return for a slip of paper; they never questioned his honesty; after all, he was an Ingledew, wasn't he? and all Ingledews have always been honest.

The other misers, the ones who continued to resist, did so on the claim that it didn't matter whether prices rose or not because they never intended to spend their money anyway. "Air ye jist goin to let it stay buried after you air?" John would ask, incredulously. "Since you're the only one knows whar at it's hid, you'll carry the secret to your grave." Well, no, they said; on their deathbeds they would tell their wives or children where the money was buried. "But what if you're hit by lightnin, or a tree falls on ye, or yore heart gives out all of a suddent?" John persisted, and one by one the misers yielded, until he had them all.

But, curiously enough, John's exposure to all of those misers turned him into something of a miser himself. His children, fortunately, had all come of age before he turned into a miser, so they could support themselves without any help from him, although his firstborn, E.H., after apprenticing himself to the town dentist, wanted to set up his own practice, but was denied help from his father and had to seek elsewhere. His assumed daughter Lola, who was secretly Willis's, got a job clerking in Willis's store. Odell, Bevis and Tearle were successful farmers, but their father constantly badgered them to save every penny and deposit it in his bank. John dreaded the thought that there was a single coin anywhere in Stay More lying around loose; even more he dreaded the thought of a single coin being spent unless it was absolutely necessary. Other men continued to chat about weather and crops and Base Ball, but John never talked about anything but thrift and savings accounts, and he was a terrible bore. He had to lend money to cover the interest on the savings accounts, but he hated to, and he subjected each borrower to a merciless and embarrassing cross-examination, and then, in the rare event the loan was granted, he charged the highest interest that the law allowed. Not a few rugged farmers were known to break down and cry like babies on the other side of his desk.

But John reserved his true meanness for the city women, who, one by one, because of inflation, were using up all their savings. One by one they sat or stood, sunbonnets in hand, in front of his desk, twisting their sunbonnets and pleading for a small loan. One by one John turned them down, on the grounds that they had no employment and no prospects for income. One by one they told their pathetic plans: one intended to raise laying hens and sell eggs, one intended to weave baskets, one intended to be trained as a nurse in Doc Plowright's office, one intended to be trained as a dental assistant in E.H. Ingledew's office, one was expecting an inheritance from a wealthy aunt in Kansas City who was dying. One even asked for a job as a teller in John's bank, claiming previous experience in a Chicago bank. But John set his gloomy eyes and his doomy jaw and turned them all down. One by one they starved for a while, then packed up and went back to their cities, abandoning their humble rustic cabins to the weeds and snakes. They were not missed by the women of Stay More. .

The only man that John feared was a black-suited agent from the newly created Federal Bureau of Internal Revenue. Recently those politicians up in Washington, probably the same bunch of bastards who ran the Masonic headquarters, had got together and decided that the easiest way to raise money for the government was to put a tax on every man's earnings. It was unconstitutional, a violation of free enterprise, but the black-suited agent told John that he would go to jail unless he obeyed. John called in his attorney, Jim Tom Duckworth, and asked him if it was true he would go to jail if he didn't cough up. Jim Tom, who was having his own problems trying to fill out his annual income tax return, admitted that it was true. John asked his help in filling out the forms, and Jim Tom agreed to help as soon as he finished his own forms, in another couple of months or so. When John finally got his forms filled out and sent them in, the black-suited agent came back again and told John to prepare to be audited. John didn't know what "audited" meant, although it sounded like "indicted" or "outlawed." He asked if he should pack a suitcase.

"We aren't going anywhere. I'll do it right here," the agent replied.

John went for his revolver, but the agent didn't seem to be armed. "What do ye aim to do it *with?*" John asked.

"Why, with my ears, of course," the agent said, and sat down at John's desk and began asking him a whole bunch of questions. Beads of sweat began to break out all over John's doomy face; soon his collar was drenched, but the agent went on asking questions, and John went on sweating, and then he began squirming in his seat. "Auditing," he reflected, was not quite as bad as the frakes, but it was worse than ticks and chiggers. Finally the agent stopped asking questions and began writing some figures on his pad. At length the agent informed John that he had underpaid his taxes by $756.00 plus 8% interest and penalty. John opened the vault and got the money and gave it to the agent, who didn't even thank him for it. Every year after that, John grew to dread the appearance of the agent, who always came, always without warning except the general warning that he always came. Year by year, the people up in Washington collected so much money that they didn't know what to do with it. Like Willis Ingledew, who had collected so much money he didn't know what to do with it, and thus had bought an automobile that nobody noticed, the government, on a larger scale, began to buy battleships and tanks and submarines, which nobody noticed.

John Ingledew was not the only Stay More victim of the Federal Bureau of Internal Revenue. The black-suited agent also "got" Willis, and "got" Jim Tom Duckworth and Doc Plowright and even William Dill the wagonmaker, who wasn't making much profit now that anyone who could afford it was buying an automobile.

The black-suited agent had a younger brother, who wore a brown shirt and brown pants, and worked for a different branch of the Revenue Service, a branch that claimed a right to put a tax on the distillation of corn. That was going too far. If they would allow the government to put a tax on their right to convert corn into beverage, the government might as well put a tax on their right to have their cows convert grass into milk. The next thing you know, the government would be putting a tax on a cow's right to convert bullseed into calves. John Ingledew called an emergency meeting of T.G.A.O.T.U. to assess the situation. Stay More's best distiller, Waymon Chism, was a member, and he stood to lose most if the man in the brown shirt located his still, which wasn't hidden, but in plain view on the Right Prong Road, with a sign over the doorway, "Chism's Dew, 35¢ a gourd, W. Chism Prop."

The members suggested that the first thing he had better do is scratch out "dew" and write in something else. To fit the space, it had to be a three-letter word, and there weren't many of those. "Sip," "sup," "lap" and "nip" were suggested, but considered risky. Better to disguise it entirely with "pot," "lap," "oil," or "rot." Better still to call it "tea." Waymon Chism scratched out "dew" and painted in "tea," but the man in the brown shirt came anyway and stared at his sign and sniffed the air and asked Waymon what kind of tea was worth 35¢ a gourd. Waymon offered to sell him a gourdful, but the man claimed he was a United States government agent and was not required to pay for it. They argued awhile, and finally Waymon gave him a gourd, which contained a genuine tea that Waymon's old woman had brewed out of sassafras roots, goldenseal, wild cherry, May apple, spicebush bark, dogbane, red-clover blossoms, bloodroot, purple coneflower, peach leaves, wild cherry bitters, saffron, sheep manure, and a generous dollop of Chism dew, the excellent taste of which was camouflaged by the other ingredients. The man in the brown shirt had to allow that it was the beatin'est tea ever he tasted, and he quaffed off the gourd in a few lusty swallows. All of the ingredients, including the last, were known to thin and purify the blood, and the brown-shirted man's blood became so thin and pure that he was absolutely lighthearted and euphoric. "Hotcha!" he exclaimed, and paid 35¢ to Waymon, and then went on his way, exclaiming from time to time, "Zippy-umph!" and "Diggety-gee!" and "Mmmm Mamma!"

He had no heart for searching further for moonshiners, not for several days at least, so he checked into a hotel at Jasper, where, several days later, the Jasper *Disaster* noted the fact under a headline reading MANIAC AT LARGE IN TOWN. People barred their doors and the sheriff got up a posse. The man in the brown shirt was run to earth on the courthouse lawn. He flashed his I.R.S. badge. The sheriff asked him what he had been drinking, and he replied, "Chism's Tea." "Wal, did ye cut down his still?" the sheriff wanted to know. "What for?" the revenuer said. "That tea is the best stuff I ever drunk." The sheriff and his posse looked at one another and grinned, and winked. "I'll let ye go," said the sheriff, "but next time don't drink a whole gourdful," The revenuer went on his way, busting up stills all over the Ozarks, but after a few weeks of such hard work, he developed an overpowering thirst for some more tea, so he returned to Stay More again and hiked up the Ring Prong road to Waymon Chism's. He asked if he could buy just half a gourdful, explaining that the county sheriff had ordered him not to drink a whole gourd. Waymon said he was sorry but a gourd was the least amount he could see his way to sell. The revenuer asked if Waymon would loan him a Mason jar to pour half of it in; Waymon didn't have any Mason jars but he poured half of the gourd into a stone jug stoppered with a corncob and gave it to the revenuer, who drank the other half and went off swinging the jug in his hand. He found that taking a small nip from the jug just before raiding a still gave him energy, and he went on busting up stills all over the Ozarks and returning periodically to Stay More to refill his jug with Chism's tea, and he would have lived happily ever after, but he was a bachelor with no dependents and because of that fact he was drafted into the army and shipped overseas, where he died at Verdun.

Bachelors with no dependents made up the entire United States Army, and almost all the Ingledews were bachelors without dependents, but none of them were drafted, and if they had been they would not have served, because they couldn't see any sense in going across the sea to fight some other countries' battles for them. When the Jasper *Disaster* ran a banner headline, AMERICA ENTERS WAR, the people of Stay More assembled at Isaac's mill and discussed the situation for three-and-a-half minutes, then put it out of their minds. They had nothing personal against the Germans. Stay Morons were not isolationists because of their isolation but because of their patriotism, which they thought of as loving and protecting their country, and they couldn't see any way that fighting in France had to do with their country. There were only two Stay Morons who fought in France during that war, and they were not drafted but volunteered. One was Raymond Ingledew, whom we met in the previous chapter, he of the libidinous urges, which were not gratified at the age of fifteen, nor at any time by the city women. At the age of sixteen, however, following a square dance at which much of Chism's Dew was consumed, he successfully enticed a somewhat homely Dinsmore girl off into the bushes, and removed both their virginities. At seventeen, he attended a pie supper, and was the highest bidder on a pie that had been baked by one of the Whitter girls, not as homely as the Dinsmore girl but still not a "looker"; she yielded easily to his debauchment. At eighteen, he graduated to a Duckworth girl who was almost pretty. At twenty, he succeeded in seducing a Coe girl who actually had certain attractions. At twenty-one, he achieved his majority and sowed his wild oats between a couple of Swain and Chism girls who were quite pretty. He felt ready to take on a beautiful girl.

There was only one girl in Stay More who, without any reservation, met that standard, and I cannot utter her name here, because the utterance of her name fills me with longing and sadness, but I have uttered it elsewhere. The town fathers of Jasper erected a high school, and this Beautiful Girl, although from a very humble family, was the first graduate of Stay More grade school to qualify for admission to the high school, and just to be near her Raymond Ingledew volunteered to serve as school bus driver, or rather school wagon driver, hitching a one-horse chaise five mornings a week and driving her into Jasper, where, since he had nothing better to do while waiting to drive her home, he enrolled at the high school himself, a twenty-one-year-old freshman among fifteen-year-old freshmen. Raymond, commendably, made no attempt to seduce the Beautiful Girl when she was a fifteen-year-old freshman. He waited until she was a sixteen-year-old sophomore.

But she repulsed him, claiming she already had a boyfriend. She did; his name was...but I have a habit of uttering his name only as a magic incantation to ward off mindlessness; I can use here only his initials, which were E.D. E.D. had been the Beautiful Girl's boyfriend since she was eleven years old, but this stood as an extra challenge to Raymond, who knew that he was much more handsome than E.D. and was certainly from a much better family. He continued, during their junior and senior years, trying to seduce her, and, because her own mother continually reminded her that Raymond was a banker's son while E.D. was only a wagonmaker's son who couldn't go to high school, Raymond at last, with a promise of marriage, seduced her, discovering that her ardor in the act was a match for her beauty. But the conquest did not satisfy him. Although they were officially engaged, he continued to dissipate his oats among all his previous conquests, and he could not for long keep this a secret from the Beautiful Girl, who, when she found out that he had been keeping company with Wanda Dinsmore, gave herself again to E.D. and later boasted of it to Raymond, whose strict double standard tore at his heart and compelled him to the rash act of picking a fight with E.D., whose fists drubbed him senseless.

When Raymond recovered, he committed the rasher act of running off to Jasper and enlisting in the army. Raymond's older brothers, all five of them, ganged up on E.D. and threatened to kill him unless he went and joined the army too. So those were the only two men of Stay More to fight in France, where they wound up in the same platoon, and even became friends, or at least friendly rivals, or at least comrades-in-arms. E.D. was promoted to sergeant, and won the Croix de Guerre; Raymond was promoted to corporal, and was captured by the Germans in the Argonne forest, tied to a tree and left there as a decoy to lure other Yanks into the line of machine gun fire, but the squadron's lieutenant sensed the trap and forbade his men to rescue Raymond. E.D. disobeyed the command; the lieutenant tried to stop him; he knocked the lieutenant cold, and crawled on his belly fifty feet to the tree where Raymond was tied and began untying him; Raymond urged him to get away because it was a trap, but E.D. continued untying him, until the machine guns opened fire: both of E.D.'s legs were hit and he crumpled to the ground and would have perished had not his men opened massive fire on the machine gun nest and managed to drag E.D. out of there. Raymond wasn't hit, but he must have died in a German prison camp, or else, when liberated, he must have met some voluptuous French girl and married her and stayed over there, because he never came back to Stay More. E.D. was court-martialed for disobeying orders and striking the lieutenant, and was sent to Fort Leavenworth prison.

John Ingledew gave the Beautiful Girl a job as a teller in the Swains Creek Bank and Trust Co. and kept reassuring her that Raymond would be coming home any day now, but he never did.

Raymond's older brother Bevis, he of the sanguine humor, managed to stumble into marriage and perpetuate the Ingledew name, as we shall see; he was the only one of the six brothers to marry.

The same year the war began and ended, the same year that Bevis married, the same year that Raymond did not come home, old Isaac Ingledew gave up working in his mill. He did not tell anyone why he was quitting, but it was assumed that he was retiring on the grounds of old age, being seventy-five years old. He turned the management of the mill over to Denton and Monroe, but he continued to sit in his captain's chair on the porch of the mill, listening to the people chatting and gossiping while their meal and flour were ground. He continued as he had for many years going without sleep. A bright young reporter on the Jasper *Disaster*, freshly graduated from what was called a "journalism school," heard that there was an old man living in Stay More who never slept, and he came down to Stay More and tried to interview Isaac, without success, because among all the other things that Isaac was continuing was his taciturnity. Isaac never revealed the secret, if there was one, of why and how he never slept, but the reporter secluded himself in the bushes for at least three nights in a row to spy on Isaac and make sure he never slept; unfortunately it was too dark for the reporter to be able to see whether Isaac's eyes were open or shut, but everyone else whom the reporter interviewed said that nobody had found Isaac asleep since the beginning of the Second Spell of Darkness, which was a fairly long time ago.

The reporter finally interviewed Isaac's wife Salina, who was more than willing to talk; the reporter's major problem was to get away from her; she kept him for fourteen hours and told him the story of her own life, the story of Isaac's whole life, the stories of her children's lives, and she admitted that she had never known her husband to go to bed since the beginning of the Second Spell of Darkness, but she didn't know why, or how, or what. The reporter wanted to ask her what effect that circumstance had had on their sex lives, but he didn't know how to phrase the question, and let it go. Even if he had asked, he could not very well have printed the information that Salina still climbed Isaac with regularity in their seventies. Even if he had printed it, people wouldn't have wanted to know that such old people even had a sex life anymore. Even if people had wanted to know that, they wouldn't have wanted to picture Isaac and Salina in that particular position or posture. The reporter's article in the *Disaster* was a long one, but it didn't tell anybody anything that wasn't already commonly known.

Because Isaac sat on the mill porch, never speaking, listening to the people gossip and chatter, the people gradually began to forget that he was among them. Just as their parents and grandparents had done once upon a time, they began to talk about Isaac as if he were not there, nay, they began to talk about him as if he were no longer living, as if he had passed already into legend, and they began to reminisce about his deeds and exploits, blowing them up out of all proportion: it was almost as if they were trying to outdo one another in making a mythical hero out of him.

He sat there unnoticed, listening with what amazement we can only imagine, as The Incredible Epic of Colonel Coon Ingledew was embellished and heightened and embroidered. Perhaps he realized that there could never again be a life like that, and perhaps this saddened him, and perhaps out of sadness he quietly died. Or perhaps, as some suggested later, he had waited only long enough to be sure that at least one of his many grandsons would marry and continue the Ingledew name, and now that Bevis had married he could pass on. Whatever the case, he yielded his breath. Because no one noticed him, no one noticed this, and they went on talking, telling of his fabulous feats and heroic adventures. Although they did not notice him, they could not help but notice, in time, the smell. Denton was the first to sniff the necrosis, and he glanced at his father and declared, "I think Paw has done guv out." "How can you tell?" asked Monroe. "Shake him and see," said Denton. "Heck, *you* shake him," said Monroe. "You're closer to him," Denton pointed out. "You're older'n me," Monroe countered. After further argument, the brothers agreed to shake him simultaneously, which they did, warily. Their father did not respond. Rigor mortis was so advanced that they had to bury him still sitting in his captain's chair with his hands gripping the arms of it, and even though they used silver dollars to try to close his eyelids, they could not get them closed, and had to leave them open. The entire population of Newton County, over ten thousand people, attended the funeral and stood in the rain at the Stay More cemetery to watch entranced as Brother Stapleton delivered the eulogy, a four-hour show, "The Incredible Epic of Colonel Coon Ingledew," and then the ten thousand voices were lifted in funereal song:

> *Tempted and tried we're oft made to wonder*
> *Why it should be thus all the day long*
> *While there are others living about us*
> *Never molested though in the wrong.*

and the resplendent, mournful chorus:

> *Farther along we'll know all about it,*
> *Farther along we'll understand why;*
> *Cheer up, my brother, live in the sunshine,*
> *We'll understand it, all by and by.*

The members of the family, instead of sprinkling handfuls of dirt into the grave, substituted flour and corn meal. The headstone bore the inscription, "Now he sleeps," but some folks weren't at all too sure of that. Salina Ingledew, well aware of the fact that Jacob's wife Sarah had followed him out of existence on the day after his death, felt beholden to continue the tradition, and took to her bed, trying hard to give up the ghost, but the ghost would not give. She felt disgraced by this failure, and remained in seclusion for the rest of her life, which lasted and lasted.

The Beautiful Girl was working as a teller in the bank one day when E.D. returned to Stay More, having broken out of the military jail. He tried to persuade her to run away with him, but she did not want to leave Stay More. He tried to stay more and persuade her to marry him, but Raymond's five brothers ganged up on him and ran him out of town a second time.

The Jasper *Disaster* announced that an amendment had been added to the United States Constitution prohibiting the manufacture, sale or possession of alcoholic beverages. The Stay More Lodge of T.G.A.O.T.U. vowed to resist unto death. But Waymon Chism, just to be safe, moved his operation off up the mountain, to a remote cave concealed by a waterfall.

Time passed. The Beautiful Girl was feeding her hogs one evening after supper, when E.D. appeared once again, having once again broken out of Fort Leavenworth. Once again he tried to persuade her to run away with him: once again she protested that Stay More was her home. The argument was futile; out of futility he raped her. Then out of further futility, the following day, while she was working alone at the bank during John Ingledew's lunch hour, he appeared in disguise and pointed a revolver at her, and robbed the bank of eight thousand dollars, and was not seen again for eighteen years.

The decline of Stay More had begun.

Chapter thirteen

Bevis Ingledew was lucky. Although his father had refused to permit him to withdraw his savings in order to build a house for his new bride, Bevis had gone to the bank one day when it was being attended only by the Beautiful Girl, had made out a withdrawal slip, and had said to her, "Goldang it, I'm thirty years old and I got a right to git my own money if I wanter." The Beautiful Girl had not argued, but had given him the money, although she had later been tongue-lashed for it by John Ingledew. The Beautiful Girl could not possibly have known it then, but she was helping Bevis get the money to build a house wherein Bevis's firstborn, John Henry, would be delivered, and that that same John Henry would grow up and marry the Beautiful Girl's own daughter, conceived when E.D. raped her. We all have a way of doing things that turn out to matter, somehow. So when the father of that daughter robbed the bank, all the Ingledews lost their money, except Bevis, who had converted his money into building materials and erected the somewhat modest bungalow illustrated above. If it is not nearly as interesting as most of our earlier structures, perhaps Bevis was not as interesting as most of our earlier Ingledews. Some would argue that his house is a symbol of the beginning of Stay More's decline.

Bevis's bride's name was Emelda Duckworth; she was a great granddaughter of Elijah Duckworth, one of Stay More's early settlers, and niece of attorney Jim Tom Duckworth. She had lost her virginity to Bevis's brother Raymond, and when Raymond became engaged to the Beautiful Girl, Emelda Duckworth turned her attentions to Raymond's five brothers, but soon discovered that all of them were too woman-shy even to look at her, much less to speak to her or listen to her. Bevis, even though because of his excess of blood he was high-spirited, lighthearted, even frolicsome, was just as woman-shy as his brothers. He was also perhaps the most talkative of all the Ingledews, but he could not talk to girls. He had known Emelda Duckworth all of her life, but he had never spoken to her until the Unforgettable Picnic, and in fact he did not even speak to her there.

The Unforgettable Picnic got its name from the fact that people still talked about it for years afterward (although nobody remembers it today), and younger generations were always pestering their elders to hold another Unforgettable Picnic, which their elders had to patiently explain to them would be impossible, and so the Unforgettable Picnic acquired even more legendary memorability as one of those things of the past that would never come again. The Unforgettable Picnic was held during the last year of the War, not necessarily as a diversion, because so very few of the participants were even concerned with the War, but because that was the only year in which the Fourth of July happened to occur on the Second Tuesday of the Month, a special coincidence made even more memorable by coinciding with the peak of 'mater-pickin time and the Golden (50th) Reunion of the G.A.R. When the news of the picnic was norated around the county by the Jasper *Disaster,* everybody made plans to come, but the Stay More T.G.A.O.T.U., sponsors of the picnic, declared in a subsequent issue of the *Disaster* that the picnic was limited only to residents of Stay More and veterans of the G.A.R. Even so, this was quite a crowd. The Field of Clover was again chosen as the site; dozens of tables, hundreds of chairs were carried into the field. The older women remembered the deplorably lascivious picnic that had occurred in 'mater-pickin time during the Decade of Light, and they cautioned their daughters to go easy on the 'maters preparing dishes for the feast.

The daughters had not been born during the Decade of Light, and they ignored this caution, but the 'mater somehow wasn't as potent as it used to be; it made a body feel pretty good but not necessarily lustful. A good clean time was had by all. There was a lot of square dancing, shootin matches, games of Base Ball, as well as several booths and rides. At the most popular of the booths, a canvas wagon cover was hung up with a hole slit in it; people took turns sticking their heads through the hole from one side while from the other side, at a distance of four hats, other people threw rotten (or at least unfresh) eggs, at three eggs for ten cents or to the highest bidder; people would gladly pay more for the privilege of throwing eggs at people they didn't like, and it was understood that every person had to take his or her turn sticking his or her head through the canvas hole. When John Ingledew's turn came, a man bid five dollars for three eggs, and hit John's head with all three of them. When the old woman Whom We Cannot Name was required to take her turn, nobody would pay even ten cents for three eggs, or even accept them free, so none were thrown. When the Beautiful Girl's turn came, Tearle Ingledew bought the eggs but deliberately missed. When Bevis Ingledew's turn came, he took it cheerfully, because he was always carefree, although he hoped he had no enemies with good aim. He put his head through the hole and looked up in surprise to see Emelda Duckworth buying the eggs. Why was she mad at him? Because he had been too shy to return her attentions? But he hadn't been any more shy than E.H., Odell, Tearle and Stanfield, and they hadn't returned her attentions either. Why didn't she throw at them? *Why pick on me?* he silently demanded.

Suddenly he heard her reply, *I'm a-throwin at you 'cause I like ye best.* But she hadn't spoken, and besides she was standing four hats away, and he couldn't have heard her if she did speak. How had he heard her? It was spooky, and the flesh of Bevis crawled, but because he was lighthearted he managed to smile at her as she wound up for the throw, and he replied to her inside his head, *If that be the case, why don't ye miss my haid clean? Okay,* he distinctly heard her voice inside his head, and one by one she threw her eggs, and each one widely missed. *Thanks, gal,* he voicelessly told her, and she replied, *You're shore welcome.* Later, when the big feed was spread and everybody had filled their plates with fried chicken and 'mater dishes and pie, and sat crosslegged on the grass to eat, Bevis noticed Emelda sitting not too far away, two, three hats away from him, and he decided as an experiment to ask her inside his head, *Did you honestly say what you said? Or was I jist imaginin it?* Her mute reply was immediate: *You heared me, didn't ye? And besides, I baked that thar pie that you're eatin a piece of.* Bevis looked down at the slice of pie in his fingers as if it were haunted, and his hand began to tremble, so he stuffed the whole piece into his mouth and, being unable to speak, remarked to her soundlessly, *I'm a-gittin a bit uneasy, us a-talkin like this, though I got to admit, if we really was talkin, out loud I mean, I couldn't say a word.* She replied with sealed lips, *I know. That's how come I figgered that I've never git ye to open your mouth so iffen I was ever gonna talk together with you, we'd have to do it thisaway.* Still, Bevis found it difficult to believe that he could hear her so plainly, especially since she was sitting a good little distance away. As a further test, he tried to see if this weird telepathy would work on anybody else. Spotting his brother Tearle, he silently asked, *Hey, Tull, have you got the time?* but Tearle did not respond. He saw his father and wordlessly yelled at him, *Paw, you're full of shit!* but John Ingledew betrayed not a twitch of having heard, although Emelda's voice entered Bevis's head: *Shame on ye. That aint no way to talk to yore own poppa!* He decided that only Emelda could hear him, and he her.

Kin you read my mind? he telegraphed her, at a loss for any other way of expressing this occult phenomenon. *Shore,* she replied, which again made him feel uneasy, until he realized that there was nothing he could do about it, so he might as well get used to it, since he was cheerful, lighthearted, an optimist. *What color underwear have I got on?* he tested her. *Red,* came her quick reply. Although Bevis was sweating more than usual, he strove to remain cheerful. He tested her with several other questions. How much money did he have in the bank? What was his middle name? How many flapjacks had he eaten for breakfast? She answered all of these correctly, and then she asked him a question, *Do you think I'm pretty?* Bevis started to assure her that she was, but discovered that he could not; to his great amazement, he found himself replying, *'Naw, not exactly. There's lots of girls roundabouts who're a heap sight prettier than you, but on th'other hand you aint so bad. I seen lots worse.* Bevis realized with astonishment that in the reading of minds there can be no flattery, no dissembling, no lies. He noticed that Emelda Duckworth was smiling, although her eyes were not on him, so maybe she had not been displeased with his honest answer. Emboldened, he told her, *I'd come over there and sit beside ye, but I'm way too shy for that.* She replied, *I know,* and offered, *Would it make any difference iffen I was to come over yonder and sit by you?* He answered, *Wal, I'd git powerful red in the face if ye did, but I reckon I could stand it, so long as you never said nothin out loud.* She said, *Okay, here I come,* but even until that last moment he did not believe that she would actually do it, and when he saw her rise up from the ground and start walking in his direction, he had a strong impulse to run away, and he started to rise but heard her voice inside him say, *Don't git up. I'll be right thar.*

Participants in the afternoon's activities at the Unforgettable Picnic could not help but notice, from time to time, all afternoon long, Bevis Ingledew and Emelda Duckworth sitting side by side, alone together in the Field of Clover, never speaking nor touching nor even looking at one another. But the Stay Morons considered it a great achievement on Emelda's part even to get that close to a shy Ingledew, although they doubted that she would ever get any closer. They pitied both Bevis and Emelda because they were missing so many of the activities and attractions of the Unforgettable Picnic, but if two people could amuse themselves by sitting side by side without speaking for the whole long afternoon, then that was their business, so nobody spoke to Bevis or Emelda or tried to get them up from the ground, not even for one of the main attractions, when a furriner from out of state set up a talking machine and for five cents a head gave his customers the privilege of listening for five minutes to an accurate recording of a Negro being burned to death by a lynch mob, one of the most unforgettable sounds of the Unforgettable Picnic. Years afterwards, someone would always comment on the fact that

Bevis Ingledew had never been known to speak to his wife, whereas even old speechless Coon Ingledew had at least been heard to give his wife directions to his house when she first came to Stay More.

Emelda politely waited until Bevis Ingledew's face had stopped burning before she "spoke" to him again. And then she "said," *I know it would mortify you iffen we was to hold hands, so let's us jist play like we're a-holdin hands. Like this,* and she demonstrated: how, by keeping her hands in her lap, and his at his sides, they could pretend that they were actually linking hands and even intertwining their fingers. *How does that feel?* she asked him. *Mighty nice,* he replied. Then she suggested, *Let's play like we're takin a stroll down by the creek, to git away from all these folks.* So they pretended that they got up from the ground, linked hands again, and strolled casually across the Field of Clover and into the trees bordering Swains Creek. They pretended that they walked along the bank of the creek until they were out of earshot of the Picnic; Emelda hummed old songs while Bevis skipped pebbles across the surface of the creek, and they went on strolling, and came to a secluded place where they sat on a rock and dangled their feet in the water. It was cool and quiet.

Emelda told him that if she could read his thoughts then he could read her thoughts too. He protested that he didn't want to snoop. *Go ahead,* she invited him. *It's fun.* So he invaded her thoughts, and discovered that she was thinking about kissing. He thought of the fact that he had never kissed a girl and was too shy to start, but she invaded his thought and thought that there was really nothing to it, all they had to do was move their heads close enough together so that their lips could touch, and they both thought about that and then pretended to do it, for a long minute. *How did that feel?* she asked him, and he replied, *Mighty fine.* The kissing had aroused his procreative instincts. *My, my,* she exclaimed. *Yore jemmison is like iron. Could I pretend like I was a-touchin it?* Bevis tried to pretend that he was blushing, but could not. Emelda bargained, *You kin make believe you're squeezin my titties.* So they fondled one another in their minds. This petting was interrupted by imagined footsteps and voices approaching. *Let's turn it into dark of night,* Bevis suggested, and they were concealed by the disappearance of the sun.

The imagined footsteps and voices faded away, cursing the darkness. In the light of stars, Bevis and Emelda could just barely pretend to see one another, so they imagined that they were pretending to feel for one another with their hands. *I never heared what doing it was named,* Emelda's voice said inside his head, *but whatever it's called, let's do it anyhow. Or, I mean, let's play like we're a-doin it.* Bevis did know what it was called; in fact, he knew close to a hundred different names for it, none of them pretty or even delicate, so he couldn't tell her, but since she could read his mind she discovered them anyway and was impressed by their number and their aggressive energy, and she exclaimed *Oooh!* almost as if they were already doing it. Groaning and murmuring, she pretended to lie down on the ground and made believe that she was spreading her arms for him, also her legs. He needed no pretense of encouragement; his mind was raring to go, and he let it go, and it went.

If any visitor to the Unforgettable Picnic might have happened to glance at the couple sitting silently side by side in the grass of the Field of Clover, the visitor would have noticed, and wondered at, the fact that both of them simultaneously closed their eyes for a long moment, and smiled, as if experiencing rapture. But no visitor happened to be looking at them during their moment.

When the couple pretended to have rested from their labor of love and returned themselves to the Field of Clover and the Unforgettable Picnic, Bevis was somewhat taken aback to hear Emelda declare: *Now you've got to marry me.* He protested: *Aw, heck, we was jist playin like. We never really done it. I aint ruined ye.* She suggested, *Then let's play like we're gittin married.* He pointed out, *It wouldn't be legal.* She thought and thought about that, and he read her thoughts, and their thoughts got mixed up and were interchangeable. *Wait here a minute,* she told him, and then she actually got up off the ground and went off in search of Brother Long Jack Stapleton; he wasn't hard to find, as his Magic Bible Shows tent was a central attraction; she had to wait until the show was over before she could speak to him, and then she told him about Bevis Ingledew and herself and what had happened to them, or what they had allowed themselves to believe had happened.

Brother Stapleton was of course a great respecter of imagination, illusion, make-believe, and he was in sympathy with her situation. He told her just to leave everything up to him and he would take care of it. The conclusion of the Unforgettable Picnic, late in the afternoon, was a triple-feature show by Brother Stapleton: "The Marriage of the Virgin," with Mary and Joseph dressed in Stay More costumes of the last Century, "The Marriage at Cana," with more elaborate costumes and orchestral accompaniment, and "The Marriage at Stay More," which depicted the wedding of Bevis Ingledew and Emelda Duckworth. The bride and groom attended more as spectators than participants, and it made Emelda weep to see herself getting married, and it made Bevis get awful red in the face to see how much he was blushing during the ceremony. He was tortured with suspense, wondering if, when the time came, the man who was Bevis could muster the nerve to say "I do" out loud. The other spectators, which included everybody at the Picnic, were caught up with the show, and cheered the couple on; bets were made among the men; the women who were not weeping made loud exclamations about the beauty of the bride's gown, which indeed Brother Stapleton had made elegant. Finally the big moment came when the groom was called upon to open his mouth, but he could not. Bevis hated to watch that part. He wanted to cover his face in his hands; at the breaking point he choked back his mortification and yelled at the groom, "Speak up, you damn fool!" and at this urging the groom croaked, "I do," and the crowd went wild.

Brother Stapleton brought the show to a dramatic conclusion, perhaps even overdoing it somewhat by having twelve pipe organs playing together as the bride and groom departed. The shivaree they gave that night for Bevis and Emelda was not imaginary; it was, as one participant remarked, the "shivareest shivaree ever shivered," with an incredible amount of noise and harassment of the newlyweds, who were given not a moment to themselves to think any thoughts or read each other's or even pretend to transmit a word into the other's head. It was just as well that they were given no opportunity for sleep that night, because Bevis would have been much too shy to share a bed with his bride. The second night of their marriage, they slept in separate beds, although before falling asleep they enjoyed a lusty copulation in their minds, and when they fell asleep their dreams were all mixed together and exchanged; in the morning he was awakened by the "sound" of Emelda doing a perfect imitation of a rooster's matinal crow. It required several more weeks of sleep to sort out the dreams and properly apportion them so that each had their fair share of nightmares. After a year of marriage, Emelda silently declared that although she had enormously enjoyed 365 incidents of imaginary albeit almost exhaustingly true-to-life intercourse, it was obvious that she would never conceive anything other than an imaginary baby in that fashion. Biology is biology, after all, and has nothing to do with make-believe.

The year of imaginary intimacy had made Bevis not quite so shy with his bride, so it was not too difficult for him to permit her to slip into his bed one night. Yet both afterwards agreed that actuality is a weak stepsister of imagination, although it was successful in begetting their firstborn, John Henry. As soon as Emelda was got with him, she and Bevis reverted gladly to their old way of intercourses, sexual and verbal, and when Bevis withdrew his savings from the bank and built his house, its bigeminality was intended literally to make separate rooms for the two of them, where they went on sleeping apart and coming together in their minds, and mixing their dreams and nightmares in fair proportion. There must have been at least three occasions thereafter when one of them physically crossed through the interior door that joined the rooms, because they had three additional sons: Jackson, William Robert ("Billy Bob") and Tracy. Along with John Henry, these four boys each noticed, in growing up, that their mother and father slept in separate rooms and never spoke to one another; since the only times the boys would not speak to one another was when they were angry, they assumed that their mother and father were always angry at one another, and therefore never on speaking terms. The boys had playmates whose parents were often heard to speak to one another, and some of the playmates claimed that their mothers and fathers actually slept in the same bed, and a few of the playmates went so far as to tell what their mothers and fathers did with one another when they were in bed.

The Ingledew boys disbelieved this, but they still felt isolated; they felt that their own parents were eccentric; they knew their father was full of blood and always cheerful and animated; they couldn't understand why their mother didn't like him enough even to say "howdy" to him. On the other hand, their mother was sweet-natured herself, and a good cook besides; they couldn't understand why their father didn't like her enough even to say, "Them shore was good biscuit, Maw." Their father talked freely and cheerfully to everybody else, but never to their mother.

One by one each of the sons grew old enough to understand the meaning and mystery of sex; one by one each was forced to accept the uncomfortable truth that in order for them to have been born, their happy father had to have slept with their mother, and that since their mother and father never slept together and weren't even on speaking terms, they couldn't possibly have been born and were therefore only imagining that they existed.

Imagination begets imagination. What lasting psychological effect all of this had upon the four boys may be imagined. The population of Stay More was declining, and one by one the Ingledew boys mentally subtracted themselves from it.

The population of Stay More declined for several reasons. People who lost their money when the bank was robbed worked twice as hard in order to replace the money, and by working twice as hard were afflicted with the frakes, and after recovering from the long lethargy and sense of futility that follows a bout with the frakes they wandered out of Stay More and were never seen again. The ones that stayed never really worked very hard again.

Tearle Ingledew, for example, who had been the most industrious of all the Ingledews because he had an excess of sweat, had worked so hard to replace his lost savings that he came down with perhaps the severest case of the frakes that anyone had ever seen: the rash was not confined to the genital area but spread all over his body; he was anointed with all the traditional remedies with all the traditional lack of effect; what little money he had reearned by working so hard he spent entirely for large quantities of Chism's Dew, and by staying in a constant state of intoxication managed to slight if not ignore his affliction, and in their own time his blisters festered and healed, and he was left with the characteristic feeling that life is a joke. The strange thing was, the joke struck him not as bad and pointless but hilarious. For the rest of his long life, he worked only hard enough to pay for his heavy consumption of Chism's Dew, and was full of good humor and could tell excellent jokes. He never gave up believing that life is futile, but the futility of it was always good for a laugh, and he was always laughing and causing others to laugh, and I believe I like Tearle Ingledew better than any of the others, even apart from his many kindnesses to me when I was young.

If he does not loom large in this particular saga, it is only because nothing much ever really happened to Tearle Ingledew, which is as it should be for persons who can laugh at the futility of life. He sat on the store porch or the mill porch, depending on where the shrinking crowds were, and told jokes and swapped yarns until he began to feel sober, then he would walk up to Waymon Chism's place and buy a gourdful to drink on the premises, then meander back to the village. "Meander" is the only word to describe Tearle's style of walking, and it is revealed as a symbol of the whole Ozarks, where everything meanders. All the rivers, streams, creeks and branches meander. The limbs of trees, especially sycamores, meander. Snakes meander. Tearle Ingledew meandered not so much because of alcohol in his brain as because he had nowhere to get to, and loads of time to get there in. When creeks and snakes and tree limbs and men are young, they go in pretty much of a straight line. When they get older, they meander. A rushing brook becomes a river and meanders. A boy becomes a man and meanders. A story becomes a book and meanders. There is always an end, but no hurry to get there; indeed, there is almost a strong wish *not* to get there. Let Tearle's meander, therefore, stand as a symbol both of the Ozarks themselves and of this, our study of its architecture.

Nothing ever happened to Tearle, not even death, although he might be dying as you read this; one would hope not, unless he has laughed at the futility of life for so long that he has at last realized that that very humorousness of life's futility is precisely the reason that life is precious, and, valuing it, loses it. Tearle, like all of his brothers save Bevis, never married, and has no descendants, and when he dies he will not be the last of the Ingledews to pass away, but he will be the last of the Ingledews born in that Century, and his death will seal the last vestige of that Century, so we have much reason for hoping that he is not on his last legs and that his liver is holding out.

Others continued to die, though. One day the loafers on the store porch got to reminiscing again about various people they hadn't seen for a long time, and the name of Eli Willard was mentioned, and they wondered if he were dead or if he would ever come back. The subject was good for a few minutes of speculation and then they tried to think of anybody else they hadn't seen for a long time, and somebody suddenly realized that the woman Whom We Cannot Name had not been seen since the day of the Unforgettable Picnic. The loafers got up off their nail kegs and crossed the road to her house and politely knocked on the door for several minutes before opening it. They went into her room but she wasn't there. They crossed the interior door into Jacob's room and found her upon Jacob's bed, dressed in her best dress with her hands folded upon her waist. They wondered why she had chosen Jacob's bed to die on, and they decided that in her old age she must have become somewhat confused. Anyway, she was dead, and they took her up to the cemetery and buried her beside Sarah. Brother Stapleton apologized that he couldn't show a eulogy because he claimed he didn't know a blessed thing about the woman but he offered a five-minute short subject showing the scene where Jacob's carriage is leaving Little Rock for his return to Stay More and he discovers that his wife Sarah is taking her social secretary home with her. Then the few people attending the funeral sang one chorus of:

> *Farther along we'll know all about it,*
> *Farther along we'll understand why;*
> *Cheer up, my brother, live in the sunshine,*
> *We'll understand it, all by and by.*

The woman had not left a will. Attorney Jim Tom Duckworth was consulted, and he advised that the house and contents should go to Isaac's heir, who was his wife Salina. Salina did not want the house; she refused to leave the dogtrot, where she remained in seclusion. Next in line was the oldest son, Denton, but he didn't want the house either. John wanted the house badly, but he had to wait his turn, because Monroe was next in line; Monroe thought about it and thought about it, deliberately taking his time because he knew how much John craved to have the house; it was, after all, the biggest house in town, one of the oldest and most impressive buildings in Stay More. The house that John was living in, and had reared his large family in, isn't even illustrated in this study, not necessarily because of my personal bias against John but because the house is unnoteworthy in all respects, at least in my opinion. John would have made a large leap up in the world if he could have inherited his grandfather's house. And for that very reason, Monroe kept it…or, rather, he accepted his inheritance of it, although he didn't care to live there any more than Denton did; he and Denton had shared the same bed all their lives, and saw no reason to discontinue the habit in their fifties, although this is not in any way to suggest that anything funny was going on; it was common practice for bachelor or spinster siblings to share a bed all their lives: so while Monroe did not abandon his accustomed bed, he deeded the house to his and John's younger brother Willis, making it convenient to Willis's store, and Willis moved into it with his younger sister Drussie, who, noting the trigeminality of the house and counting upon her fingers, realized that she and Willis made two, whereas the house was three, so she converted the house into a hotel, and hung a small sign over the porch that said simply "HOTEL." She gave the place a good cleaning, and ordered new linen and china and flatware from Sears, Roebuck and dressed up the three-hole privy out back with lace and chromolithographs of children rolling hoops, and ordered a case of expensive Nippon crepe toilet paper; then she sat in a rocker on the front porch day after day eagerly waiting her first guest, but the only people who came to her hotel were various neighbors, friends and relatives who did not intend to spend the night but only wanted to try out the novelty of using Nippon crepe toilet paper and discovering how superior it was to corncobs, sticks, leaves, mail order catalogs and old songbooks. Drussie had to order another case of rolls.

But still no paying guests arrived to spend the night at her hotel.

The economy was in bad shape, at least locally. The Jasper *Disaster* ran side-by-side stories about how Newton County was going to the dogs while nationally the city folks were all getting rich and lavishing their money on bootlegged booze and fancy autos and a strange music called jazz. Letters-to-the-editor poured in to the *Disaster* asking him to please stop rubbing it in. Drussie wrote pointing out that such stories of local poverty might frighten off potential guests for her hotel. The people of Stay More might not even have known they were poor if that dadblasted newspaper hadn't told them so.

John Ingledew asked Jim Tom Duckworth to bring suit against the newspaper, but it was too late: one by one the customers of John's bank withdrew their savings in order to make the down payment on crank-up phonographs and records, player pianos, cream separators, fancy cast-iron cooking stoves, inner-spring mattresses, wristwatches, and new radiators for their Fords. After all their savings were spent, they tried to float loans from John, but he had nothing to loan them, and the bank failed. There was no need for a bank; every penny that was earned was spent to meet the installments on credit purchases. And not many pennies were earned, because the land itself had been used up over the years, worn out from one-crop farming: year by year the average size of an ear of corn became smaller and smaller, until the nubbins were too tiny to husk and shell, and there was no grain for Denton and Monroe to grind in the mill, and the mill closed down. Denton and Monroe had no choice but return to farming full time, but the earth was too poor to farm, and they talked of going off to a city and finding work, although they hated the idea, and did not want to leave Stay More, or at least Newton County, or at least the Ozarks, but since there were not yet any cities in the Ozarks, at least not in Arkansas, and since the only city in Arkansas was Little Rock,

Denton and Monroe went there and found work and lived in a board-
ing house and were not seen again in Stay More for several years.

Bevis Ingledew, who had a wife and four sons to support, was no
more lucky at farming than Denton and Monroe, but he wouldn't
move to Little Rock, and he kept on farming, refusing to accept the
fact that there was no profit in it. As soon as his four sons were old
enough, he got them out of bed before daylight and put them to
work until past sunset, and Emelda cried because she couldn't scare up
enough grub to feed them sufficiently for all that work. Nightly her
dreams were shared with Bevis, but more often than not their dreams
were nightmares, until the only dream that Emelda had remaining
consisted of a doll fashioned from cornhusks. When they were awake,
Emelda silently "discussed" with Bevis the possible significance of this
cornhusk doll, but he, who had had his share of that image in their
remaining common dream, did not know its meaning any better than
she. Emelda treasured the humble cornhusk doll because it was the
only pleasant dream that still came to her at night, and it appeared
faithfully every night. In time, during a spare moment, Emelda
fashioned a real cornhusk doll and clothed it with mother-hubbard
and sunbonnet made of calico from a flour sack. Her sons admired
it and wished their father would speak up and admire it too, not
knowing he already had. Having created the female cornhusk doll,
Emelda next created a male one dressed in dungarees. Having created
thus a pair female and male, she couldn't stop, and went on making
cornhusk dolls until the house was filled with them, the females in
her room, the males in Bevis's.

Bevis was embarrassed by this useless activity and was afraid
that somebody might come and see it and spread the word around
the village that Emelda Ingledew had slipped a cog. He realized,
however, because he could read her mind, that she couldn't stop. He
knew also that she had given an individual name to each and every
one of the dolls, from Abella to Zona for the females and from
Aaron to Zuriel for the males. Furthermore, each of the dolls had a
distinct personality, and in the dreams they shared at night these dolls

began interpersonal relationships, usually of a happy manner that managed to crowd out many of their unpleasant nightmares. There were so many dolls that Bevis and Emelda might not have had any nightmares at all but for the fact that it was a drought year and the crops were failing and John Ingledew had no money to lend them even if he were willing to, which he was not, and Uncle Willis could not extend their credit at the store, and Aunt Drussie was unable to furnish them a free dinner at her hotel, and the only way they could eat at all was for their sons to go down to the bank of Swains Creek each night with a lantern and fish for a mess of catfish, which were always easy to catch after dark, until the Ingledews had caught and eaten them all. They went hungry for four days and then the boys asked permission from their mother to eat a couple of her cornhusk dolls, but Emelda was shocked at the thought of what would amount to cannibalism to her, and could not permit it. Since all of them had given up work, they sat most of the day on the store porch, slightly consoled by listening to Uncle Tearle make jokes about the futility of life. Out of compassion Uncle Willis gave them a can of Vienna sausages; they each had one and saved the rest for breakfast. Surely, otherwise, they would have starved.

One day a fancy automobile, in fact a Cadillac Four-Passenger Sport Phaeton with its top down, came into Stay More and drove around. The passengers were tourists, two ladies and two gentlemen, all wearing baggy knickers, golf hose and bow ties. They did not stop nor get out. They looked at the buildings and pointed at the people, and drove on. When they passed Bevis Ingledew's house, one of the women shouted "Stop!" to the man driving, and he applied his brakes. "Look at that," said the woman to her companions, pointing at Emelda Ingledew, who was sitting on the porch in her rocker, making a cornhusk doll named Romola. She was applying the finishing touch: a gingham sunbonnet. "I want one of those, Harry," the woman said to her companion, and Harry dutifully opened the door of the Sport Phaeton and stepped out, extracting his wallet.

"How much?" he said to Emelda, gesturing at the cornhusk doll.

"Huh?" she replied, never having suspected that anyone would attach a cash value to a cornhusk doll, any more than to a human life.

"*That,*" he said, clearly aiming his index finger at the doll. "It. Whatever. You sell? Me pay."

"I never sold one afore," she informed him.

"Fifty cents? A dollar?" he bargained.

"My lands," Emelda said, "it aint but some cornshucks and scraps of flour sacks."

"Harry!" called the woman from the car. "Louise says that she wants one too!"

"You got any more of them?" Harry asked Emelda.

"Aw, shore," Emelda admitted. "House is full of 'em. You want a he-doll or a she-doll?"

"Louise," Harry called to the car, "do you want a boy dolly or a girlie?"

"Oh, get one of each, Harry!" Louise said, and the other woman said, "For me too!"

Harry held up four fingers to Emelda; she went into Bevis's room and got two male dolls, then into her room for another female.

"How much?" he asked her again.

"Whate'er ye think they're worth," she said modestly.

"Four bits apiece?" he offered, and laid two one-dollar bills in her hand.

"Thank ye kindly," she said, and Harry took the dolls to the Sports Phaeton and gave a pair to each of the ladies.

The ladies examined their dolls and one said, "Aren't they the cat's meow?" and the other said, "Aren't they the bee's knees?" Then both told Harry that nothing would do but that they must also get a pair each as gifts for their friends Maxie, Lila, Isadora, Nikki, Maisie, Lydia and Stacia, and maybe they shouldn't forget Winnie and Daisie.

Harry returned to the porch and said to Emelda, "Make me a wholesale offer. Whaddayasay three for a buck? Gimme eighteen." She fetched the dolls for him, loaded his arms with them. He packed them into the trunk of the Sports Phaeton, then gave Emelda six more dollars, and the tourists drove away. As they passed back through the town, the women were seen to point together at the HOTEL sign on Drussie's hotel. Drussie watched the car slow down. The women seemed to be pleading with the men to stop at the hotel, and Drussie hoped the men would agree to stop, but apparently they did not, for the Sports Phaeton went on out of town and was not seen again.

Emelda Ingledew, however, had eight dollars, which was more money of her own than she had ever held in her hand before. She ran all the way to Willis's store, where Bevis and the boys were loafing, and, forgetting herself, spoke aloud publicly to Bevis for the first time, showing him the money and saying, "Lookee what them tourists paid me for a passel of cornshuck dolls!" Bevis was extremely embarrassed on several counts: he was embarrassed because a female was speaking to him, because she was publicly displaying money, because she was admitting that she made corn-husk dolls, and above all because he did not believe that tourists would pay eight dollars for any amount of cornhusk dolls, although, since he could read her mind, he knew that she was not lying to him. Together, and with the help of their four sons, they went into Willis's store and bought eight dollars' worth of Corn Flakes, Quaker Oats, Vienna sausages, sardines, sody crackers, coffee, flour, and fistfuls of Hershey bars, O Henrys and Baby Ruths. The latter items were not good for their teeth, and they all developed cavities which the dentist, Bevis's oldest brother E.H., refused to treat for less than cash money. They resigned themselves to letting their teeth rot until they fell out, but they were saved from this fate by the arrival of a letter at the post office addressed simply to: The Dollmaker, Stay More, Ark. By then, everybody knew that Emelda made cornhusk dolls, and they didn't dare laugh at her since she had sold eight dollars' worth of them.

Postmaster Uncle Willis delivered the letter to her. It was signed by a St. Louis woman named Isadora Lubitschi, and it said: "Dear Madame: My good friend Louise Goldstein recently returned from a delightful tour of the woodsy mountains and presented me with a pair of dolls which she had purchased from you, if you are the person in question who manufactures these items, which consist of some sort of dried plant material covered with bits of cloth in the fashion of women's long dresses and men's working overhalls. If you are the person in question who manufactures these charming curios, I would be pleased to inform you that I am in the business of middleman, or middlewoman, to the trade in *objets d'art,* and I am able to quote you an offer of $36.00 (thirty-six dollars) per gross for whatever quantities of such items you can supply. Please ship them parcel post to the above address." Emelda was dumbfounded. She did not know what "gross" meant, unless the St. Louis woman considered her cornhusk dolls coarse, vulgar or obscene. Emelda asked Bevis telepathically what "gross" meant, but he had only heard the word when Jim Tom Duckworth spoke of "gross injustice" in court. So they asked Uncle Jim Tom what it meant and he said it meant something so mighty awful or misdone that it can't be pardoned. Emelda showed him one of her dolls and asked him for his opinion, but he opined that as far as his taste was concerned, the doll might look pretty awful but it wasn't so gross that it couldn't be pardoned. He, for one, was willing to pardon it. Emelda showed him the letter from the St. Louis woman. He read it, and called her attention to the structure of the phrasing, "per gross." "That's *a* gross," he said. "It means how many of something, but I disremember the figure. Why'n't ye ask Uncle Willis. He orter know."

They were reluctant to ask Uncle Willis, because nobody ever believed anything that Uncle Willis said, but they had nowhere else to turn, so they asked Uncle Willis and he told them that a gross was a dozen dozen. They thought that was unbelievable, but they sat down on the store porch and counted up on their fingers, trying to figure out what a dozen dozen were. Since they each had only ten fingers, it was difficult to count up to a dozen, and get another dozen on top of that. Uncle Willis watched them for as long as he could stand it, which was pretty long, and then he took from his storeroom a cardboard carton marked "One Gross, White Thread" and gave it to them and told them to count the spools, which they did, finding that there were 144 spools. Emelda and Bevis went home and counted the dolls, and discovered that there were 432 male dolls and 432 female dolls. They divided these into piles of 144 each, and discovered that they had exactly six gross of dolls. Emelda hated to see them go, but she could always make more. They shipped the six gross off to St. Louis and received in return the woman's check for $216. Although John's bank had failed and he could not cash the check for them, he decided to reopen the bank and let them deposit their check and draw upon it as they needed. John had never given up hope of reopening his bank; he still subscribed to and faithfully read *The Bankers' and Investors' Weekly;* I doubt if his conscience was troubled at all by the fact that he was enabled to reopen his bank by a deposit from the same son whom he had denied permission to withdraw his savings years before.

Bevis Ingledew took his wagon and drove around to all of the farms in Stay More, buying cornhusks for 5¢ a bushel. No one thought him crazy, because word had quickly spread of Emelda's talent for converting cornhusks into money, and most of the other women were dying to learn her secret, but Emelda pulled down all the shades in all her windows and arranged her four sons into an assembly line, and together, with Bevis guarding the exterior of the house to ward off peepers, they turned out cornhusk dolls by the thousand, and shipped them off to St. Louis, and made a fantastic lot of money, more than they knew what to do with, so much more that they were easily persuaded by John, whose bank they practically owned now, to invest it. John faithfully read *The Bankers' and Investors' Weekly,* and he had dreamed for years of dabbling in securities analysis or becoming a "Customer's Man," but he had no potential customers until his own son Bevis had more money than he knew what to do with. He took Bevis's surplus money and sent it off to a brokerage office in Little Rock and invested it in those issues which *The Bankers' and Investors' Weekly* recommended as growth stocks, and sure enough they grew and grew. It mattered naught that their growingest stock was General Electric although they had never seen electricity and did not believe in it. They made so much money in the stock market that John's commissions from this one customer were enough for a full salary, and John was thinking of renovating his bank, while Emelda telepathically pestered Bevis to build a larger and finer house for them. John began to pay attention to those issues which *The Bankers' and Investors' Weekly* classified as "high risk speculative ventures," investment in which was practically gambling, but John began to gamble, and to win. One stock in particular, Poupée Industries Inc. of St. Louis, was particularly attractive, and John bought more and more shares of it, and it continued to rise, until it was one of the highest priced stocks on the under-the-counter market, and Bevis and Emelda owned practically all of it. A lavishly printed annual stockholders' report was mailed to them, and they discovered that Poupée Industries Inc. was merely the distributor of quaint dolls "which consist of some sort of dried plant material covered with bits of cloth in the fashion of women's long dresses and men's working overhalls and are manufactured at a secret location in the enchanted Ozarks."

Then the stock market crashed. It wasn't John D. Ingledew's fault any more than it was John D. Rockefeller's, but the latter survived while the former didn't. A small headline in the Jasper *Disaster* noted the fact: "Stay More Stockholders Wiped Out in Panic of Wall Street" and a small editorial said simply "We hope some lesson has been learned from all of this."

Bevis Ingledew was always cheerful and full of blood, and he took the bad news in good part, but John D. Ingledew took to bed, and stayed there, looking gloomier and doomier than he ever had, if that were possible. Doc Colvin Swain was called in. Doc Swain was not only the best of Stay More's physicians, but he was also the seventh son of a seventh son (who was Gilbert Swain, Lizzie's seventh), and a seventh son of a seventh son has the power to cure any sickness known to man except the frakes. But even with this power, Doc Swain could not cure John D. Ingledew, and John D. died. Doc Swain was so puzzled as to the cause of death that he asked for permission to perform an autopsy, expecting to find perhaps a broken heart, but John D.'s heart, when Doc Swain finally succeeded in finding it, was not broken but only atrophied, severely.

At the funeral, Brother Long Jack Stapleton discovered that he was unable to show the eulogy. Something had gone wrong with his power; it wouldn't work. The show would not go on. He tried and tried to turn it on, but not a single image appeared. So he said a short prayer and they sang several choruses of "Farther along we'll know all about it" and Brother Stapleton went home, wondering if farther along he ever would understand why he had lost his power to show. He never did, and he never regained it, and some folks said that the loss of his power was the reason he himself died, not long after, leaving Stay More without a resident pastor for the rest of its life.

Chapter fourteen

When John Henry "Hank" Ingledew was ten years old, he ran away from home, to join the circus. The year before, he had grown mighty tired of making cornhusk dolls. Making cornhusk dolls all day long leaves the mind idle to think idle thoughts, and although Hank was pretty good at thinking no thoughts at all, he could not help but continue to speculate upon the fact that he probably did not exist because he could not have been born if his mother and father did not sleep together and were not even on speaking terms with one another although they did seem to cooperate at least in the making of cornhusk dolls. Other boys his age did not have to make cornhusk dolls, and that was one more reason for feeling that he did not really exist but was only imagining things. His reasoning was that if he did not exist he might as well not exist someplace else instead of here in Stay More. The trouble was, he couldn't conceive of someplace else, until one day in the late summer of his tenth year, when a billposter in a bow tie and a straw boater, driving a Ford truck, came into town and received permission to glue an enormous circus bill to the side of the barn that had been built by Denton and Monroe and was prominently located in the center of town. Hank Ingledew, along with all the other children of Stay More, gazed in awe at the poster, which showed in garish colors pictures of ferocious tropical animals, women in tight clothes standing up on the backs of prancing horses, acrobats leaping through the air, and announced that Foogle Bros. Three-Ring Shows would play at Jasper, Ark, three days only, Aug. 24–27, with a Grand Midway.

It occurred to Hank that a circus was a someplace else that would beat hell out of not existing in Stay More, even though he wasn't required to make cornhusk dolls anymore since the stock market collapsed and people out in the world were spending their money on apples and pencils instead of cornhusk dolls. Hank began to hatch a plan: he would sneak off to Jasper in time to be there when the circus arrived, and he would get a job with the circus, so when his folks showed up to attend the circus they would see that he already had a job, and might even be proud of him, and they wouldn't make a big fuss when the circus moved on and took him with it. So on the eve of August 24th, when nobody was looking, he "borrowed" one of his father's mules without telling anyone and rode it bareback into Jasper, where he found to his dismay that the circus had already arrived in town and was being erected, by the light of strings of intensely burning glass bulbs. Jasper had not yet received electricity, but the circus had its own portable generator.

Hank could do nothing at first but stare with fascination at all of the light bulbs, until one of the workmen said to him, "Show aint open yet, kid. Come back tomorrow." Hank told the man he was hoping to get him a job of work. "See the punk pusher," the man replied, and directed him to a tough-looking man in a teeshirt, who was supervising a bunch of local boys, many of whom Hank recognized. "No cash. Free ticket only," the man said to him. "Go help those punks hold that rope." Hank said that he wanted to join the circus for keeps and do something important like impossible stunts. The man laughed at him and asked what kind of impossible stunt he could do. Well, Hank said, he could touch his elbows together behind his back. He demonstrated. "Hey, that's pretty good, kid," the man remarked sincerely. "Come with me." The man took him to a trailer where another man in a teeshirt was just sitting in a canvas chair, doing nothing but smoking a cigarette. "Hey, Cholly, get a load of this," the first man said and told Hank to repeat his impossible stunt of touching his elbows together behind his back. Hank did. Cholly pursed his lips and stared at Hank through squinted lids. "He'll do," Cholly said and took Hank and fitted him out with a clown suit and showed him how to tie a rubber ball over his nose and put white and purple paint on his face. Then Cholly took him to another man in a teeshirt and said, "Phil, watch the kid," and as Phil watched Hank touched his elbows together behind his back several times in quick succession. "What else can he do?" Phil wanted to know. Hank said that he could also pat his stomach while rotating his other hand on top of his head, and vice versa. "Great," said Phil. "Can you juggle?" Hank couldn't, so Phil took three oranges and began to show him how. Hank was getting sleepy, but he kept practicing until he could not only juggle the three balls but throw them all up in the air, touch his elbows behind his back three times, and catch them as they came down.

The putting up of the circus was finished, and all the other local boys were run off the grounds, but Hank was allowed to stay. It must have been close to midnight, but none of the circus people seemed to be sleepy. They sat around and played cards and smoked cigarettes and told dirty jokes. Phil said to him, "Well, let's meet some of the finkers and geeks," and he took him around and introduced him as "the new joey" to several of the circus people: the other clowns, acrobats, horsemen, and even to the sideshow people, who made him uneasy: a bearded lady, a very fat lady, a midget, a man covered with tatoos, another man who seemed normal but Phil whispered into Hank's ear that the man did an act of biting the heads off of chickens, and a man who was very, very old, who Phil said was billed as "the World's Oldest Man." None of these people showed any particular interest in meeting Hank, but the man who was the World's Oldest Man seemed to be studying him keenly behind his wrinkled eyelids. The old man's eyes seemed to be still working, although none of the rest of him looked like it would work; Hank doubted that the old man could speak, so he was surprised and momentarily disbeliev- ing when the old man asked him a question, "Where are you from,

Joey?" After Hank had persuaded himself that the old man's mouth actually had moved and that he had spoken, Hank answered, telling him that he was from Stay More, which was a small town about ten miles south of here. He was required to repeat himself, loudly, for the old man was nearly deaf. Then the old man nodded his head almost imperceptibly and spoke again: "You're an Ingledew, aren't you? I would recognize an Ingledew anywhere, even behind that rubber nose and that greasepaint."

Hank went away wondering how the old man had known he was an Ingledew, but he decided that anybody as old as that man was probably knew everything that was to be known. And then the magic electric bulbs were going out, and Phil told Hank that he would have to do a star pitch. When Hank looked puzzled and asked what a star pitch was, Phil laughed and slapped him on the shoulder and said, "You'll have to learn the circus lingo, kid. A star pitch is sleeping out in the open, on the grass."

Hank slept on the grass, sleeping fitfully, having dreams of performing his stunts in his clown suit in front of a whole bunch of people, many of whom might recognize him behind his rubber nose and his greasepaint, as the old man had done. When he woke and rose up from the grass, he discovered that nobody else in the camp was awake even though the sun was well up in the sky. He figured that people who stayed up so late at night probably slept late in the morning. He smelled coffee a-making somewhere, and tracing it, found a trailer with the back end open and a man inside cooking up a bunch of flapjacks.

It was the first time Hank had ever seen or heard of a man doing the cooking; maybe the man was also one of the freaks. But Hank was hungry, and he eyed the flapjacks hungrily, licking his lips, until the cooking man noticed him, and said, "New kid, huh? Welcome to the crumb castle." The cooking man loaded a plate with flapjacks and gave them to him along with a mug of coffee. Hank sat down at a nearby table to eat but the cooking man explained to him that that was the "long end," reserved for the circus workmen; the performers had to eat at the "short end." Hank moved, and ate his breakfast, joined gradually by other clowns and acrobats. He learned that the

Midway would not open until noon, and the first performance under the Big Top was not scheduled until two o'clock.

After watering his mule, Hank wandered around the grounds, treating himself to a free preview of the animals. There was a lion in an iron cage on wheels and it roared at him, giving him a slight start. There was an elephant tethered by one enormous ankle to a stake; he had never seen an elephant before, but he knew what it was because he had studied African geography in the fourth grade. It did not roar at him; it seemed to be very slow and calm and gentle, lifting an enormous foot slightly from time to time. He patted it on its tremendously long snout; suddenly the elephant coiled its snout and uncoiled it with such force that Hank was flung through the air a distance of nearly two hats and landed on his back in pain. He got up gingerly, resolved to go no closer to the elephant; he fingered himself all over for broken bones; none were, but his upper lip was beginning to swell, and by the time the Big Top opened his lip would be so swollen that he would have the most comical face of all the clowns. He stared malevolently at the elephant and said to it, "If Godalmighty made you, He orter make one more and quit." He wandered on, and found a monkey in a cage; the monkey was so small and timid-looking that he couldn't possibly do Hank any harm, but when Hank tried to shake hands the monkey scratched him, leaving bleeding lines halfway up his arm. Hank decided to leave the animals alone, and wandered over to the area where the sideshow people were loafing around in the morning sunshine. A reporter from the Jasper *Disaster* had arrived, and was interviewing the fat lady, asking her questions about her diet and how much she weighed, and did she have any trouble rolling over in her sleep at night? Then the reporter interviewed the midget, the bearded lady, the world's strongest man, and he tried to interview the man who bit heads off of chickens, but the man would answer no questions, so the reporter went on to the World's Oldest Man and asked him, "How old are you?" There was no response.

Hank told the reporter, "He's near deef. Talk loud." The reporter repeated the question loudly.

"I can't be certain," replied the World's Oldest Man, "but several years past a hundred, I can assure you."

"How did you manage to live that long?" asked the reporter. "Are you an abstainer?"

"I've never tasted alcohol, no," replied the old man, "but I don't think that had anything to do with it."

"Well—?" the reporter waited, then persisted, "To what do you attribute your longevity?"

The old man was silent, as if thinking, then he said quietly, "I kept moving. I never slowed down long enough for death to catch me."

The reporter admired that answer and commented, "You seem to have all of your wits about you."

"Thank you," replied the old man. "I do."

The reporter pursued the question. "But why did you keep moving?"

Again the old man was silent, as if meditating and discovering the answer for the first time, and when he spoke the answer it was with a self-wonderment. "I felt there was something I had to do. Ought to do. Was foreordained to do."

"No fooling?" said the reporter. "And what was that something?"

"Whatever I have done," said the old man, and would not elaborate.

"How long have you been with this circus?" asked the reporter.

"Oh, it's hard to remember. Maybe twenty years."

"And what did you do before that?"

"I traveled. I was engaged in various sales campaigns."

"Where are you from, originally?"

"Connecticut."

The reporter thanked the old man for the interview and went on to interview the tattooed man. Hank wandered back to the crumb castle or chuck wagon or whatever it was to see if dinner was ready yet. After eating, he saw that the Midway was open, and he strolled it, keeping an eye out for any of his folks, whom he did not want to see until he had his clown suit and make-up on. But there weren't many people on the Midway. He had two dollars and seventy-five cents in his pocket, which was all of his life's savings after the stock market crashed, so he spent some of this to ride the Ferris Wheel and get a cone of cotton candy. Then he realized he'd better go practice his juggling before the Big Top opened. As he was leaving the Midway, he passed a peanut vendor and was surprised to discover that the peanut vendor was the World's Oldest Man, hawking peanuts out of a tray that was suspended from his neck on a string. Not very loudly, the old peanut vendor was calling, "Fresh roasted peanuts! A nickel a bag!" Hank went up to him and gave him a nickel. The old man looked at him and gave him a bag of peanuts but refused his nickel.

"You're an Ingledew," said the old man. "I can't charge an Ingledew anything."

Hank commented, speaking loudly, "That thar sideshow must not pay ye very well, that you're obliged to sell goobers on the side."

The old man shook his head. "No, boy, I don't need to sell peanuts. I've been selling things all my life, and I just can't give up the confounded habit." And he hobbled off down the Midway, croaking, "Fresh roasted peanuts! A nickel a bag!" Hank wondered again about how the old man was so old that he knew everything and therefore knew that Hank was an Ingledew, although that didn't explain why he would give away a bag of peanuts free of charge to any Ingledew.

Hank went to Phil's trailer and with Phil's help put on his clown suit and his rubber nose and greasepaint. He confessed to Phil that he was a bit nervous about appearing in front of all those people. Phil snorted. "What's the name of this place? Jasper? Well, in circus lingo a 'jasper' is a local person who buys a ticket. There're not many jaspers in Jasper."

Phil was right: when Hank went into the Big Top for the first time, he discovered that there weren't more than fifty people in the audience, and none of them were Stay Morons. Although there were three rings in the circus, only one of them was being used. With the other clowns, Hank went around the ring, doing his elbow-touching and juggling act. Nobody laughed, although the younger members of the audience giggled and pointed. Hank was disappointed; it hadn't been much of a thrill. He suffered the sourhours while waiting for the evening performance. The attendance at the night show wasn't much better, and again there was no one from Stay More. Hank knew it had been a bad drought summer and people didn't have much money, and his own folks didn't have any money at all. But he wished that at least one of his uncles or brothers would show up in the audience and recognize him. Maybe tomorrow. But when the evening performance was over, Phil assembled all the circus people and said to them, "Okay, let's blow this morgue. Everybody up at dawn and tear down the rags." Hank was surprised to discover that his friend Phil was apparently the boss of the whole circus, and he asked him if he meant that they were leaving in the morning, and Phil said, "Yeah, kid, this town is a total blank," so Hank asked him if he could go with them to whatever next town they were going to, and Phil said, "Sure, kid, but the pay is lousy." Hank realized that he hadn't been paid anything for his two performances so far, but he'd had plenty of free food. He went to bed early on the grass and had dreams of doing his act in front of big crowds in the cities.

He was awakened just before dawn by a hand on his shoulder. It was the World's Oldest Man. "Get up, Ingledew," he said. Hank rose quickly to his feet. "Let's go home," the old man said. "The circus is over."

"But I'm a-gorn with 'em. Phil said I could," Hank protested, then remembered he would have to speak loudly for the old man to hear him. He began to repeat himself loudly, but the old man hissed "Sshh!" and put a finger to his lips and clamped the other hand over Hank's mouth. "Wait 'till we're out of here," the old man said and took his arm and began to lead him out of the circus lot. Hank couldn't understand why the old man intended to go with him. Or maybe the old man just intended to escort him out of the circus. If the old man was so old that he knew everything, even Hank's last name, then maybe the old man knew some reason why Hank should not join the circus for keeps and go with them to the next town. Suddenly Hank remembered his mule, and by mute sign language or pantomime he tried to convey this to the old man, and was finally required to whisper loudly in the old man's ear, "My mule," and the old man let him go and get it. Then the old man slipped into a tent and got a fifty-pound sack of peanuts and hoisted it up onto the back of the mule. Hank led the mule and they left the grounds of the circus. When they were out of earshot of anyone in the circus, Hank raised his voice and said to the old man, "I was fixin to jine the circus fer keeps. Phil said I could. Aint he the boss?"

"Philip Foogle and his brother Charles own the circus, yes," the old man said. "But he isn't the boss, and neither is Charles."

"Who is?"

"I am. Or, rather, I'm an agent of the boss."

"Why won't you let me jine the circus? I don't want to go back to Stay More."

"You don't? That's dreadful. You shouldn't have left it in the first place. Didn't anyone ever tell you the story of your great-great-uncle Benjamin Ingledew?"

Hank had heard of the story of his great-grandpap's older brother Benjamin, who had headed for California to hunt for gold and died in the Mountain Meadows Massacre, but he didn't understand what that had to do with his joining the circus, and he wondered how the old man knew about Benjamin Ingledew, but realized that the old man was so old that he knew everything. They were well outside of Jasper by now, halfway to Parthenon, and the old man was still hobbling along beside him. Was he actually going all the way to Stay More with him? It would sure wear him out.

"You wanter ride the mule?" Hank offered.

"Thank you," the old man said. "I would be very grateful." Hank helped him to climb up on the mule's back, and they went on. The sun was rising.

Hank indicated the fifty-pound sack of peanuts on the mule's shoulders, and asked, "You aim to sell them goobers in Stay More?"

"If I can," the old man said.

They walked on, and passed through Parthenon. They did not talk much, because the old man would only speak if Hank asked him a question and although there were many questions which Hank could have asked him Hank didn't know which one to start with, so he remained silent. Hank wondered if the old man was quitting the circus for good, or maybe he just intended to sell his peanuts in

Stay More and then catch up with the circus later on. Maybe in the meantime Hank could persuade him to let him join the circus, if he really was the boss.

It was almost noon when they reached Stay More. Hank began to worry if his folks would give him a licking for sneaking off from home and taking the mule with him. He had a feeling that maybe the old man could protect him, so when the old man asked to get down from the mule at Willis's store, Hank asked him if he didn't mind staying with him until he took the mule home, and the old man smiled a small smile and nodded his head. Thus, the old man did not get off the mule until they reached Hank's house, where Hank's father and brothers were sitting on the porch waiting for dinner, and Hank's mother came running out of the kitchen as soon as Bevis Ingledew telepathically informed her that their errant son had returned with the mule and that an unbelievably old man was sitting on the mule.

"Boy, whar on earth have ye—" Bevis Ingledew started to demand of Hank but then he stared fixedly at the old man for a long moment and exclaimed, "Strike me blind! If it aint ole Eli Willard! But it caint be! I've not laid eyes on ye since I was 'bout twenty, and I'm past forty now, and back then you was already senile."

"He's the World's Oldest Man," Hank declared proudly, as if he had invented, or at least discovered, him. But he had heard stories about Eli Willard and knew that he had already been in Stay More again and again and again long before Hank was born.

"Jist in time for dinner," Emelda remarked, and invited Eli Willard into her kitchen, where she served him and Bevis and the boys a frugal but filling lunch. During the meal, Eli Willard was brought up to date on the current condition of Stay More: who had died, who had been born, the opening and closing of the bank, the closing of the mill, the coming and going of the city-women homesteaders, the Unforgettable Picnic, the making and selling of corn-husk dolls, the failure of crops, and so forth.

Eli Willard showed no particular interest or emotion at any of this news, although he remarked that he was happy to have noticed that there was now a gasoline pump standing in the road beside Willis's store, which implied that there was now an abundance of horseless carriages in the neighborhood. He asked if there had been any more lawsuits against hapless motorists whose vehicles had frightened livestock. The Ingledews were embarrassed at his bringing up the subject, and they apologized on behalf of the departed Uncle Denton, and said that there was a legend in the Ingledew family that Uncle Denton had a peculiar sense of humor and had intended the lawsuit only as a joke. Eli Willard smiled a wan smile. Then he thanked them for the dinner and asked Hank to take him back to the general store. Eli Willard's reappearance had caused so much excitement to Bevis and Emelda that they forgot to reprimand Hank for running away from home, or even to ask where he had been. Hank helped Eli Willard up on the mule's back once again and took him and his fifty-pound sack of peanuts to Willis's store, where Eli Willard attempted to buy a hundred small paper sacks from Willis, who was so astonished and delighted to find the Connecticut peddler still among the living that he refused to accept payment for the tiny sacks, but, when Eli Willard had transferred the contents of the fifty-pound sack of peanuts into one hundred half-pound sacks, with Hank's help, Willis accepted the gift of one sack free gratis. Then Eli Willard sat on the store porch and attempted to sell peanuts at five cents a bag.

Business was not very brisk. Willis tactfully pointed out to Eli Willard that the word "bag" means scrotum throughout the Ozarks, and that instead of saying "Fresh roasted peanuts! A nickel a bag!" Eli Willard should say "Fresh roasted peanuts! A nickel a poke!" Therefore the peanut peddler altered his pitch, but business did not improve. Willis offered the further opinion that the word "peanuts" itself was suspect, because it suggested not only the testicles but also micturition. "Goobers" also suggested the male genitals, but was not as suggestive as peanuts. So Eli Willard began to say, "Fresh roasted goobers! A nickel a poke!" whenever anyone came along, which wasn't often. He sold a few pokes. Hank decided that maybe Eli Willard intended to rejoin the circus as soon as he had sold all of the peanuts. To test this notion, he casually asked the old man if he knew where the circus was going after it left Jasper. Eli Willard nodded. Hank left the store and went around from house to house in Stay

More, telling everybody that old Eli Willard was back in town, and offering a whole half-pound of goobers for just five cents. Soon the store porch was crowded with people cracking and eating peanuts, and before long they were up to their ankles in peanut shells. As the afternoon waned, Eli Willard sold his last poke of peanuts. Willis Ingledew swept the peanut shells off the store porch, and closed his store and went home to eat supper. Eli Willard and Hank were alone. The profits from the sale of peanuts had come to exactly five dollars, which Eli Willard gave to Hank, saying it was payment for the ride from Jasper to Stay More.

"How you gorn to git back?" Hank wanted to know.

"I'm not."

"Huh? You aint givin up on the circus fer good, air ye?"

Eli Willard nodded.

"Wal, will ye tell me whar they went, so's I can fine 'em?"

Eli Willard shook his head. Then he asked, "What's your name, Ingledew?"

"John Henry. Everbody calls me Hank."

Eli Willard seemed to be only thinking about that, without comment. Then he unbuttoned his left sleeve and removed from his wrist a dazzling gold wristwatch; even the band was gold. He handed it to Hank. "It's a chronometer," he explained. "Keeps perfect time. Never loses a second. Not a fraction of a second. But it isn't for you, except in trust. Keep it for your son."

"My son?" Hank said. "Heck, I ain't but ten year old."

"Yes, but you'll have a son some day."

Hank thought about that. He realized that in order to have a son you first had to find a girl and sweet-talk her into marrying you, and then you had to persuade her to get into bed with you and let you do it to her, and more than once if it wasn't the right time of month. Hank could never do anything like that, and he told Eli Willard so, but the old man just laughed and assured him that he would indeed eventually do all of those things, and more.

"But what if it aint a son but a daughter?"

"Try again. And again. And when your son is old enough to appreciate, give him that chronometer and tell him my story."

"What's your story?"

"Four score and ten years ago, I sold a clock to your great-great-grandfather, who, as you probably know, was the first white settler of Stay More. It wasn't a very good clock, I must confess…" Eli Willard went on, and told Hank the whole long story of his many many returns to Stay More, what merchandise he had offered if not sold, the experiences he had had, not excluding the humiliations and the boredom. He talked through and past suppertime, and Hank was getting mighty hungry, but he figured the least he could do in return for such a fine gold watch, even if he couldn't wear it himself but only keep it for his son, was to listen carefully to the old man's story and try to remember it so that he could tell it to his son on the day that he would give him the fine gold watch, and maybe his son could make some sense out of the story even if Hank couldn't.

It was a very interesting story, Hank thought, although he didn't see any particular significance in it, unless it was just about time in general, time passing, time coming and staying awhile and going away forever not never to come back anymore. It was kind of sad, he thought. It was almost like not knowing whether or not you really existed because in order for you to have been born your mother and father had to speak to one another and go to bed together, and as far as he knew his mother and father never had. Eli Willard seemed to be a very wise old man, and Hank decided that when the old man got finished telling his story Hank would ask him for his opinion on whether or not a person could exist if his parents had never spoken to one another or gone to bed together.

It seemed to be getting late. The lightning bugs had all come out and filled the air. The old man's voice was becoming weak and hoarse, but he seemed to be near the finish. He was at the part where he drove the first horseless carriage into Stay More and Uncle Denton sued him for it and he went away and joined a circus and didn't come back again for twenty years.

He's almost done, Hank realized, and then Hank could ask him some questions. He had to strain his ears to hear what the old man was saying in his weak, hoarse voice. And then he could not hear him at all. The old man's lips were still moving, but Hank couldn't catch a word. Hank put his ear up close to the old man's mouth and managed to catch one feeble word that sounded like "peanuts" but then he couldn't hear anything else. Eli Willard's lips went on moving. "I caint hear you!" Hank hollered into his ear, but Eli Willard just closed his eyes, and his lips went on moving for a while and then stopped moving, and his chin fell to his chest. Hank gave his shoulder a shake and Eli Willard fell over.

Hank ran up the road to Doc Swain's place and fetched Doc Swain, who came and inspected Eli Willard and declared that it looked as if he had been dead for many years. Doc Swain took his shoulders and Hank took his legs and they carried him over to E.H. Ingledew's dentist shop, where E.H., who was a mortician as well as a dentist, carefully embalmed him. The next day the people of Stay More assembled and discussed the situation. They didn't know where to ship the body, and even if they did they couldn't afford it. A search of the dead man's pockets had produced just a tiny amount of cash, not even enough for a box coffin. Hank Ingledew didn't tell anyone about the gold wristwatch, which rightfully belonged to his future son; he wrapped the watch in flannel and put it into a tin lard pail and buried it in a place that not even I know. Eli Willard was not buried. The Stay More cemetery, after all, was for Stay Morons, and Eli Willard was not a Stay Moron. Willis Ingledew offered in place of a coffin an unused glass showcase in the rear of his general store, and Eli Willard's well-preserved body was laid to rest in this showcase, and all of the Ingledews, at least, gathered around it and sang:

> *Farther along we'll know all about it,*
> *Farther along we'll understand why;*
> *Cheer up, my brother, live in the sunshine,*
> *We'll understand it, all by and by.*

One day Hank Ingledew laboriously hand-lettered a sign, "WURL'S OLDISS MAN," and took it into the store and, with Willis's permission, placed it on top of the showcase. Hank brooded sometimes because Eli Willard had not lived long enough for Hank to ask him the question about whether or not Hank could exist if his parents had never spoken to one another or slept together. Sometimes when Willis was sitting out on the store porch, Hank would slip into the rear of the store and sit down beside the showcase and make believe that he was talking to Eli Willard and asking him questions. In this way, over a period of time, he came to understand the power of make-believe, and this was a consolation to him.

Eli Willard rested in peace in the showcase for several years, and people came from all over Newton County to see him, and while they were in the store they would usually buy a candy bar or a plug of chewing tobacco or something, and this business helped Willis Ingledew survive the lean years of the Great Depression and even to make modest loans to all the other Ingledews to help them survive.

Willis was totally forgiven for whatever errors of credulity he had made long ago; people began to believe him; they believed anything he said; they even believed, all of a sudden one day, that he actually possessed an automobile. On the day they believed he possessed an automobile he was driving it into Jasper for repairs when he lost control on a sharp curve and plunged down a steep embankment, totally wrecking the car. He died instantly and they buried him, singing "Farther Along" over his grave. He was the last male of his line.

His niece Lola, whom nobody realized was secretly his daughter, inherited the general store, and her first act as proprietress was to insist that the other Ingledews kindly remove the glass showcase with the body of Eli Willard in it. She said she would not set foot in the store until they did. So she did not set foot in the store, which was all right with just about anybody, because nobody had any money to spend there, although unfortunately the post office was also inside the store. But Lola did not inherit the postmastership, because U.S. government positions are not inheritable. When Willis Ingledew died, the Beautiful Girl, who had returned to Stay More after a long and mysterious absence and had purchased Bob Cluley's little general store up at the other end of Main Street, purchased it with money that nobody knew how or where or why she had obtained, now applied to the U.S. government for the post of postmistress, and was granted it, much to the chagrin of Lola, who could only watch helplessly as

Tearle Ingledew loaded the cabinet of post office boxes into a wagon and hauled it up Main Street to the Beautiful Girl's general store. Lola and the Beautiful Girl had in common that they were spinsters and that they were general store proprietresses, but they had absolutely nothing else in common.

The Jasper *Disaster* ran a feature story on the corpse of Eli Willard under the title, "Connecticut Itinerant Has No Final Resting Place, Even in Death." One of the national wire services picked up the story, and soon it was running in papers all over the country. A family of Willards in Rhode Island wrote to the Newton County coroner, claiming that Eli Willard was their longlost great-grandfather, but the coroner replied that Eli Willard was a lifelong bachelor who had no kin or descendants. The students of Yale University took up a collection for the purpose of having the showcase shipped to Yale's Dwight Chapel, but the university administration vetoed the idea. The Governor of Connecticut wrote the Governor of Arkansas suggesting that something ought to be done, and the latter replied that his staff was investigating, with the main problem being to locate Newton County in general and Stay More in particular. Meanwhile a man drove up to Lola's store and introduced himself as Philip Foogle and asked to be allowed to view the remains. Lola said she wouldn't set foot inside the store, but she would unlock it for him, and did, and the man went in and later came back out and said that the deceased had been, when last seen, wearing an extremely expensive gold chronometer wristwatch which was not now on the deceased's person. Foogle claimed that he had loaned a considerable sum of money to the deceased, who had spent it on the wristwatch. In short, he, Foogle, wanted the wristwatch. Lola said she didn't know nothing about no wristwatch. Foogle asked who had been with the deceased at the time of his deceasement, and Lola told him Hank Ingledew, and gave him directions to Hank's house, and Foogle went there and was mildly surprised to discover that Hank Ingledew was a grown-up version of the same ten-year-old kid whom he had almost converted into a permanent clown several years before.

"Aha!" said Foogle, and then, "Okay, kid, come clean. What did you do with the wristwatch?"

"What wristwatch?" said Hank, having learned in the school of life how to maintain a perfect deadpan and a tone of innocence.

Foogle, forgetting momentarily that he was no longer dealing with a ten-year-old circus punk, began to twist Hank's arm, whereupon the grown-up Hank flung Foogle all the way back to his car. Foogle drove back to Lola's store, thinking he might at least salvage something if he could lay claim to the showcase and contents, and exhibit it in his sideshow. Lola was more than happy to let him have it, if he would haul it off. It wouldn't fit in his car. He drove off to Jasper to hire a truck, and Lola gloatingly boasted to the Ingledews that she had worked her will, and that soon she would set foot inside her store.

But before Foogle could get back with the truck, Hank rounded up his three younger brothers and the four of them gained entrance to the store through the rear door, and transferred the showcase and contents to the abandoned mill, where they concealed it inside the wheat roller machine, and where it remained for many years. The Ingledew brothers pledged one another to secrecy. Lola set foot in her store. She had no idea on earth, she told Foogle, where the showcase might have gone. She was just glad it was gone.

What has all of this to do with the illustration at the head of this chapter? That curious "carpenter gothic" house, located a mile up Banty Creek from downtown Stay More, was built by a man who, like Eli Willard, was not a Stay Moron, but that in itself is no reason for making his house the headpiece for this whole chapter. The man was also a native of Connecticut and was also, like Eli Willard, a wanderer, but neither are those any reasons. I will offer a reasonably good reason in just a few minutes, but for the moment I need only point out that, chronologically, the house was built during one of those years that Eli Willard lay in state in Willis's store, the same year that Bob Cluley sold his little general store to the Beautiful Girl (although there is no connection) so that this carpenter gothic house represents those years and that year, not only chronologically but also symbolically, because the *retardataire* gothicism of the house relates to Eli Willard and his death. Nobody knew well the man who built it, but they knew he must have been a carpenter, not just because of all the carpenter gothic details but because it was well-built and is still standing, although it was vacant for some twenty years after the violent death of the builder.

The man was known only as "Dan." He was already in his fifties when he first came to Stay More and although he did not have a wife he had a young child, a girl as reclusive as her father. Neither of them was seen in the village more often than the Second Tuesday of the Month. People sat on the porch of Lola's store and speculated that the man was an escaped convict. Then one by one the people moved to the porch of the Beautiful Girl's store not only because it had become the post office but also because they liked her better than Lola, and on that porch they speculated that Dan was a runaway bank embezzler and had a pile of money stashed away somewhere in his fancy carpenter gothic house. Now and then someone would come upon the man out in the woods hunting, and marvel at his marksmanship, extraordinary even by Stay More standards. A lucky few people happened to be within earshot on several occasions when the man was playing his fiddle, and they agreed that there had never been a better fiddler, not even the legendary Colonel Coon Ingledew.

During the years of the Great Depression, the Stay Morons all of a sudden revived their interest in the old-timey music and the old-timey ways, and both the Stay Morons and the Parthenonians tried to persuade Dan to play his fiddle for public events, but he would not, not out of shyness but because he knew that square dances fostered drunken fighting, and, as he said, he had been in enough fights to last him for the rest of his life. So, in effect, unlike Eli Willard, who over the years kept bringing things *to* Stay More, the strange near-hermit named Dan contributed nothing to Stay More, but rather took *from* it, in the form of a meticulous observation of its history and culture that resulted, indirectly, through means I have discussed in some other place, in the present volume. If Dan himself has no place in the present volume, he was responsible for it, and his house has a place in it, for it was in his house, after Dan was killed and the house was abandoned, that the Ingledews deposited the glass showcase with the remains of Eli Willard, after a flood had undermined the foundations of the abandoned mill. Even in death Eli Willard kept traveling, but once he was deposited in the abandoned house of the near-hermit Dan he was left in relative peace for another twenty years.

Just in passing, we might note that the house was, and still slightly is, yellow. It was one of the few painted houses of Stay More. We need not get involved with the architectural significance of painted vs. unpainted houses, but we should consider the symbolism of the color, as Dan saw it. It had nothing to do with cowardice, for Dan was one of the bravest men who ever lived. If he had been an Ingledew, which he was not, his legend would have equaled anything in this book. Nor did yellow have anything to do with jaundice, lemons, Fusarium wilt, Orientals, or egg yolks. The Indo-European root of yellow is *ghel*, a formation which also produces gold, gleam, felon, glimpse, glitter, glisten, gloss, glow, glib and gloaming. All of these apply to Dan, but he painted his house yellow as a symbol of fair-haired women, and of the rising sun.

Chapter fifteen

Recognize it? The practiced student of architecture should be able to examine an altered building and determine the form of the original—"read" it in translation, as it were. Here we see the somewhat imaginative, if architecturally uncomely, result of Oren Duckworth's attempt to convert the unused barn that Denton and Monroe Ingledew built four chapters back into an industry, specifically a canning factory, or "Cannon Fact'ry" as they pronounced it. Unless we count the present-day ham processing operation of Vernon Ingledew as an industry, the Cannon Fact'ry was the only modern industry that Stay More ever had. Rare was the Stay Moron who enjoyed working *for* someone else, for wages. No farm in Stay More ever had a hired hand. Just as Jacob Ingledew had never even considered owning slaves because he felt that a man shouldn't own more land than he and his sons were capable of cultivating, successive generations of Stay Morons felt that they should not hire help; if they needed extra hands during haying time or threshing time, they swapped help with one another. But during the Great Depression, the farms of Stay More were reduced to bare subsistence enterprises, yielding the families a meager larder and nothing else. To earn even enough to pay for staples like salt and pepper and chewing tobacco, it was necessary to find a job, and the only jobs to be found in Stay More was the seasonal labor in Oren Duckworth's Cannon Fact'ry. Later the w.p.a. and the c.c.c. and the a.a.a. and the rest of the New Deal's alphabet soup brought relief to some, but most Stay Morons considered those government agencies a form of welfare or even charity, which was worse than working for somebody else.

Oren Duckworth started his canning factory not to provide jobs for his neighbors but because with the death of John Ingledew Stay More was without a leading citizen and Oren Duckworth desired to become a leading citizen. He was Jim Tom Duckworth's oldest boy, and attorneys' sons were always expected to amount to something, although Oren was past forty before he thought of the idea of taking the old engine from behind the abandoned mill and putting it alongside the abandoned barn to convert it into a factory. I've always wondered why he didn't simply convert the abandoned mill into a factory; possibly E.H. Ingledew, the oldest of his line and therefore the legatee of the mill, wouldn't sell it to him. At any rate, when old Jim Tom Duckworth went to his reward, he left behind a modest amount of accumulated lawyer's fees, which Oren used to purchase the simple machinery for his factory: conveyors, cleaning trough, canner and cooker.

Unconsciously no doubt, in planning his factory, Oren Duckworth preserved the bigeminality of the original barn: the left crib was where the women cleaned and prepared the snaps and 'maters and put them into cans; the right crib was where the men sealed the cans and cooked them, and the male-female division of labor was always clear in the minds of those who worked there. Snaps and 'maters were the only products of the factory; the former were canned during June and the latter during July and August; both vegetables grew abundantly all over the place. Additional jobs were provided for the pickers. Farmers hired women, teenagers and even children to pick, paying them usually a few pennies per bushel, and hauled the bushels by wagon to Oren Duckworth's factory, where a stout girl unloaded them into a trough around which sat a dozen women who cleaned, snapped the snaps or peeled the 'maters, pressed them into tin cans being loaded on the chute up in the loft by another person, also female, and placed them on a conveyor belt which carried them over into the other crib, where a group of men manned the machine that put a lid on each can and then arranged them in large iron bails that were lowered into a vat of boiling water; after the cans had cooked and cooled, they were conveyed up into the loft of that crib where another person, also male, packed them into cardboard cartons.

In the early days of the operation, the cans bore Oren Duckworth's own gaudily chromolithographed labels, imprinted with the legends "Duckworth's Finust Snaps" and "Duckworth's Finust Maters," but, even though the former clearly pictured a luscious mound of plump green beans while the latter showed a huge red tomato, nobody in the cities, where the cans were shipped, appeared to know that "snap" means green beans and "mater" means tomato, and the cans did not sell. Eventually Oren Duckworth made contact with a large and well-known food processor in Kansas City, a company whose lawyers will not permit me to mention its name, and thereafter Duckworth's finust snaps and maters were sent in unlabeled cans to Kansas City, where the Big Name Food Processor attached his own label, and you and I were unknowingly eating them when we were children, although the Cannon Fact'ry closed down before we were grown up.

The Stay More 'mater had of course not retained its full aphrodisiac properties, although the 'mater of that time was surely far more erogenous than the hybridized objects that are marketed as "tomatoes" today.

Whatever might be said against Oren Duckworth's materialistic motives for operating the canning factory, it must be acknowledged that the operation granted Stay More a reprieve, to live as a town a little longer. Without the canning factory, people would have been forced to leave Stay More and search for work in the larger towns and cities. The canning factory not only created jobs but also, because the big motortruck which came to get the cans and take them to Kansas City had to ford Banty Creek where it crosses the main road and because Banty Creek overflowed its banks six different times during the first summer the canning factory was in operation, making it impossible of passage not only for the big motortruck but also for any wagons hauling snaps and 'maters from the north side of the creek, and because Oren Duckworth's crews had to construct a raft and laboriously float not only the raw product but also the finished product back and forth across the creek when it was flooded, which caused Oren Duckworth not only to curse but also to moan, and because he was noticed cursing and moaning not only by his employees and family but also by a federal government agent, a "spotter" from the Works Progress Administration, who wore not only a pair of binoculars but also a telescope suspended from leather thongs around his neck, and who spotted not only Banty Creek in flood but also Oren Duckworth cursing and moaning, and who told the Stay Morons that not only could he do something about it but also *would* he do something about it, and did: he brought in an engineer who not only surveyed Banty Creek and drew up plans for a cement bridge over it but also hired some of the local boys to assist in the labor of constructing the bridge, which took all summer. Oren Duckworth was all in favor of the bridge, and so were the local boys given jobs by the w.p.a., but, nobody else was, because a bridge was the worst form of PROG RESS and was against all tradition.

The w.p.a. bridge is not illustrated here, partly for that reason. No architectural history of the United States is complete without an illustration of the Brooklyn Bridge, and it should follow that our history should not omit the w.p.a. bridge, but it is scarcely comparable, being only three hats long, about three feet above the natural water level of the creek, and consisting of poured cement with the sides formed of a row of crenelated piers, fifteen to the side. Year by year the floods of Banty Creek would wash logs and other debris against those crenelated piers, where it would jam up, and to break the jam the Stay Morons would sledgehammer those crenellations away, until eventually only the roadway of the bridge itself remained, with one pier of the crenellation embossed like a tombstone with the legend "Built by w.p.a." Bevis Ingledew often remarked that he would just as soon get aholt of some dynamite and obliterate the whole bridge, but for one reason or another he never got around to it, and what is left of it is still there.

Most of John Henry "Hank" Ingledew's children do not even know what "w.p.a." stands for, and they have had some fun conjecturing the possibilities: Well Plastered Alcoholics, Washout Prevention Association, Way Past Absurdity, What Possible Accident, Wet Persons Anonymous, etc. The fact that the "P" in w.p.a. actually did stand for PROG RESS was not lost upon the Stay Morons of the time, who helplessly watched the bridge being poured, and wondered what the world was coming to.

After work, the w.p.a. gang got into fights with local boys, but they were fighting not out of ideological controversy so much as for recreation and for the purpose of showing off in front of a very pretty teenage redhead girl named Sonora Twichell who was presumed to be the niece of the Beautiful Girl and was spending the summer with her, as she had been doing for several summers, going back home each August to her presumed mother in Little Rock. John Henry "Hank" Ingledew was one of the local boys who fought with the w.p.a. gang for the purpose of showing off in front of Sonora, although he didn't need to, because she had eyes only for him, although he didn't know it; because he was just as shy of females as any Ingledew had ever been, although he never forgot about Eli Willard's chronometer wristwatch which he had buried; because he knew that some day he would have a son to give the watch to, although he couldn't conceive of how he would ever approach a girl and get up his nerve to ask her to marry him so that they could have a son; because that was something well beyond the powers of an Ingledew, although he knew that in order for him to exist his own father somehow had to have approached his mother. The very pretty redhead Sonora thought that Hank Ingledew was the best-looking boy she had ever seen, and from the age of thirteen onward, when she first started spending summers with the woman she thought was her aunt but guessed was her mother, she decided that she would marry Hank someday. But every time she even looked at him, let alone spoke to him, he would get red in the face and turn away. Her mother, whom she presumed to be her aunt, told her about the legendary woman-shyness of all the Ingledews extending back into history. The Beautiful Girl knew the whole history of Stay More and told Sonora about the cornbread that Sarah had baked for Jacob Ingledew, so Sonora baked some corn-bread for Hank the summer she turned sixteen, and she took it to him and gave it to him, but nobody (except Eli Willard) had ever bothered to tell Hank anything about his great-great-grandfather (and Eli Willard hadn't mentioned the cornbread) so Hank didn't know the significance of the cornbread, except as something to eat, and he did eat it, but didn't think it was as good as the cornbread his mother made, although he didn't say this to Sonora, because he wasn't capable of saying anything to her.

When Sonora went back home to Little Rock that year after the summer was over, she was emboldened to write a letter to Hank, saying things that she dared not say to his face, things that he dared not listen to, to his face. She told him that although she was only sixteen years old she already felt grown up and that she didn't like any of the boys in Little Rock as much as she liked him and she was very sorry that he wasn't able to talk to her and she hoped that even though he couldn't talk to her he might be able to write to her, and she signed it "Your friend, Sonora."

Just holding this letter in his hands made Hank get very red in the face, especially because Sonora was the prettiest girl he had ever seen, which made it all the harder for him to conceive of ever being able to say anything to her. But he suddenly realized that saying something to her in a letter wouldn't be the same as saying something to her face. She wouldn't be looking at him when he said it; she couldn't even see him. So he sat down and got out a sheet of writing paper and took his pencil and licked on it and chewed it for a while, and managed to write, "Dear Sonora:" That was as far as he got. He waited for a better day, but the day never came, so he took the sheet of paper saying only "Dear Sonora:" and put it in an envelope and mailed it to her.

She was thrilled, and responded with a letter pouring out her heart to him, telling him how she liked Stay More so much better than Little Rock and how she wished she could live there all year around instead of just in the summertime. She even told him who her favorite film actors and actresses were.

These names meant nothing to Hank because he had never

seen a film, and yet, as if by magic, the same week Hank received this letter, a man drove a truck into Stay More and hung dark curtains over the windows of the school house and set up a screen and a projector and allowed everybody to come and pay ten cents to see real shows that were almost as good as the shows that Brother Long Jack Stapleton used to show before he lost the power, and there on the screen were the actual persons that Sonora had mentioned to Hank in her letter, so that after he had seen ten of the shows, he was able to write Sonora and say, "Dear Sonora: I saw some of them shows too, and my favorites is also Barbara Stanwyck and James Stewart. Your friend, Hank."

This was the most that he had ever said to any female except his mother, and Sonora realized it, and was greatly flattered. She replied at great length, saying she hoped that when she came back to Stay More the following summer to stay with her aunt, she hoped that she and Hank could go together to watch a picture show. If the show were romantic, she speculated, they might find themselves holding hands. Hank read this letter several times, and thought about it carefully. Movies, he had discovered, were shown in the dark, and in the dark it wouldn't be so difficult for him to hold hands with a girl, especially Sonora, since they had already broken the ice by mail. In his next letter he told her so, and she was so excited that she replied by suggesting that if the movie were romantic enough, and they held hands, it might develop that when he took her home afterwards they would want to sit in the porch swing together for a little while, and if they did that they might kiss. Hank memorized this letter but was uncertain as to whether or not he could ever get up the nerve to kiss Sonora, certainly not in broad daylight, and he conveyed these doubts to her in his next letter. She replied, "Silly. It would be night." All of the movies that Hank had seen had been shown in broad daylight with dark curtains over the schoolhouse windows, but after thinking about it, he decided that maybe he could persuade the movie man, if he ever came back to Stay More the next summer, to show some of the shows at night. When he mentioned this in his next letter to Sonora, she was so aroused that she wrote back to him saying that if they saw a lot of movies and did a lot of hand-holding, and sat in the porch swing afterwards kissing for a long enough time, they might want to sneak out to the corncrib where they could lie down together. John Henry "Hank" Ingledew lost his virginity by mail.

When Sonora returned to Stay More the following June to spend the summer with her aunt/mother, she and Hank were such old friends that they didn't even bother with the preliminaries of movie-going and hand-holding and kissing. As soon as it got dark on the first night Sonora was back in Stay More, they met in a thicket alongside Swains Creek, embraced, and made a love that eclipsed anything in the U.S. mails. Hank was amazed at how superior reality is to words. To experience such a thing, he realized, was proof that he existed, even if his parents had never done it. And he knew that now that he had done it, he had created a son to wear Eli Willard's chronometer.

But he was mistaken. He did not realize that every act of love does not result in offspring; he did not know that there are many days in each month when a girl is infertile. He offered to marry Sonora, and was confused when she laughed and said she was too young, although she would be happy to marry him after she finished high school in another year. The high school that Hank had finished at Jasper had not permitted pregnant girls to attend, but possibly, he realized, the big-city high school at Little Rock was more broadminded. He was further confused when, the very following night, she wanted to do it again. He wondered if that would produce twins, but he did it. By the end of the week, he was worrying about supporting quintuplets, but he thoroughly enjoyed doing it and went on doing it, until Sonora said they had to stop for a while because it was the "wrong" time. He didn't know what was wrong with it, but he obligingly stopped. "We can pet, though," she told him. He didn't know that word, but she showed him what it meant.

It was a great summer. I was there. Even though I was only a child I knew what Hank and Sonora were up to. Several times I spied on them and envied their pleasure. But the only other person who knew, rather than simply guessed, what they were up to, was the Beautiful Girl, to whom Sonora confessed. As postmistress of Stay More, the Beautiful Girl knew that her daughter, whom everybody else thought was her niece, had been carrying on a lengthy correspondence with Hank Ingledew, and she was glad for Sonora, because Hank was one of the best in a long line of fine Ingledews. He was tall, and strong, and good-looking. So the Beautiful Girl, who once upon a time had been courted and bedded by Hank's Uncle Raymond, was not at all surprised when Sonora confessed that she had lost her virginity to Hank and that they indulged themselves in their bodies almost daily. Sonora assured her that they were "careful." The Beautiful Girl thought that was a beautiful thing, and she lived vicariously through Sonora, enjoying Sonora's descriptions of the myriad ways that she and Hank took advantage of the fact that they had miraculously been created female and male.

It was also miraculous that Sonora did not get pregnant that summer. Hank was puzzled. He knew that certain women are sterile. He asked Sonora if she had ever had a bad case of the mumps, but she hadn't. Then he began to wonder if he himself might be sterile. Perhaps, after all, he was only imagining that he existed. Or maybe, he speculated, he only existed in Sonora's imagination; she had created him for the purpose of giving her pleasure. He did not much like the thought, but there it was.

Thought can be a shattering experience. Sonora, for her part, did not think thoughts, except to remember when it was the wrong time of month; she simply enjoyed herself. Hank couldn't tell her what was gnawing away at his brain, and yet, compulsively, he went ahead. He was quite fond of 'maters, but that had nothing to do with it. There was simply something about Sonora: the way she looked, the shape of her, her red hair that had a wonderful smell in all its locations, her eyes even, her voice too, the movements of her hands and feet, the shape and capacity of her arms, and above all the shape and capacity of her principal openings, that never failed to animate him and his responsive part. Thinking about this, as he often did, he came to the conclusion that her openings were, after all, sockets, hollows, voids, and therefore if it were possible that somebody did not exist, it was more likely she rather than he, and he arrived at the momentous truth that woman is but the creation of man, his fancy and his delight. He could live with this, and he did: having settled the problem, he endured it.

After the true maternity and paternity of Sonora became known, she did not have to return to Little Rock to her adoptive mother, who was in fact her aunt, but remained in Stay More, finishing her education at Jasper High School. Her father, E.D., had acquired religion, and when he learned from her mother of Sonora's affair with Hank Ingledew, he attempted to put a stop to it. He was only partly successful. Sonora would not accommodate Hank on school nights, limiting him to weekends. Because weekends often occurred at the wrong time, she also acquired, from a high school girlfriend who clerked in the Jasper drugstore, a package of prophylactics, which she insisted that Hank use. "What's that fool thang for?" he wanted to know. "Heck, that won't be no fun," he protested. "Let's try it and see," she suggested, and they did.

But after graduation, in June, she threw away the prophylactics, and she and Hank ran off into the woods, in broad daylight, mornings, afternoons, evenings, and corresponded themselves silly, even in the wrong time, until Sonora was unquestionably pregnant, whereupon they were dutifully married, and on the wedding night, after the shivaree party had been served refreshments and departed, Hank told Sonora of the gold chronometer wristwatch which Eli Willard had given him and which he had buried to await the appropriate time when Hank could give it to his son. Sonora thought that was the marvelousest thing she had ever heard, and she said they ought to name their son Eli Willard Ingledew, and Hank agreed that would be very appropriate. For nine months, they talked every day about Eli Willard Ingledew; they could even picture him grown up, wearing the magic watch that kept perfect time and never lost even a second. They knew he would be somebody very important in the world, maybe even President of the United States, or at the very least Vice President. When Sonora could feel the baby stirring in her womb, she began to picture him, and she and Hank knew that Eli Willard would be the most handsome of all the Ingledews.

Sonora took up sewing, and made all of Eli Willard Ingledew's clothing up to the age at which he would receive the wristwatch, which would be sixteen. They not only talked about Eli Willard Ingledew to one another, but also to all their family and friends, so that the whole village began to look forward to his birth, almost as if the baby would be an actual reincarnation of the Connecticut peddler. When Sonora went into labor, instead of fetching Doc Swain and having her baby at home like everybody else had always done, she was taken all the way to Harrison, where the nearest hospital was, and the car in which she traveled was followed by every available conveyance in Stay More, with the entire population, in that year just about a hundred, being transported. The waiting room at the hospital wouldn't hold a fraction of them, but they milled about in the corridors and outside on the lawn. Sonora's labor was a long one, yet nobody seemed to mind. News of the advent or nativity or simply parturition spread through the town of Harrison, and the members of the Harrison High School precision marching band donned their new uniforms and assembled in formation on the hospital lawn, where they played "A Babe in Mother's Arms," "A Child at Mother's Knee," "A Boy Grows Up," "The Stars and Stripes Forever," and the Harrison High School *alma mater.*

At last the obstetrician lifted the baby by its ankles, slapped its bottom to induce crying, and Sonora discovered that Eli Willard Ingledew had no penis. "A mighty fine gal," said the obstetrician, and Sonora told him to break the news gently to her husband. Hank Ingledew hung around for a while, but everybody else went home, and the following week's issue of the Jasper *Disaster* carried the event in seventeen words at the bottom of the last page: "Last Friday a daughter, unnamed, was born to Mr. and Mrs. J.H. Ingledew of Stay More." Hank and Sonora got their heads together and considered naming the baby Ela Willa or Elise Wilma or Eleanor Willardine, but finally Sonora named her simply Latha, after her mother. Then, as soon as Sonora was able, they got busy again, in the morning, afternoon and evening, and tried to create Eli Willard on the second chance.

Sonora's conception was quick; the new infant would be born less than ten months after the first one. That summer Sonora went to work in the canning factory, to earn money for a second layette. Sonora parked her baby in the "baby-trough" at the canning factory, which was one of the former cow cribs reserved for the babies of the women who sat around the cleaning-trough snapping snaps and peeling 'maters. The several babies did not socialize much; mainly they lay or sat watching their mothers snapping snaps or peeling 'maters and wondering what in the name of heaven was going on, all day long. At night Sonora protested to Hank that she was simply too tired to make love, much as she wanted to, and her refraining from it overloaded Hank with new reserves of life, so that he was compelled to work harder, and even began clearing some new land, the first time that that had been done in Stay More for ages and ages. As a result of this labor, he was waylaid with a severe case of the frakes. His mother, Emelda, attempted to administer the old but unproven remedies, but he would not let her, because, although he had no interest in superstitions, folklore nor old-timey ways in general, he had at least heard that there was really no earthly cure for the frakes. Sonora's old high school chum who clerked in the Jasper drugstore furnished an ointment containing ACTH, and this, although it didn't cure Hank's frakes, was at least as effective as the panther urine ointment had been a century before, which is to say, it was worthless. Hank took to his bed and waited in agony for the itching to stop, and then gave himself up to the deep feeling of utter futility that came afterward. When news of the birth of his second child reached his bed, he remarked, "I don't give a shit what it is."

It was another girl. Sonora solicited his help in naming it, but he said she could name it Eulalee Wilhelmina for all he cared. Sonora named it simply Eva. She pointed out to Hank that while all of his siblings were male and all of his many uncles were male, this was no guarantee that his children would be male, because, after all, her mother's siblings had been female, and there had been a lot of females in her father's lineage. Hank said he didn't care. He really didn't. He would just as soon have girls as boys, or neither. He would just as soon have nothing. He didn't give a damn. It was all the same to him, one way or the other. He could straddle the fence and leave well enough alone. In fact, he could leave everything alone and didn't feel like making the effort to straddle the fence, even. Nothing mattered. It made him no difference whatever.

Hank's case of the frakes was one of the worst. In the winter, beneath their heavy quilts, Sonora would cuddle up to him and try to warm him, but he would not be warmed. She was scared, because she had grown up in the city and had never seen anyone get the frakes before. She told him that she loved him, and that therefore she loved his frakes too, but he did not even bother to reply. He couldn't care less. Sonora's mother counseled her that she would just have to wait and be patient. "How long? Oh, Mother, *how long*?" Sonora wailed. But her mother could only say that nobody ever knew.

Then the world went to war again. This time, the Stay More town meeting lasted for a little longer than the three-and-a-half-minute discussion of the previous war, but not much: the general consensus was that if this feller Hitler wanted Europe, why shouldn't he have it? But he was also trying to get England, and that was where our foreparents came from, and we oughtn't to let him have that, so we ought to at least help the British hang on to their lands. Several Stay More boys went off and joined the service. Sonora hoped that maybe the war would rouse Hank from his lethargy and despondency. It did not.

But then some yellow people who lived halfway around the world sent their ships and planes to a place called Pearl that was part of America even though it was out in the middle of the ocean, and bombed hell out of it. That was going too far. Hank got out of bed, dressed, kissed his wife and babies goodbye, and said so long to his parents and brothers and uncles, and went off to join the service. He didn't know which branch of the service to join. The Army offered to teach him a trade, and the Marines offered to make a real man out of him, but he kept thinking of Pearl, which was way out in the ocean, and he decided the best way to get to it would be the Navy. So he joined it, and after basic training they let him come home for a little while to show off his uniform and get his picture in the *Disaster* and impregnate Sonora again. Then they sent him to a school where they taught him how to take apart and repair and put together radio equipment. There was hardly any trace of his frakes remaining, so he studied hard, and by the time he was shipped to sea he could write to Sonora and tell her that he was "Semen First Class," to which she replied, "You sure are, honey."

He was the first Stay Moron ever to see the sea. His ship went all over the ocean, but it didn't go to Pearl. Because the enemy commenced shooting at and trying to bomb his ship, they raised his pay, and he didn't have anything to spend it on, so he sent most all of it home, and Sonora and her babies were able to live a good life. Hank was so good at patching up and operating radios that he was transferred to a bigger ship, and promoted to petty officer. He survived the sinkings of two destroyers, a battleship, and an aircraft carrier, and by then he was a master chief petty officer (and also the father of a third daughter, Janice). Eventually they shipped him back stateside for shore leave, and once again he came home to show off his uniform and to attempt once again to create Eli Willard Ingledew.

The Jasper *Disaster* took his portrait and printed it on their front page, and noted that he was eligible for commission as ensign. Hank was saddened to learn that some of his childhood friends had been killed in France and on the beaches of the Pacific. His brothers Jackson and Tracy had been drafted and were fighting in Europe, and his youngest brother William Robert ("Billy Bob") would have been drafted, except that he was the last son in the family, and there was a law against it.

There were very few young men in Stay More; in the previous war there had been very few young men out of Stay More. The canning factory was no longer operating, on account of a shortage of tin, but the women and boys and old men went on harvesting the snap crop and 'mater crop and canning it in re-used Mason jars. The war was good for Stay More in the sense that all its young men fighting overseas sent most of their paychecks home, and there was so much mail from them and to them that the post office was permitted to reopen for the duration of the war, and of course both general stores did a fair business. Odell Ingledew even thought of reopening his father's bank, but Tearle talked him out of it, saying that the war was only a temporary thing and would probably be over before Odell could install a new floor and replace the busted-out winder lights, not to mention the vault door that had been ripped off and gone God knows where.

Hank returned to the Pacific with the rank of ensign, and his ships began invading islands and atolls all over the place. He himself never fired a gun, nor killed an enemy, but his expertise with radio helped conquer the foe, and by the time of the invasion of Iwo Jima his rank was captain, in charge of all the radio operations of his entire fleet. The officers and enlisted men under his command still referred to him as "Rube" behind his back, and did bad imitations of his country accent, but they respected him and never gave him any trouble. In the invasion of Iwo Jima, another Stay More boy, Gerald Coe, who had been a boyhood friend of Hank's, made a heroic charge of a machine gun nest that was instrumental in taking the island, but was killed in the process, and posthumously awarded the Congressional Medal of Honor. There is a bronze plaque in his memory in a hallway of Jasper High School. When the war ended after the surrender of the enemy, Hank was promoted to commodore and offered a stateside desk job, but he wasn't interested, and came home to Stay More just in time for the birth of his fourth daughter, Patricia.

He didn't hold it against Sonora, but he somehow felt that it cast aspersions on his manhood that he had been unable to produce a son. It was hard for him to hold his head up in Stay More. Also, there wasn't much use in Stay More for a highly trained electronics technician. Stay More didn't even have electricity yet. Also, Swains Creek and Banty Creek put together weren't much water compared with the ocean. Hank dreamed, nearly every night, of that ocean. Finally he could stand it no longer, and said to Sonora:

"Let's go to California."

"Anytime," she replied, thinking he only meant to show her the place. She did not know the story of Benjamin Ingledew, who had tried to go to California and got as far as Mountain Meadows. Nor did she know of the curse that Jacob Ingledew had placed on any Stay Moron who dared try it again.

When they left for California, Hank had forgotten about the gold chronometer wristwatch. Perhaps he had even forgotten where he had buried it.

Chapter sixteen

During the war there came to maturity, in Stay More, two twin sisters, Jelena and Doris Dinsmore, who were destined to intrude, indirectly, into the Ingledew saga. It was Bevis Ingledew who first referred to them as "the Siamese twins." Those listening to him didn't know what that meant, but he could remember being taken as a child to the St. Louis World's Fair, where he had seen a pair of Siamese twins in a sideshow. So when Bevis started joking in his high-spirited fashion about Jelena and Doris Dinsmore as the Siamese twins, the rest of the Stay Morons picked up the habit.

Jelena and Doris (their full names were Jelena Cloris and Helena Doris, but this confused their mother when she was yelling at them) were inseparable, not physically, but in all other ways. One was never seen without the other. Never. The men loafing and joking on the store porch had a ready mine of mirth in the inseparability of the Dinsmore sisters, speculating, for instance, that the two girls probably "went out back" together too, since it was known that the Dinsmore outhouse, though primitive and airy, was a two-holer. Although they were twins, there was a very slight difference between them, which gave rise to rumors that their fathers had not both been Jake Dinsmore, who, when the sisters were five years old, had gone out to California looking for a job, and had never returned, abandoning a family of fourteen children to a mother who did her poor best to feed them.

The mother's name was Selena—her father had named her that because he had been an admirer of Salina Ingledew but didn't know how to spell. Selena Dinsmore had first noticed the closeness of Jelena and Doris when they were infants: she had only one crib, and the two girls began very early the practice they would continue for the rest of their lives: sleeping in the same bed. Their mother nursed them together one to a breast, a not very difficult balancing act to those who saw her doing it. As soon as they were old enough to sit up and eat at the table with the other children, they always made certain that their chairs were side-by-side and their identical chipped bowls contained the same amount of gruel. From the first through the eighth and last grades, the two sisters shared the same desk, and the teacher of those years, Estalee Jerram, could scarcely ever tell them apart and was always calling upon one of them by the other's name. The difficulty was compounded because Jelena and Doris insisted that their mother sew their clothes from identical patterns of flour-sack gingham and calico. If one of them was punished in school for some infraction of the rules, the other would insist that Miss Jerram mete the same punishment to her. If one of them was hurt and cried, the other's tears were no less profound. They had few friends and seemed to need none.

The men who loafed on the store porch and made joking allusions to "the Siamese twins" began to speculate jokingly about what was going to happen now that the sisters were growing up and filling out. There were not, to anyone's knowledge, two brothers anywhere hereabouts who were sufficiently twinned themselves to make a proper match for Jelena and Doris. But that was not what Jelena and Doris had in mind anyway, it seemed. What they had in mind became apparent at the first play-party they attended, Etta Whitter's birthday celebration, where the games played were "Marching 'round the Levee," "Build the Bridge," "Post Office," and "Snap." All of these were kissing games, and whichever boy kissed Jelena had to kiss Doris too. Some of these games involved being "it," and whenever Jelena was "it," Doris would also be "it" at the same time, which some of the others felt was unfair in the running and catching games, because it made the sisters doubly quicker to catch when they were "it." Usually, when they were caught by the boy who was "it," they would both kiss him at the same time, Jelena on the right cheek, Doris on the left. The men on the store porch, hearing about the party afterward, made jokes about what was going to happen when Jelena and Doris were old enough to start going to square dances. As a matter of fact, the sisters did nearly wreck the first square dance they attended. Tobe Chism, the caller, had to stop the music and take the girls aside and try to explain to them that it is simply impossible for two girls to square dance with the same partner at the same time. When he was unable to persuade them to take turns, one doing one dance and one the next, he at least worked it out so that they wouldn't both be moving with the partner at the same time, although this didn't work too well either because Jelena or Doris or both would be inclined to forget to stand still and let the other do the moving. Folks were laughing at them so, they finally walked home together and didn't go to any more of those romps.

They decided to get religion, because religion held that any kind of dancing was sinful, and even frowned upon the play-parties, because kissing was involved. On the next rare Sunday when a passing evangelist came to Stay More to give a meeting and baptism, the sisters offered themselves up for salvation, but when the congregation gathered at the creek for the baptizing, the revivalist discovered that the sisters wished to be baptized simultaneously. He argued that they ought to be baptized in the order of their birth, Jelena going first, but they refused. He protested that he didn't think he was stout enough to submerse them both at the same time.

"You got two hands, ain't ye?" Jelena observed.

"Yeah," said the minister, "but generally I clamp one of 'em on yore face to keep the water out of yore nose and mouth."

"We kin clamp our own faces," declared Doris.

So the baptist, after studying and pantomiming the possibilities for a while, standing with his legs spread wide in the waist-deep water, had the girls face one another, and put one of his hands on the back of each, and lowered Jelena to his right and Doris to his left into the water. But to get them both completely under in this position required him to go under too, and there was no sign of any of them for a long moment; then the man's head emerged, his hair plastered and his spectacles all wet, struggling mightily to get both girls back out of the water.

The men on the store porch got a lot of mileage out of that story, and began to make jokes about what would happen when Jelena and Doris were old enough to receive their first caller.

Although most of the old-timey ways were forgotten or unused, courtship was still formal and old-fashioned. Couples, especially those who had got religion, did not go off on "dates"; a respectable girl would never find herself alone with a young fellow before marriage, which was why Sonora Twichell's premarital conduct with Hank Ingledew had scandalized a small segment of the population. For proper folks, the suitor or swain, if he had matrimony in prospect, would call at the girl's house, be invited to spend the night, and have the privilege of staying up late and talking with his intended after the others had gone to bed—in the same room, usually within earshot of anyone who could not, or did not want to, sleep.

The Dinsmore hovel (there is no other name for it), shown in our illustration, is perhaps typical of lower class dwellings built throughout the "Hoover" years when "things was so bad we'uns jist stood around lookin at one another and wonderin who to eat next." In fact, it was built during the Roosevelt administration, but it still represents the decline of architecture in the Ozarks. It had but two rooms, and when Mont Duckworth, son of the canning factory owner, came to court Jelena, he would sleep in one room, in a bed with three of her brothers, Willard (named after some peddler), Tilbert and Baby Jim. In the other room he would do his courting while Mrs. Dinsmore slept with Ella Jean, Norma and—Mont hoped—Doris. But Doris, and Jelena too, could not conceive that anyone would court one of them without the other. Thus, when the others had gone to bed, Mont found himself sitting in front of the woodstove, Jelena on one side, Doris on the other.

"Well, uh…" Mont began. He had heard some of the jokes that

the men on the store porch had made. If he had listened well enough, he could have remembered what they had suggested that he say or do in a situation like this, but he could not. To help his nervousness, he bit off a chaw of tobacco and began chewing. From time to time he would make some idle talk such as: "Right airish tonight, aint it?" and from time to time he would spit accurately into the open door of the stove. Doris and Jelena would both smile and make dove's eyes at him. After midnight, when the fire in the stove was almost out and no move had been made to rekindle it, Mont announced, "Well, uh, reckon I'd best turn in," and he went and slept with their brothers and departed early on the dawn.

The men on the store porch made jokes at the expense of Mont as well as Doris and Jelena. But one of the younger of them, Boden Whitter, declared, "By God, ole Mont aint got the melt to spark them gals proper, but *I* kin shore give it a try." Boden Whitter did not report back to the men on the store porch about the outcome of his attempt, but word got around anyway, and Boden became no less a victim of the men's jokes than Mont had been. It seems that at one point during the evening he had suggested to Jelena, "Well, honey, you keer to traipse out fer a look at the moon, or somethin?" and Jelena said she didn't mind, and rose, and went out, but Doris was right on her heels. Boden followed, trying politely to get them to take turns, but Jelena said, "It's jist as much her moon as it is mine." Boden sat down on a big rock, and the sisters sat on either side of him; by and by he put an arm around each of them, and a little later he started in to kissing Jelena, but then he had to kiss Doris too. The kisses got longer and harder and Boden began to think he could talk Jelena into lying down, but then he realized that Doris would be watching or, worse, lying down beside Jelena, and he began to doubt if he could do anything if he was being watched, and in any case he might be expected to do Doris too, and he wasn't at all certain that he could. The more he thought about it all, the less sure and more nervous he became, and finally he gave it up.

The men on the store porch speculated endlessly about alternative outcomes to Boden's experience, and had a lot of fun.

A year or so went by, both Mont and Boden got married to

other girls, and Jelena and Doris were getting to the far end of marriageable age, and then the war came and took away nearly all the
young bachelors of Stay More. When news came of the first of several
deaths of Stay Morons in the war, the people threw a pie supper at
the canning factory for the purpose of raising funds for some kind of
War Memorial. Ostensibly a pie supper is for the purpose of raising
funds, but it is also a means of promoting conviviality and courtship
between males and females. All the women and girls bake a pie, and
these are wrapped and sealed and auctioned off one by one to the
highest bidders among the men and boys. The males aren't supposed
to know who baked which pie, and are thus obliged to sit with, and
eat with, and talk with, the female who baked the pie that they bid
on. The organizers of the pie supper paid a visit to Mrs. Dinsmore
and said she ought to make sure that both Doris and Jelena each
baked a separate pie, no foolishness of both doing the same pie, and
Mrs. Dinsmore said she would see to it that each girl did her separate
pie, and sure enough, Jelena and Doris showed up at the pie supper
with two different pies.

To the men on the store porch who had missed the pie supper,
it was afterward Uncle Tearle Ingledew who told the tale, told it on
his own nephew, William Robert Ingledew. "Billy Bob," as we have
seen, was Hank's youngest brother, and was not drafted into the service because all three of his brothers were already serving. Although
just as tall and strong and handsome as his oldest brother, he was, if
anything, even shyer toward females, the shyest of his generation of
shy Ingledews, but he somehow persuaded himself that there was no
connection between bidding on a pie, of which he was uncommonly
fond, and courting a girl. "So he made him a good bid," related Uncle
Tearle to the men on the store porch, "and he got this here pie that
Jelena had fixed, and he took the wrappers off, and saw it was sweet
pertater, which he don't keer fer too mighty well, so he figgered he'd
take him another chance, and bid on the next pie that come up, and
damn if he didn't git the one Doris fixed! It was coconut cream. The
folks thar got pervoked and says you wasn't supposed to bid on but
one pie, but ole Billy Bob, he says by God he likes coconut cream
and for that matter he aint too *un*partial to sweet pertater neither,

and he reckons he'll jist eat 'em both. And he did. Jelena and Doris set on each side of him while he et their pies, but he never minded. They never bothered him much, and he give 'em a slice or two of their pies. After they done eatin, he was right well full and satisfied, and didn't even mind when both them gals set in to talkin his ear off." Strangely, the men on the store porch did not make any jokes over this news. They nodded their heads gravely, spat their tobacco juice, whittled their sticks, stretched in their chairs. At length one of them remarked, "Wal, if they is a-gorn to be jist one, then maybe ole Billy Bob is the one, atter all."

He was. The next summer, Billy Bob, who was a carpenter by trade, more or less, built himself a modest frame house on the south bench of Ingledew Mountain. It too resembled the plain, modest dwelling which is the headpiece of this chapter and which represents the further architectural decline of the Ozarks. The only difference between Billy Bob's house and the one illustrated here is that while the latter is bigeminal the former is trigeminal. When Hank Ingledew came home on another shore leave, he paid a visit to his kid brother's house, and reported back to the village the news that Billy Bob had two housekeepers who were sisters, Dinsmore girls, and everybody knew who he meant, but one of them said to Hank, "Yeah, but they aint exactly housekeepers."

The next time the revivalist who had revived the Dinsmore sisters happened to be passing through Stay More again, he learned of the situation and paid a call on the sisters and pointed out to them that their "man" wasn't even a member of the church; in fact, like all Ingledews, he was an atheist; but even if he was a member of the church they would still be living in sin and they had better agree to one of them getting legally married to Billy Bob. When this had no effect, the minister went to their mother and reasoned with her, but Selena told him, "Why, Reverend, them gals is happier than I ever seed 'em in their whole life, and I aint aimin to git in the way of their happiness." The preacher gave up. But the men on the store porch did not. Whenever Billy Bob came to the store, which was seldom, they would pester him with questions which made him blush all the redder and at last manage to stammer out, "Aw, you fellers is all wet."

But were they? To their sharp eyes it began to appear increasingly plain that Billy Bob, who had never been noted for great energy, was becoming almost indolent. He moved with slow, unstudied aimlessness, not exactly abstracted but with the corners of his mouth ever so slightly uptilted in what was not a grin nor a smirk so much as an expression of felicity. If the store-porchers' conjectures were true, they could not help but feel, to a man, a profound envy which they never dared express to one another. Yet the only question which Billy Bob ever deigned answer was a question that one of the men on the store porch posed in the most general terms and as a kind of observation, twelve months after the sisters had gone to live with him: "Hit's been all of a year now, Billy Bob. How you like it?"

And Billy Bob scratched under his hat reflectingly and, with that expression on the corners of his mouth, allowed, "Wal, they tend to kind of talk a little more than I keer to listen."

Not long after, Tilbert Dinsmore circulated the report that not one but both of his sisters, he had observed on a recent visit to Billy Bob's place, seemed to be swelling out around the middle. Now he didn't know what others thought, he said, but as for himself he didn't take kindly to the idea of having a damn pair of woodscolts for nephews or nieces or one of each. The next time the preacher happened to be passing through Stay More, Billy Bob's many uncles, led by Tearle, ganged up on him and "persuaded" him to join William Robert Ingledew in holy matrimony with Jelena Cloris Dinsmore *and* Helena Doris Dinsmore. They were no longer referred to as "the Siamese twins" but rather as "the Mizzes Ingledew."

Several months later, strangest of all to relate, only one child was born. According to whoever heard it from Billy Bob, who himself did not understand it, Jelena and Doris with their bellies approaching term had gone down to the creek to bathe, and when they returned, Jelena was carrying the baby swathed in a towel.

What happened to the other baby? Or had there been another one? Had it been stillborn and they had buried it? Or had it drowned in the creek? But how could two sisters, even if they had conceived within minutes of one another, have managed to give birth at the same instant?

No, the people thought, only one of the girls had been pregnant, and the other girl had a sympathetic false pregnancy or else just stuffed a pillow of ever-increasing size inside her dress. But Billy Bob himself didn't know which sister it was, and within a short time, in the last year of the war, his brother Jackson was wounded in France and sent home, and since Billy Bob was no longer the only brother at home he was drafted into the service and flown almost immediately to Germany.

The baby was a girl, and its name was Jelena. This news threw the men on the store porch, and the whole village, into endless speculation. Before long, all of the Stay Morons were divided almost equally into two factions: (1) The Jelenists, who held that Jelena must have been the mother because she named the infant after herself, as a kind of "Jelena Junior," and (2) The Dorisites, who held that Doris must have been the mother because she named it for her sister, out of love. These two factions debated endlessly, occasionally quarreled, and caused some disruption of family ties. Men, by and large, were more inclined to join the Jelenists, while more women than men leaned toward the Dorisite persuasion.

Mrs. Dinsmore, the sisters' mother, was invited to become a leader of the Dorisites but did not want to show favoritism, so, before joining either faction she determined upon a simple way of deciding which sect to join: she would ask her daughters which one was the mother. She did. Afterwards, fanning herself and mopping her brow in the parlor of the arch-Dorisite, she announced to the other ladies present, "I swear, if them gals didn't jist both look at me and both say the same words at the same time, word by word: 'We both of us are.'"

So the debates raged on, until every Stay Moron had declared as a staunch Jelenist or a devout Dorisite. Everyone, that is, except Jelena and Doris themselves, and nobody ever thought of the idea of asking them to join. One day Jelena told her mother that she would like to join the Dorisites, which the Dorisites took as unquestionable proof of their position. But Jelena said she could not join the Dorisites because Doris wanted to join the Jelenists, which the Jelenists declared was unquestionable proof of *their* position. Neither sister could join their respective sects because it would involve their separation, and they had never been separated from the moment of Doris's birth. So neither did, but their respective sects went on claiming that because the sisters had *wanted* to join, it was unquestionable proof of their position.

Jelenists, by and large, are individualists, holding that a person is responsible for himself, that if one conducts one's life with due responsibility, everything will go all right. Jelenism teaches us to be alert, to watch what is occurring in the everyday life, to observe closely sensory input to ourselves. Jelenism gives us a sense of our own uniqueness. No two people are ever alike; if we meet someone like ourself, it is only proof of our uniqueness. A true Jelenist who also happens to believe in God can comfortably believe that God did indeed create man in His own image. But it isn't necessary for a Jelenist to believe in God. The atheistic Jelenist can believe that man created God in his own image, while the solipsistic Jelenist can believe that he himself has created everything and everyone to his own liking. All Jelenists have a strong sense of personal identity, and, usually, a sense of personal purpose, of having something to do that needs to be done and can best be done by oneself. Jelenists may be chauvinistic, and it is true that they are more proselytizing than Dorisites, but this is because of their belief that a strong sense of identity and purpose also requires a strong sense of conviction. It is very difficult to prove a Jelenist wrong on any question.

Dorisites, on the other hand, are altruistic, cooperative, lenient, and so respectful of the opinions of others that they tolerate the Jelenists much more than the reverse. A Jelenist cannot understand why anyone would want to be a Dorisite, while a Dorisite not only understands why Jelenists are as they are, but also appreciates it or at least sympathizes with it. Dorisites are very good at empathy and sympathy. To a Dorisite, the most wonderful fact of existence is that there is somebody else besides oneself. A true Dorisite who also happens to believe in God usually believes that God really does love him or her and everybody else. The atheistic Dorisite believes that although there is no God, if there were a God He would be an easy person to talk to, while the solipsistic Dorisite, which is almost a contradiction in terms, believes that he has created everybody else because he needs somebody to play with. Dorisites make excellent mothers, and also but less often, excellent fathers. Above all, Dorisites make excellent lovers. Even in the physical act itself, a Dorisite is always aware of mutuality. Outside such intimate dealings, Dorisites are sociable to the point of gregariousness. Every Dorisite has many friends and is always on the lookout for more. It would be easily possible to imagine a hermit Jelenist; an anchorite Dorisite is inconceivable.

Human nature is not perfect, and both Jelenists and Dorisites have their shortcomings. Jelenists are inclined to be secretive, while Dorisites are so incapable of keeping a secret that they are not trustworthy. Dorisites can be overprotective, while Jelenists may be inclined to be unconcerned. Some Jelenists are acknowledged swell-heads, while just as many Dorisites are shrinking violets. In the area of perversion, Jelenists are sadists and Dorisites are masochists. There are Jelenists known for their compulsive lying or compulsive stealing, while Dorisitism has produced its share of prostitutes and bad politicians. There have been six U.S. Presidents since the time of Jelena and Doris; of those six, three have been Dorisites, while the other three were Jelenists.

But it is of the Stay More factions that we must speak. The Jelenists were no longer on speaking terms with the Dorisites, and the latter, although perfectly willing to speak to the former, understood the former's feelings, respected them, and made no move. In families containing members of both factions, difficulties arose. Bevis Ingledew, for example, was one of the leaders of the Jelenists, while his wife Emelda was an upstanding Dorisite. Being no longer on speaking terms with her was no problem, since he never spoke to her anyway, but there was the problem of shutting her out of his thoughts. Every now and then he would "hear" her say something like, *Dorisitism teaches us to be charitable. Why don't ye take that leftover ham to them pore Coes?* and he would be inclined to retort that Jelenism teaches us to be self-sufficient, but he would remember that Jelenists were not on speaking terms with Dorisites, and then realize that just by thinking these thoughts he had communicated them to her. The "argument" would begin, their thoughts furiously debating charity vs. self-sufficiency. She couldn't prove him wrong, because a Jelenist can never be proved wrong, but in the end he would wind up taking the leftover ham to the poor Coes, where he would find that while Ed Herb Coe was a Dorisite and grateful for the ham, Viola Coe was a Jelenist and wouldn't let him accept it. "Shame on ye, Bevis! A good Jelenist like you! I got a mine to tell the other members on ye!"

The schoolhouse, which had been the church once upon a time, was expropriated by the Jelenists for their sanctuary, which is what Jelenists call their meeting place. Being accommodating, the Dorisites did not object: instead, they held their meetin place, which is what Dorisites call their meeting place, in the unused canning factory. The Jelenists also expropriated the Second Tuesday of the Month for their meetings; the Dorisites instituted the Third Tuesday of the Month. Dorisite meetings were little more than sociables, where everybody greeted one another and exchanged secrets and sang convivial songs and hatched charitable plots and declared their love for Doris Ingledew and her daughter Jelena and everybody else, including the Jelenists. The Jelenist meetings were more somber, or more staid; without singing, they solemnly repeated their list of 101 reasons why Jelena Ingledew could not possibly be the daughter of Doris, and then their more complicated list of 1001 shortcomings of Dorisites, then each member of the congregation rose in turn to proclaim that he or she was an individual, unlike anybody else present, and could be depended upon to do his or her share of keeping the world going, and didn't need no help from nobody.

This factionalism continued strong until the War Department sent news that Pfc. William Robert Ingledew had been killed in combat in the siege of Berlin.

The Jelenists and the Dorisites united for a memorial service in Billy Bob's honor, and all together sang:

> *Farther along we'll know all about it,*
> *Farther along we'll understand why;*
> *Cheer up, my brother, live in the sunshine,*
> *We'll understand it, all by and by.*

The Dorisites praised the Jelenists, and the latter grudgingly admitted that while they couldn't understand why anybody would want to be a Dorisite it was pretty obvious that Dorisites weren't *all* bad, in fact Dorisites had a lot to recommend them, and they suggested that the Jelenists and Dorisites bury the hatchet and become united. The Dorisites squealed their approval of this suggestion, and everyone embraced.

Toward the end of the service, all were surprised by the appearance of Jelena and Doris themselves, carrying between them, or taking turns carrying, the infant Jelena. There was absolute silence as they came down the aisle and took seats, Jelena sitting on the Dorisite side, Doris sitting on the Jelenist side, with the baby being permitted to crawl around in the aisle between them. It was the first time that Doris and Jelena had been separated, in a sense, but no one thought of them as being separated. Spontaneously the girls began singing "Farther Along," and the rest of the congregation quickly picked it up, and were alert enough to notice and follow the slight alteration that the girls made in the line, "Cheer up, my *sister,* live in the sunshine…"

Then it was time for the eulogy, but nobody could think of anything to say about Billy Bob. Oren Duckworth remarked that he had died in the service of his country, but that was about all. Doc Swain, who was acting as master of ceremonies even though he was a Jelenist, invited Jelena and Doris to make concluding remarks if they wished to do so. They rose together, faced the gathering, and, as one, declared: "He was both of ours."

Doc Swain adjourned the meeting. He would have one more duty to perform, sadly, a few days later, standing with his pen in one hand and the certificates in the other, looking down upon the reddened earth where the sisters lay, hundreds of feet beneath Leapin Rock, tightly holding hands though lifeless. On each certificate, where the blank said "Cause of death," Doc Swain wrote: "*Broken heart.*"

And at the funeral, when they tried to sing "Farther Along," Doc Swain interrupted them, saying, "Farther along, hell! We done already understood it."

Even afterward there were people who still thought of themselves as being Jelenists or Dorisites, or who at least remembered that they once were. But the factions never met as separate groups again.

The baby Jelena was taken to live with Sonora Ingledew and her four daughters, but when Hank came home from the war, and decided to go to California, he and Sonora discussed it and agreed that they had too many girls already, so they asked Hank's brother Jackson, who was a bachelor, if he wouldn't mind rearing the child, and Jackson said it was the least he could do. When the little girl was old enough to go to kindergarten, Jackson moved with her to Harrison, where she grew up, and became a beautiful woman, and is going to reappear significantly in the end of this saga. Like so many of the Ingledews, Jackson didn't talk much, and unless he ever told it to her, which I doubt, she's never heard this story.

Chapter seventeen

Southeast of Los Angeles, in neighboring Orange County, California, is the city of Anaheim; founded by Germans in the middle of the last Century, it was discovered early in this Century by a wandering Stay Moron, who was struck by the novelty of having an orange tree in one's own front yard, from which one could help oneself when the oranges are ripe. He settled there, and from time to time wrote his various cousins back home in Stay More to tell them about the excellent winterless climate, high pay, and the fact of being able to pick an orange in one's own front yard, in some cases the backyard too, and by the end of the war, the Second one, there were a dozen Stay Morons living in Anaheim, as well as several hundred persons from other places in the Ozarks, so that the atmosphere of Anaheim was distinctly Ozarkian although there was no topographic, climatic or architectural resemblance. (The illustration to the left is of a house not in Anaheim but in Stay More, and was not built until the end of this dreadful chapter.)

People from the Ozarks transplanted to Anaheim still greeted one another with "Howdy" and dropped their "g's" and periodically they observed "Old-timey Days," particularly the Second Tuesday of the Month, and some of the men whittled, and some of the women held quilting bees, although all of the old-timey superstitions and remedies were forgotten, and there was no condemnation of PROG RESS, because PROG RESS was going on all around them: Anaheim was growing at a phenomenal rate, everybody was prospering. When John Henry Ingledew arrived with Sonora and his four daughters, the other Stay Morons gave them a big welcome party, because they were delighted to have at last a genuine Ingledew among them, since they already had a Dinsmore, a Whitter, a Duckworth, a Coe, a Chism, a Plowright, a Swain and a Stapleton.

John Henry "Hank" Ingledew quickly found employment, at high pay, as an electronics technician for a huge canning factory, an operation that made Oren Duckworth's snap and 'mater canning factory look like nothing to write home about. (The Duckworth factory did reopen for a few summers after the war, but the competition, most of it coming from California, killed it, and Duckworth too moved to Anaheim.) The factory Hank Ingledew worked for was automated, and his job was to service the electronic apparatus which automated it. Also he "moonlighted," after hours, as a repairman of television sets, and made so much money that he and his family could afford to live in an opulent twelve-room "Spanish colonial" house (which will never be illustrated in any history of architecture). Sonora joined a women's club, and the daughters went to good kindergartens and schools. Every weekend, if somebody's TV set wasn't in urgent need of repair, they all went to the beach, where Hank could stare at his ocean, or rather John Henry could, because as soon as he arrived in California he let it be known that he would prefer not to be addressed by the nickname of his Stay More boyhood, although it took Sonora a full two years to get out of the habit of calling him Hank, and even after two years she would sometimes forget herself, especially when she was being endearing, as she often was, unhampered by worry since a California gynecologist fitted her out with a diaphragm.

But when her youngest daughter, Patricia, was old enough to leave home and go to kindergarten, Sonora found that her days were empty. She thought of getting a job, but John Henry pointed out to her that they already had more money than they knew what to do with. Sonora became addicted to daytime soap operas and quiz shows on television, and her days were long and lonely and repetitious. When she simply could not stand to watch the tube, she began to write long letters, to her mother and a few other chums back home in Stay More. She told them of all the things she did, and all the things she possessed, and how happy her daughters were, and how busy John Henry was. They replied with what little news Stay More yielded: deaths mostly, the changing of the seasons (which Sonora missed), drought, flood, a rare wedding, and Decoration Day at the cemetery.

Without discussing it with John Henry, out of fear that he would say no, Sonora took to leaving her diaphragm in its case. She was, after all, only twenty-seven, and they could, after all, quite easily afford a large family, and there was always a chance, after all, that they might have a son. For three months Sonora went without her diaphragm, and took her husband into her at least every bedtime and often on waking, so that John Henry no longer had any enthusiasm for moonlighting, and gave up his sideline repair of television sets, with some loss of income, offset by an automatic generous raise at the automated canning factory.

In the middle of the fourth month, it worked: Sonora knew the night she had conceived, and her days thereafter were still dull with television and an occasional women's club meeting, but she no longer felt purposeless. She was five months pregnant before John Henry even noticed, and that was because she said "Ow" when his paunch was bearing down too hard upon her middle, whereupon he looked down between them and observed, "Hey, you're gettin a potbelly too." She just smiled, and he went on, "Unless..." He finished what they were doing, and then lay beside her and asked, "Have you not been wearin that thing?" She shook her head. He asked, "Wal, what was the sense in gettin it, then?" She shrugged her shoulders. John Henry did not get angry. He concluded, "Well, it durn well better be a boy, this time." Not only was he well aware of the heavy responsibility he carried to perpetuate the Ingledew name, but also his daughters were spoiled and they were all over the place. He was constantly tripping on their toys, and constantly bringing home more toys for them to leave for him to trip on. And when all four of the girls were gathered around their mother, gossiping away like some gabby hen party, John Henry felt excluded from his family.

He missed males. He missed his uncles and his father and his brother. Twice a year, on the average, the Stay Morons of Anaheim would get together with the other Ozarkers of Anaheim for an Old-timey Day, where the women would load tables with platters of fried chicken and 'mater dishes and every manner of pie and cake, and the men would congregate to themselves to swap remembered hunting and fishing yarns, or to attempt to remember and relate the old jokes, although nobody was very good at it. These bull sessions always wound up with each of the men declaring fervently that, while, yes, he shore missed them ole Ozarks and shore aimed to git back fer a visit one of these days, it was frankly obvious that after all has been said and done, in this day and age California is the place to be endowed with this world's goods and to feel well repaid for our efforts and to entertain high hopes of enjoying the finer side of life or even be cradled in luxury or at least live the even tenor of one's ways to the heart's content.

John Henry thought these men seemed a little bit runny around the edges. He had grown up with some of the men, and they seemed to have changed. Maybe, he realized, he was runny around the edges himself, and didn't know it. He touched his potbelly and noticed that the other men had potbellies too. He ought to walk more, he decided, but there weren't many sidewalks in Anaheim outside of downtown, and pedestrians on the roads were stared at by drivers as if they were in trouble. John Henry had taken a long walk, once, and seventeen cars had stopped and offered him a ride. Dogs had barked and howled at him. Children had stared and pointed. A housewife had come out of her house and offered him the use of her telephone, and when he had said he was just walking for exercise, she had invited him into her house for a beer, and after he had finished it she had opened her housecoat revealing nothing underneath and had thrown herself upon him, and he had marveled at the novelty of fucking an absolute stranger, but he hadn't gone for any more walks since then.

He told himself that he would make up for it whenever they went back to Stay More for a visit. He promised himself that if they went back to Stay More for a visit he would walk up and down every road in Newton County. But every year, when his two-week vacation came, they went to Yosemite or Grand Canyon or San Francisco or down into Mexico. There were a few Stay Morons in Anaheim who went back for a visit, and returned to report that Stay More was dying and just about gone, and this saddened John Henry and Sonora, who told themselves and each other that this was the reason they didn't want to go back, but they both knew, without telling each other, that the real reason was that if they ever did go back to Stay More they would not be able to leave it. Few if any of the Stay Morons in Anaheim remembered the curse that Jacob Ingledew had placed on any Stay Moron who would leave it to go west, but one by one the Stay Morons in Anaheim began to experience calamities and misfortunes: one was killed in a freeway crash, one died of lung cancer, one was wiped out at a Las Vegas crap table, one was mangled in the machinery of a factory, one drowned in the surf of the Pacific, one was murdered by a jealous husband, one choked to death on an orange, and so on. Nothing ever happened to John Henry, but he kept wondering if something would.

During her fifth pregnancy, Sonora put on an exceptional amount of extra weight, so that toward the end of the pregnancy she felt that she was fat and gross and ugly and could not understand why John Henry would want to keep making love to her, so she stopped him from it. It was a bad time to do such a thing, because there was a girl, one of the secretaries at the factory where John Henry worked, who had been flirting with John Henry for a long time although she too was married. They sometimes had a cocktail together after work at a lounge near the factory, and during one of these meetings he revealed to the secretary that his wife was no longer permitting him to have relations with her. "Call her and tell her you have to work late," the secretary suggested. He did, and the secretary likewise called her husband and told him the boss was keeping her overtime, and then they got into the secretary's convertible and drove up into the hills, and walked into a dense grove of orange trees and lay down on the ground and spent an hour doing it and redoing it with variations, and that was the beginning of their affair.

The secretary told John Henry that he had shown her what sex could really be like. She was always flattering him. Sometimes they would lie around tired after doing it and she would take his part in her hands and admire it, making original complimentary remarks about it. On weekends, the secretary's husband, who was an ardent sports fan, often went off to a ball game, leaving his wife alone, or, now, alone with John Henry, so that they did not have to lie upon the hard ground but on a soft bed, soft rug, soft sofa, or standing up together in the shower.

It was on one of these Saturdays that Sonora went into labor. She didn't know how to find John Henry; he had told her he was going to some ball game. She phoned for a taxicab to take her to the hospital, and decided that her oldest girl, Latha, who was nearly ten, could baby-sit. John Henry came home from his tryst to find Latha trying to break up a fight among her younger sisters, who were wrecking the house. He found a teenaged baby-sitter for the four of them, and went off to the hospital, where Sonora was in her room napping after the delivery. He did not wake her, but went to the glass wall to view the baby. There were many of them. He asked a passing nurse, "Which'un's mine? Ingledew's the name." The nurse pointed, to the second row. John Henry couldn't see the baby very clearly, but he noticed that each bassinet had a card affixed to it, some of the cards were trimmed in blue and some in pink, and the bassinet the nurse was pointing at had a pink-edged card on it. "Shit," said John Henry. "Oh, shit." The nurse gave him a distasteful look and walked away. He found another nurse and told her that when his wife woke up to tell her that he had come and seen the baby and would come back tomorrow. Then he telephoned the secretary's house, but her husband answered, so he hung up, and went out to a cocktail lounge and got drunk, and came home in the wee hours of the morning to find the baby-sitter's irate parents taking her place and asking him if he didn't have any idea of what time it was, and if he didn't have the common sense to let the sitter know where he could be reached. When he got rid of them he fell into bed, and had no dreams until well after daylight, when he had dreams of Stay More alternating with dreams of running off to Mexico with the secretary.

It was almost noon when he woke, and found that his daughters had tried to prepare a breakfast for him, but had burned the coffee and overcooked the eggs. "Girls! Girls! Girls! Girls! Girls! Girls!" he said, and the smaller ones began to cry. "Aw, cut it out, and let's all go out to Howard Johnson's for breakfast," he suggested. They told him that they had had their breakfast at breakfasttime and it was almost lunchtime. So he took them out to eat their lunch while he had his breakfast, and then, because children aren't allowed in maternity wards, he had them stay in the car reading comic books while he went into the hospital. He kissed Sonora on her forehead, and she took his hand and held it and said "Poor Hank," then looked at him apologetically.

"Wal," he observed philosophically, "it don't look like there's going to be any more Ingledews."

"This one's the prettiest of them all," Sonora declared. "Wait till you see her."

They named the fifth daughter Sharon and she did indeed grow up to be the prettiest of them all, although they were all pretty. John Henry decided that he had better go back to repairing television sets on the side, and save his money in order to be able to pay for five fancy weddings eventually. When he met the secretary at the cocktail lounge after work on Monday, he remarked, not facetiously, "Maybe if I was married to you, I'd have a boy." The secretary shook her head, telling him that she didn't want to have any children. That struck John Henry as peculiar; he had never heard of a woman who didn't want to have children. "How come?" he asked. She explained that she liked sex so much that she didn't want to spoil it by having children. That struck John Henry as ironic: to refrain from procreation for the sake of enjoying the procreative process. The secretary asked, "Do you want to marry me?" He said he had given it a thought or two. She laughed and held his hand and told him to hurry and finish his drink so they could drive up into the hills, but he said not this evening, because he had decided to return to the nocturnal repairing of television sets as an extra source of income, to finance his many daughters' eventual weddings. "I didn't know you could fix tv's," she said. "Come and fix ours. You can meet my husband." So that night, on his rounds, he stopped by the secretary's house in the guise of repairman, and met her husband. He was a tall fellow, but not as tall as John Henry. Sure enough, the television set needed a new tube.

The husband didn't pay much attention while John Henry replaced the tube, and when it was finished the husband just took out his wallet and said "How much?" The secretary said, "I think that other one up in the bedroom has something wrong with the channel selector. Come on, I'll show you." She took him up to the bedroom and closed the door and giggled and unzipped his pants and knelt before him. Soon they were doing a sixty-nine on the bed, with John Henry on the bottom, when the door opened and the husband came in and said, "Well, well, this is interesting. But don't let me interrupt you." John Henry tried to get up, but he was on the bottom, and the secretary whispered to him "I think he means it," and she went on doing him until she had finished him off. John Henry wasn't worrying about getting beaten up afterwards, not by that guy, but maybe the fellow had a pistol somewhere. When the secretary had finished him, the husband remarked, "Lovely. Doesn't she give wonderful head?" and then went out and back downstairs.

John Henry asked the secretary if her husband had a gun, and she said not that she knew of. He checked the bedroom's television set; there was nothing wrong with it. He went downstairs, where he found the husband mixing drinks, and offering him a glass. John Henry's drink was Scotch, whereas he preferred bourbon, but he didn't quibble. They sipped their drinks, and the secretary introduced them, saying, "This is John Henry Ingledew. He's in charge of electronics at the plant, but he repairs televisions on his own." "Glad to meet you, Jack," said the husband. "How's your wife?" "She's fine," John Henry replied. "Just had a baby." "I mean," said the husband, "how is she at giving head?" "Oh, pretty good, I guess," John Henry said uncomfortably, feeling that his privacy was being twice invaded. "Would she give it to me?" the husband asked. "Now, look here…" John Henry said, getting angry. He didn't have to listen to this. He would just as soon bash in the guy's face for him. "Turn about is fair play," the husband insisted, "don't you think?" "You don't even know my wife," John Henry pointed out. "No, but wouldn't it be easy to get to know her? Let's have a party." "No, thanks. I'm too busy," John Henry said, and he set down his unfinished drink and went out the door and got into his van and went on to the next house that needed its television set repaired. The lone occupant of this house was a woman who said her husband was out playing cards and told him the bedroom television set also needed repairs. "No thanks, lady," he said, and got away from there.

He avoided the secretary thereafter, but after he had been avoiding her for several weeks she came into the electronics shop at the factory at the end of the day and said, "Couldn't we have a drink and a little talk, like old times?" He gave in, and took her to the cocktail lounge again. When their drinks were before them, the secretary began, "After all, these are modern times we are living in," and she proceeded to elaborate an argument in favor of free love. She loved having sex with him, she said, and she had been missing it terribly these past few weeks, and she was awfully glad to know that her husband actually didn't mind, one teensy bit. "But he wants me to return him the favor," John Henry said. "And you honestly can't?" the secretary wanted to know. "I don't think so," he said. "At least, I sure as hell wouldn't care to watch."

He had tried to imagine what it would be like, watching Sonora going down on the secretary's husband, and he couldn't even get the picture in focus. "He wouldn't insist on that," the secretary assured him. "I just don't like the whole idea!" John Henry said so loudly that several other customers in the bar turned to stare at him. "Well," the secretary concluded, "we're giving a party Saturday night. Would you consider coming to that? It wouldn't be just the four of us. There will be a lot of other couples there." "I'll think about it," John Henry told her, and for the rest of the week he thought about it. He didn't want to go, and he wondered what kind of party it would be, whether they would play games or even start fooling around. But Sonora was depressed lately, as she always was several weeks after the birth of a baby, and he thought it might do her good to get out of the house and meet people and have some good clean fun or even some good unclean fun if that was what it was all about. These are modern times we are living in, he kept remembering, over and over. So he said to

371

Sonora, How would you like to go to a party? and when she said whose? he said some people at the factory were giving it. She didn't have anything to wear, because she was still overweight and didn't have her figure back, but he offered to buy her a new dress and she was dying to get out of the house for an evening, so she gave in, and they went to the party at the secretary's and her husband's house.

It was not a wild party. There was plenty of drinking, but no fooling around. The secretary's husband complimented John Henry on his wife's beauty, but he made no passes at her. Sonora seemed to be enjoying herself. Several men made decorous small talk with her, and one man flirted with her, but nobody laid a hand on her. Occasionally a couple would disappear upstairs for a while, but all in all it was a warm and sociable occasion, and John Henry thanked the secretary's husband for inviting them. On the way home, Sonora, who was tipsy, babbled on about what a good time she had had, and in bed that night she was exceptionally passionate and adventurous. Just two days later, one of the men they had met at the party phoned and invited them to another party the very next weekend. The secretary and her husband were also at the second party, but there were a lot of people who had not been at the first, and the Ingledews broadened their circle of acquaintances. Toward the end of the party, Sonora was deep in conversation with two men on the sofa, and did not notice when the secretary came and took John Henry's hand and led him off to a bedroom.

When the Ingledews got home that night and went to bed, John Henry wasn't in the mood, and Sonora accused him of drinking too much. As they were dressing for the third party the following Saturday, she made him promise not to drink so much. At the party, he told the secretary, "Look, let's do it early so I'll have time to recuperate before bedtime." Sonora lost interest in the man she was talking to, and noticed John Henry was missing. When he reappeared, she asked, "Where did you go?" He replied, "I was out in the kitchen, talking to some guys."

Later in the evening, Sonora found herself in conversation with the secretary's husband, who kept refilling her drink until she was too tipsy too early. She had made John Henry promise not to drink so much and now here she herself was drinking too much. She liked the secretary's husband, and thought he was witty. Every time he finished a joke he would lean down and kiss her underneath her ear. One time when he did that, he whispered in her ear, "Let's get some fresh air." The room was stuffy with cigarette smoke, and also hot, and she thought they could continue their conversation out on the porch, so she stepped outside with him. There weren't any chairs on the porch. "Let's sit in my car," the man suggested. They sat in the car. The man put his arm around her, but she brushed it off. He put it around her again, and she was too tipsy to bother brushing it off again. She didn't care. After a while he took one of her hands and placed it on his groin and she felt him swell; she tried to take her hand away but he held it there. "Let me go," she protested. He whispered in her ear, "I'll let you go if you'll kiss it a while." She slapped him, hard, and got out of the car and returned to the party, where she found Hank and apologized to him for having drunk so much and asked to go home.

At the next party, she avoided the secretary's husband. But late in the evening everybody started taking their clothes off, declaring they were going to have an orgy. John Henry and Sonora argued; she wanted to go, he wanted to stay. She left, saying he could get some-body else to drive him home. After the orgy, which John Henry didn't particularly enjoy, the secretary and her husband drove him home. "You ought to have a talk with that girl," the secretary's husband told him. Sonora was in bed, but she turned on the light when he came in, and they had a talk. It was quite a talk. Sonora began by demanding to know if he had had sex at the orgy, and when he told her that was the point of the whole thing, she was furious. "Do you think I would ever do a thing like that?" she demanded. "You'd have to get used to it, gradually," he said. "You think I would?" she said. "Would you *want* me to?" "I don't know," he admitted, but allowed, "I guess if I was doing it I couldn't object if you were." "Oh ho!" she said. "Did you know that that man, that…what's his name…the husband of one of the secretaries at your plant…when we were at the last party he somehow talked me into sitting in his car with him, and then he tried to get me to give him a blow job! Would you have let me give him a blow job?" John Henry did not answer, because he had still not settled the question in his own mind. In order for him to settle the question, he would have to permit himself to visualize the act, and he was unable to get the picture in focus. The tube was blown. "Would you?" she persisted. At length he admitted, "I honestly don't know. His wife has done it to me. With him watching."

Sonora began beating at him with her fists, yelling "Get out! Get out of here! Get out of here and don't ever come back!" He resisted, but her fists drove him out of the bedroom and down the hall and down the stairs and out the front door and down the steps. He spent the night in a motel, and returned to his house the following day. She wouldn't let him in. He protested that all his clothes and things were in the house. She began dumping his clothes and things out the window. "Sonora, for crying out loud!" he complained, but she continued throwing his effects out of the house, until there was nothing of his remaining in the house and the front yard was littered and the neighbors were standing on their porches watching and whispering as John Henry loaded all his effects into his van and drove to the motel.

After a week he returned to his house and rang the doorbell and then pounded on the door and hollered, "Sonora, at least let me say goodbye to the girls!" But she would not open the door. He lived in the motel for another two weeks, and called her every day on the telephone, but as soon as she recognized his voice she would hang up. He tried to write her a letter, but got as far as "Dear Sonora," which caused him to remember the first letter he had ever sent her, and made him sad, but he mailed these two words to her anyway, with the return address of his motel; there was no reply.

Of course, he went to no more parties, and when the secretary came into his electronics shop to find out why he was avoiding her, before she could get a word out of her mouth he said, "Just skip it. Just git the hell out of here and don't bother me anymore," and the tone with which he said these words was such that she left him alone and he never saw her again. After work Friday he drew his paycheck and got it cashed and checked out of the motel, and wrote Sonora one more note: "Dear Sonora: I'm going home. Going home. Love,

Hank." He mailed this, and pointed his van eastward and drove all night across the desert and up into the mountains and beyond. He parked and napped beside the road a couple of brief times, and kept moving; on the morning of the third day he reached Fort Smith, Arkansas, and turned northeastward toward home.

On the road from Jasper to Stay More he noticed an abandoned house. And then another one. Parthenon was all run down. At the church/schoolhouse outside Stay More he stopped and got out and walked for a while among the headstones in the cemetery: a dozen Ingledews, many Swains and Plowrights and Coes and Dinsmores and Chisms and Duckworths and Stapletons. He drove on into the village. There was no village. His mother-in-law's small general store seemed to be still in operation; at least its front door was open, but he did not stop to speak to her. The bank was a shell of stone. The dentists' and doctors' offices were empty or gone. The mill was rotting and seemed as if it would collapse any moment. Aunt Lola's big general store was boarded up, its gasoline pump immobile with rust. The canning factory was stuffed with bales of hay. Someone seemed to be still living in the old hotel, but he did not stop. He drove on to his folks' house and was almost surprised to find it lived in. His mother and father stared at his van as if it had come from the moon, and read the lettering on the door: "Ingledew Television Service, Anaheim, Calif. 433-8991." To his father and mother, he said simply that Sonora had kicked him out of the house and it was purely his own fault because he had been fooling around, but he was awful glad to come back to Stay More because he never cared much for California anyway.

After his mother fed him dinner, he left his van at their house and went for a long walk, to start getting rid of his potbelly. The walk took him past many more abandoned houses; he tried to remember the names of the people who had lived in them. The ones he could remember all lived, if they still lived, in Anaheim or Fullerton or other California towns. But while the human habitations were abandoned, nature was not, and nature welcomed Hank back to Stay More: the air was nice and had a fragrance that he had never found anywhere out west. The smell of weeds that he had taken for granted all his life was a new perfume for him. A car stopped beside him and its driver said "If it aint ole Hank! Git in, Hank. No sense walkin," and Hank was obliged to explain that he was walking for exercise and then to offer some reasonable explanation for why he had come back from California.

During his long walk, which lasted most of the afternoon, seventeen cars stopped and offered him a ride, and each time he had to explain why he had come back from California. One of the drivers said, "I heared that Snory and the gals didn't come with ye," and Hank, remembering that news travels fast in the backbrush, said "Naw, but they'll be along, directly." "You and Snory busted up?" another driver asked, and Hank replied, "Jist fer a little spell." His walk took him in a roundabout way almost to Jasper, and walking back from Jasper on the main road he remembered that the last time he had traveled this road on foot he was only ten years old and was accompanied by the World's Oldest Man, who had died after giving Hank a gold chronometer wristwatch for his son and telling him the whole story of his many visits to Stay More. Hank could still remember most of the story, but damned if he could remember where he had buried that wristwatch. It didn't matter. He had no son to give it to.

Hank hoped to avoid explanations to his mother-in-law, but when he walked into Stay More she was sitting in her rocker on the porch of her store, and he couldn't very well just walk on past her. So he stopped and sat on a porch chair and told her that her daughter had evicted him because he had foolishly "been with" another woman, but he hoped that time would heal all wounds, and that Sonora would bring the girls and come back to Stay More to live, because as far as he was concerned he wasn't ever going to leave Stay More again. His mother-in-law said she was very glad to hear that, and she hoped that Sonora would forgive him and come home too. They chatted a while longer about other things, and then the subject came up of Hank's regret over having fathered no son. His mother-in-law laughed, and she, who probably knew more about the old-timey ways than anybody else in Stay More, told him of an old tried-and-true superstition that had never been known to fail: if a husband sits on the roof of his house near the chimney for seven hours his next child will be a boy. Hank scoffed, but his mother-in-law named all of the men of Stay More who had been born males as a result of their fathers sitting on the roofs of their houses for seven hours. Hank was impressed, but he observed, "Heck, I aint even got a roof to set on."

That set him to thinking, and the following day he began construction of the ranch-style house which is the illustration for this chapter. It is located at a higher elevation of Ingledew Mountain than any of the other Ingledew buildings, and has a fine view of what is left of Stay More, as well as the mountains around. The architecture of it might seem Californian, but while there are many houses similar to it in California, there are also many houses similar to it elsewhere in the Ozarks. Hank didn't know anything about carpentry, having never done any before, but he was good with his hands, and could learn. Stay More still did not have electricity, so he couldn't use power tools, but he went to Harrison and persuaded the electric company to run a line from Jasper, and thus it might be said that the building of this house was indirectly responsible for the coming of electricity to Stay More. Hank's uncles dropped by from time to time to give him advice and to saw a board.

When the foundation was laid, he wrote a letter to Sonora, telling her what he was doing. She did reply, but he wished she hadn't: it was a very cool letter mentioning the fact that she had run into the secretary's husband at a supermarket and gone with him to his car in broad daylight and knelt on the floorboards and blown him. Pure spite. Hank was tempted to modify his plan for the house, eliminating all of the extra bedrooms for his daughters, but he was convinced that even if Sonora never came back to Stay More, his daughters would come, at least to visit. So he went ahead and built five bedrooms in the house, one for himself (and Sonora if she ever came back), three for his daughters to share, and one, finally, for the son that he never gave up hoping to have.

Chapter eighteen

John Henry "Hank" Ingledew worked so hard on his house that, expectedly (although he had forgotten to expect it), he came down with the frakes when he was finished with it. It is of course quite possible to get the frakes more than once; having them does not produce immunity as in the case of so many other dread diseases. His second attack of the frakes was, however, not quite as uncomfortable as the first, because the experience of the first had taught him that the itching would be terrible and that afterwards he would sink into irrevocable despair, and there was nothing he could do about it, so he resigned himself to it, and his resignation kept him from suffering quite so much. Still, he was bedfast, and would have starved to death, had not his mother, taking him a pie she had baked, discovered he needed far more than pie. After she had cooked a meal and forced him to eat it, she told Sonora's mother of his condition, and his mother-in-law had his father-in-law drive her into Jasper, where there was a telephone. She put in a long distance call to California, and told Sonora that Hank had the frakes, and Sonora immediately booked airplane passage for herself and her five daughters, and was picked up by her father at the Fort Smith airport and driven to Stay

More, where she burst into Hank's bedroom hollering "Why didn't you tell me?" He replied, "Who cares?"

She threw herself upon him, weeping, and the five daughters crowded timidly into the doorway, staring at their father. "Is he dead?" one of the younger asked the oldest. "No," the oldest assured her, "he just wishes he was." Then the girls wandered off for a tour of their new home, and fought over whose bedroom was whose, and who would get a room all to herself. It was decided that the oldest would have that privilege. There was no furniture in any of the rooms, except the bed in Hank's bedroom, so the girls spent the night at their grandparents'. Sonora slept with Hank and even tried to interest him in intercourse, but he wasn't interested. She apologized for the nasty letter she had sent and the awful thing she had done with the secretary's husband, but Hank honestly felt no animosity, nor, for that matter, anything. Wasn't he the least bit glad that she had come home? Sonora persisted. Well, he observed, it would be convenient because he wasn't able to cook for himself, provided he was interested in eating, but since he didn't give a shit about eating, it wasn't convenient, so she might as well go back to California. No, she said, it was too late: before she left she had placed their house on the market and instructed a mover to pack up all their furniture and stuff and transport it to Stay More. So see? she said. Hank shrugged. She sighed and went to sleep. Hank knew that the purpose of sleep is to restore the mind and body for the challenge of the coming day, and since the coming day held no challenges for him he didn't care whether he slept or not, but Nature, who runs this show, put him to sleep anyway.

Because there was no longer a school at Stay More, the daughters of school age were driven into Jasper each day by Sonora's father, who worked as a mechanic in the Jasper Ford agency. The daughters came home each day complaining of the school's shortcomings compared with the schools they had attended in Anaheim. Sonora was sad about this, even though it meant nothing to Hank. She tried to assure the girls that they would get used to it. She tried to instill in them a respect, if not a love, for their native state, reminding them that all of them except the baby had been born in the Ozarks. And in fact, one by one, eventually, they no longer complained of their school but even reported on the more positive aspects of it. They began complaining that their father was indifferent to them. Even though he was no longer bedridden, and could move around just as easy as anyone, he wasn't interested in anything, and his daughters couldn't talk to him, although they tried.

Gradually he regained his interest in eating, if in nothing else, and one evening at supper when Sonora served some heated-up beans out of a can he actually grumbled. "It's all we can afford," Sonora retorted. "We've used up all our savings building this house and moving our things here and living for weeks and weeks without any income. Do you want me to look for a job? Will you stay home and take care of the baby while I'm working? I intend to start a garden patch next spring, and get some chickens, but what will we do until then?"

"Aw, heck," Hank replied, and the next day he painted out the letters "Anaheim, Calif." on the side of his van, and painted in the letters "Jasper, Ark." and drove into Jasper and rented one of the vacant buildings on the square, the little brick-painted-white store whose illustration heads this chapter. It is the only building illustrated in this book which is not in Stay More, but there would be no more buildings in Stay More, except one, and that is our last chapter.

Although Jasper had been wired for electricity it had no television sets, and it dawned on Hank that before he could service television sets there would first have to *be* television sets, and not only that but they would also have to be around long enough, a week at least, for something to go wrong with them. So he got out his paintbrush again and added "and Sales" after "Service" on the sides of his van and the front of his shop. General Electric generously shipped him a dozen sets on credit, and he put these in his show windows, and waited for customers. Everybody who came into Jasper, especially on Saturdays, would wander around the square to Hank's shop and look in the windows at his television sets, but no body came into the store.

It occurred to Hank that if he turned the sets on, the people could see how an actual picture appears. So he plugged the sets in and turned them on, but the reception was terrible. He realized he would need not only a high antenna atop his shop, but also a "booster." He sent off to Little Rock for these items. When they arrived, Hank was finally in business. Crowds gathered at his windows, and stayed for hours to watch whole games of Base Ball coming from St. Louis and Chicago and Kansas City and everywhere else. The sheriff complained that the crowds were blocking traffic on the street, and requested that Hank bring some of the sets out into the square, but Hank explained that television requires dim light for the picture to be seen clearly. He suggested to the sheriff that the sheriff could help matters by ordering the crowd to go inside and buy one of the damn things so they could watch it in the comfort of their own living room.

The sheriff went up in front of the crowd and hollered, "OKAY, FOLKS! YOU'RE BLOCKING TRAFFIC! WHY DON'T YOU GO INSIDE AND BUY ONE OF THE DAMN THINGS SO YOU CAN WATCH 'EM IN THE COMFORT OF YOUR OWN LIVING ROOM?" The crowd surged through the door, and Hank was sold out within five minutes, and booked up for a month to install the antennas and boosters at their homes. When he arrived at some of their homes to install the antennas and boosters, he discovered that these homes were so far out in the wilds that they didn't have electricity; he was instrumental in getting power lines erected in the remotest recesses of Newton County. The desire for television brought with it the means for operating washing machines, dryers, deep freezes, ranges, phonographs, blenders, electric clocks, vacuum cleaners, radial arm saws, toothbrushes, shoe polishers, shavers, typewriters, not to mention lamps and chandeliers and porch lights and every manner of ceiling fixture. Labor was so saved that there never again was a single case of the frakes in Newton County—no, there was *one* case, but he is our last chapter.

We may rightly question whether or not Hank Ingledew's contribution to the way of life was a gross violation of the time-worn strictures against PROG RESS, and there is no denying that the company which manufactured the television sets he sold, as well as all the other aforementioned electrical appliances, had (and still has) as its motto, "PROG RESS is our most important product," but I seriously doubt that Hank Ingledew ever gave the matter any thought. Selling television was a good way of earning a living, and he grew prosperous. Then too, innumerable sourhours were banished by the tube. There is one school of opinion which would argue that if literacy spoiled the Ozarks by diminishing the oral tradition, television restored something by requiring no literacy—but just what that something is would be hard to pin down.

When the money began rolling in, Hank decided that the time had come to try, once more, one last time, to have a son. He never forgot the superstition that his mother-in-law had told him about, and although he was totally without belief in superstition he could not deny the evidence of the efficacy of this particular superstition, that so many males born in Stay More had been males because their fathers had sat on the roofs of their houses for seven hours, and when Hank built the house that he now lived in, he had given it a low-pitched roof not only because low-pitched roofs are fashionable for ranch-style houses but also in order to facilitate his eventual ascent to the roof's ridge. One evening when Hank and Sonora were talking in bed before going to sleep, he asked her,

"Snory, do you want to have another kid?"

"Oh, don't worry about that," she replied. "I went to a gynecologist up at Harrison and had myself fitted out for a new diaphragm."

"I don't mean that," he said. "I mean, would you? Could you stand to have one more?"

She was silent, thinking. Then she said, "It probably wouldn't be a boy, either. You still want a boy. You won't ever give up."

"Your mother told me something, once," he said. "I know it sounds silly, but there's an old, old superstition that if a man sits on his roof for seven hours near the chimney his next child will be a boy."

Sonora laughed uproariously. "My mother never told *me* that."

"But it works, she said. Lots of men were born male because their fathers sat on their roofs. Her own father. Your dad's father. Your dad. And she said me too, although not on purpose: my father was nailing on the shingles of his roof one day, and he was up there seven hours. At least that's what your mother said."

"When did you get so chummy with my mother?"

"It was the day I came home from California."

"Oh? As soon as you got back, you went running to my mother to complain because I won't give you a son?"

"Not like that. I was just talking to her and the subject came up."

"Are you going to sit on the roof for seven hours?"

"I've been thinking about it."

"*Really,* Hank! What if somebody comes along and sees you?"

"Well, I could just tell 'em I'm adjusting the TV antenna or something."

"Oh sure. Just when are you supposed to sit on the roof? Right before knocking me up, or right before the baby is born?"

"I hadn't thought of that. Your mother didn't say."

"Why don't you ask her?"

"Heck, I couldn't ask her *that.*"

Sonora didn't say anything more. But just before going to sleep, she drowsily mumbled, "Maybe I will ask her." And she did. The next time she saw her mother, she casually mentioned the subject, never having had any difficulty discussing sex with her mother, and told her, "Hank wants to sit on the roof for seven hours. When's he supposed to do it? Before conception or before birth?" Her mother told her that it was supposed to happen just prior to conception. Sonora relayed this information to Hank, who declared,

"Well, I'm ready anytime you are."

Sonora calculated the best time of her month and answered, "Any time this weekend," so the following Sunday, after the noon dinner, when there weren't any television sets that needed urgent repairs, Hank filled a quart Mason jar with ice and water (it was a hot day), propped a ladder against the eaves of his house, kissed Sonora for good luck, and climbed to the roof, stepped onto it, then climbed the roof to its ridge. He put his ice water on the top of the chimney, the only flat surface up there. He sat down on the ridge, lighted a cigarette, smoked it, and dropped the butt down the chimney. His daughters came out of the house and stared up at him, pointing at him and giggling among themselves fit to burst. After an hour of it, they grew tired of giggling and went back into the house.

It was one hell of a hot day, and the sun reflecting off the roof made it even hotter. Hank was soaked with sweat; he uncapped the Mason jar and took a lusty drink of ice water. The ice was rapidly melting. The pressure of the ridge against his buttocks was uncomfortable. He hollered down the chimney, "Hey, Snory!" His wife came out of the house, and he called to her, "Could you throw me up a sofa cushion or a pillow or something?" She laughed and went back into the house and brought out a sofa cushion; she threw it; it didn't reach him; he had to fetch it halfway down the roof. He put it on the roof ridge and sat on it. That was much more comfortable. A pickup truck pulled into his driveway, and in it was his father and all four of his uncles. "Hey, Hank!" Uncle Tearle called up to him. "Ball game down at Deer. Let's go." "I got to fix this damn antenna," Hank replied, taking hold of the antenna and pretending to turn it. "We can wait," Bevis said, and got out of the truck and began climbing the ladder. At the top of the ladder he asked, "Need a hand?" "That's okay, Dad," Hank said. "I can do it, but it takes a while to get it right. You boys go on to the ball game." Bevis protested that they could wait, and it took several minutes of argument for Hank to persuade them to leave. They were scarcely out of sight when another pickup truck pulled into his driveway, and Bill Chism jumped out and called to him, "Hey, Hank. My Tee Vee just won't go on. I don't know what's the matter with it." "Well, Bill, I'm sorry," Hank replied. "I'm messin with this here antenna, and I'll probably be up here all afternoon." "Aw, durn," Bill said, "I was gonna watch the Cardinals."

"Did you check to see if it was plugged in?" Hank asked. "Hadn't thought of that," Bill said and got back into his pickup and drove off. Half an hour later he was back. "Yeah, it's plugged in, all right, and I can get some sound, but there jist aint ary picture." Hank replied, "Try the brightness and contrast knobs. Could be you've dimmed the tube out." Bill left again, and returned in another half hour. "I reckon I've missed that there Cardinal game by now. But my old woman is givin me hell on account of she has to watch 'I Love Lucy.' You sure are takin a long time with that antenna. What's wrong with it anyhow?" "Caint git it adjusted just right," Hank said, but he was at a loss for any way to get rid of Bill Chism. He could keep sending him back to fool around with various knobs and screws on his television set, but ole Bill would just keep on coming back until Hank had fixed it. Now Bill showed no inclination to leave, but was just hanging around watching Hank pretending to twist the TV antenna. Hank kept up the pretense until he realized that he wasn't fooling Bill, and then he asked, "Bill, can you keep a secret? I'll tell you the truth. I know it's plumb ridiculous, but what I'm doing up here on the roof, see, is an old superstition. Learned it from Snory's mother. I've got to sit here on the roof for seven hours, and I've just been here about three."

"No foolin?" Bill said, with an ill-suppressed grin. "What's it supposed to cure?" "It don't cure anything, exactly," Hank replied, "it just sorta brings a certain kind of good luck." "Is that a fact?" Bill said. "Well, I declare. I hope it works fer ye. But will you come and fix my Tee Vee as soon as you git down?" Bill consulted his wristwatch and added, "That'd be about eight o'clock. If you hurry, maybe my old woman can watch her program." "I'm sure sorry, Bill," Hank said. "But as soon as I git down, I've got to do something else."

"What's that?"

"I caint tell ye, Bill, but it's part of the superstition too."

Bill hung around a while longer, dejected, and then complained, "What if you was a doctor, and my old woman was a-dying? You'd come down then, I bet."

"Yeah, Bill, I sure would, but I aint a doctor and your old woman aint a-dying, and I've done put my mind to this here superstition, and you'd have to burn my house down to get me off of here." Bill went away.

Hank's jar of water was empty; he hollered down the chimney for more, and Sonora climbed the ladder and got his jar and refilled it, and brought it back up with a ham sandwich. He ate his sandwich and drank his ice water, then he realized that he needed to urinate. He went down the back slope of the roof and stood at the edge of the roof and urinated. Inside the house one of his daughters observed, "Mommy, it's raining, although the sun is out. I bet there'll be a rainbow." All of the girls ran out of the house looking for a rainbow. Then they went back in. Late in the afternoon, a carload of Stay Morons drove into the driveway and stared at him and then drove away. "Damn that Bill Chism," Hank said aloud. Another carload of Stay Morons arrived. Then another. The population of Stay More at that time had shrunk to only about sixty, but before the afternoon was over every last one of them had had a chance to see Hank Ingledew sitting on his roof. Most of them shouted, "Good luck, Hank" as they were driving away, but many of them made joking remarks. The last visitor was a reporter from the Jasper *Disaster,* carrying a Graphlex camera. "You point that thing at me," Hank warned, "and I'll smash it to flinders."

"Could I ask a few questions?" the reporter asked.

"I jist as soon ye didn't," Hank said.

"It isn't every day that I get a chance like this," the reporter persisted. "Imagine the headline: 'STAY MORE MAN SITS ON ROOF SEVEN HOURS.'"

Hank grimaced, and said, "There better not be a word in your paper. A man has got the right to do whatever he wants so long as he aint harmin anyone. I'm on my own property, and you're trespassing. I'll take ye to court if you print this." The reporter retreated, and nobody else came. He had just a couple of hours to go. He was tired. His bones ached. He felt silly. But he believed it would work. Faith fortifies.

When his seven hours were up, Sonora climbed to the top of the ladder and smiled at him and asked, "Shall I climb on up there, and we'll do it on the roof?" Hank didn't know if she was serious or not, but he observed, "It's still light. I'll come down." He went down off the roof. She pointed out that the girls wouldn't be going to bed for another hour. "Are we supposed to do it right away?" Hank wondered. "I guess," she said. "Well, let's go for a little walk," he suggested. Sonora went inside to tell the oldest girl that they were going for a walk and would be back soon. Then Sonora and Hank went into the woods behind their house; within a few hats they were lost from sight. On a thick blanket of old leaves Sonora sat and removed her slacks and panties; Hank removed his pants and shorts. They embraced and kissed for a while, but Hank discovered that his part was not only not standing but also it wasn't even rising. Hank could not explain it. He tried: "I guess maybe I'm just all wore out from sitting on the roof so long."

"But what about all of those other men that it worked for, who sat on their roofs and then had sons?" Sonora said. "Were they worn out too? How did *they* get it in?"

"I don't know," Hank said, and he climbed on top of her and put it between her legs and went through all the motions of intercourse, but his part refused to stiffen. Sonora thrust her hips vigorously against his, but it wouldn't help. He did, however, after prolonged movement, spill his seed, which Sonora collected on her fingertips and inserted into herself. It was this which impregnated her.

Nine months later she gave birth to, sure enough, a son. She was ecstatic, and there is no word to apply to Hank, who made a fool of himself out of pride and happiness. But after the celebrating was over, he frowned and asked Sonora, "What was the name of that guy we were going to name him after? You know, the World's Oldest Man, that peddler from Connecticut?" "Yeah, I know who you mean," Sonora said, frowning; "His name is right on the tip of my tongue… Eh…Eh…Elmer? No. What *was* it?" She couldn't remember. Hank asked his father. Bevis said, "It was one of them funny Yankee names, Esau or something." Hank's Uncle Tearle thought the first name was "Ezra" but none of his uncles could help him.

Wasn't the name written down anywhere? Maybe it was written on the glass showcase which served as the man's coffin. Hank went into the old mill; its timbers were thoroughly rotten; he worried that the mill would collapse upon his head, but he found the glass showcase and dusted it off. The old man hadn't changed a bit, but the sight of him didn't refresh Hank's memory as to what his name had been. "What was your name, old-timer?" Hank said aloud, and wouldn't have been surprised if he got a reply, but he didn't. He inspected the glass showcase closely, but there was nothing written on it except the name of the manufacturer, "Acme Display Fixtures, Inc." He told Sonora that they might as well name their son Acme Display Fixture Ingledew, but Sonora rejected that because of the resemblance between "Acme" and "Acne." Sonora suggested finding the oldest person in Stay More and asking him or her if he or she could remember the name of the Connecticut peddler. That turned out to be Drussie Ingledew, Grandpa Doomy's kid sister, in her early eighties, still living in the Stay More Hotel, still operating it in fact, although the last customer to spend the night there was back during the Second War.

"Aunt Drussie," Hank said, "what was the name of that old peddler who used to come back to Stay More again and again and finally died here when I was a kid?" "Aw, shore," Drussie replied, "everybody knows his name. I'm ashamed of ye, thet you've forgot it. Why, when I was just a little girl, I remember the year he brought the whale oil when the bar oil guv out, and then again when the whale oil guv out he brought coal oil. Then there was the time—" "Aunt Drussie," Hank interrupted, "what was his *name?*" "He used to give me candy," Drussie recalled, "and ask me if I had been a good girl, and if I was being as good a girl as I knew how. I'll never forget him, to the day I die." "But you don't remember his name?" Hank asked. "Ellis Wilkins?" Drussie said. "Ellery Wilkes? Ephriam Wilson? Elton Wallace? Ennis Willoughby? Any of them sound right to you?" Hank shook his head. "Wal, I'll tell ye," Drussie offered, "there was a time he druv up to Stay More in the first hossless ker-ridge, and my oldest brother Denton took 'im to court fer spookin his livestock' in the building whar the cannin fact'ry used to be, that one time was Denton and Monroe's barn, and the Jasper newspaper printed a give-out on the court trial. Maybe if you was to find that old newspaper, it would have his name in it." "What year was it?" Hank asked. "Year?" said Drussie. "Why, I reckon that was the same year, or the year after, that Doomy organized the Masons." "What year was that? Do you know the number of the year?" "Number of the year? Law, boy, years don't have numbers!" "Don't you know the number of *this* year?" "No. Do you?" Hank said goodbye to his great-aunt and drove into Jasper to search the files of old *Disasters*, but the fellow on duty in the *Disaster* office was the same person that Hank had refused permission to photograph him on his rooftop or even to interview him, and the fellow was peevish and wouldn't give Hank permission to look at old issues. It didn't matter; Hank didn't even know what year it was. Even if he knew the exact year, he probably wouldn't have been able to find the item. He went home to Sonora and said, "Let's just name him Hank Junior and you can call me Big Hank and call him Little Hank."

No, Sonora wasn't buying that. For one thing, she knew that the boy would eventually grow to be bigger than his father, and therefore the Little Hank designation would be as absurd as "Li'l Abner." For another thing, she had been thinking that names ought to *mean* something. Her own name, Sonora, had been given to her by her mother because it meant "little song" and her newborn cries had been like little songs. "John Henry" didn't mean anything. Taken literally, it meant "God is gracious and is the ruler of an enclosure, or private property," which, even apart from the fact that the Ingledews didn't even believe in God, was contradictory: a gracious John cannot be a tightfisted Henry. Sonora wanted a meaningful name. It was springtime; things were growing; she wanted her baby to grow and flourish. So she named him Vernon. Hank didn't much like that, but there wasn't much he could do. He hoped that before the ink was dry on the birth certificate the name of the Connecticut peddler might suddenly return to him, but it never did. Vernon Ingledew it was, and remained.

We come now to a difficult matter. What psychological effect would it have upon a growing boy to have five older sisters? Wouldn't he be dreadfully spoiled? Would he become effeminate? Or wouldn't his congenital Ingledew woman-shyness be magnified a hundredfold? It was true his sisters doted on him—and during the summers there were not five but six of them, in a sense: his first cousin Jelena, raised by his Uncle Jackson in Harrison during the school year, spent all her summers, every summer, in Stay More and was such a close friend of his sisters, especially of Patricia, who was the same age, that as far as Vernon was concerned she was one more sister. She and Patricia were eight years old when Vernon was born, and that is an age for being particularly interested in watching Sonora change Vernon's diapers. Soon Patricia and Jelena were volunteering to change Vernon's diapers.

Jelena was to claim, years afterward, that she fell in love with him the first time she laid eyes on him. Was he aware of her in infancy?

Dubitable; to him, her face was just one of seven female faces that came constantly in and out of his field of vision. But he was four years old before he understood that he was in any way different from these seven persons. By the age of four he had begun to misbehave, and his father, in order to induce good behavior, threatened to cut off his tallywhacker unless he behaved himself. He could not help but notice that the other seven persons did not possess tallywhackers, and assumed that they had all flagrantly misbehaved, and were doomed to go through life tallywhackerless and wearing dresses and sitting down to pee.

He did not want to wear a dress, nor did he want to have to sit down to pee, so he tried his best to behave. In the years of his growing up, Vernon was preoccupied with behaving himself. He felt sorry for the seven persons who had lost their tallywhackers, but he tried to avoid all of them except the one who was his mother, for whom he felt an emotion that was not pity or compassion or wonder but a deep feeling that he could not understand, and which frightened him in its intensity, causing him to do his best to suppress the feeling, lest it lead him into misbehavior and the loss of his tallywhacker.

There are two things that can happen to a boy who has five (or six) older sisters and a mother with whom he is unknowingly deeply in love: on the one hand he can lose all of his courage and self-confidence and be a pampered emotional cripple for the rest of his life, or, conversely on the other hand, growing up masculine in a feminine household, fiercely determined to keep his tally-whacker, he may be forced by himself into great achievements. Vernon Ingledew forced himself into great achievements.

His first great achievement, however, was almost accidental, and occurred at the age of sixteen. On one of his many solitary walks in the fastnesses of Ingledew Mountain, he discovered a razorback boar. It had been thought that the razorback, if it ever existed at all outside of legend, was long extinct in the Ozarks, but to Vernon, who had seen pictures of them, there was no mistaking that this was indeed a razorback boar. In the end of the following, penultimate chapter, we will have to witness Vernon's struggle to capture the boar. And in the final chapter we will learn what he did with it.

Chapter nineteen

Jackson Ingledew was a janitor in the Harrison public school system. He got the job in the same year that Jelena, who had become his ward, was old enough to start to school. During the summer months, when school was not in session, he was unemployed, and the two of them returned to Stay More for the entire summer. That is part of the reason why he bought the "mobile home," shown here; the other part of the reason was that he thought the mobile home looked "modern." The Ozarks were filling up with mobile homes, and Jackson got the latest model. Stay More was full of abandoned houses that were his for the asking, but he opted for the modernity and the convenience of a mobile home. For nine months of the year, while school was in session, Jackson's mobile home was parked in a "trailer camp" in the small city of Harrison; for the other three months it was parked beside Swains Creek in Stay More, halfway between the old canning factory and the sycamore tree which had held Noah Ingledew's treehouse.

In many ways Jackson Ingledew resembled Noah Ingledew, or at least Noah is the only other Ingledew to whom Jackson is comparable in any respect. Jackson's favorite (but not exclusive) oath was also "shitfire" but he always pronounced it as a drawn-out "sheeeut far," and he never uttered it in the presence of his niece and ward Jelena. He was extremely conscientious about his responsibilities as substitute father; the position did not rest lightly on his shoulders, but he tried his best: for instance, when Jelena grew up and became a beautiful and highly desirable girl, Jackson highly desired her, and it required the highest exercise of self-control to keep him from seducing her, but he never seduced her, which more than any other fact tells us what kind of man he was. When she was only one year old she climbed into his lap and uttered her first word, "Da da." He put her down, perhaps literally as well as figuratively, and said, "Not Dada. *Uncle*." She looked at him strangely and tried to pronounce "uncle," but it came out "ugla" and he is still Ugla Jackson to her to this day.

Although he was unable to give her the affection of fatherhood, he was at least attentive to her; whenever she requested, he would read her storybooks to her, so often that she already knew how to read by herself even before she started school. When school was over, each day, Jackson had to sweep the halls and rooms for a couple of hours, so during those two hours he would leave her in the school's library, where she read and reread every book over the years. She loved reading, but it was a dull way to grow up, and she always eagerly looked forward to the summers, when Jackson would hitch the mobile home to his pickup truck and haul it back to Stay More. It was even more fun for Jelena when Hank and Sonora Ingledew came back from California with their five daughters and Jelena discovered that she had a first cousin, Patricia, who was the same age as she. Jelena never read a book in the summertime.

One summer when Jelena was eight, she arrived in Stay More to discover that she had another cousin, recently born, and that this cousin had a tail, or rather a tail that was on backwards, or rather frontwards, a tail on the front of him, just an inch or less long. When she looked at his face, she fell in love with him. Although she had not ever seen one of those tails before, she knew that all the world was divided into boys and girls, and that when boys and girls grew up they got married and became mothers and fathers, although she herself for some reason had no mother and father, and she decided on the spot that when Vernon Ingledew grew up she was going to marry him. She couldn't wait for him to grow up, but he took such a long time doing it, and by the time she herself was already grown up he was just a little kid starting the first grade of school. What was worse, he wouldn't have anything to do with her. He ignored her. She and his sisters played "house," frequently, but Vernon refused to join them. They also played "mobile home," but he would not even volunteer to drive the "truck." They played "school" and "store" and "bank," and tried their best to recruit him as a "pupil" or "customer," but he would have none of it. They played "church" and told him he would go to hell unless he joined them, but he opted for hell.

One summer old Doc Swain died, and his little clinic on Main Street was abandoned, along with the other abandoned doctors' and dentists' offices, and the abandoned bank and mill and general store—in fact, everything on Main Street was abandoned except the old hotel, which was no longer a hotel but just a residence for Drussie and her niece Lola, both old ladies who sat on the porch all summer long staring at the boarded-up general store. When Doc Swain's office was abandoned, all of the contents of it were left in it, and Vernon's sisters and Jelena decided to play "doctor" and again they tried to persuade Vernon to join them, telling him that he could be the doctor and they would be the nurses and patients. This time Vernon, who was six, at least thought the matter over without flatly rejecting it, and at length decided that he didn't mind being a doctor, so for the very first time he joined them in their play. The clinic was as fully equipped as country doctors' clinics ever were; they dressed Vernon in the doctor's smock, rolling up the sleeves until they fit him; and put a stethoscope around his neck and a round reflex mirror on his forehead. Sharon was the nurse, Eva the receptionist, and the rest of them patients. Vernon at the age of six had been taken to the doctor often enough, with whooping cough and measles and mumps and chicken pox, to know how a doctor deports himself, and he gave a reasonably good performance. He felt each patient's pulse and put his stethoscope to their chests and listened—with some awe—to their heartbeats. Jelena's breasts were well developed at the age of fourteen, and it thrilled her when Vernon's hand put the stethoscope on her breast. "What's your complaint?" the six-year-old boy said to her in as deep a voice as he could manage. It was the first time he had ever spoken to her. "I'm going to have a baby," she told him. "Hhmm," he said, and gave her a bottle of yellow pills. "Well, take two of these a day, and come back if it doesn't go away." The girls laughed, embarrassing him, and "Nurse" Sharon told him, "You're 'sposed to examine her. She's 'sposed to git on that table and have you take a look at her." Jelena was reluctant but also excited at the idea, and she climbed onto the examination table and raised her skirt and removed her panties. Vernon came and took a look, but wouldn't come close. "Nothing wrong with you," he said, "'ceptin they cut off yore tallywhacker fer bein bad." The girls laughed uproariously, and Vernon threw off his smock and stethoscope and marched out, declaring "I don't want to play dumb games." He never again joined any of their games, and then they were too old to play games.

When Vernon was six, he noticed for the first time that his father also had a tallywhacker, which he had already guessed, since his father wore pants and had short hair, so the next time he saw his grandfather he asked Bevis, "Grampaw, was Daddy always a good boy?" Bevis replied by telling him of the time that Hank had "stolen" one of the mules and run away to join the circus. "But you didn't cut off his tallywhacker for it?" Vernon wanted to know. "Didn't he never do nothing that was bad enough for you to cut off his tallywhacker?" "Huh?" said Bevis, and Vernon revealed to his grandfather that his father had on several occasions threatened to cut off his tallywhacker and make him into a girl unless he behaved himself. "Aw, he was jist a-funnin you," Bevis told him. "He'd never do nothin like that, and even if he did, that wouldn't make ye into a girl. Girls are born that way." "Why?" Vernon wanted to know. "Wal," Bevis hedged, "you're a mite too young to understand things like that. Why don't ye jist put it out of your mind 'till you're older?"

But Vernon could never put it out of his mind, nor could he completely shake off the fear that his father might cut off his tallywhacker unless he behaved himself, so he continued to behave himself, and he continued to be obsessed with the subject of sex, although he continued to withstand the efforts of his sisters to involve him in their activities and the efforts of his cousin Jelena to get him to notice her.

There were no boys in Stay More his own age, although he had a few friends at the Jasper school, with whom he played boys' games during recess. He excelled in sports. But he would just as soon stay home by himself, or help his mother; he was always striving to do things for his mother, whom he loved. She loved him too, perhaps too much, because her husband never did completely regain his potency after sitting on the roof for seven hours; he suffered recurring bouts of impotency, and went to see a specialist at Little Rock, who examined him and talked about "distinctly low testosterone assay" and prescribed medicine that didn't help much; he later went all the way to St. Louis to see another specialist, who examined him and talked about "estimation of urinary 17-ketosteroid excretion" and prescribed another medicine which was just a little better, but didn't cure the problem; so, during a national convention of televison salesmen in Chicago, he slipped off to see a psychiatrist, who traced the problem back to the episode of sitting on the roof for seven hours but was unable to help Hank understand how sitting on the roof for seven hours would make him impotent, so he traced the problem further back to Hank's childhood when Hank had often wondered whether or not he actually existed because in order to exist his mother and father would have had to have gone to bed together, which they had never done.

"How do you know they didn't?" asked the psychiatrist. Because they had separate beds, and never slept together, Hank told him. "But," said the psychiatrist, "that doesn't mean they couldn't have had intercourse somewhere, at some time." Well, anyway, Hank said, the problem never bothered him anymore so he didn't think it had anything to do with his impotency. "Aha!" said the psychiatrist. "The roots of our problems lie where we least expect them," and he suggested that Hank commence psychoanalysis, but Hank told him that he was just temporarily in Chicago for a convention, and he went on back to Stay More. Because he didn't make love to Sonora very often, she was somewhat frustrated, but she had determined never to "cheat" on him again, so she remained a faithful wife but compensated for her frustration by being overaffectionate to Vernon, who returned her affection. They frequently slept together, until he was nine years old, when his growing manhood tempted her and made her ashamed of her temptations, so that she never slept with him thereafter, which he could not understand. There were so many things that he could not understand, although in his fantasy he concocted elaborate and even outrageous explanations for them. When he was ten years old, his mother discovered that she had irreversible breast cancer. At her funeral Vernon listened to them singing:

> *Farther along we'll know all about it,*
> *Farther along we'll understand why;*
> *Cheer up, my brother, live in the sunshine,*
> *We'll understand it, all by and by.*

He did not understand this. He did not understand that what was meant by "by and by" was the "sweet by and by" of the hereafter. Even if he believed in a hereafter, which he did not, he understood the song to mean that there would come a time, on this earth, when we will finally know the meaning of life, and time, and death, and he was determined, from that moment forward, to learn the meaning, if it took him all his life.

The rain that fell during Sonora's funeral was the hardest that had fallen on the Ozarks since the flood of Noah Ingledew's time, and it caused all the creeks to overflow their banks. Hank, grieving though he was, had the presence of mind to realize that the old mill and probably the store too would be swept away in the flood, so after the funeral, he and his brother Jackson backed a pickup truck, up to its hubcaps in swirling muddy water, to the porch of the old mill, and they went into the mill, feeling its floor trembling, and lifted the glass showcase containing the body of the old Connecticut peddler, whatever his name was, and loaded it into the pickup truck and got it away just in the nick of time: with a thunderous roar the old mill collapsed and was swept away down the creek. They transported the showcase to higher ground, to the abandoned yellow house of the old near-hermit Dan, where they left it in an upstairs bedroom, and then returned to the village, and with the help of the other men of Stay More used sledgehammers to demolish the old abandoned bank building and stack its stones against the side of the road in an effort to keep the swollen creek from washing away the road. The effort did not succeed; the road was washed away; but after the creek had returned to its normal level, they partially rebuilt the road.

Jelena graduated from Harrison High School at the age of eighteen; she was the valedictorian of her class, and undoubtedly could have won a college scholarship if she had applied for one, but after the death of Vernon's mother, Jelena was old enough and smart enough to realize that it had been foolish of her to plan, all her life, to marry Vernon when he grew up. When he grew up, she would be twenty-six, at least, past marriageable age. Even if that wasn't past marriageable age, he was her first cousin, and nowadays first cousins did not marry. Even if first cousins could marry, she could never get him to notice her, except for that one time when they had played "doctor." At his mother's funeral, when Jelena had tried to embrace him and say something comforting to him, he did not seem to be aware of her existence. So, if she could not be his wife, perhaps at least she could become his mother, or his stepmother. Waiting for a suitable time some months after the funeral, she said to Hank, "Would you like to marry me?" "That's real kind of ye, Jelena," Hank replied, "but I'm your uncle and I caint marry you." "Vernon needs a mother," Jelena insisted. "I don't know about that," Hank observed. "I reckon he's jist about old enough to take care of hisself. And he's got lots of sisters to look after 'im." "You won't marry me?" Jelena tried one last time. "I have to tell you somethin, honey," Hank replied. "I don't know how to say it, but even apart from me bein twenty-four years older than you, I aint able to…well, you know what a man is supposed to do to his woman, well, I aint able." "I don't care," Jelena replied, "we don't have to do that." "Don't ye want children?" Hank asked. "No," she said, "Vernon can be my child." "Tell you the honest truth, Jelena," Hank said, "nothin against you personal, but I don't honestly believe that Vernon would want to be your child."

Crestfallen, Jelena gave up on the idea. Mark Duckworth, son of Mont, son of Oren the erstwhile canning factory operator, and Jelena's third cousin twice removed, asked Jelena for a date, took her to the drive-in movies at Harrison, kissed her during intermission, took her there again the following Saturday, petted her some, was petted in return on the third date, and after the fifth date persuaded her to get into the back seat with him. The movies bored Jelena, but there was nothing else to do, and she soon discovered that she really liked the things that she and Mark could do with their bodies. When he proposed marriage to her, she turned him down, telling him that she was waiting for Vernon Ingledew to grow up. He laughed at that, and went on proposing, pointing out that his chicken ranch was just about the best chicken ranch in Newton County and that he intended to make it even bigger. (While we have Jelena and Mark in his car at the drive-in movies, we might notice that the car too is bigeminal, usually having two doors, his side, *her* side, and that cars have traditionally been used for "making out," which in essence is what bigeminality is all about.)

Mark was a good-looking chicken farmer, twenty-two years old; Jelena was a beautiful brunette close to nineteen. We have not yet reached the point where we could tap her on the shoulder, as it were, and point out to her that she could never have a happy marriage with Mark Duckworth because of the discrepancy between their respective intelligences. He was no dumbbell, by any means, but Jelena Ingledew was just about the most intelligent female in the history of Stay More. If she had been willing to leave Stay More, she could have found boundless opportunities elsewhere, and boundlessly more attractive prospects for husbands, but she was not willing to leave Stay More. So she married Mark Duckworth. The old abandoned school/church-house was given a good dusting, a minister was imported from Jasper, and everybody (there were only twenty-nine Stay Morons that year) came to the wedding. Jelena was even surprised to find Vernon there, dressed in his first suit and his first necktie. As Uncle Jackson was leading her down the aisle, she paused and bent down and whispered in Vernon's ear, "I was going to wait and marry you when you grew up. Will you marry me when you grow up? If you say 'yes,' I'll call off this wedding." Vernon looked into her eyes to understand if she were teasing him, and, understanding that she was serious, shook his head and declared, "I will never marry." And he was right. He never will. He is the last of all the Ingledews. There will be no more.

We are so close to the end of this epic that if it were a snake it would bite us, as folks used to say in Stay More, but don't anymore, because there are so few folks remaining. Yet endings make me nervous, not because I don't know what to expect but simply because they are endings, and there is nothing beyond them, as there is nothing beyond death and nothing beyond the universe. There *will* be something beyond this ending, but not for now. We do not have time to accompany Vernon on one of his numerous solitary walks in the woods, when he studied nature as intently as possible, trying to understand it. We do not have time to listen to one of the heated quarrels between Jelena and her husband Mark, who discovered very quickly that marriage takes something out of romance. Jelena bore Mark two children, both sons, and with his permission had herself sterilized after the birth of the second son. She was a good mother, but eventually decided that she could not stand her husband; it was a loveless marriage, and the chores of a chicken farmer's wife were endlessly boring. She had fantasies, sometimes, of taking her life, and once she even walked up the mountain to Leapin Rock and stood on the edge of it, looking down. Vernon, on one of his woods walks, spotted her. He was fourteen then, and as big as she, and he sneaked up behind her and threw his arms around her and pulled her away from the precipice. "I was just enjoying the view," she told him. "Oh," he said, hangdog, "I thought ye were fixin to jump." "Why should I jump?" she said. He studied her eyes, trying to understand whether or not she had intended to jump, and understood that she had, and told her, "You're unhappy." "Why should I be unhappy?" she demanded, but then she broke down, not weeping but just losing control of herself, and told him all her problems. He was embarrassed, not only because she was a woman talking to him and he was shy of women, but also, and more so, because he had not reached a level of understanding to be able to tell her what she should do or even to offer her words of comfort or solace. "Well," she observed at length, "it did me good to talk to you," and she went back home.

On one of his weekend woods walks, at the age of sixteen, Vernon discovered the abandoned yellow house of the old near-hermit Dan, who was buried on the hill behind it. Exploring the interior of

the house, he found upstairs a feather mattress, and lay down on it;
he had never lain on a feather mattress before and was surprised at
how comfortable it was, so comfortable that he fell asleep and slept
for several hours. When he got up he went into the other of the
two bedrooms of the house and was startled to discover an old glass
showcase containing the body of an old, old man. He stared at it for
a moment, trying to understand, then he ran all the way home and
said, "Dad, there's a dead body in a showcase in an old yellow house
about a mile up Banty Creek."

Hank said, "Sit down, son. Can you spare an hour or two?"
It took more than an hour or two, more like three, but Hank told
Vernon the story of the old peddler from Connecticut. Vernon was
delighted. Even more delighted than by the story of the old peddler,
he was delighted by the past of Stay More; he had known that Stay
More had a past, and he had explored all of its abandoned buildings,
but he had never inquired into that past. "We was even going to
name ye after him," Hank informed his son, "but we plumb fergot
what his name was, and nobody could recall it. The reason we was
even going to name ye after him was that he left somethin fer ye, let
me see if I caint remember whar I buried the thing." Hank took his
shovel and went to Bevis's house and asked his father if he could dig
up something in the backyard. Bevis was seventy-eight years old, and
his mind had begun to fail him, but he could still use Emelda's mind,
which he did, and she said okay. Hank dug his hole, but that wasn't
the spot. He dug another hole, and then another. Darkness came and
he had to give up digging for the day, but rose early the next morning and resumed digging, until the backyard of his parents' house
looked as if it had been bombed. The reporter of the Jasper *Disaster*,
who had been a mere reporter when Hank had sat on his roof for
seven hours, was now the editor, and showed up and began taking
pictures before Hank could stop him. "What are you looking for?"
the editor wanted to know. "Oil? Gold?" "None of your business,"
Hank replied. The editor beseeched, "Nothing ever happens in this
county anymore. Give me a story." Hank would not.

The *Disaster* folded with the next week's issue, which consisted
only of grocery ads and a picture of Hank destroying his parents'

backyard with a caption, "Stay More citizen, J.H. Ingledew, 48, shown with shovel in left background, is mysteriously excavating the rear yard of the home of his parents, Mr. and Mrs. B.H. Ingledew, also of Stay More, this county. We were unable to determine his motive, and, after reflection, we ceased to care. This is the last issue." There have been no more newspapers in Newton County.

But Hank found the watch. The lard pail was so rusted it disintegrated in his hands, but the heavy wad of flannel within the lard pail was still intact, and in the heart of the wad of flannel was the gold chronometer wristwatch, in perfect condition.

As Hank winds up the watch, time changes to the present tense. Now. The watch runs. Hank apologizes to his parents for having torn up their yard, and promises to smooth it out and reseed it as soon as he gets the chance. "You jist better," says Bevis, whose mind has failed but who is using Emelda's. Hank takes the watch home and gives it to Vernon. He says, "This is it. This is what that old peddler left for you. He made me promise to keep it for you."

"Gosh dawg," exclaims Vernon, dazzled by the sight of the expensive gold chronometer, whose band is gold too. He takes it and looks at it closely, turning it over and over in his hand. He discovers on the reverse of the gold case, which is not gold but some kind of polished silvery alloy, an inscription, engraved into the metal: "For Vernon Ingledew, from Eli Willard. *Tempus fugit. Carpe diem.* Etc." He calls this to the attention of his father, who reads it and exclaims, "That's him! That's his name! *Eli Willard.* That's *your* name, boy! That's what we were fixin to name ye." "No," Vernon points out, his name is "Vernon," as can plainly be seen in the inscription. There is something puzzling about that circumstance to Hank. He rereads the inscription. "Hhmmm," he says. "What's this here 'ect.' for?" "Not ect," says Vernon, "*etc.* Et cetera. It means everything else." He says again, "Everything," he is so proud to have that watch. He holds the watch to his ear and listens to its precise, firm, assertive ticking. Then he slips the watch over his hand and onto his wrist.

As Vernon puts the watch on his wrist, he becomes aware of us.

He stares at us. We stare back at him. We notice how, at the age of sixteen, he is already a full-grown Ingledew, past six feet tall, eyes as blue as his great-great-great-grandfather's.

"Who are those people?" Vernon asks his father.

"What people?" says his father.

Vernon realizes that he is aware of us because he wears the watch. We make him uncomfortable, self-conscious, and the women among us make him extremely woman-shy. He takes off the wrist-watch and puts it in his pocket, losing his awareness of us.

"You aint gon wear it?" his father asks.

"Not yet," says Vernon. "I aint ready for it. But I'll carry it around."

He carries it around, in his pocket, and at night leaves it on his bureau with his pocket change, rabbit's foot, etc. Sometimes in the middle of the night, he wakes up, in pitch dark, takes the watch and puts it on, to see if we are still here. We still are.

Toward the end of his sixteenth year he leaves the house and goes off into the forest of Ingledew Mountain and into a deep dark cave, where he hides and puts on his watch again. We are still here. "What do you folks want with me?" he asks.

As our spokesman, I reply, "Listen, Vernon, we've got great plans for you."

"Who are you?" he wants to know.

"We are students of the architecture of the Arkansas Ozarks who have become interested in Stay More and particularly in the Ingledews. You, Vernon, could become the greatest Ingledew of them all. You know already that you're the last Ingledew, because you aren't going to marry or have any children."

"That's right," he acknowledges, "but I aint so certain that I'd care to be the greatest Ingledew of them all, and even if I did, I don't want you folks following me around. Darn it, that lady there is a-laughin at me, and if you folks is such students of the Ingledews you know how shy Ingledews is toward women. Make her stop."

Madam, *please*.

"Look, Vernon," I continue, "we already know practically everything about you, and about all of your ancestors. Our study is just about finished, and we want to conclude it with something important. The building that heads this chapter, if you can call it a 'building,' is just a trite mobile home, like trite mobile homes all over the Ozarks and elsewhere. Architecturally, it's a cipher, even if it is bigeminal, a duple, which means that it is divisible by two: two rooms, two doors, two bays, whatever, symbolizing the division of creatures into male and female, and of sexuality, although in the case of this particular mobile home, which belonged to your Uncle Jackson and in which Jelena represented the female side, there was no sex between them. But speaking of Jelena, haven't you ever had sexual fantasies about her?"

"That aint none of your business!" he says, and grasps the watch as if to remove it from his wrist.

"Oh, indeed it *is* our business," I declare, "but let it go, for the moment. Our immediate problem is to construct the building of the next chapter, the last chapter. *You* are going to do it by yourself."

"What am I supposed to do? Get out a saw and hammer?"

"No. First you must do something that will make a lot of money, for your house is going to be expensive. You will be twenty-two when you build it, and you're only sixteen now, which means that you have six years to raise the money."

"How? Jobs are pretty scarce hereabouts."

"Create your own job."

"Doing what?"

"Growing and selling something."

"Jelena's husband Mark Duckworth grows and sells chickens, but he aint gittin rich."

"Not chickens. Pigs. Vernon, aren't you awfully fond of ham?"

"That's right."

"But haven't you been constantly suspicious that nobody makes really good ham anymore?"

"Sure. It troubles me."

"Then do something about it."

"Okay. Where do I start?"

"Find a razorback."

"There aren't any razorbacks anymore."

"You seem to know an awful lot for a boy your age."

"Aw, heck. Everbody knows there aren't any razorbacks."

"Get up and walk outside of this cave."

Vernon obeys. Outside the cave, foraging on acorn mast, is a razorback boar. He softly whistles in recognition of it. "Say, thanks," he says to us, and removes his wristwatch and puts it into his pocket. It is too bad he cannot put us into his pocket too, to spare us the sight of the terrible contest that is about to occur.

Vernon improvises a halter out of black-jack vines, and sneaks up on the boar. Having had no experience in capturing razorbacks, because there have been no razorbacks to capture, he does not realize that razorbacks will fiercely defend themselves. When the boar sees Vernon, it does not run, but stands its ground until Vernon is close to it, then it charges him, toppling his legs out from under him, goring his calves with inch-deep wounds. Razorbacks are not nearly as big as domestic swine, but they are much swifter and meaner for that reason. Vernon can hardly stand up, and as soon as he is on his feet, the boar charges him again, but he sidesteps like a matador and throws the halter over the boar's head as it charges past, keeping a firm grip on the other end of the line. He is pulled off his feet and dragged along the ground, and the wristwatch in his pocket is broken.

Chapter twenty

Our last illustration, regrettably, is smudged and obscure. Vernon Ingledew refuses our request to view the final dwelling of Stay More. We can just barely determine that it has certain things in common with the first dwelling in our study, which perhaps suggests that time, and architecture, are cyclical: we began with an ending, we end with a beginning. But I have not seen this building myself; Vernon refuses to divulge its exact location in the forest fastnesses of Stay More; our illustration, or what is left of it, is based upon a Polaroid snapshot taken by a young couple who are friends of mine, and the last "outsiders" to immigrate into Stay More. But Vernon will not build this structure until his twenty-second year, and he is still only sixteen.

Yes, he finally succeeds in capturing that razorback boar, tethering him to a tree while he hobbles home to dress his wounds, then borrows his father's four-wheel-drive truck, which he drives up old logging trails to the place where he has captured the boar. He drops a ramp from the truck-bed, and forces the boar up the ramp and into the truck, and takes it home and pens it up. Word quickly spreads that Vernon Ingledew has captured a real live razorback. This is so fantastic that the editor of the defunct *Disaster* is tempted to start it up again, but he has already sold his printing press. A Harrison newspaper publishes the story, and the students at the University of Arkansas, whose mascot the razorback is, take up a collection of two thousand dollars for the purpose of buying Vernon's razorback, but two thousand dollars isn't enough to pay for the building of the house of this chapter, so he rejects the offer.

Vernon sets about breeding the boar to three Poland China gilts. The boar is disdainful, but a gilt in heat is too much for him. Vernon turns seventeen, and after three-and-a-half months the Poland China sows farrow a total of twenty-six pigs. Instead of black-and-white like Poland China pigs, they are red-and-brown, and have bristly spines like razorbacks. Vernon fattens them; instead of feeding them corn, as domestic swine are fed, he feeds them the diet of razorbacks: acorn mast and wild fruits, all they can eat. One of the Chism boys up on the mountain is still distilling Chism's Dew, and Vernon asks permission to haul off the corn mash that is used in the distillation process, and he feeds this also to his pigs; there is enough alcohol in it to keep his pigs constantly happy. In hot weather, when most pigs suffer, and wallow in mud to alleviate their suffering, Vernon regularly showers down his pigs with cold water from a hose, which makes them actually smile and grunt with pleasure. All of this contributes to a superior type of pig. When the gilts are old enough to go into heat, Vernon breeds them to their father, producing pigs that are even more razorback than themselves. Normally, wild razorback sows farrow only four to six pigs, but Vernon's hogs have become so contented and domesticated that they farrow eight to twelve pigs each.

Vernon's great-great-aunt Drussie Ingledew, ninety-eight years old, is on her deathbed, but before she dies she tells Vernon how people used to cure ham back in the old days when there were still razorbacks at large, but Vernon refuses to share his secrets with us. He will not reveal the special time of year when he slaughters his hogs, nor will he reveal the arcane but humane method he uses to slaughter them. He smokes the meat for an amount of time that he will not reveal, using smoke from burning objects the composition of which is a closely guarded secret. Many spies try to learn his secrets, but they do not succeed.

"Ingledew Ham" is the best stuff in the history of ham-making. There is nothing else comparable; it practically melts in your mouth, and is much sweeter than ordinary ham. At first Vernon sells his total output to the supermarkets of Jasper and Harrison, but the demand for it keeps forcing the price up, until the local supermarkets cannot carry it, and it becomes a mail order item affordable only by the wealthy. Vernon's five sisters, who are married to, respectively, a Whitter, a Chism, a Coe, a Plowright, and a Stapleton, help him raise and process his hams, as do their husbands; it becomes an increasingly large operation. Vernon branches off into smoked sausage, cased in cornhusks the old-fashioned way, and far superior to commercial sausage. Then he branches off into sugar-cured and smoked bacon; also spareribs and head cheese, letting nothing go to waste.

One day he takes his watch to Harrison to be repaired. The watch repairman examines it, declaring he's never seen one like it. The repairman gently opens the case, and shakes his head; he says it will take him months, maybe years, to find replacements for the damaged parts and to put the watch back together. "Take your time," Vernon assures him. He is only eighteen years old. (It's really too bad about that watch. I had planned to tell Vernon what the next step was: he was to go away to college, to the University of Arkansas, where he would play football, becoming a "Razorback" himself, making the first string in his sophomore year, as a defensive end, and becoming the best defensive end in the history of the Razorbacks, making All-American in his senior year. That would have made a great sports story, which we could call simply *Razorback*, but the watch is broken and we cannot get to him to tell him about it. So he does not go to college. But he studies.)

On the same trip to Harrison to take his watch to be repaired, he discovers a store that sells a kind of book with soft covers called "paperback." The paperback more than the razorback is a momentous discovery for Vernon. He buys a handful of paperbacks on astronomy, geology, genetics, anthropology, linguistics, and architecture, which he takes home and reads in his spare time when he is not supervising his swine industry. Periodically he returns to Harrison to see if his watch has been repaired, and finding that it hasn't, he buys more paperbacks, on chemistry, geometry, zoology, history, philosophy, musicology and literature.

His sisters, and his father too, to a lesser extent, tease him about becoming a "bookworm." The only other person in Stay More who reads books is his cousin Jelena. When Vernon finishes his paperbacks, he takes them to Jelena and trades them to her for her paperbacks on physics, biology, art history, theater, sociology and eschatology, which is a subject that interests him most because he is still trying to understand why his mother died. One day Jelena swaps him a book on sexology. He has not been exactly ignorant of the subject, for, after all, he has been personally responsible for breeding his razorback boar to many Poland China gilts and their offspring, the sight of which has given him many a throb. And yes, although he refuses to admit it, he has had sexual fantasies involving his cousin Jelena. When he swaps books with her, he is careful not to get too close to her, because she has a certain venereal scent or fragrance that drives him wild.

The next time he goes to swap books with her, he finds her alone, her children in school and her husband off somewhere for the day selling his chickens. She gives him a Coke, and asks him what he thought of the book on sexology. He admits it was "interesting." She asks him if there is anything he doesn't understand. He understands just about everything, he allows, but he doesn't quite understand why it is that animals "mate" only at certain times whereas humans apparently do it all the time. "Sit down, Vernon," she suggests, "and we'll talk about it." He sits down, careful not to sit too close to her. She says, "You're nineteen. Are you still a virgin?" That isn't any of her business, he tells her. "I'm just trying to find out if you know what sex feels like," she says. I can imagine, he says. "Then you have a rich imagination," she comments, and begins her mini-lecture: "If sex is pleasurable for all creatures, why is it that for animals it is confined only to the time of rutting or 'heat'? Did you know, by the way, that compared with animals, it is more exceptional for women than for men to be able to indulge in sex at any time of the year?" Vernon admits that he had not thought of that. "It's true," she goes on, "and since it's plain that the purpose of human sex is not for procreation but for pleasure, more often than not, then this pleasure, and the absence of it, and the strong emotions inspired by both the desire and the unfulfillment of the desire, are on one hand the source of art, literature, music, religion and science, and on the other hand greed, selfishness, malice, envy and war. We are different from animals because we have a mind, imagination and an ability to reason, and these attributes originate out of our longings and desires for sex. Does that make any sense to you?"

Vernon thinks it over and grants that it does. "But our sexuality also leads us into 'civilization,'" Jelena points out, "and civilization imposes restrictions on our sexuality. Civilization creates the institution of marriage, and standards of 'morality.' Marriage is a trap. But I needn't warn you of that, because you are never going to marry, are you?"

Vernon reaffirms the intention that he first declared to her on her wedding day. "Are you," she asks, "like so many of your uncles and great-uncles and great-great-uncles, going to remain celibate all your life?" Vernon does not answer. "We're alone, you know," she points out. "Mark won't be home until suppertime." Vernon makes no response. "Don't you want me, Vernon?" she asks, a trifle desperately. "Am I too old for you?" Vernon can bring himself neither to nod nor shake his head. Jelena stands up. "I'm going into the bedroom," she announces, "and I'm going to take off all my clothes and lie down on the bed." She leaves the room. Vernon just sits there. I wish he had on that wristwatch so that we could shout at him. But perhaps he does not need it; we see him finally rise, and walk slowly to Jelena's bedroom, where he finds her reclining on the bed, smiling at him. It is the most beautiful sight he has ever seen, and he understands it. He understands that he must quickly get out of his clothes, and does. He understands that he must climb upon the bed and suspend himself above her, and does. She takes hold of him and guides him into her; the entrance entrances him; Vernon will remember that first entrance for the rest of his life: he cannot understand how anything could be so far beyond understanding as the feeling of her warm moist interior.

He sighs aloud at the wonder of it, and so does she. And as soon as he has absorbed the wonder of it, they both begin moving their hips, urgently, as if, having discovered the wonder, they are eager to find how much of it can be found. Vernon does not last long; his quaking burst paralyzes him, but she holds him to her and will not let him go, whispering a question in his ear, "How did that feel?"

Vernon studies the heuristic inquiry, and replies, "It felt…it felt like I was being turned inside out." She laughs, and says, "That's beautiful," and her laughter causes her body to shake, and the shaking of her body rearouses Vernon and he begins to move again, they both again, for a longer time this time, alternately fast and slow as if searching for the right tempo, and finding it, which causes Jelena to begin to tremble, slowly at first, then uncontrollably, violently, amazing Vernon, who is more amazed by the sound that comes deep from her throat, but he seeks to understand it, and understands it, and in the understanding of it reaches his own second crisis and explosion and release.

Then they lie side by side holding one another and breathing deeply, and Jelena teases, "See what you've been missing all these years." He does, but has a worry: "What if you get pregnant?" "I can't," she replies. "When Monty was born, I requested that the doctor tie my tubes." "Oh," says Vernon, "then you can do it all the time?" "*All* the time," she says, hugging him tighter.

The "affair" between Vernon and Jelena, for that is what it is, continues; it is a rare day that her husband Mark is gone from home all day long, but Jelena finds excuses to get out of the house, and she and Vernon begin meeting in the woods, where they remove their clothes and cavort like animals. One day she tells him that she wants to get a divorce from Mark and marry Vernon. Divorces are unheard of in Stay More; at least we have not heard of one yet. Vernon tells her again that he loves her but he reminds her of his declaration that he will never marry. She does not understand it, but she wishes that she could live with him all the time, and not have to go on meeting him clandestinely. If they keep that up long enough they will be discovered.

And sure enough, they are discovered: Luke Duckworth, Mark's brother, hunting squirrel in the woods, happens to spot the couple, and reports it to Mark, who does not believe it, but confronts Jelena and says, "Somebody tole me they seen you and Vernon out in the woods together without your clothes on. Tell me it aint true." She knows she can't go on covering it up. "It's true," she says. He slaps her, knocking her to the floor, kicks her, then takes his rifle and goes to Vernon's swine processing plant and points the rifle at Vernon and says, "If you even look at Jelena again, I'll kill you."

Soon everybody in Stay More (there are only twenty-one people this year) knows about the affair between Vernon and Jelena, and several of Vernon's sisters remark to him that he ought to be ashamed of himself, and his father says to him, "You're too old for me to cut off your tallywhacker, but I got a good mind to do it anyhow." Vernon goes to Harrison to see if his watch has been repaired; it hasn't, so he buys paperbacks on law, psychology, archaeology and an assortment of pornography, and secludes himself with his books, until he discovers one day that there is a boy his own age in Stay More, for the first time since he was born. The boy's name is Day Whittacker and he is accompanied by a girl who does not give her name, but who may or may not be the wife of the boy, because she is several months pregnant. The boy, who like Vernon is nineteen years old, says that they have been wandering around exploring various ghost towns, and they like Stay More, even if it isn't completely a ghost town, and they would like to use the old yellow house if nobody else wants it, but one of the upstairs bedrooms contains a glass showcase with the dead body of a very old man in it, and they can't very well live in the same house with a dead body. Vernon explains to them the historical significance of the dead body, and tells them that if they really want to live in the yellow house he will ask his father if they can move the body to some other place. Then Vernon remembers that his father is angry with him because of his affair with Jelena, so he says to Day Whittacker, "On second thought, let's you and me jist move it ourself. I'll git my truck." He gets his truck and with Day's help they transport the showcase back to its original location, appropriately, in the abandoned Ingledew general store.

Day Whittacker and Vernon Ingledew become good friends; they have in common not only their age but also a boundless curiosity about nature. Day Whittacker is an expert in forestry, and knows everything about wood. I have partially examined the story of his visit to Stay More in another volume; his significance in the present volume is merely that he provides Vernon Ingledew with many hours of companionship, and for that matter will continue to be Vernon's best buddy for the rest of their lives.

Now in particular he and his wife or girlfriend or whoever she is help to divert Vernon's attention from Jelena. Vernon tells them all that he knows of the history of Stay More, and they tell him of their adventures and exploits exploring ghost towns in Connecticut, Vermont and North Carolina. They are "tracking" the old near-hermit Dan, who had lived in all those places, and who has died, or been killed, here in Stay More. Vernon takes an interest in the story of Dan, particularly Dan's place in the history of Stay More.

Vernon is shown something that he had not noticed before, thinking it only wallpaper: the plaster walls of Dan's bedroom are covered with writings, in pencil: aphorisms, epigrams, mottoes, observations on nature and on human nature, including references to various Ingledews. Vernon learns, for instance, something that neither he nor his father ever knew: that the reason his grandfather Bevis Ingledew never spoke to his grandmother Emelda was not that they were not on speaking terms but that they could communicate telepathically. Bevis and Emelda are both now dead. Vernon learns also that his great-uncle Tearle, who is not dead, knows several secrets about his great-grandfather John "Doomy" Ingledew. Vernon copies all of the writings on the walls into a leather-bound journal. He becomes obsessed with the history of Stay More, and even forgets about Jelena. He searches attics. In the attic of the double-doored house of Bevis and Emelda, now abandoned, he finds a box of dozens of photographs, taken early in this Century by Eli Willard, and showing just about everybody who lived in Stay More when its population was over four hundred. In the attic of the old hotel that had been built originally as Jacob Ingledew's trigeminal house, Vernon finds the unfinished but nearly complete manuscript of *The Memoirs of Former Arkansas Governor Jacob Ingledew*. He also finds there, in a trunk containing women's old clothing, concealed beneath the clothing, eighty-nine small journals, diaries, a daily record of the existence of the Woman Whom We Cannot Name from her fourteenth year until the day of her death. He breaks open a rusted safe in the back room of the abandoned general store and finds record books which reveal all of the activities of: (1) the store, (2) the post office and (3) the fraternal organization that was at first the Free and Accepted Masons and later The Grinning and Ogling Tipplers' Union. It is all there; the chronicle of the birth and growth and decline of Stay More is complete. Our story is, to all intents and purposes, over.

But that gold chronometer wristwatch still has to be repaired. Once again Vernon returns to Harrison, and, after buying paperbacks on genealogy, cosmology, oriental philosophy, folklore, and my three previous novels, he timidly ventures into the watch repairman's shop, and finds the watch repairman bent over the gold chronometer, delicately making adjustments. The watch repairman looks up and says, "Just a few more minutes, and I'm done with it. But I can't let you have it. I'll give you a thousand dollars for it." Sorry, Vernon says. "Two thousand," the watch repairman offers. It's not for sale, Vernon tells him. "Three thousand, for God's sake," the watch repairman offers. It's kind of a heirloom, Vernon points out, and has no price. "Four thousand? Five? Six? You name it," says the watch repairman. Could I have my watch, please? Vernon requests. "Well, heck, just a minute," the watch repairman says, and finishes his adjustments and closes the case.

The watch repairman will wind up the watch, and as he does so, time will change to the future tense. The watch repairman will say, "I will have to charge you three hundred and forty-seven dollars and fifty cents for parts and repairs." Vernon will write him a check, then he will take the watch and go home. One day, he will show the watch to his friends, Day Whittacker and his wife or girlfriend or whoever she is. He will explain to them that if he puts on the watch he will become aware of us. Then he will put on the watch. "Howdy," he will say to us. He will indicate the couple beside him and will ask us, "Is there anything you would like to say to them?"

"Just give them our regards," I will reply. And Vernon will give them our regards, and his own, and go on home, where he will find Jelena waiting for him. At the sight of her, he will instantly close his eyes. She will ask, "Why are your eyes closed, Vernon?" He will reply, "Mark said he'd kill me if I ever laid eyes on ye again." "Are you afraid of him?" she will ask. "I don't care to git shot," he will declare, "but man to man without a gun I'm not afraid of him." "Open your eyes, Vernon," she will request, "I want to tell you something." He will point out, "I don't hear with my eyes." "Open your eyes, Vernon, or I will go away," she tells him. That will be what he will want her to do, and he will keep his eyes closed, and she will go away. "You numbskull," I will tell him, after she is gone, "she wanted to inform you that her husband Mark has taken their two sons and moved to California." "Oh," he will say, and will run after her, but will not be able to find her. She will not be at her house, which has a "For Sale" sign on the front of it (but nobody will ever buy it). "Where is she?" he will ask us, and we could, if we would, tell him, but we must let him find her by himself. He will look all over Stay More, he will look all over this book, examining it page by page, picture by picture; he will call our attention, as if we would not know, to the architecture of the book itself: it will be architectural, and he will analyze the architecture of it, showing how the base is heavier, the upper part lighter, and how the roof is pitched, and we will be over the ridge, on the downslope of the roof. He will call our attention to something else that we will not have noticed: that there is a typographical error on page 393, a spelling error on page 144, a grammatical error on page 84, and a historical error on page 251. He will also demonstrate something else that we will not have been aware of: that the initials of the title of the book, *The Architecture of the Arkansas Ozarks,* form the acronym TAOTAO, which, he will explain, means "double Tao," or *bigeminal* Tao, and for those of us who will not have known, he will point out that "Tao" means "the Way" or "the Path" and refers to a philosophy of life which may be cryptic or paradoxical but seeks to understand the basic order and creativity underlying all architecture and personality and life.

We will find this all very illuminating, but we will be more interested in whether or not he will find Jelena, and we will urge him on. He will return to the moment of her conception, on page 354, and will determine that it was Doris who was in fact her mother, so the Dorisites were right all along, and Vernon, who is a Jelenist, will cease being one and become a Dorisite, and being a Dorisite he will search all the harder for Jelena, tracing her page by page through this book; he will shed a tear over her lonely childhood and he will curse himself for having ignored her when they were growing up, and he will ask for permission to change page 400 so that when on her wedding day she asks him if he will marry her when she grows up he will be able to answer that he will, but we will not be able to grant him that permission, for what will have been done will have been done, so he will go on, turning the page, and when he turns to page 401 he will find her standing at the edge of Leapin Rock, and then he will begin running, running as hard as he has ever run, until he reaches page 419, and reaches Leapin Rock again. She will see him and say, "Don't come near me, Vernon. I'm going to jump and you can't stop me. If you come near me, I'm going to jump."

"If you jump," he will tell her, "I will jump too."

"You will?" she will say.

He will nod.

"What reason would you have to jump?" she will want to know. "I've got all kinds of reasons. Mark has taken the boys and left me, and you won't ever marry me."

He will ask our permission to tell her that he will marry her, but we will be constrained to point out that he has firmly declared that he will never marry.

"Aint a feller got a right to change his mind?" he will ask us.

"You mean you *will*?" she will say.

"I wasn't exactly talkin to you, Jelena," he will say.

Her face will fall. But then he will say, "We could live together, couldn't we? We don't have to git married." And her face will light up again, and she will move away from the precipice and embrace him, and they will make desperate love right there on top of Leapin Rock. Leapin Rock is a hard rock, but they will not seem to notice.

Walking down from the mountain, hand in hand, she will ask him, "How did you know I was up there?"

"It's a long, long story, Jelena," he will reply, but he will begin to tell it to her, and when he reaches the third line of page 420 she will remark, "Isn't this wonderful?" and then she will suggest, "Vernon, let's run away. You've got loads of money, haven't you? Let's run away, and go clear around the world, so that we can find out how much we want to stay in Stay More."

The adventures of Vernon and Jelena in their trip around the world will perhaps furnish material for another volume, but we might notice here that Vernon will find, in an old basement bookstore in Rome, an ancient volume, whose Latin title will translate roughly as *The Archaic Architecture of Arcadia*; it will be expensive, but he will have, as Jelena will have observed, loads of money, and he will purchase it.

When they will have returned to Stay More after their trip around the world, he will study and learn Latin for the purpose of being able to decipher it; then he will read the volume, which will be about the architecture of a mountain village in ancient Arcadia. The author of the volume will have been a Roman writing at the time of the Decline of the Roman Empire, writing out of nostalgia because of the contrast between his life and the life of ancient Arcadia. Vernon will be amazed to discover that the book, although ostensibly architectural, will actually be about the lives of six generations of a peasant family named Anqualdou, the first of whom, Iakobus, despite being a peasant, will become provincial eparch of Arkhadia, and the last of whom, Vernealos, who will be the last of his line because the woman he will love will not be able to bear children, will discover an ancient Persian manuscript which will trace this whole process back further to a Mesopotamian cylinder cycle and thence to a sheaf of Egyptian papyruses, and on back to the beginning of language.

We don't change much, Vernon will reflect, and will be further amazed to discover that the person of Vernealos will be himself and that the book will predict everything that will happen to him for the rest of his life. When he will realize this, he will stop reading, just at the page describing one of his epic marathon love-makings with Jelena, and he will close the book and wrap it up and mail it off to the Library of Congress with a covering letter saying the book is theirs on condition that they never let him see it. Vernon will never know what is going to happen to him in the end. He will know only that he will be the last of the Ingledews, that there will be no more, until in some distant future century this whole cycle will be repeated once again.

Being the last of the Ingledews, he will want to stay, for as more as he can. He will not want to end. On his trip around the world, he will have discovered, and been appalled at, how very little the sciences really do understand, all by and by. He will have been struck with wonder at the way mankind is using—and misusing—the resources of this earth, sucking it dry and gouging it bare of its fossil fuels while letting the energy of the sun go to waste, the energy of the wind go to waste, the energy of the tides go to waste. In the obscure illustration of this final chapter, we will at least be able to discern what seems to be a windmill, and conjecture that part of the energy for Vernon's last domicile is furnished by wind, and we will further assume that the roofs or domes of this domicile will be wired or rigged for solar energy. In fact, Vernon will work so hard just in *planning* this house that the very planning itself will give him a bad case of the frakes, which will be the last case of the frakes in Newton County. No one, ever again, will have to work hard enough to get the frakes. Frakes, like the plague and smallpox and typhoid fever, will become obsolete. But Vernon will have the last case, from his labors in planning his house. Trying to cure it, he will search again all through this book for the many cases of it, and will discover that not a single one of them was ever cured. Fighting against the terrible itching and the despair that he knows will follow it, Vernon will suddenly discover the cure for the frakes.

To Jelena he will announce, "I do not have the frakes." "But you do," she will point out. "Yeah, but I choose to ignore them," Vernon will say. And, ignoring them, they will go away. They will be no more. Never again will man be punished for his efforts to accomplish something.

And Vernon will accomplish something: ignoring his frakes, he will build this house. Although it will be smudged and obscure to us, it will be very real to him and to Jelena, who will live in it and love in it, for the rest of their days. Although they will enjoy their privacy, they will not be exactly recluses, for they will invite their friends, Day Whittacker and his wife or girlfriend (whose name, we will now know, is Diana Stoving) to visit them. Vernon's sisters and their husbands will never visit, because his sisters will be ashamed that Vernon will be "living with" and "running around with" his own cousin, and because, in fact, all but one of his sisters will leave Stay More and move to California and St. Louis and Kansas City and Eureka Springs, respectively. (The population of Stay More will be only nine.) The one sister who will stay more will be Patricia, who will be Jelena's age and will have been her best friend in childhood and who will at least *speak* to Jelena whenever she sees her, but who will not visit her at home. Vernon's father will visit occasionally, because, as Hank will remark, "If a feller is crazy enough to build a house like this, I reckon I'm crazy enough to come and see it now and again." Also Vernon's great-uncle Tearle, the last survivor of his generation of the Ingledews, will visit occasionally, complaining, "It aint got no porch. Nobody builds a porch to set on no more." But Jelena will have a beautiful garden bordering the cool spring that bubbles up out of the property, and there will be lawn furniture to sit on in that garden.

I will hope that on my next visit to Stay More I will be invited to sit with them in that garden. I will also hope that Vernon will be willing to discuss the architecture of his house. I will expect him to let me have a look at some of those documents he will have found. I will look forward to sampling some of that fabled Ingledew Ham. The old Ingledew General Store will be disintegrating, and I will attempt to persuade Vernon and his father to allow me to assist them in removing the glass showcase containing the body of Eli Willard and giving it a proper burial in the Stay More cemetery, for even if Eli Willard was not a Stay Moron, he will have to have a permanent resting place, with a permanent headstone, the inscription of which I will be glad to furnish.

I'm sure that Vernon will understand.

Acknowledgments

*T*he Architecture of the Arkansas Ozarks is not purely a work of the imagination. Over the years I have attempted to read everything about the Ozarks that has been written, as some small consolation for not being able to go there and dwell there as long as I would like. My ancestral roots are deep in the Ozarks, and I know its people and its architecture and its traditions intimately, but I have tried to write this book with a self-imposed detachment which required a geographical detachment too. During the time of the writing of this book, I was able to visit the Ozarks on only one occasion, of one day's duration, and the roll of film I shot that day did not develop. But here in my small room I am surrounded by books and magazines on the Ozarks, piles of photographs taken earlier, souvenirs of my childhood, letters from Ozark friends and relatives, and a mountainous landscape of notes that I obsessively write to myself. The view from my window is of a sycamore tree exactly like Noah Ingledew's, backed by a meadow and a mountain.

Some of the more unbelievable situations and people in this novel are based upon "reality"; indeed, the more implausible or incredible an episode or person may seem to be, the more likely that true history is being imitated. For example, John Cecil was an actual person and the Battle of Whiteley's Mill was an actual battle, fought as described here. The governor of Arkansas during Reconstruction actually was a blue-eyed Ozarks mountaineer. The woman home-steaders from the cities actually did homestead in Newton County. Of course there is an actual Newton County in the actual location of the Ozarks given, with a county seat named Jasper, and another town named Parthenon, and, as far as you and I are concerned, another town named Stay More. I would be happy to show it to you, but I feel I have.

Walter F. Lackey's *History of Newton County, Arkansas* was the principle reference for this book, but I have also been influenced by the Ozark writings of Vance Randolph, Otto Ernest Rayburn, Way-mon Hogue, Charles Morrow Wilson, John Gould Fletcher and many others, as well as such periodicals as *The Ozarks Mountaineer.*

Before writing the novel, I corresponded with many persons in the Ozarks. Mrs. Oliver Howard, reference librarian of the State Historical Society of Missouri at Columbia, was especially helpful, and her colleague, Lynn M. Roberts, editorial secretary of the *Missouri Historical Review,* furnished me with Xerox copies of several illustrations in their collection of Missouri Ozarks buildings, which are strikingly similar to Arkansas Ozarks buildings. Amanda Sarr of the University of Arkansas library furnished me with a complete bib-liography of books and articles on Arkansas architecture, and Martha McK. Blum, graduate assistant in the University of Missouri library, did the same for Missouri architecture. I exchanged several letters with Professor Cyrus Sutherland of the Department of Architecture at the University of Arkansas, and I am grateful for his help. I also exchanged several letters with Tom Butler, a resident of Newton County, and with Day Whittacker and Diana Stoving, also residents of that enchanted county. My letters were generously acknowledged by Dorothy Doering of the Drury College library, Christopher Dar-rouzet of the Missouri State library, John L. Ferguson of the Arkansas History Commission, Robert E. Anderson of the School of the Ozarks library, Charles McRaven, also of the School of the Ozarks, and the anonymous librarian of the *Arkansas Gazette.*

In its original form, this novel was much more sexually explicit than it is now, replete with such language as "joist," "beam," "stud," "timber," "pole," "erection," "rear elevation," "door," "gable," "sill," "rail," and "jamb." I am very grateful to my editor, Llewellyn Howland III, for persuading me to leave such things to the reader's imagination, and I trust that the reader's imagination has succeeded. My editor was the first person to hear of this project, the first person to encourage it, and the first person to see it when it was finished. In addition to removing certain passages, he made two other sweeping changes of an important nature.

His devoted secretary, Rosemary Gaffney, not only spent many hours making his letters to me legible and coherent, but also spent days tracking down a crucial but elusive doctoral dissertation in the archives of Harvard University. She is simply a wonderful person.

Helpful in a way they did not realize were the few people who wrote letters of appreciation for my previous volumes, and I would like to list them here: George Eades, Katherine Berry, Sandee Jo Joy, Rhode Rapp, Weld Henshaw, Juanita Melchert, Sue Anderson, Mrs. John Ingle, Gretchen Keiser, Linda Gray, Alex Humez, Sharon Karpinski, Joanna Noe, Willie Allen, John Braden, Carol Cross, Eleanor Jacobson, my two United Kingdom "fans," Capt. Archibald A.J. Dinsmore and Gayle Harrison...and Dione, wherever you are. Without the encouragement of these good people, this book would not exist.

To my students in my architecture classes at Windham College, I am indebted for a spirited give-and-take over the years that has taught me much about architecture, and I apologize to them for never discussing the architecture treated in the present volume.

As to the chapter head illustrations, there is no point in claiming that any resemblance between these buildings and actual buildings living or dead is purely coincidental. Most of these structures no longer stand, but that fact makes them no less "real." They stood, and that is, like all of us, what matters.

About the Author

Donald Harington

Although he was born and raised in Little Rock, Donald Harington spent nearly all of his early summers in the Ozark mountain hamlet of Drakes Creek, his mother's hometown, where his grandparents operated the general store and post office. There, before he lost his hearing to meningitis at the age of twelve, he listened carefully to the vanishing Ozark folk language and the old tales told by storytellers.

His academic career is in art and art history and he has taught art history at a variety of colleges, including his alma mater, the University of Arkansas, Fayetteville, where he has been lecturing for fifteen years. He lives in Fayetteville with his wife Kim.

His first novel, *The Cherry Pit*, was published by Random House in 1965, and since then he has published eleven other novels, most of them set in the Ozark hamlet of his own creation, Stay More, based loosely upon Drakes Creek. He has also written books about artists.

He won the Robert Penn Warren Award in 2003, the Porter Prize in 1987, the Heasley Prize at Lyon College in 1998, was inducted into the Arkansas Writers' Hall of Fame in 1999 and that same year won the Arkansas Fiction Award of the Arkansas Library Association. He has been called "an undiscovered continent" (Fred Chappell) and "America's Greatest Unknown Novelist" (Entertainment Weekly).

The fonts used in this book are from the Garamond family